NYC ANGELS:
UN
DR

LAURA IDING

NYC ANGELS:
THE WALLFLOWER'S SECRET

BY

SUSAN CARLISLE

Step into the world of NYC Angels

Looking out over Central Park,
the Angel Mendez Children's Hospital,
affectionately known as Angel's, is famed
throughout America for being at the forefront
of paediatric medicine, with talented staff
who always go that extra mile for their little patients.
Their lives are full of highs, lows, drama and emotion.

In the city that never sleeps,
the life-saving docs at Angel's Hospital work hard,
play hard and love even harder. There's always time
for some sizzling after-hours romance…

And striding the halls of the hospital, leaving
a sea of fluttering hearts behind him, is the
dangerously charismatic new head of neurosurgery
Alejandro Rodriguez. But there's one woman,
paediatrician Layla Woods, who's left an
indelible mark on his no-go-area heart.
Expect their reunion to be explosive!

NYC Angels

Children's doctors who work hard and love even harder…in the city that never sleeps!

NYC ANGELS: UNMASKING DR SERIOUS

BY

LAURA IDING

To the Thursday Morning Breakfast Club.
I value your support more than I can ever say.

All the characters in this book have no existence outside the imagination of the author, and have no relation whatsoever to anyone bearing the same name or names. They are not even distantly inspired by any individual known or unknown to the author, and all the incidents are pure invention.

First published in Great Britain 2013
by Mills & Boon, an imprint of Harlequin (UK) Limited.
Harlequin (UK) Limited, Eton House, 18-24 Paradise Road,
Richmond, Surrey TW9 1SR

Special thanks and acknowledgement are given to Laura Iding for her contribution to the *NYC Angels* series

ISBN: 978 0 263 89886 6

Harlequin (UK) policy is to use papers that are natural, renewable and recyclable products and made from wood grown in sustainable forests. The logging and manufacturing process conform to the legal environmental regulations of the country of origin.

Printed and bound in Spain
by Blackprint CPI, Barcelona

Dear Reader

I need one of those T-shirts that say 'I love New York'! Visiting the Big Apple is fun as there are so many things to do and to see. I especially like seeing Broadway plays, the Statue of Liberty and jogging in Central Park (just to name a few).

So I was thrilled and honoured when I was asked to participate in the *NYC Angels* series by writing the third book.

Dan Morris is a top-notch paediatric cardiothoracic surgeon who meets his match in physical therapist Molly Shriver. Molly makes it clear she is the one running the show when it comes to helping Dan's son Josh to walk again.

Both Dan and Molly have been burned by relationships in the past, but as they work together for Josh's sake is it possible they'll get a second chance at love and family?

I hope you enjoy Dan and Molly's story as much as I enjoyed writing it. Don't hesitate to visit my website or find me on Facebook—I love to hear from my readers.

Sincerely

Laura Iding

www.lauraiding.com

Laura Iding loved reading as a child, and when she ran out of books she readily made up her own, completing a little detective mini-series when she was twelve. But, despite her aspirations for being an author, her parents insisted she look into a 'real' career. So the summer after she turned thirteen she volunteered as a Candy Striper, and fell in love with nursing. Now, after twenty years of experience in trauma/critical care, she's thrilled to combine her career and her hobby into one—writing Medical Romances™ for Mills & Boon. Laura lives in the northern part of the United States, and spends all her spare time with her two teenage kids (help!)—a daughter and a son—and her husband. Enjoy!

Recent titles by Laura Iding:

Mills & Boon® Medical Romance™

HER LITTLE SPANISH SECRET
DATING DR DELICIOUS
A KNIGHT FOR NURSE HART
THE NURSE'S BROODING BOSS
THE SURGEON'S NEW YEAR WEDDING WISH
EXPECTING A CHRISTMAS MIRACLE

CHAPTER ONE

"No-o-o-o!" Josh wailed, throwing his arms around the nanny's neck when Dan tried to lift the boy off the sofa. "I want Gemma to take me!"

Dan Morris gnashed his teeth, his gut burning with guilt as Josh showed him once again how much he preferred the company of Gemma, the middle-aged woman who'd been caring for him the past six months, over that of his father. But with the ease of long practice he buried his true feelings and kept his tone soft as he gently prised Josh away from Gemma, lifting his small frame into his arms.

"It's okay, Josh. Remember how I told you I'm going to be home with you for the next few weeks? We're going to attend physical therapy together. There's nothing to be afraid of. I'm going to be with you the whole time."

Josh didn't look too impressed with his vow but thankfully stopped struggling, leaning against his father's chest as if willing to accept his fate. He'd stopped crying too, but the occasional loud sniffle was just as difficult to bear.

Dan tucked Josh into his booster seat in the backseat of the black BMW, buckling him securely into the harness before he himself slid into the driver's seat, trying to think of a way to breach the chasm between them. He wanted Josh to know he was loved. Cherished. But how? Words alone hadn't worked so far.

"Daddy, is therapy going to hurt?"

Helpless fury and guilt nearly choked him at his son's innocent question. How many times had Josh asked him that same thing in the hospital? How many times had he been forced to answer yes? He cleared his throat and smiled at Josh, using the rearview mirror. "No, Josh, therapy isn't going to hurt. The therapist will exercise your legs. There won't be any needles, I promise."

Josh settled back, seemingly reassured. Dan drove carefully through the busy Manhattan streets to the physiotherapy clinic located within the brick walls of Manhattan's Angel Mendez Children's Hospital, affectionately known as Angel's, where his pediatric cardiothoracic surgery practice was located. He hoped physical therapist Molly Shriver was everything she'd been reported to be.

He'd wanted the best, *demanded* the best for his son. He couldn't bear to think about the grim possibility that Josh might never walk again. If this Molly Shriver was half as good as her reputation heralded her to be, he was convinced she was the one who could make that happen.

He and Josh arrived ten minutes early because he despised being late. They'd barely settled into their seats in the waiting room when a young woman with bright green eyes and reddish-gold hair pulled back in a perky ponytail came out to greet them.

"Good morning," she said, smiling brightly, her attention focused, rightly so, on Josh. Dan had stood when she'd entered the room, but Josh was obviously still seated in the waiting-room chair, wearing shorts and a

T-shirt as requested. She knelt beside Josh so that her eyes were level with his. "You must be Josh Morris, although you look much older than seven. Are you sure you're not eight or nine?" she asked, her voice full of doubt.

Josh giggled, and shook his head. "Nope. I'm seven but my birthday is in three weeks."

"Oh, goody! I love birthdays! We'll have a party to celebrate!" she exclaimed, making Josh giggle again. "And that must be why you look so much older. My name is Molly and I'm so happy you came in to see me today."

Dan tucked his hands into the back pockets of his jeans and watched, reluctantly impressed with how she'd immediately established a connection with his son. She seemed to know a lot about kids.

No doubt, far more than he did.

"We're going to have lots of fun today, Josh," Molly confided. She held out her hand to his son. "Are you ready to play some games with me?"

All evidence of his former tears gone, Josh nodded eagerly as he reached for her hand. Fearing that she didn't realize his son couldn't walk, Dan quickly swooped down to swing Josh into his arms. "We're ready," he said gruffly, sending her a dark look.

For a moment her gaze narrowed and her smile dimmed. "Did you leave Josh's wheelchair out in the car?" she asked with feigned sweetness.

Just the thought of seeing his son confined to a wheelchair made him break out in a cold sweat. He could spend twelve hours in surgery, meticulously reconnecting coronary arteries and veins to repair tiny damaged hearts, but those hours he'd sat at his son's hospital bedside after the car crash had been the longest, darkest hours of his life. "No," he said bluntly. "Josh won't need a wheelchair. He has me. And now he has you, to help him learn how to walk again."

Her lips thinned and her smile faded even more. He thought she was going to pursue the issue, but instead she led the way through the doorway into another, much larger room. There were all kinds of exercise equipment scattered about, along with what appeared to be toys. Lots of toys, like brightly colored balls of every shape and size, jump ropes, bean bags and hula hoops. She gestured toward a padded table located on the right-hand side of the room. "Josh needs to sit right here. And why don't you take a seat here, on his left?"

He gently set Josh on the padded table, taken aback by how she wanted him right next to Josh, since he'd planned to just sit back and watch. "I can sit over there," he said, indicating a hard plastic chair tucked in the corner of the room.

"I'm afraid that won't work," Molly said cheerfully. "We'll need you close by in order to help. Right, Josh?"

"Right," Josh agreed enthusiastically, although Dan was sure the boy had no idea what he was agreeing to.

While it grated against his nerves to take orders from this petite woman, whose head barely reached the level of his chin, he'd vowed to do whatever was necessary for his son. And belatedly he realized she probably wanted to teach him the same exercises that she'd be doing with Josh, so he could reinforce them at home. "All right, then." He pulled up a rolling stool to sit close to his son's left side.

"Excellent." Molly grabbed a red plastic ball that was slightly smaller in circumference than a basketball, and took a seat on another rolling stool, positioning herself off to Josh's right side. "We're going to play catch, okay, Josh?"

He nodded enthusiastically.

"Watch carefully. I need you to toss the ball high in the air, like this..." She demonstrated what she meant, throwing her arms in the air and then keeping them over her head to catch the ball again. "And then catch it again like this. Are you ready?" she asked.

When Josh nodded, she tossed the ball in a high arch, so that Josh had to lift up his arms to catch it. "Great!" she called with enthusiasm. "Now toss it back up in the air toward your dad."

Before Dan realized what was happening, Josh did as she requested, the ball going high in the air and crookedly off to one side, so that Dan had to react quickly in order to catch it. He wanted to scowl at the obvious amusement in Molly's gaze, but as usual kept his feelings to himself. Besides, he found her enthusiasm and laughter oddly relaxing.

"Good job, Josh. Now, Mr. Morris, toss the ball back to your son."

It was on the tip of his tongue to correct her, *Dr. Morris, pediatric cardiothoracic surgeon,* but right now the focus needed to be on his son. He didn't mind taking the role of a concerned father. After all, he was currently on leave of absence from the hospital, with one of his partners covering his patients. "Dan," he said shortly, as he did as she requested, tossing the ball up in the air so his son could reach out for it. "Call me Dan."

She didn't answer, as if she couldn't have cared less what his name was, and her gaze remained trained on his son. He tried to squelch a flash of annoyance. "Now, throw the ball back up in the air, toward me, Josh," Molly said. "Up as high as you can."

This time Josh's aim was a little better, although the ball still veered off to the side. They repeated this game several times, and Dan couldn't help glancing at the clock with growing annoyance. Okay, maybe he could understand her need to establish a bond with his son, but was this really what their medical insurance was paying for? What good would tossing the ball in the air do for Josh's legs? When was she going to start with his muscle-strengthening exercises?

"Great job, Josh," Molly said with another broad, cheerful smile. She looked and acted as if she absolutely loved her job. "Okay, now we're going to work with a hacky sack." She put the red ball back on the shelf and brought over a small round beanbag. "Have you ever played with a hacky sack, Josh?"

"No," he said, a tiny frown furrowing his brow as he watched Molly. She tossed the hacky sack into the air and bounced it off her elbow, aiming up so that she could catch it again. Then she repeated the motion with the other elbow, and then with her knee.

It was on the tip of Dan's tongue to remind her, again, that his son couldn't walk or stand for any length of time to play the goofy game of hacky sack, but then she sat down on the rolling stool, still holding the small beanbag.

"This isn't an easy game, so you have to concentrate very hard," she warned. "Do you think you can do that for me?"

Josh's big brown eyes were wide as he nodded.

"Maybe we should get your dad to play, too," Molly said, with a mischievous glint in her eye. Without warning she tossed the hacky sack into the air and then bounced it off her elbow and then her knee, aiming toward him. She hit it hard enough to make him scramble to reach up and grab it before the beanbag could smack him in the center of his forehead.

His temper snapped as he tossed the hacky sack back in her lap. "Maybe you should quit playing games and get to work." The moment the sharp words left his mouth he wanted to call them back, especially when Josh's brown eyes darkened with wounded sorrow.

Slicing his heart like the sharp blade of a scalpel.

It took everything Molly had to keep her relaxed smile on her face, when in reality she wanted to sweep Josh into her arms and take him far away from his ogre of a father.

"Hmm, I think your dad got up on the wrong side of the bed this morning, Josh," she murmured, picking up the hacky sack and turning in her seat so that she faced Josh. She lowered her voice and leaned forward as if he was her coconspirator. "Or maybe it's just that he doesn't know how to play games," she said as if they were sharing a big secret. "You and I are going to have to help teach him, okay?"

Josh bit his lip and ducked his head, sending a worried glance at his father. "Okay," he said in a very small voice, as if torn between siding with her and trying to protect his father.

She did her best to ignore Dr. Morris's piercing gaze. She knew very well who he was, of course. After all, she'd seen him at the ribbon-cutting ceremony when Angel's had opened the new neonatal wing, although he hadn't noticed her. Plus, she'd cared for many patients who'd had surgery performed by him. Parents raved about what a great surgeon he was.

Dr. Morris had an amazing reputation within the hospital, but she couldn't say she was nearly as impressed with the guy in person. Granted, he was devastatingly attractive—tall and broad-shouldered, with mink-colored close-cropped hair and big, melting chocolate-brown eyes. But she wasn't easily swayed these days by a good-looking guy. Especially one who rarely, if ever, smiled.

In fact, they'd be far better off if he'd put his frowning energy into his son's therapy instead. She was still seething with the fact that he'd denied his son the freedom of a wheelchair.

But there would be time to talk to Dr. Morris about that later. Right now she needed to concentrate on poor Josh, who deserved every bit of her attention. "Okay, here's what I need you to do for me," she said with a smile and a secret wink. Josh rewarded her with a tremulous smile, so heartbreakingly sweet she had to crush the urge to sweep him into her arms and promise him that she'd never let anything bad happen to him.

Ridiculous, as Josh was her patient, not part of her family. He belonged to the stern-faced surgeon sitting next to him. And she'd do well to remember that.

Don't get emotionally involved. You'll only lose another piece of your heart once this adorable little boy doesn't need you anymore.

She made a career out of helping her small patients not need her anymore. So, of course, she needed to keep a safe emotional distance from them. However, telling herself not to get emotionally involved was easier than actually doing it. Still, she gave it her best shot. "I want you to bounce the hacky sack in the air with your elbows and your knees." She demonstrated what she wanted him to do. "Now, you try it."

Josh did his best, which was more than she could say about his father, who watched him like a hawk. More than once he almost came out of his chair to help his son, even though she sent him a glance that clearly told him to back off.

Josh's ability was hampered a bit by the fact that he sat on the exam table, he would have done better in a wheelchair, but soon he managed to get a decent rhythm going. She was glad that he had the ability to move his knees because that meant his hips were in good shape.

"Excellent job," she lavishly praised him. "Now, let's try something else. Try to kick my hands with your toes. Kick me as hard as you can."

Josh tried to lift up his legs so that he could kick her hands, but his leg muscles were too weak. The bright angry red scars that marred his youthful skin weren't easy to ignore. But the weakness in his legs was even worse. She hid her dismay at how little he could raise them upward. He would need a lot of work to get his strength back.

Good thing she had plenty of patience. Unlike his father.

"Let's try something else," she quickly improvised, since he couldn't kick the palms of her hands. She reached over to lift him up and quickly set him down on the floor before Dr. Morris could jump up to take over. She grabbed the red plastic ball again and placed it between Josh's feet. "Try and kick the ball sideways toward your other foot, but keep your leg straight like this." She gently moved his right leg, showing him what she wanted him to do.

Josh did as she asked, shifting his right leg enough to move the ball, although it went barely a few inches before rolling to a stop far away from his left foot.

"Great, that's wonderful, Josh." She quickly moved the ball so that it was located near his left foot. "Now, kick it back again."

He scrunched up his face with the effort to concentrate on doing what she'd asked. He tried a couple more times but only moved the ball scant inches. And suddenly he crumpled into tears. "I can't," he wailed. "I can't kick the b-ball!"

This time she did wrap her arms around him in comfort. How could she not? "Don't cry, please don't cry," she crooned softly. "You're doing very well, Josh. Remember how I said some of the games were hard? Believe me, very soon you'll be kicking that ball between your feet just fine. Just don't give up on me, okay? I promise we'll keep working on these games together. But I need you to do your part."

He quieted against her, and eventually nodded his head against her breast. She was relieved that Josh had got over his breakdown quickly—some patients took much longer, even her teenage patients. This type of frustration wasn't new to her by any means.

When she glanced up at Dr. Morris to reassure him that Josh's reaction was completely normal, she caught her breath at the starkness of his gaze as he stared at his son. Pain shadowed the brown depths, mixed with what appeared to be guilt and a hint of longing.

She took a deep breath and let it out slowly. Apparently Josh wasn't the only one who needed help. And no matter how much she wanted to, she couldn't turn her back on his father.

She could only hope and pray that she could get through this new challenge without too many emotional scars.

If it wasn't too late already.

CHAPTER TWO

BATTLING A WAVE of helplessness, Dan clenched his hands into tight fists, wishing he could be the one to comfort his son. But Josh didn't often turn to his father for comfort.

Because he hadn't been there enough for him. Not because he didn't want to be but because his career was demanding. His young patients didn't just need open heart surgery during the day. He was on call every third evening and every third weekend. And that meant he'd often been forced to leave Josh in the care of his nanny.

At least the nannies were better to Josh than his mother had been. Although that didn't stop Josh from asking for her, especially when he was stressed. Dan rubbed the ache at his temples. He hated knowing that his son was still suffering for the mistakes he himself had made in marrying Suzy. But despite the awful things she'd done, he couldn't hate the woman who'd borne him a son. But he sure as hell resented her. He'd been stupid to believe she'd ever loved him.

Thankfully, Josh's tears had stopped almost as abruptly as they'd started. Dan was glad, even though there was no possible way the ache in his heart would go away as easily.

Watching the light play across Molly's red-gold hair

as she cuddled Josh close was only a partial distraction. He knew it was his fault that Josh was suffering right now. His fault that he'd been too distracted by Josh's mother, who'd called out of the blue after six years of absence, asking for money, to notice the car barreling through the intersection, straight toward them.

Even now, he could hear the screeching tires, the sickening *thunk* of metal crushing against metal. The agonizing sound of Josh's high-pitched scream.

He wanted to put his hands up to cover his ears, but that would be useless as he knew the noise would reverberate over and over in his mind, where nobody else could hear it but him. With a herculean effort he dragged himself out of the dark past to the just-barely-lighter present.

He couldn't ever make up for the injuries Josh had suffered that fateful night. All he could do was to try and start over. He'd taken a leave of absence from work so that he could rebuild his relationship with his son, at the same time doing whatever was necessary to ensure his son would walk again.

"Okay, Josh, we're going to sit back on the exam table here, so that I can massage your legs a bit before we use the ultrasound machine," Molly was saying now, lifting Josh up, despite her slim build, and setting him back on the table, as if Josh hadn't suffered a meltdown five minutes ago. "Do you know what an ultrasound machine is?"

Slowly Josh shook his head. "Will it hurt?" he asked.

Dan's heart squeezed in his chest. His son had suffered several surgeries to his injured legs, and every single one of them had hurt him.

He wanted to promise Josh that nothing would ever

hurt him again. but obviously that wasn't exactly realistic.

"Not one bit," Molly assured him. "I'll show you how it feels on your hand. And we can try it on your dad first, so that you know I'm telling you the truth."

Dan roused himself to respond to Molly's unspoken demand. "I don't mind trying the ultrasound," he managed, even though he couldn't believe that Josh's first therapy session was almost over. In his mind Molly hadn't done nearly enough work with his son, and now the session was winding down. He silently vowed to get a few minutes alone with her to find out what sort of exercises he should be doing with Josh at home.

He stood, and helped Molly maneuver Josh into position so that she could massage his legs. Dan had to give her credit, Molly never once stared in horror at Josh's numerous surgical scars.

"Try to relax, Josh," she murmured, as she smoothed some sort of paste substance on her fingertips, before gently beginning to massage Josh's right leg. The leg that had taken the brunt of the crash. "Now, you let me know if I'm hurting you, okay?"

Josh nodded, and he grimaced a bit when she gently massaged the knot in his calf muscle.

"You have a very tense muscle right here," she said, using her thumb to smooth over the area. "I know it's a little sore, but you'll feel much better afterward if I work on it now."

"I know," Josh said bravely, and once again Dan's heart squeezed in his chest for what his young son was going through. If he could have taken the pain for Josh, he would have. But of course he'd walked away from the crash virtually unscathed.

And felt guilty about that part, too.

He tuned out a bit as Molly and Josh chatted about his school, as she asked him what his favorite subjects and teachers were. Since the crash, he'd hired a tutor to work with Josh so that he could keep up with his classes while he attended therapy every day.

But his ears pricked up when he heard his son talking about Mr. Iverson, the tutor he'd hired. "I don't like him. He's mean."

"What did you say?" he demanded, before Molly could respond. "What did Mr. Iverson do that was mean?"

Josh's lower lip trembled. "He yells at me. He makes me do adding and subtracting over and over again, even though I don't understand it. But he doesn't explain anything, just keeps making me fill out the worksheets and yelling at me when they're not right."

Dan frowned darkly. How was it that he hadn't known about the problems Josh was having with his teacher before now? "Well, I'll get rid of Mr. Iverson. You should have told me sooner, Josh."

Instantly Josh's eyes brightened. "Really? No more math?"

"Now, Josh," Molly admonished gently, inserting herself into the conversation, "do you really think you can pass first grade to go on to second grade without learning to add and subtract?"

Josh gave a very adultlike sigh. "No, I suppose not."

"Sometimes school is hard, just like therapy," Molly said, moving over to massage Josh's other leg. "But there are things we can do to make them both fun."

Was he imagining it, or was that last comment directed squarely at him? He tried not to scowl but since when was school supposed to be fun? Kids had to learn, but tests, writing essays, memorizing history and practicing your sums wasn't exactly fun.

Was it?

"The muscles in your left leg aren't nearly as tied up in knots as those in your right leg," Molly said, turning the conversation back to the issue of therapy. "Do you feel the difference?"

Josh nodded vigorously. "Yep. Doesn't ache very much at all."

"I'm glad. Now we're going to use the ultrasound machine. Here's the wand, feel how smooth it is?" She picked up what looked like a stout hammer, except that the base of it was much wider and very smooth to the touch.

Josh tentatively put his hand over the end of the wand. "Yeah, it's very smooth."

"I'm going to move it in small circles over your skin, like this." Molly demonstrated again, on the palm of his hand. "Now, when I turn the machine on, it's going to make some noise and you'll feel a very faint vibration but it won't hurt. Do you want me to show you on your dad first?"

Josh nodded again, and watched with wide eyes as Dan extended his arm so that Molly could use the ultrasound machine on him.

She squirted cool gel on his arm, and then flipped the switch on the machine and moved the ball of the wand over his skin in a circular motion. He frowned. "I can barely feel the vibration. Are you sure it's turned on?"

"I'm sure. I told you this wouldn't hurt a bit." She glanced over at Josh with a bright smile. "Are you ready to try it?"

"I'm ready." Josh braced himself, and Dan couldn't help moving closer to his son, putting his arms around Josh's thin shoulders. When she squirted the ultrasound gel on his skin, Josh jumped. "It's cold!"

"I know. And that's the worst of it, I promise." Molly pressed the ball of the ultrasound wand against Josh's leg and moved it in small circles.

Instantly Josh relaxed. "It really doesn't hurt!" he exclaimed in surprise.

"Josh, I will never lie to you," Molly said solemnly as she continued with the ultrasound therapy. "Remember when I told you the exercises were going to be hard to do? And they were, right? I will always be honest about what we're going to do, okay?"

Josh grinned. "Okay."

Dan waited patiently, as Molly finished up the ultrasound treatments, doing eight minutes on Josh's right leg and four minutes on his left. He didn't understand what good the treatments would be, though, as he honestly hadn't felt a thing when she'd practiced on his arm.

So far all they'd done had been to play several games, get a massage and then this weird, painless ultrasound therapy. Not that he wanted his son to be in pain, but surely there had to be more to therapy than what he'd seen today?

Was this Molly Shriver really the best in the business?

If so, maybe he needed to consider other alternatives.

Molly could tell that Dr. Morris wasn't thrilled with how Josh's therapy had gone today, and while she wished he'd trust in her knowledge and judgment, she figured that allowing anyone else to be in control went against the grain of a top-notch cardiothoracic surgeon.

And she still needed to talk to him about Josh's wheelchair.

"We're all finished, Josh," she said, scooting her chair back and putting the ultrasound machine away. She took out a towel to wipe the ultrasound goop from Josh's legs. "Now, I'm going to have you sit here for a few minutes while I talk to your dad, okay?"

"Okay."

"Heavens, I almost forgot!" She whirled round and picked up a candy jar full of lollipops. "Here, what's your favorite flavor? You get to pick any one you like for working so hard today."

She thought she heard a faint snort from Josh's father, an indication perhaps that he didn't think Josh had worked hard at all, but she ignored him. Josh debated the multitude of flavors. He took his time, as if this was the most important decision he'd make in his life, so she waited patiently until his fingers delved into the jar. "Grape," he announced, pulling out the lollipop with the purple wrapper. "I like grape."

"Grape is one of my favorite flavors, too," she confided, putting the lid back on the candy jar and setting it aside. "Now, wait here for a minute, okay?"

He was too busy sucking on his lollipop to answer. She gestured for Josh's dad to follow her out into her private office.

Once they were alone, she didn't beat around the bush. "I want you to get Josh a wheelchair." Dan, er—*Dr. Morris*—towered over her, topping her in height by a good eight inches. But she refused to be intimidated even though he was clearly angry.

"Josh isn't permanently handicapped," he said tersely. "He doesn't need a wheelchair. He's going to learn how to walk again. At least, he would if you were doing more than playing silly games."

The cutting edge of his tongue only made her square her shoulders to face him with renewed determination. "This isn't about what you want or need, Dr. Morris, it's about your son. It's about giving him the freedom to move around without waiting for you or someone else to carry him. It's about giving him independence. And lastly it's about strengthening his core muscles, his torso." She was growing angrier by the second.

"Don't you understand how important core body strength is when it comes to walking? You stand there and mock what I've done today, but those games I played with Josh were core-strengthening games. And therapy doesn't have to hurt in order to achieve results!"

He actually stared in shocked surprise at her outburst. A tiny voice in the back of her mind warned her to stop while she was ahead, but she was on a roll.

"Furthermore, how dare you question my methods? I have good outcomes, the best in the region. Do I stand over your shoulder and tell you how to operate on a damaged heart? This is my job, my career, and I'm damn good at it."

Her temper flared easily, she didn't have red hair for nothing, but it dissolved as quickly as it ignited. She took several deep breaths, immediately feeling bad at how she'd lost control. Was she crazy? A powerful surgeon like Dr. Dan Morris could make or break her career.

Well, he probably couldn't totally break her career,

as she really did have excellent outcomes that spoke for themselves. But he could make her life miserable.

And what if he stopped referring patients to her? The very idea made her gut clench and roll.

Why, oh, why hadn't she bitten her tongue?

The silence stretched interminably between them, until she decided he was waiting for an apology.

One he honestly deserved.

But before she could take her foot out of her mouth to formulate the words, he totally surprised her. "Where can I get a pediatric wheelchair?" he demanded.

"Um, right here. I can get you one from the storage room." She didn't move, though, afraid that he'd capitulated too easily. She licked her lips nervously. "Look, I'm—"

"If you wouldn't mind getting it now, I'd be happy to reimburse you for it," he interrupted, as if impatient to get the wheelchair now that he'd decided Josh really did, in fact, need one.

She nodded and quickly left the office to rummage around in the back storeroom. She found a perfect-sized wheelchair for Josh, and brought it back to his father.

He stared at it for a long moment, before dragging his gaze up to meet hers. "I never meant to take away Josh's independence," he murmured, his gaze full of stark agony. "That's the last thing I would ever want to do."

She felt her eyes prick with tears, hardly able to bear to see the lines of tortured self-reproach grooved in his cheeks. "I know. You were seeing the wheelchair as a sign of giving up. But encouraging Josh to use an assistive device isn't giving up at all. Trust me, this is just the first step on the road to Josh walking again."

His jaw tensed and his intense gaze seemed to drill

all the way down to her soul. "Do you really believe that?" he asked hoarsely. "Do you really believe he'll walk again?"

"Yes." She couldn't stop herself from stepping closer and placing a reassuring hand on his forearm. The warmth of his skin shot tingles of awareness dancing along her nerves. But she kept her gaze centered on his, ignoring her inappropriate reaction. "I believe he will. I won't lie to you, though. Josh's leg muscles are weak, so this isn't going to happen overnight. He has a long way to go. But I know he'll be able to walk again."

He covered her hand with his, surrounding her with even more heat. "I'm going to hold you to that," he said wearily.

She gave his arm a reassuring squeeze, and then subtly pulled out of his grip. "No more than I'm holding myself accountable," she assured him. They'd gotten past the first hurdle, but there would be more. She took a deep breath and let it out slowly. "You're going to have to help," she added. "Because Josh can't do this on his own. He'll need your support."

To her surprise, he nodded in agreement. "I know and that's perfectly fine with me. Obviously, he's not going to be able to walk with just one hour of therapy a day. I expect you to give me a list of leg-strengthening exercises to do with him at home."

She wanted to roll her eyes heavenward at his determination to direct the physiotherapy of his son. She supposed this tendency of his was part of being a surgeon but, really, hadn't they already gone through all this? She was the one in charge, here, not him.

The sooner he recognized that fact, the further along they'd be.

"Now that you mention it, I do have a list for you," she agreed as she headed over to her desk. She picked up the bright blue folder, and then came back over to hand it to him. "Inside you'll find everything you'll need. And, of course, I'll be seeing Josh five days a week. You've asked for early morning appointments, so he's scheduled every day at 9:00 a.m."

"No problem," he agreed readily, as he opened the folder to peek inside. He scanned the printed pages she'd tucked in the pockets, and then looked up at her with a deep frown. "These aren't exercises," he accused. "They're *games*." He emphasized the last word as if it was a curse.

She tried not to smile, but her mouth quirked up at the corners despite her best effort. "Yes, I'm aware of that, Dr. Morris. Your son is seven years old. Surely you know how to play games with him?"

She could have sworn there was a momentarily blank look in his eyes, before he snapped the folder shut with a flash of annoyance. "Of course I do."

This time she couldn't stop the smile from blossoming on her face. "Don't worry," she said, patting his arm as if he were one of her small patients, rather than a big, broad-shouldered heart surgeon. "You'll get better with practice."

CHAPTER THREE

MOLLY WAS PHYSICALLY exhausted by the time she finished her day, and while she'd cared for many patients during her nine-hour shift, it was young Josh and his enigmatic father who lingered in her mind as she took the subway home.

She tried to scan the newspaper she'd purchased at the hospital, as she normally did, but her mind kept wandering. She couldn't help wondering about how Josh was handling his new wheelchair, and whether or not Dr. Morris had unwound enough to play a few games with his son.

And she found herself hoping that the uptight surgeon wouldn't overdo things with Josh in his eagerness to get the boy walking again. If he pushed Josh too hard, the poor kid would be too sore to participate in her games tomorrow. Moderation was an important aspect of physical therapy and she realized now that she should have made a point of reinforcing that fact before they'd left.

She doubted Dr. Morris knew anything about moderation. The way he'd watched her, with his incredibly intense gaze, had made her feel extremely self-conscious. And far too aware of him.

Her cheeks burned as she remembered the way she'd

let him have it in her office. Normally she didn't find it at all difficult to keep her temper under control, at least within a professional setting. But somehow Josh's father had pushed her buttons in a big way. The memory of her tirade made her wince. She'd have to make sure she kept her cool during their session tomorrow.

Would Dr. Morris bring his son in again? Or would he send Josh to someone else? Everyone knew that Dan Morris was single—there was a lot of talk about him being one of Angel's most eligible bachelors, especially now that Dr. Tyler Donaldson had been snagged by Dr. Eleanor Aston.

But whereas Tyler was a flirt, Dan was an enigma. Composed. Aloof. She didn't doubt for a moment that he had a nanny to help care for his son. The thought that she might not see Dr. Morris in the morning left her feeling curiously disappointed. That was crazy, because it wasn't as if she had any interest in the guy, other than how he needed to learn how to unbend enough to help his son.

She was so lost in her thoughts that she nearly missed her subway stop. At the last moment she grabbed her backpack and her newspaper and elbowed her way through the crowd to dash out the door seconds before they closed. Thankfully, the weather was mild for spring, so it was no hardship to walk the few blocks home to her tiny apartment.

Inside, she quickly heated up some leftovers and forced herself to finish reading the newspaper. She liked being up to date on current events, especially as the length of her commute didn't provide any time to watch the news.

When she opened the entertainment section, she

stared in shock when she recognized her sister, Sally, and boyfriend, Mike, smiling together in a huge photo announcing their engagement.

Sally and Mike were engaged? Since when? And why hadn't anyone called her?

She couldn't seem to drag her gaze away from the beautiful, happy couple. Her sister was as dark as she herself was fair, making it even more noticeable that they weren't bonded by blood. Molly had been adopted by the Shrivers when she'd been four years old, but shortly thereafter her adoptive mother had discovered she was pregnant.

When Sally was born, Molly had been thrilled to have a younger sister to play with, but as they'd grown older, it had become clear that Sally, as the biological daughter, had been the favorite and she herself had too often been simply an afterthought.

Nothing had changed in the years since they'd both grown up. No matter how hard she tried to belong, when it came to her family, she remained the outsider, looking in.

Seeing her sister's engagement photo soured her appetite, so she shoved the newspaper aside and carried her dishes to the sink. She shouldn't be so upset at how Sally had gotten engaged without telling her, but she was. She knew her family hadn't done this to her on purpose, they weren't mean-spirited, it was more that they often forgot about her.

If she called her mother now to ask about Sally's engagement, Jenny would profusely apologize and offer some weak excuse to try to cover the fact that Molly hadn't been included.

For a moment, a deep sense of loneliness weighed

down her shoulders like a heavy blanket. All she'd ever wanted was to be a part of a family. She'd thought her prayers had been answered when the Shrivers had adopted her, but over time she'd become less and less a true member of the family.

And since she'd graduated from college her one attempt to have a family of her own had backfired. James had been several years older than she was, a divorced father with two young boys. She'd met him when one of his boys had been injured playing soccer and she'd performed his therapy. They'd dated for five years, and she'd been sure he'd propose marriage, but instead he'd called off their relationship, claiming he'd fallen in love with someone else.

He'd broken her heart, although now, a year later, she could admit she'd loved his two young sons more than she'd loved him.

Not seeing James's boys anymore had left a huge, aching hole in her life. In her soul.

Her heart squeezed painfully in her chest. She didn't belong, not with the Shrivers and certainly not with James. On a professional level she belonged at Angel's, and working there had been the best decision of her life.

It was too bad that on a personal level it seemed she was destined to live her life alone.

Dan swallowed a curse as he wrestled to get Josh's wheelchair back into the trunk of his car. Josh didn't seem to like the stupid chair, despite Molly's insistence that having it would give him more independence. And Dan hadn't appreciated the sympathetic stares aimed at his son when they'd ridden down in the elevator together. One of the reasons he had balked at using the chair had been to save Josh from being teased about it.

Although maybe if he'd used the wheelchair with Josh from the very beginning, his son would be that much further along with his therapy.

More to feel guilty about. As if everything Josh had been through, the prolonged hospital stay and multiple surgeries, hadn't been enough. With an effort he shoved his dark thoughts aside.

"Ready, Josh?" he asked, as he slid behind the wheel.

"Yep." One good thing was that Josh hadn't been upset about going to therapy this morning. And he hadn't clung to Gemma, his nanny, begging her to take him. Dan knew part of the reason was that Josh was looking forward to seeing Molly again. However, he hoped there were also tentative bonds forming between him and his son.

Yesterday, when they'd gotten home, he'd fired the tutor who'd been mean to Josh and had called the school to arrange for a replacement. This time a young college freshman by the name of Mitch came to the house and Josh seemed to flourish under the kid's fun and somewhat laid-back approach.

As he'd watched them together, he couldn't help thinking Molly would approve.

After Josh's lessons they'd played the ball game again and the entire time Molly's parting words had played over and over in his mind. *Don't worry, you'll get better with practice.*

His gut still burned with the memory. He hadn't felt that inadequate since his internship year.

Despite being seriously annoyed with her, he had to admit to feeling some grudging admiration for Molly.

No one had ever dared to stand up to him the way she had. And what was that she'd said? Something about how she wouldn't stand over his shoulder and tell him how to do heart surgery? Earlier in the session she'd called him Mr. Morris, but she'd obviously known who he was the whole time.

He supposed it was possible that she'd only figured it out after spending more time together. While he often referred patients to her, based on her reputation for being the best, it wasn't as if they'd worked together side by side. He simply wrote the order and then asked his patients and their parents how things were going when they came in for their routine follow-up visits. They'd always given him rave reviews about her care.

As far as his own opinion of her went, the jury was still out. She might be a pretty woman, with a bright, sunny attitude, but he wasn't going to be happy until Josh was walking again. And despite what she claimed, he had trouble believing these games of hers would really work.

The traffic was heavier this morning, and he drummed his fingers impatiently on the steering wheel as they waited for yet another red light. This time, when they arrived at Angel's physical therapy clinic, they only had five minutes to spare.

Five minutes that was taken up by wrestling once again with the stubborn wheelchair. Once he got the thing unfolded and the footrests put back together, he lifted Josh out of the car and placed him in the seat.

This time Molly was waiting for them when they arrived. "Wow, you look awesome in that wheelchair, Josh."

His son brightened under her admiration. "Really? You think so?"

"Absolutely. And today we're going to practice getting in and out of it, okay?"

"Okay."

"This way," Molly said, gesturing for them to follow her into the large therapy room. Dan pushed Josh's wheelchair forward. "If you wouldn't mind stopping right there," she said, when he reached the center of the room, "I'd like to see what Josh can do on his own."

Letting go of the chair and backing off to watch his son struggle to move the large wheels forward was difficult. Josh's small arms seemed far too skinny to be of much use, although he did manage to wheel the chair all the way over to Molly.

"Excellent." Once again she knelt before Josh so they were at the same eye level. "I need you to practice wheeling yourself around, Josh. I know your arms will get tired, but you still need to practice. It's the only way to get your arms stronger, all right?"

"All right."

"Good." Molly's smile was bright enough to light up the whole room. For the first time Dan wondered just what her life was like to make her so happy all the time. He'd noticed that she wasn't wearing a wedding or engagement ring, but that didn't mean she wasn't seeing someone. He couldn't imagine a woman like Molly being without a man, so he had to assume she was involved. Why that thought made him feel depressed, he had no clue. The last thing he needed was a woman to further complicate his life.

After Suzy had upped and left six years ago, he'd vowed to never let a woman get close to him again. Josh needed stability in his life more than he himself needed female companionship. He'd willingly thrown himself into his career. Maybe a little too enthusiastically, now that he thought about it.

"I'm going to help you stand up, okay? First we have to set the brakes." She put her hands over his smaller ones to show him how to move the levers forward. "Now, I'm going to put my arms underneath yours, but I need you to push up on the arms of your wheelchair at the same time."

He watched Josh struggle to stand, noticing that Molly took a good portion of his weight in order for him to accomplish the task. Although once he was standing, she made him balance there for a few seconds.

"I'm going to fall," Josh whined. "Don't let me go or I'll fall!"

"I won't let you go, Josh, I promise," Molly assured him. "Just try and stand here for a little bit."

After another ten seconds she let him sit back down in the chair. Dan watched intently so that he could practice this at home with Josh.

"Good job," she praised his son. "Did you play any games with your dad last night?"

Josh nodded. "Yep, we played the ball game before dinner. It was fun. And I have a new tutor, too. His name is Mitch. I like him way better than Mr. Iverson." Josh screwed up his face in an apparent attempt to mimic the stern tutor.

Molly's lips twitched as she fought a smile, but when she lifted her gaze over Josh's head to meet his, Dan could see frank approval reflected in her gaze. And despite the fact he shouldn't care what she thought of him, he was secretly glad to have earned her favor.

The session went on, with more games that she dragged him into playing, and he was thrilled to notice that Josh was able to move his legs a little better today when Molly instructed him to kick the ball between his feet.

When she ended Josh's session with another massage and the ultrasound treatment, he couldn't help voicing his concern. "What exactly is the purpose of doing the ultrasound on his legs for eight minutes? I don't see what good it can possibly do for him."

She arched a brow, as she continued providing the treatment. "These are very intense ultrasound waves that are focused directly on the injured muscles. They help increase blood flow, which in turn helps to reduce pain and swelling," she said patiently, as if speaking to a first-year medical student.

"Really?" He frowned, trying to work through the pathophysiology of what she described. "And ultrasound waves are safe and harmless?"

"Definitely safe and harmless," she agreed. "But that doesn't mean they don't have helpful properties, as well. I also wanted to mention that you shouldn't let Josh overdo the games at home. What you did yesterday was perfect. An hour in the evening is enough so that Josh doesn't overwork his injured muscles. We wouldn't want him to suffer from muscle spasms."

He nodded, unwilling to admit how much he'd wanted to push Josh into playing her therapy games for longer than he had. Not because he wanted Josh to overwork his injured muscles but because he desperately wanted to see his son walk again.

Patience was a virtue, he reminded himself. Although having patience while performing heart surgery was far easier than having patience with his son struggling to learn how to stand and walk.

When she'd finished the ultrasound therapy, she handed Josh the candy jar, and this time it didn't take him long to choose a cherry-flavored lollipop. Dan figured that by the time they'd completed the initial twelve weeks of therapy, his son would have tried every flavor several times over.

"Okay, Josh, I'm going to talk to your dad again for a few minutes," Molly said as she put the candy jar away. "Wait here and I'll help you get into your wheelchair when I return."

Josh nodded, the skin around his lips already stained red from the cherry sucker.

Dan followed Molly's petite frame back to her office, trying not to imagine what her figure looked like beneath the baggy scrubs.

"Dr. Morris—" she began, but he quickly interrupted her.

"I asked you to call me Dan," he reminded. "I'll be attending therapy with Josh because I'm his father, not because I'm a surgeon here at Angel's."

"Ah, okay, Dan, then," she murmured. She paused, as if she'd lost her train of thought, and he took a moment to savor the way she'd said his name. For the first time in six years he preferred hearing his first name to his formal title.

"I want you to consider getting a wheelchair, too," she said.

He blinked, and tried to gather his scattered thoughts. "You mean one for Josh to use here as well as the one he'll use at home?"

"No, I mean one for you to use specially while we're

working together with Josh." She tilted her chin in a gesture he already knew meant that this was a topic she felt strongly about. "Josh needs you to be a role model for him. And he needs to learn how to get in and out of it by himself. I think he would find that easier to do if you were learning alongside him."

Was she crazy? He'd never heard anything more ridiculous. What good would it do for him to be in a wheelchair, too? "I appreciate your advice but I don't see the need to get myself a wheelchair."

"Dr. Morris—Dan," she corrected swiftly, "You don't have the option to refuse. You have to stop questioning everything I do or suggest. Like the ultrasound treatments, and now getting a wheelchair of your own. For years you referred your pediatric patients to me, but now suddenly you're acting as if I have no clue what I'm doing. Why can't you believe I only have your son's best interests at heart?"

"I do believe that," he said slowly. He forced himself to meet her emerald-green gaze. "It's just..." He trailed off, unable to find the words to express how he felt. Because she was right. He was acting as if she didn't have a clue what she was doing. Just because he wasn't an expert in physical therapy, it didn't mean she wasn't. He had to trust her expertise and knowledge.

But getting a wheelchair of his own seemed over the top. He wasn't the one who'd been injured.

Yet it was his fault that Josh had been.

He swallowed against the hard lump of the bitter truth. Did it matter if he felt stupid using a wheelchair? Wasn't Josh's recovery worth it?

"Look, we need to settle this now, before we go any

further in treating Josh because if you can't or won't trust me, there's no point in us continuing."

Her last sentence made him scowl. "Are you threatening me?"

"It's not a threat. I'm only telling you that you either heed my advice and do what I say as it relates to Josh's therapy, or you find someone else to work with." She shrugged, as if she didn't care what he would decide to do. "I'm not the only therapist here, there are many others equally qualified."

He clenched his jaw, unable to believe she was actually handing him an ultimatum. He couldn't help it that it was his nature to question things. To make sure he understood what was going on.

"A good therapist-patient relationship is the key to success. Maybe I'm not the best fit for you," she said, when he didn't respond.

"But you are the best fit for my son." The moment he'd uttered the words, he knew they were true. Molly had a way with children, and it was obvious that Josh was already anxious to please her. Not to mention none of the other therapists had her amazing outcomes.

He'd tolerate whatever she decreed in order to help Josh. "I'll accept your terms," he said, roughly shoving his ego aside. "I'll get a wheelchair so Josh and I can learn how to use them together. And I promise not to question your methods from this point forward. I'll place my son's care in your capable hands."

She stared at him for a few seconds, as if struggling to see inside his mind, to believe he actually meant what he'd said. He didn't know what else to say, to help her understand how he'd meant every word seriously.

Nothing was going to get in the way of Josh's ability to learn how to walk again.

Nothing!

If Molly Shriver had been hoping to get rid of him, she would be sorely disappointed. He was in this for the long haul. For Josh's sake.

No matter what.

CHAPTER FOUR

MOLLY WAS SECRETLY relieved that Josh's father hadn't decided to move his son's care to another therapist. Remembering how she'd issued her ultimatum made her cheeks burn with embarrassment. Once again she'd allowed her redhead temper to get the better of her. Why on earth did Dan Morris bring out the worst in her?

She took a deep breath and tried to prepare herself for their upcoming appointment. If she was smart, she would have insisted Josh be assigned to someone else. Emotionally, it would be better for her, as the young boy was already wiggling his way into her heart. And once he didn't need her anymore, he'd take a piece of her with him, leaving a tiny hole behind.

But somehow her instinct for self-preservation seemed to have abandoned her. Because it wasn't just Josh she was beginning to care about.

His stern-faced father was even more intriguing.

Watching the two of them navigating their wheelchairs in the gym had given her a deep sense of satisfaction. The proud and hopeful expression on Dan's face when Josh successfully transferred himself from the wheelchair to the therapy table and back again had been heartbreaking. It was clear how much he cared for his son. And she had to give Dan credit for keeping his promise. He hadn't questioned her or interfered in her treatment plan in the past two days.

Today was Friday, their last session before the weekend. She had a surprise for Josh, and hoped his father wouldn't revert back to his old ways. She'd learned as the week had progressed that Dan did better with structure rather than impulsiveness. Maybe that's what made him such a good cardiothoracic surgeon.

That was too bad. She worked better by following her instincts. And today her instinct was to get outside and have some fun. Especially on this unseasonably warm day in early March. Why stay inside when the temperature was in the fifties and the sun was shining?

When she was paged by the front desk to let her know that Josh and his father had arrived, she picked up her jacket and the red plastic ball before heading out to the waiting room to greet them.

"Good morning, Josh, Dan." Calling Josh's father by his first name was getting easier. In fact, he was looking less and less like the strait-laced cardiothoracic surgeon who'd shown up here four days ago. Especially dressed in his well-worn jeans and Yankee sweatshirt that only enhanced his broad shoulders.

"Hi, Molly," Josh greeted her enthusiastically from his wheelchair. "We're ready for therapy, right, Dad?"

"Right," Dan agreed with a rare smile. He looked surprisingly comfortable seated in the adult wheelchair alongside his son.

"I'm glad, especially as I have a surprise for both of you." She fought a smile as Dan immediately tensed up. Heaven forbid she plan a surprise. "We're going on a little field trip to Central Park!"

"We are?" Dan said with a frown. "That seems too far out of the way for an hour of therapy."

"The patient who was scheduled to see me after Josh cancelled so we have two hours free. Most of the snow has melted and as it's a beautiful day, we may as well enjoy the sunshine." She could tell he wasn't thrilled with the idea. "Come on, we'll have fun."

Dan opened his mouth as if to argue, but then closed it again without saying a word.

"Yippee!" Josh said with exuberance. "I love field trips!"

She grinned, relieved to see her patient was happy with the idea. And because Dan had promised not to question her motives, he couldn't very well disagree.

She walked alongside Josh as he wheeled his chair back down the hall toward the elevator. Dan followed in his own wheelchair right behind them, and while he didn't utter a single word of complaint, she could feel his displeasure radiating off him.

She sighed, hoping he wasn't regretting their bargain, because if he switched therapists now, Josh would certainly suffer.

Thankfully, Josh kept up a steady stream of chatter as they made their way outside. The sun was warm, but the air still held a hint of coolness as winter slowly gave way to spring, perfect weather for Josh and Dan, who'd be exerting themselves in order to use their wheelchairs.

The park was just a couple of blocks down from the hospital so it didn't take long to get there. The hardest part of the trip was navigating around the people crowding the sidewalks. Good ole New Yorkers, couldn't move over to give two people in wheelchairs room to maneuver.

They reached the south end of the park and followed the sidewalk inside. "Okay, Josh, you have to find us a good place to play ball," she instructed him.

"How about right over there?" he suggested a few minutes later, pointing to a relatively isolated grassy area.

"Perfect," she murmured. "Do you need help going over the grass?"

"I can do it," Josh said, his face intent as he exerted extra pressure to wheel himself over the bumpy terrain. Dan followed his son's example, even though he remained unusually quiet.

She plopped down on a park bench and tossed the ball up in the air, enjoying the sun on her face as she caught it again. "Remember the game we played that first day you came into the office?" she asked, directing her question to Josh.

"Yeah," Josh said, stopping his wheelchair not far from where she was seated. "Are we going to play catch again?"

"We are. But I want you and your dad to spread out a bit, so we're like the three points of a triangle."

Josh obediently moved his wheelchair back a foot. When she glanced over at Dan, he was doing the same thing.

"Excellent. Now, remember how we did it before, okay?" She tossed the ball high in the air toward Josh, who caught it easily.

"Good job, Josh," Dan said, breaking his silence.

Josh flushed with pleasure and turned his chair so that he was facing his father, before he tossed the ball up in the air. Dan had to lean over the side of the chair a bit to catch the ball, but he managed just fine. He tossed it back up in the air toward Josh.

"Molly!" Josh called, mere seconds before the ball landed on her head and then bounced off erratically. She laughed and jumped up to race after the ball.

"Caught you napping, didn't he?" Dan drawled, a smile tugging at one corner of his mouth.

She grinned and nodded. "I can't tell a lie, he certainly did."

"Good thing you have a hard head," he teased.

"Good thing." Her smile widened. She could hardly believe he'd made a joke. "I bet yours is harder," she goaded as she quickly tossed the ball at him.

She'd used a little too much force, though, and the ball caught the wind, veering off to the left, out of his reach. But that didn't stop him from stretching up and over the side of the chair in a valiant attempt to reach it.

And suddenly the wheelchair tipped sideways, dumping him onto the ground.

"Dan!" she said.

At the same time Josh yelled, "Daddy!"

She rushed over to his side. "Oh, my gosh, are you all right?" she asked anxiously.

"Fine," he muttered, his cheeks stained red with embarrassment.

"Tell me where it hurts," she murmured, pulling the chair out of the way.

He groaned and rolled onto his back, staring up at her. "Mostly hit my shoulder, but I'm fine."

"Let me see." She leaned over him, running her fingers up his muscled arm to his shoulder. Thankfully there was no bump or obvious injury that she could feel.

But when she looked down at him, their faces were so close she shivered from the intensity of his gaze.

Time hung suspended between them as he reached up and cupped her cheek with the palm of his hand. For a moment she completely forgot that Dan was a cardiothoracic surgeon. And a single father.

She leaned into his caress, catching her breath at the way his thumb slid across her cheek.

"Daddy!" Josh's cry broke the moment and she quickly pulled away from Dan, glancing up at his son.

"Don't worry, Josh, he's fine," she assured him, trying to calm her own racing heart.

What was wrong with her? What was she thinking? Getting close to her patient and, worse, to his father would be nothing more than a detour to disaster.

A path she couldn't afford to take.

Dan chided himself for thinking about what Molly would taste like if he dared to kiss her.

He must have fried a few brain cells in the sun to even contemplate such a thing. But that moment she'd leaned over him, her expression so full of care and concern, had made him ache to touch her. To hold her.

To kiss her.

And the way she'd pressed her cheek into the palm of his hand made him think that the attraction wasn't one-sided. In fact, he'd noticed her eyes had darkened with the same desire that shimmered through him.

It had been so long since he'd felt anything remotely like it that he wondered if he'd dreamed up the flash of desire?

"Do you need help?" she asked, reaching down as if to help him up.

"I'll get there by myself," he said, more gruffly than he'd intended. She snatched her hand back and then moved closer to Josh. For a moment he sat on the ground, trying to figure out how he'd get back into the wheelchair if he truly couldn't use his legs.

He prided himself on getting to the gym whenever possible between surgeries, but to lever himself up off the ground using only his arm strength to get back into the dreaded wheelchair was more than he could manage.

Feeling like a wimp, he gave up the pretense. He rose to his feet and plopped back into his chair. Seeing Josh's concerned gaze made him feel even worse, because for a few minutes there he hadn't thought about Josh at all.

Just Molly. Pretty, cheerful, stubborn Molly.

"Hey, don't worry, Josh. I'm not hurt a bit." He wheeled himself closer to his son. "Make sure you don't make the same mistake I did, okay?"

"Okay." Josh's worried expression eased.

Dan risked a glance at Molly, and immediately felt bad when he noted the tiny frown puckering her brow. He hated knowing that he was the source of the frown. Especially when she was always so cheerful.

Just another reason for him to keep his distance. He wasn't ready to get involved in a relationship. Clearly, after what happened with Suzy he didn't even know how to function in a true relationship. He'd forever remember the accusations Suzy had hurled at him when she'd walked out. She'd called him cold and heartless, blaming him for everything that had gone wrong in their marriage.

Molly deserved better than someone like him.

He wasn't stupid enough to believe the failure was all his fault, but unfortunately he knew much of what she'd said was true. He did work long hours. His patients did often come first.

He hadn't always been there for her. For Josh. Especially in those first difficult months after Josh's birth. And later, once the lure of spending his money had worn off, she'd moved on to someone else.

Pushing the dark memories aside wasn't easy, but dwelling on the past wasn't going to help. He needed to focus on the present. On Josh.

He was relieved when the tenseness between him and Molly faded as the morning went on. They sat on the grass and played the game Molly called kick the ball, and he was encouraged by how well Josh was doing even after just four days of therapy.

Josh was able to move his legs from side to side, kicking the ball from one foot to the other, something that he hadn't been able to do earlier in the week. A huge accomplishment, one that he knew he owed to Molly and her unorthodox approach to therapy.

Just another reason he needed to maintain a professional relationship with Molly. He refused to give her a reason to switch Josh to another therapist.

His son needed Molly, far more than he did.

Watching Molly's slim figure as she chased after the ball made his gut clench with awareness. He couldn't remember the last time he'd been with a woman. Too long. Maybe that's why he'd overreacted to the pressure of her hands against his shoulder. Any woman would probably have inspired the same response.

When the next ball Josh sent in her direction bounced up and hit her on the nose, she laughed, and he couldn't help smiling at the light, musical sound.

Who was he kidding? He hadn't been this acutely aware of a woman since well before Josh had been born.

"I think we'll have to head back," Molly said with obvious regret as she set the red ball aside. "I have another patient scheduled at eleven."

"No-o-o," Josh wailed, his previous good humor vanishing in a flash. He pounded his fist on the padded arm of the wheelchair. "I don't wanna go."

Dan empathized with his son, feeling the same sense of regret at knowing their time together was over. The reminder that this had been nothing more than a job for Molly was like a cold slap to the face.

"We'll come back again soon, Josh," Molly said as she crossed over and put her arm around Josh's thin shoulders, giving him a reassuring hug. "We sure had fun today, didn't we?"

Josh buried his face into her side and nodded.

"We don't have to leave yet, Josh," Dan found himself saying. Molly swung toward him, her face registering surprise, and he hastily clarified, "I know you have other patients to see, but there's no reason we can't stay longer."

"Oh, no, of course not." Was he imagining the flash of disappointment in her eyes? He must have been because now she sounded downright happy. "Would you like that, Josh?" she asked with a smile. "Wouldn't it be great to stay here longer with your dad?"

His son clutched at Molly and shook his head, sending a spear of disappointment straight through his heart.

Molly looked surprised and upset by his son's response but the last thing he wanted or needed was her pity. "It's okay, Josh. I'm sure you're tired, so maybe it's just better if we head home. Mitch will be coming over after lunch anyway."

Josh still didn't respond, so Molly spoke up, filling the abrupt silence. "Sounds good, then. Let's go." Molly gently eased away from Josh and smiled, even though he could tell she was troubled. As they headed out of the park her pager went off.

"Are we late?" Dan asked, mindful of the fact that her next patient could already be there, waiting for her back at the hospital.

"No, it's not that," she said slowly. "Apparently my eleven o'clock patient cancelled, too."

He shouldn't have been relieved by the news but he was. "Do your patients cancel a lot?" he asked, perplexed. "I mean, two in a row seems a bit much."

She grimaced and nodded. "Actually, this happens more than you'd think. Especially on days like today, when it's nice out. Or on bad-weather days. Or days close to the holidays…" Her voice trailed off and she shrugged. "Hey, it's part of the business. Some people just don't think physical therapy is important. But the good news is that now we don't have to hurry back."

"Did you hear that, Josh? We can stay another hour."

The way Josh brightened at the news that they could stay longer only reinforced the fact that he wasn't feeling too tired after all.

Josh just hadn't wanted to stay without Molly.

And, heaven help him, he couldn't blame his son. Not when he felt exactly the same way.

Molly shouldn't deny the wave of relief she felt that she didn't have to return to the hospital just yet. Being outside was glorious, but she knew it was more than that.

Josh and Dan were getting to her. She knew they needed this time together just as much, if not more so, than Josh needed his physical therapy.

"Daddy, can we have hot dogs?" Josh asked excitedly, when a hot dog vendor pushed his cart into view. "I'm hungry!"

"Why not?" Dan said with a smile. "I'm hungry too."

"I'll race you over there," Josh challenged, wheeling himself quickly along the path.

"You're on," Dan shouted, taking off after his son.

Molly laughed when Josh reached the hot dog stand first and then raised his hands over his head in a gesture of victory when he beat his father. She suspected Dan had let him win, and couldn't deny the warm glow she felt seeing them interact together.

Not for the first time she wondered what had happened to Josh's mother. Not that it was any of her business but, still, she couldn't imagine a woman giving up her husband and her son.

Her entire family.

For a moment her smile dimmed, but just then Dan turned and called over to her. "Molly, are you up for a hot dog, too?"

"Sure," she agreed, striding over. She couldn't explain why, but she was suddenly ravenously hungry.

"My treat," Dan said gruffly, when she pulled money out of her pocket. She stared at him with indecision until he added, "Please? It's the least I can do."

"All right," she agreed, shoving the money back into her pocket. She took the hot dog and loaded it up with ketchup and mustard, before following Dan and Josh over to the closest picnic table.

As they enjoyed the impromptu meal, she couldn't

help noticing that the three of them looked just like any other family enjoying a day at the park.

But of course this wasn't a date. It was therapy.

No matter how much she wanted to pretend otherwise, Josh and Dan did not belong to her. They weren't her family.

She needed to remember that as soon as Josh was able, they'd both walk away.

CHAPTER FIVE

DAN PACED THE LENGTH of the kitchen while Josh ate cereal for breakfast. He felt at a loss as to what to do with himself now that he had so much time on his hands. He'd given Gemma the weekend off to visit her daughter and granddaughter, and now the hours stretched endlessly ahead of him. When was the last time he'd had a week off work? Or a weekend that wasn't filled with peewee football, birthday parties and soccer?

He felt bad that Josh couldn't take part in sports anymore, although he sincerely hoped his son would be able to join again next year. And he couldn't help feeling guilty that he'd been a little annoyed with the chore of driving his son around prior to the car accident.

Now he'd give anything to see his son running up and down the soccer field again.

He flexed his sore muscles, having already worked out in his weight room, trying to sweat thoughts of Molly from his system. It was ridiculous to lose sleep over a woman.

Not just any woman, he corrected himself grimly. His son's physical therapist, a woman who wore sunshine and happiness like a brightly colored dress.

A woman so different from him that they may as well be suspended in different solar systems.

The phone rang, and he welcomed the distraction, jumping to answer it. "Hello?"

"Dan, Marcus here. One of your patients, Carrie Allen, came into clinic with pneumonia. I just wanted you to know I started her on antibiotics again."

He frowned, thinking he should go in to see little Carrie for himself. "Did you admit her?"

"No, luckily her mother brought her in early, so I think she'll be all right. I'm going to see her again next week and if anything changes, I'll admit her to Angel's."

Dan rubbed the back of his neck, trying to relax. "Okay, great. Thanks for letting me know."

"Are you planning to attend Jack Carter's going-away party next Friday?" Marcus asked.

"Where is Carter going?"

"He resigned as Chief of General Pediatrics to work with Nina Wilson at her pro bono clinic."

"Really?" He felt like he'd been away from Angel's for months, instead of just a few weeks. "Our loss. I would like to attend the party. Where is it?"

"Eight o'clock at the Ritz Carlton. Nothing but the best for Jack."

Dan made a note of the date and time. "By the way, what do you know about Molly Shriver, the physical therapist?" he asked, trying, and failing, to sound casual. "Do you know if she's seeing anyone?"

"I don't know, but I think one of the nurses here is a friend of hers. Just a minute." Before Dan could stop him, he put Emily on the line, who cheerfully explained how Molly had broken up with some guy a little over a year ago.

Feeling like a fool, he thanked her for the information and quickly ended the call. He wasn't proud of himself for eliciting gossip about Molly, but he couldn't help feeling pleased that she wasn't seeing anyone at the moment.

"I'm finished, Daddy," Josh said, pushing away from the table. Before he could move over to help him, Josh had swung himself from the kitchen chair into the wheelchair.

He'd been amazed at how quickly Josh had adapted to using the wheelchair and had found getting from one place to another far harder than he'd ever imagined, giving him a new perspective for what his patients had to go through.

Heck, he'd even fallen out of the stupid contraption yesterday at the park. Although the minute Molly had come over to tend to him, embarrassment hadn't been his biggest concern. Instantly, he'd wanted nothing more than to kiss her.

An impulse that he thankfully hadn't acted on.

He needed to stop thinking about her, or he was going to drive himself crazy.

"What are we going to do, today, Daddy?" Josh asked.

Good question. How pathetic that he had no idea how to entertain his son. What did other parents do with their kids on the weekends? He had no clue. He racked his brains.

"We could try that new indoor game place," he offered. What was the name of it? Fun and Games? "Even with your wheelchair, I think there are lots of things you can do."

"Really?" Josh's eyes lit up with excitement. "Can we ask Molly to come, too?"

It was on the tip of his tongue to refuse, except for

the fact that he'd had the same idea. "I'll give her a call, but I don't know if she'll agree to come," he cautioned Josh. The last thing Dan wanted was to get his son's hopes up. "She might already have plans for today."

Or she might refuse, simply because going with them was crossing the line of professionalism.

His hands were damp as he dialed her number. She didn't answer so he left a message, giving his phone number and asking her to call him back if she was interested in going to Fun and Games with him and Josh. When he hung up the phone, he had the depressing thought that she might not bother to return his call.

He hid his disappointment when he turned back to his son. "Sorry, champ, but Molly wasn't home. I left her a message, but I think we're on our own today. But we'll have a great time anyway, right?"

"Right," Josh agreed without enthusiasm.

Dan wished there was something he could do or say to cheer him up. But it was hard to be upbeat when he felt the same way.

He was worse than Josh, counting the hours until Monday when they'd see Molly again.

Molly listened to the voice-mail message at least three times, secretly thrilled at hearing Dan's husky voice inviting her to go along with them to Fun and Games. She'd managed to push him from her mind during her three-mile run, but now he was back there, front and center.

Although it wasn't as if he'd invited her out on a date or anything, as Josh would be with them. And the indoor games place was hardly a romantic setting but even so, she was tempted, oh, so tempted to say yes.

She tried to rationalize her desire to go, telling herself this little outing could be just an extension of Josh's therapy. Josh had already made great progress in just five days—surely he'd be even further along if she helped him today?

Before she could talk herself out of it, she dialed Dan's phone number. He picked it up on the first ring and for a moment she couldn't speak.

"Hello?" he asked again. "Is this Molly?"

"Ah, yes, this is Molly," she blurted out, finally finding her voice. "I'm, um, returning your phone call." Brilliant conversation, she told herself, rolling her eyes. Just brilliant. Could she sound like a bigger dope?

"Molly, I'm so glad you called back. Would you be willing to go to Fun and Games with me and Josh? We'd love you to."

The eagerness in his tone soothed her frayed nerves. "Sure, what time?"

"Well, I thought we'd go later this afternoon and then stay for dinner, although they mostly serve pizzas and burgers. With the traffic in New York, I could pick you up at two or two-thirty. If that's all right with you." Was it her imagination or did Dan sound nervous? "We could also play more of your games before heading out, if you think that would be all right."

"No, of course I wouldn't mind. Two o'clock sounds fine. Would you rather I meet you at the clinic? That way you don't have to drive all the way out here to the Bronx."

"Josh and I will pick you up, right, Josh?"

She had to grin when she heard Josh yelling "Yeah!" in the background.

"All right, I'll see you around two." She was about

to hang up when Dan asked for her address. Feeling a little embarrassed, she rattled off the number of her apartment building. She knew it wasn't exactly in the best neighborhood, but it was all she could afford on her therapist's salary.

"See you soon," Dan murmured huskily.

"All right," she managed, before hanging up. For a moment she couldn't move, stunned by what she'd just agreed to. Was she crazy? Didn't she have any self-preservation left after James had dumped her last year?

Apparently not, since she didn't make a move to cancel her plans. No matter how stupid, she was looking forward to seeing Dan and Josh again.

She usually cleaned on Saturdays, and as she had a few hours to kill, she stuck to her routine. When she'd finished, she showered and dried her hair, deciding to keep her hair down rather than pulling it back into a ponytail, the way she usually wore it at work.

This wasn't a date, but she still managed to try on just about every article of casual clothing that she owned, which admittedly wasn't much. She wore scrubs to work and didn't have enough money to be a clotheshorse. In the end, she settled on a pair of well-worn jeans and a bright green short-sleeved shirt that brought out the color of her eyes. Perfect attire for Fun and Games, although she wished she had something to wear that would make her look nice for Dan.

Stop it, she lectured herself. She was going along to help Josh with his therapy. Nothing more.

And maybe if she repeated that several more times, she'd find a way to believe it.

When her apartment buzzer went off at five minutes before two, she quickly crossed over to answer it. "I'll be right down," she said through the intercom, not wanting Dan to see her sparse furnishings. She'd gotten most of them from a secondhand store, and nothing matched.

She was surprised when only Dan was there, waiting for her in the minuscule lobby. "Where's Josh?" she asked.

"He's in the car, I'm double-parked outside," Dan admitted with a wry grin. "Let's go before I get a ticket."

She laughed and shook her head. "They wouldn't dare give Dr. Daniel Morris, renowned pediatric cardiothoracic surgeon at Angel's, a ticket."

He didn't say anything in response, but when he put his hand in the small of her back, gently urging her forward, she felt his light touch all the way down to her toes.

Get a grip, she told herself sternly.

Thankfully, Josh was excited to see her, diverting her attention from the ridiculous attraction she felt for his father. "Hi, Molly!"

"Hi, Josh. How are you feeling?"

"Good. Are we gonna play some more games today?" he asked. "I have more fun with you."

She winced at Josh's blunt statement and glanced over at Dan, noticing his mouth was set in a grim line. She knew he cared deeply about his son, and it couldn't be easy for him to hear Josh express his feelings.

No wonder Dan had asked her to come along today.

"Sure, we'll play some more games," she agreed, covering the awkward silence.

She was relieved that Josh kept up a steady stream of chatter as Dan drove back to their place. When they arrived, she waited patiently for him to pull Josh's wheelchair out of the trunk of the car, before heading to the elevator. She wasn't the least bit surprised to see that Dan lived in a luxurious apartment on the top floor, one that no doubt cost twenty times her annual salary. She tried not to feel intimidated as Dan showed her to the playroom.

"Where are you going?" she asked, when he turned to leave. "You have to play with us, right, Josh?"

"Right," Josh agreed.

She thought Dan's smile dimmed a bit, although he stayed in the playroom with them. Determined to make the most of the time they had, she ran them through a series of games, which had Josh giggling with enjoyment by the time they were through.

"Enough," Dan cried, throwing his hands in the air. "I give up!"

"What do you think, Josh?" she asked. "Should we let your dad off the hook?"

"No," Josh said, shaking his head. "Let's beat him again!"

She felt bad for ganging up with Josh against his father. "No, that's not fair. This time I think you and your dad should go against me."

"Actually, I don't think we have time," Dan said gently. "We have to get going, if you want to eat dinner any time soon."

She glanced guiltily at her watch, realizing they'd played far longer than planned. "All right, then, let's go."

Technically, after the time she had just spent with them, there was no need for her to really go to Fun and Games with them. For a moment, it crossed her mind to beg off. She could easily take the subway home.

But she held her tongue as Dan helped Josh put on

jeans and a T-shirt. "Look, Molly, we match!" Josh said excitedly, pointing to his green shirt.

"So we do," she murmured, knowing that she didn't have the heart to disappoint Josh by backing out of their plans now.

Not even to save herself from more heartache.

"I'm hungry, Daddy," Josh complained as he drove to Fun and Games.

He glanced at his son, in the rearview mirror. "I know. We'll be there soon, okay?"

"Okay," Josh agreed.

"I'm hungry too, Josh," Molly said, swiveling in her seat so she could face him. "What are you going to have? Pizza? Or a burger?"

"Pizza!" Josh shouted.

Dan smiled, but kept quiet as Molly chatted with Josh. When he'd first picked her up at her rundown apartment building, he'd almost turned round and left. The fact that Molly didn't have a lot of money made him wonder, just for a brief moment, if she was looking for a rich husband, the way Suzy had been. But it wasn't fair to compare her to Suzy, so he thrust the thought aside.

And when she'd come down to the lobby, a bright smile on her face, he'd nearly swallowed his tongue. She was stunning, even wearing simple figure-hugging jeans and a bright green blouse. He appreciated the curves that had previously been hidden by her baggy scrubs. And she'd left her red-gold hair down, gently framing her heart-shaped face, leaving him to wonder if the strands would feel as silky soft as they looked.

Did she have any idea the effect she had on him?

How distracted he'd been by her the entire time they'd played therapy games with Josh? He'd hardly been able to tear his gaze off her long enough to catch the ball. He didn't even care that they'd ganged up on him, not when the sound of their laughter rang through his home.

He couldn't remember the last time Josh had laughed so much. Too long, he decided. Far too long.

And he had Molly to thank for it.

He pulled into the jammed parking lot, realizing that many other parents must have had the same idea to bring their kids here to play. Normally, he'd avoid these types of places like the plague, yet for some reason, tonight he was looking forward to it.

Something else he could thank Molly for.

He pulled out Josh's wheelchair, and quickly unfolded it. He'd become an expert over the past few days.

"Wow," Molly murmured in awe, when they took the ramp into the building. There were games lining all the walls, a bouncy house in the middle of the room and of course plenty of picnic table type seating. "This is amazing!"

"It's loud, that's for sure," Dan mumbled with a sigh. He had to smile at the way Molly glanced around in awe, as if she'd never been inside a place like this.

"What do you want to play first?" she asked Josh.

"I want to hit the gophers!"

He grimaced and led his son and Molly over to the video game where several gophers popped out of holes and the goal was to bop them on the head to push them back in. The player scored a point for every gopher they hit.

Molly giggled as Josh started smacking the gophers. "Get 'em, Josh, get 'em!"

"Are you hungry?" Dan asked, once Josh had finished his game. "There's an empty table right over there."

Molly nodded, and quickly crossed over to the table. He was impressed at how well Josh managed to finagle his way through the games room with his wheelchair.

"What will you have?" he asked.

"Well, Josh wants pizza, so that would be fine with me," she admitted.

"No problem. I'll put in our order." He felt a little guilty that the only food he'd provided for her so far had been fast food, but when the pizza arrived, she and Josh both dove into the meal with such relish that he suspected she didn't mind. Besides, there was no point in wishing he could take her to a nice restaurant, where they could enjoy a quiet meal by candlelight.

This evening was for Josh. Not for him.

He discovered Molly was a kid at heart and she threw herself into the games with gusto. She also had a highly competitive streak, getting frustrated when he beat her score on the gopher game. And when she finally topped his score, she jumped up, whooping as loudly as his son.

"I think you've lost your voice," he said, when they made their way back out to the car some hours later.

"I know," she said hoarsely, with a tired smile. "But it was worth it."

He gave her credit for thinking that, since his ears were still ringing from the bells and whistles shrieking from the various games.

Josh yawned widely, trying to keep his eyes open. "That was so fun, Molly. I'm glad you came with us."

"Me, too," she whispered.

Dan watched his son in the rearview mirror, smiling to himself at how hard Josh fought to stay awake on the way home. But they'd only been in the car for fifteen minutes when his head dropped off to the side and he fell asleep.

Now that he was essentially alone with Molly, he found he couldn't come up with a safe topic of conversation.

"You're doing a good job with Josh," she said hoarsely, breaking the silence. "How is it that you're able to come to all his therapy appointments?"

"I took a leave of absence from work," he admitted. "And it's well worth it because he's responding so well to therapy."

"Yes. He is."

He was tempted to reach over to take her small hand in his when suddenly Josh cried out. "Ow, Daddy, it hurts. It hurts!"

"What's wrong, Josh?" Instantly, Molly twisted in her seat, reaching back for Josh. "What hurts? Tell me what hurts?"

"My legs," he cried. "Make it stop! They hurt so bad!"

"What's going on, Molly?" Dan asked, keeping his attention on the road. He'd been about to head for Molly's apartment to drop her off, but they were closer to his place, which was only five minutes away.

"I think he's having muscle cramps," Molly said, with a worried expression on her face. She quickly unbuckled her seat belt and managed to climb into the backseat. "I'll work on massaging his legs, but it would work better if he was lying down."

"We'll be home in less than five minutes," he told her.

Dan could hear Molly trying to talk soothingly to

Josh as she worked on his legs, but his son was still crying out in pain.

"Mommy!" Josh cried, sobbing as he arched his back in the booster seat. "I want my mommy!"

Helpless fury banded Dan's lungs, making it difficult to breathe. He gripped the steering wheel tightly, listening in agony to his son's suffering, as he pushed the car as fast as he dared to get Josh home.

CHAPTER SIX

MOLLY DID HER BEST TO massage the cramping from Josh's legs, knowing that it was her fault the child was in pain. She wouldn't blame Dan for switching therapists after this. She barely registered the fact that they'd arrived back at Dan's until he opened the door of the backseat and reached for Josh.

She unsnapped the belt holding Josh in. Wordlessly, his features tense, Dan scooped Josh from the booster seat and into his arms before striding toward the elevator, leaving her to scramble along behind them. Thankfully the elevator arrived quickly and she continued to massage the muscles in Josh's legs as they rode up to the thirty-second floor.

"His room is this way," Dan said gruffly, as he swung through the condo to Josh's bedroom. The boy had ceased screaming for his mother, but he was still crying. Each gulping sob broke her heart.

"I need some lotion," she said to Dan when he'd gently set Josh down. She climbed up onto Josh's bed in order to have a better angle that would enable her to use more pressure on his leg muscles. Dan returned quickly with a small tube of hand lotion.

She ignored the fatigue in her own fingers as she worked over Josh's legs. After about twenty minutes he stopped crying, but she still continued to massage his legs until she only felt the smoothness of relaxed muscles beneath the angry red scars.

She nearly jumped when she felt Dan's hand on her shoulder. "He's asleep, Molly. I think you can stop now."

With a brief nod she awkwardly tried to climb off Josh's bed, wincing as the muscles in her back cramped painfully from being bent over for so long. When she managed to get back on the floor, she stumbled and would have fallen if not for Dan's strong arms wrapping around her waist, holding her up.

For a moment she could only lean against him, reveling in the strength of his arms surrounding her as she breathed in his unique musky scent.

After a long moment she forced herself to break away, standing up on her own two feet. She avoided Dan's gaze as she made her way back to the main living area. She dropped onto the sofa and mentally braced herself as she slowly raised her gaze to meet his, fully expecting to feel the scathing edge of his tongue.

"Thank you," he murmured. He sat down heavily beside her, scrubbing his hand over his jaw. "I don't know what I would have done if you hadn't been there."

She blinked in surprise at his gratitude. "It's my fault, Dan," she said, unable to take credit for helping Josh through the crisis when it had been her fault from the beginning. "I shouldn't have allowed him to overdo things this afternoon. I should have realized that he'd be moving around a lot with all the games."

"Josh was enjoying himself," he pointed out with a tired sigh. "If anyone is to blame, it's me."

She shook her head, knowing he was shouldering blame that wasn't his. She was glad Josh had fallen asleep and prayed that the muscle cramps wouldn't return.

When Dan didn't say anything for several long seconds she remembered how Josh had called out for his mother. She had to assume that Dan had joint custody of his son, but surely the boy needed his mother at times like this? "Are you planning to call Josh's mother?"

Instantly, his expression turned grim. "No."

She was shocked at his blunt refusal. How could he turn his back on his son like that? "Why not?" she pressed, refusing to listen to the tiny voice in the back of her mind telling her to mind her own business. "Josh was calling for her. He obviously needs his mother."

Dan muttered something that sounded like a curse under this breath as he rose to his feet. "Despite what you heard, Josh hasn't seen his mother in six years."

She sucked in a harsh breath, wondering if she'd heard him correctly. He'd raised Josh since he was a one-year-old? "Six years? Really?"

He rubbed the back of his neck. "Besides, my ex wouldn't come, even if I did call her," he finally admitted. "Not unless I offered her money. And I refuse to pay her another dime to be a mother to her son."

She opened her mouth and then closed it again, unable to think of anything to say in response. She found it impossible to imagine what had caused Dan's ex to turn her back on her husband and her son. "Her loss," she finally managed.

Dan's tense facial features relaxed. "I think so, too," he agreed softly. Then he cleared his throat and glanced toward his son's room. "Look, Molly, it's late and I know you probably want to get home, but I would rather you stayed here in case Josh's muscle cramps return."

His request caught her completely off guard. “Here?” she squeaked.

“In the guest room,” he hastily clarified, ramming his hands into the front pockets of his jeans, looking distinctly uncomfortable. “It’s the room right next to Josh’s.”

She didn’t have any of her things, not even a toothbrush or a comb, but the thought of Josh’s muscle cramps returning was enough that she couldn’t bring herself to refuse. Staying to ease the child’s pain was the least she could do. “Of course I’ll stay.”

Relief flooded his features. “Thank you. I have spare toiletries and will leave them in the bathroom you’ll share with Josh.”

She wanted to smile at the way he’d made a point of letting her know she wouldn’t have to worry about stumbling across him in the middle of the night. She assumed that his master suite had its own bathroom. Not that she should even imagine him in his master suite. She quickly pulled her thoughts away from the image that bloomed in her mind. “Um, great! Sounds good.”

“This way,” he said, gesturing to the doorway of the spare bedroom with one hand.

She rose to her feet and followed him across the living room to the guest room. He paused next to her, so close she could feel the heat radiating off his skin.

“Thanks again, Molly,” he murmured, staring down at her intently.

For a moment she thought he was going to kiss her, but instead he simply took her hand and squeezed it gently. She was glad it was dark, so he wouldn’t see how she blushed. “You’re welcome,” she murmured, forcing herself to tug her hand gently from his when all she really wanted to do was to throw herself into his arms.

When he finally left, she leaned against the door and took several deep breaths, trying to calm her racing heart.

She needed to remember that he'd only asked her to stay for his son's sake, not because he wanted to be alone with her or anything. If she hadn't been able to hold on to James, there was really no way in the world she had a chance with someone like Dan. He was way, way out of her league.

She brushed her teeth and vowed to take the subway home first thing in the morning, putting their relationship back on a professional level.

Where it belonged.

Dan didn't sleep very well, and while he'd have liked to blame his son's leg cramps, he knew the real reason was because Molly was just down the hall in the guest room.

So close.

Too close.

He finally crawled out of his bed at five-thirty, knowing that trying to sleep any longer was useless. And there was a tiny part of him that looked forward to seeing Molly this morning.

After a quick shower, he padded softly to the kitchen and peered inside the fridge. He wanted to make a nice big breakfast as a way to thank Molly for helping Josh through his crisis and staying last night.

He hadn't heard Josh wake up at all, and since he'd been awake half the night, he could only assume his son had slept peacefully.

After brewing a pot of coffee, he began pulling out

the ingredients for French toast, Josh's favorite. He prepared the egg mixture so that he'd have things ready to go when Molly and Josh woke up. His stomach rumbled with hunger so he decided to cook thick slabs of bacon, as well.

"Do your patients know you eat like that?"

He spun round to find Molly hovering in the doorway, dressed in the clothing she'd worn the day before, only this time she'd pulled her long red-gold hair back into its usual ponytail, a style that made her look incredibly young.

Or maybe he was just incredibly old.

"Ah, good morning, Molly." What was it about her that made it difficult for him to think straight? He glanced down at the bacon with a guilty flush. "My patients are children, not adults. And, besides, having bacon once in a while isn't too bad, right?"

She laughed softly and hitched her purse over her shoulder. "I guess not, although I must confess I would have imagined you making wholegrain pancakes or granola and yogurt for breakfast."

He grimaced wryly. "Guess I've tarnished my image, huh? Come in, have a seat. Would you care for coffee?"

She gazed longingly toward the coffeepot, but slowly shook her head. "No, I should probably head home. I just wanted to thank you for your hospitality."

"You can't leave without eating breakfast," he said in a rush of panic, ridiculously upset that she intended to leave so early. "Did you really think I was cooking all of this for me?" he asked, gesturing to the meal in progress incredulously.

"Well…" she said doubtfully. "I don't want to impose on your family time."

He didn't have the heart to admit that he and Josh didn't exactly have family time, at least not in the way she probably thought. They had more of a trying-to-rekindle-their-broken-relationship-time, which consisted of awkward silences more than anything else.

"If you leave now, you would be imposing on me and Josh to eat all this food by ourselves," he teased, trying to keep his tone light. "Please sit down, and are you sure you wouldn't like a cup of coffee?"

She chewed her lower lip nervously, but then ventured farther into the kitchen, taking a seat on the stool in front of the breakfast nook. "I'd love some coffee. The mere scent was enough to wake me up from a sound sleep."

He busied himself with pouring her a mug of coffee, sliding it over to her before getting one for himself. "Cream, sugar?" he asked.

"Cream or milk, if you have some." She cupped her hands around the mug as if needing the warmth.

He brought out the milk, and then frowned. "Are you cold? I'll turn up the heat."

"Maybe a little," she admitted, rubbing her hands up and down her arms. "It's been so nice the past few days, but now I can see frost outside."

"Welcome to spring in New York," he muttered. "Hang on a minute, I'll get you a sweatshirt."

He flipped the bacon strips before he retreated to his bedroom, looking for one of his sweatshirts. He brought it out for her, oddly pleased at how she looked wearing his clothing.

"Thank you."

"It's the least I can do," he responded. "I, uh, hope

you like French toast," he said, crossing back over to the stove. "It's Josh's favorite."

"I love it," she assured him. She took a sip of her coffee and he couldn't help thinking how pretty she was. Suzy had worn enough makeup to paint a clown, but he preferred Molly's fresh-scrubbed beauty any day of the week.

Forcing his gaze to the task at hand, he dunked the bread slices in the egg mixture and set them into the sizzling fry pan.

"Dan, I have a question for you and I hope you don't think I'm intruding or anything."

He glanced up from the French toast. "You can ask me anything, Molly," he said truthfully. After baring his soul to her last night about Josh's mother, he couldn't imagine what could be too intrusive.

"It's, uh, about Josh's birthday." She was staring down at her coffee as if afraid to look him in the eye. "I was wondering if you'd made any plans?"

He tightened his jaw, and spent a few minutes flipping the bread slices before answering. "No, I haven't planned anything yet," he said slowly. "But I'm guessing you think I should have some sort of party?"

"I don't want to tell you what to do," she said hesitantly. "But if you were going to have a party, I'd offer to help."

"You would?" He glanced up and caught her gaze. She looked so hopeful he found he couldn't deny her anything. "What sort of party are you imagining?" he asked with a mock frown.

"Here's what I've been thinking," she said, leaning forward eagerly. "We could get a whole bunch of wheelchairs from the clinic and invite Josh's friends to a game of wheelchair football. That way he could play with them, and I think his friends would get a kick out of it, too. We could serve either hot dogs and hamburgers or pizza for dinner. What do you think?"

He had to admit she'd nailed the best idea he'd ever heard. "I think it's a perfect idea. If the weather co-operates."

"I know. March is dicey," she murmured. "But as long as it's not snowing, they can bundle up and we don't have to play for hours. If it's cold, we can start at the park and then come here afterward." She glanced around at his immaculate apartment and frowned. "If you don't mind the fact that the kids will likely make a mess," she added doubtfully.

Normally, he wasn't ashamed at the fact that he liked his life neat and orderly, but the way she looked at his things made him feel slightly embarrassed. Since when was having a clean home more important than his son's happiness?

"I don't mind at all," he quickly interjected. "All that matters is that Josh and his friends have fun."

She relaxed, a bright smile blooming on her face. His gut tightened with awareness. He'd never been more attracted to a woman than he was to Molly. She was a beacon of light in his otherwise drab existence. "Great. There's no time to lose. We have to invite his friends as soon as possible."

"I'll call his teacher, I'm sure she'll give me the names of the kids in his classroom."

"You should invite all of them, girls, too," Molly informed him.

"Girls?" He didn't try to hide his surprise. "Really? Isn't first grade a little young for having girls over?"

"It's just the polite thing to do," she said. "Besides, we're planning this at the last minute, so I'm worried a lot of the kids might not be able to come."

He scowled as he scooped the slices of French toast off the griddle and stacked them on a plate. He hoped the kids in Josh's class would come, and hoped that giving them all wheelchairs to use would keep the teasing down to a minimum.

"Breakfast is ready," he said, carrying the plate over to the breakfast nook. He pulled the bacon out of the pan, too, blotting the grease and then stacking them on another plate. Lastly he pulled out the maple syrup, before sliding into the seat beside her, so close their elbows bumped.

He watched with amusement as she doused her French toast with enough maple syrup to float a boat. She took a big bite and then closed her eyes, as if savoring the flavor. "Mmm, absolutely delicious," she announced.

"Thanks." He took a bite of his food, admitting that it was pretty darned good. But he knew the main reason he was enjoying his meal so much was because of Molly. Somehow she had the ability to brighten his day with nothing more than a smile.

Selfishly, because he didn't have much to offer her in return, he found himself wishing that she would be around to share breakfast with him every morning.

Molly told herself at least ten times to leave Dan's to return home, but somehow she ended up spending the entire morning with him. And Josh.

She was thrilled that he'd agreed to her idea for Josh's birthday party. And if she was a little annoyed that he hadn't come up with something for himself, she put those feelings aside.

She was beginning to realize that Dan needed help, not just in learning how to play games but in learning how to be a father. What his ex had done, leaving him alone with a small son to raise on his own, was appalling. And while she understood he had a very demanding career, operating on young infants and children, surely they weren't more important to him than his son?

She couldn't help wondering about him, especially his past, even as she insisted on helping to clean up the breakfast dishes. To her surprise, Dan refused to let her do the work alone. Working side by side with him in such a mundane task as washing dishes brought a strange sort of intimacy to their relationship.

"I'd like to massage Josh's legs one more time before I go," she said as she finished drying the last pan. "Too bad I don't have the ultrasound machine here for him. He could really benefit from that therapy, too."

Dan scowled as he took the damp dishtowel from her. "I could buy one, if you think that would help."

"Buy one?" she echoed, aghast. "Do you have any idea how expensive they are?"

"Doesn't matter," he said with a shrug. "I'll buy one today, if you think it would help."

She could hardly believe he was really offering to purchase an expensive piece of equipment for Josh to use for such a short time.

But then again, wasn't she surrounded by luxury? Dan Morris obviously could afford an ultrasound machine. Or anything else he or Josh desired.

"Don't be ridiculous," she muttered. "We can stop by the clinic and use the ultrasound there just as easily."

"Great. And then maybe we can take in a movie this afternoon, too."

"Yeah!" Josh said with barely repressed enthusiasm. "Come on, Molly. Please? Please come see a movie with us?"

She wanted to say no. Needed desperately to put distance between them. Maybe Dan cooked breakfast like a normal person, but he was a pediatric cardiothoracic surgeon, for heaven's sake. Wasn't this fancy condo proof of how he moved in much higher circles than she could even fathom? She'd heard rumors that his salary was seven figures. Talk about a mind-boggling amount. She didn't make a tenth of what he did.

This…friendship, or camaraderie or whatever they had couldn't go anywhere. Why was she setting herself up for more heartache? She was destined to remain an outsider, and nothing was going to change that. Dan only thought he needed her now, but as soon as he'd repaired his relationship with his son, he'd move on.

"Please, Molly?" Josh said again. And looking down at Josh's big brown eyes, mirror images of his father's, she couldn't bring herself to say no.

"Yes, Josh, I'd love to see a movie with you."

CHAPTER SEVEN

GOING INTO THE physical therapy clinic on Sunday, when no one was around, felt strange. Molly didn't think she would get into trouble or anything but, still, she knew she'd be glad when she'd finished the ultrasound treatments to Josh's legs.

While she worked on Josh, she did her best to ignore Dan's intense gaze, but it wasn't easy. At this point she didn't think he was watching her because he didn't believe in her technique.

No, this time she had the distinct impression he was watching her out of some sort of personal interest. Not a romantic interest, she told herself quickly, but more as if she were some sort of alien creature that he couldn't quite figure out.

Maybe because she was so different from his ex? Hearing Josh cry for his mother had really bothered her. She couldn't imagine how Dan managed to cope with the demands of being a single parent.

"Can we go to the movie now?" Josh asked eagerly, after choosing a root-beer-flavored lollipop. She hid a smile, figuring he was planning to try every single flavor in the jar before starting over with grape.

"Sure thing, champ," Dan said with a gentle smile. Was it her imagination or was he already getting closer to his son? “We have plenty of time to get there before the show starts, no problem.”

“Yay,” Josh said, using his arms to propel his wheelchair forward as they made their way back out to the car. “I can’t wait.”

Dan sent Molly a wry smile over Josh’s head. He’d already explained that Josh wanted to see the latest Disney film, and she honestly didn’t mind. The last cartoon film she’d seen had been one that she’d watched with James’s two sons.

And if she remembered correctly, James had begged off, claiming he had work to do. Now she wondered if he’d been seeing that other woman even then.

No reason to torture herself over that now. Her friend Kara had told her she was much better off without James, and while that had been difficult to believe at first, it was easier now. Today was about Josh, not her. She was determined to enjoy herself, while protecting her heart.

Getting to the movie theater didn’t take long and once Dan had spent a small fortune on popcorn and soft drinks, they found a place in the back where Josh could sit in his wheelchair at the end of an aisle.

“Sit next to me, Molly. Sit next to me!”

She did as Josh asked, hoping Dan wouldn’t mind. He didn’t say anything, simply took the seat to her right, the action causing their shoulders to brush lightly. She settled back in her seat, telling herself to focus on the ultra-wide screen.

Flanked on either side by the Morris men made it difficult for her to concentrate on the movie. As the one in the middle she was the one stuck holding the bucket of popcorn. She grew acutely aware of Dan leaning over to help himself, especially when his arm stayed pressed against hers. Warmth radiated from his skin, sending shivers of awareness rippling along her arm.

But she didn't move away, despite knowing she should.

The movie was a cute story and she soon found herself giggling right along with Josh. And when she heard Dan laughing softly, she was secretly thrilled he'd unbent enough to enjoy the show.

"That was fun. Thanks for bringing me along," she said after the movie ended.

"I'll drive you home," Dan offered quickly. "Unless Josh and I could convince you to stay for dinner?"

"I couldn't eat a thing after all that popcorn," she protested. "Besides, I really need to get home."

"I understand," he murmured, although she caught a glimpse of disappointment shadowing his gaze.

Her resolve almost wavered. Almost. But she'd already let this go on long enough. What was she thinking, spending time with Dan and Josh as if they were more than friends? The last thing she needed was to make the same mistake with Dan and Josh as she had with James.

The ride to her apartment didn't take long. When Dan pulled up, he jumped out before she could stop him, coming over to open her door for her.

"Bye, Josh, see you tomorrow," she said as she climbed out of the car. When Dan drew her toward him so he could close the door, she had the insane thought he was going to haul her into his arms and kiss her, but then he whispered in her ear, "I'll call you later to finalize the details about Josh's party."

She flushed and ducked her head, hoping he wouldn't

notice her embarrassment. "Okay, sounds good." With a final wave to Josh she turned and hurried inside.

Feeling Dan's gaze boring into her back with every step.

Dan forced himself to get back into the car with Josh, when every cell in his body wanted to follow Molly. He was getting tied up in knots over the woman, and he knew it. Yet knowing it and stopping himself from thinking about her were two entirely different things.

Molly had helped him mend his relationship with Josh, but what he was feeling for her went beyond gratitude. He knew he needed to rein in his feelings, and fast.

But despite his firm pep talk, when he and Josh returned home he couldn't help noticing that the spacious three-bedroom apartment seemed empty now that Molly was gone. Which was ridiculous. How was it possible that his home seemed complete only when Molly was here? Nothing made any sense anymore.

He turned on some music, hoping to fill the emptiness. He busied himself making arrangements for Josh's birthday party and the wheelchair football game. There wasn't much he could do on a Sunday night, but he vowed to contact Josh's teacher first thing in the morning. The party would take place in two weeks on Saturday afternoon.

So in the interim he made plans and lists, realizing that planning a party was a lot of work. And tried not to count the hours until Josh's therapy session at nine o'clock next morning.

The following morning, Dan called Josh's teacher first thing, and she was more than happy to help him give him a list of the student's names. She also offered to pass out the invitations in class, which meant he needed to get them completed as soon as possible.

He and Josh arrived for therapy in their respective wheelchairs with scarcely a minute to spare. As usual, Molly came out to greet them. She smiled warmly at Josh, but he sensed she was avoiding eye contact with him. He scowled as he wheeled into the gym behind them, wondering if she was uncomfortable around him now, after they'd spent the weekend together. If so, he couldn't understand why. He hadn't acted inappropriately at any time, although he couldn't say the same for his thoughts.

In his thoughts, he'd been extremely inappropriate. Down and dirty inappropriate.

"We're going to play a new game today. Are you ready?" Molly asked.

"Yeah!" Josh agreed enthusiastically.

"Absolutely," Dan responded, hating to admit that he was growing used to her games.

The game consisted of hitting the ball with their feet, which of course was much easier for him than it was for Josh. But he had to give his son credit, as he seemed determined to kick the ball up in the air with his toes.

He was shocked and stunned when Molly deemed it time for the massage followed by the ultrasound treatments. How had the hour gone by that fast?

When she'd finished with Josh's ultrasound, Dan quickly followed her out of the room, leaving Josh to enjoy his lime-flavored lollipop. "Josh's teacher has emailed me the names of the kids in his class, so I'm going to work on the invitations tonight."

"That's great!" For what seemed to be the first time

that morning, she looked him directly in the eye and smiled. "Josh is going to be so surprised."

Her enthusiasm was contagious. "Here's what I have planned so far," he said. "We'll meet at the park first for the wheelchair football game, and then afterward we'll eat pizza, punch, cake and ice cream either at the park if it's nice or at my place if it's not."

"That sounds perfect," she agreed. "Don't forget prizes."

"Prizes?" He stared, perplexed. "I wasn't thinking of playing any other games."

"You need to reconsider that plan. What about a scavenger hunt?"

"A scavenger hunt?" Hell, hosting a party was more complicated than he'd realized. "I don't think I want the kids going around to the other apartments, asking for things." He couldn't remember the last time he'd participated in a scavenger hunt.

"We could have a scavenger hunt at the park, after the football game." Her green eyes brightened with excitement. "I'll hide a bunch of stuff at wheelchair height or lower, and they can try to find the items I've hidden. Whatever they find are their prizes. Although you'll need to make sure there's a prize for everyone."

He suppressed a sigh. More rules. More things to buy. He needed another list. "Okay, that'll work."

"We won't know what the weather will be like, so we might need a back-up plan. Maybe check again with Josh's teacher to see if the school would let us use the gym," she suggested. But then she glanced at her watch. "Sorry, but I have to go. My next patient is here."

"Okay, no problem." He took a step back, trying to

hide a flash of disappointment. Not that he could blame her for needing to do her job. "See you tomorrow."

"Absolutely. Goodbye." Was it his imagination or was she in a hurry to get away from him?

As he went back to where Josh was waiting, he couldn't deny he felt a little lost without the connection he'd thought he had with Molly. Had he become too dependent on her?

The realization brought him up short. He couldn't afford to be too dependent on anyone. Josh's happiness was the most important thing in his life, and he needed to remember that.

Granted, he appreciated Molly's help, but he was making strides in mending his relationship with Josh. He might be new at this hosting-a-birthday-party thing, but he was determined to be a good father. He wanted—*needed*—to make sure his son knew just how much he loved him.

Molly did her best to keep her distance from Dan, but it wasn't easy. On Tuesday night she called her friend Kara.

"Molly, it's so good to hear from you!" Kara gushed.

"I know, it's been too long, hasn't it? How are you holding up?"

"I'm doing okay." Kara's crush on Tyler Donaldson hadn't been much of a secret. However, now that the handsome Texas-born neonatologist had gotten involved with Eleanor Aston, Kara had been trying to mend her bruised heart. Especially now the two were head over heels in love and rumored to be expecting a baby. "I can't be mad at the guy, not when he's obviously so happy."

"Don't worry, you'll find someone just as perfect someday," Molly said stoutly.

"Actually, I have met someone," Kara said. "But we're just friends."

"Really?" She injected warmth into her tone, refusing to be envious of her best friend. "Anyone I know?"

"His name is David Jacobson and he's a new pediatric neonatologist at Angel's." Since Kara worked in the brand-new neonatal unit, she probably interacted with the new doctor a lot. "But we're just friends."

"Hey, you can't ever have too many friends," Molly pointed out.

"I know, and I value your friendship every day," Kara said. "By the way, would you be willing to go to Jack Carter's going-away party with me this Friday night? Did you hear he's having it at the Ritz?"

"No, I hadn't heard about the party, although I did hear that he handed in his resignation." Normally, Molly avoided fancy places like the Ritz, but maybe attending Dr. Carter's going-away party would be a good distraction. "What about your new friend, is he going to be there, too?"

"Yes, he's going and, yes, I wouldn't mind bumping into him there. Come on, Molly, please? I don't want to walk into this party all alone."

Molly knew Kara wanted a good reason to attend the same party David was going to, and since she knew Kara needed to get over Tyler, she couldn't say no. Especially as her own social life was practically nonexistent. It wouldn't hurt her to get out and mingle more. "Sure. Why not? I'd love to."

"Thank you," Kara murmured. "It starts at eight o'clock and you have to wear something fancy."

She grimaced. “Oh, boy, that means I have to go shopping.”

“And when was the last time you bought yourself something nice?” Kara demanded.

Since never. She’d worn a simple black skirt and green blouse for the ribbon-cutting ceremony, unwilling to spend her hard-earned money on fancy clothes. But it wasn’t every day that the chief of pediatrics stepped down to work at a free clinic with his fiancée, so she swallowed her protest. “Okay, okay. I’ll shop. Maybe I’ll find something on sale.”

“Did you hear who’s been appointed Chief of General Pediatrics in Jack’s place?” Kara asked.

“Who?”

“Dr. Layla Woods. I think it’s awesome that a female physician was given such a prestigious position, don’t you?”

“Yes, it’s great.” Molly didn’t know Layla Woods personally, although everyone talked about the tiny blonde bombshell and her sweet Texas accent. Not to mention her brilliance as a pediatrician. “She deserves the position.”

“I agree.”

“Are you sure you’re okay?” she asked, when Kara went quiet. “I’m sure it’s not easy to see Eleanor and Tyler together all the time.”

“It was hard at first, but now they just seem so natural together that I can’t help but be happy for them.”

“You’re amazing, Kara, you know that?”

“Thanks, Molly, so are you. Hey, look, I have to run, my break is over. We’ll talk more later, okay?” Kara quickly disconnected the call and Molly could just imagine her friend running back to the unit to take care of her tiny patients.

Molly was glad Kara wasn't too heartbroken over Tyler and Eleanor's newfound love. She didn't want to be full of envy, but she hoped Eleanor knew how lucky she was. If the rumors were true about her and Tyler having a baby, a family, was the greatest gift in the world.

Images of Dan and Josh flitted into her mind, but she shoved them aside ruthlessly. The two of them were not meant for her.

Maybe Kara was right. Maybe she needed to get out more. Socialize. Meet people. Meet men. Someone other than a single father with emotional baggage from his horrible ex-wife. What if she became involved with Dan and he ended up leaving her, just like James had?

Walking into the living room, she turned on her laptop computer and logged into her bank accounts.

She needed to know how much she could afford to spend on a dress. Because maybe, just maybe, she'd meet someone at the going-away party who would help her forget about Dr. Daniel Morris and his adorable son, Josh.

The following morning, Molly did her best to keep Josh and Dan at a professional distance. Josh's therapy was coming along very nicely, and when she played the kick-my-hand game, she was thrilled at how high Josh was able to kick.

"Oomph," she grunted, playing it up a bit as she staggered backward, gazing at Josh in awe. "You nearly knocked me over!"

"I know," Josh said with exuberance. "I'm getting stronger, right, Molly?"

"You are definitely getting stronger, champ," Dan said, a wide smile on his face. "I'm so proud of you."

Despite her best efforts to stay detached from the dynamic father and son duo, her heart ached at the love shining from Dan's eyes. Her throat tightened, and for a moment she couldn't breathe.

"We have a lot to thank Molly for, don't we?" Dan said to Josh.

The boy nodded. "Yep. We love Molly, don't we, Dad?"

She couldn't talk, could barely think as Dan's gaze clung to hers. "Yes, we do," he agreed lightly.

She knew he didn't really mean it. At least, not in the guy-girl type of way. But she knew she was blushing just the same. "Enough, you two, we have more work to do before this session is over."

In truth, they only had one more game to play before it was time for the massage and the ultrasound treatment. She finished the therapy and handed Josh the jar of lollipops, watching with amusement as he chose a lemon-flavored sucker.

"Molly, do you have a minute?" Dan asked, as she was about to leave.

She glanced at the clock. "Just a minute. I have another patient waiting."

"I understand."

She walked down the hall to her office, all too aware of Dan following close behind. "Is there a problem? Has Josh been having more muscle spasms?"

"No, there's nothing wrong." Was it her imagination or did he look nervous? "I just wanted to know if you were busy on Friday night?"

For a moment she couldn't hear anything but her heart thudding in her chest. Was he really asking her out on a date? Then she realized he probably wanted her to spend time with him and Josh again. She sensed he liked having her as a buffer when he interacted with his son. Although they were clearly getting along better so she knew he didn't really need her.

"I'm sorry, but I already have plans. Maybe another time?"

The disappointment in his eyes tugged at her heart, but she did her best to ignore it. "Sure. Another time, then."

She tore her gaze away and glanced again at the clock. Of course today every one of her patients was going to show up for their appointments. "I'll see you and Josh tomorrow, okay?" Without waiting for him to say anything, she quickly left her office, heading to the waiting room to greet her next patient.

Unfortunately, Dan's invitation looped over and over like a stuck tape playing through her mind as her day progressed. Along with the distinct disappointment in his dark eyes, when she'd told him she already had plans.

How pathetic to realize that deep down she would rather spend time with Dan and Josh, instead of dressing up for some fancy going-away party at the Ritz Carlton Hotel. If not for agreeing to Kara's plans first, she might have backed out.

What in the world was wrong with her, anyway?

CHAPTER EIGHT

AFTER MOLLY SHOT DOWN his invitation before he could even ask her to go with him, Dan wasn't exactly looking forward to Jack Carter's going-away party, but as the event would be doubling as a fund-raiser for Nina's pro bono clinic, he told himself that it was all for a good cause.

Molly seemed to be back to her friendly self by Friday, and it had taken everything he had not to ask her out again, this time for Saturday night.

He sensed there was more holding her back than just the fact that he was the father of her young patient. Molly was bright and cheerful most of the time, but there were the occasional moments when she seemed a little sad. He thought about what his partner had said, about Molly breaking up with her boyfriend about a year ago, and found himself wondering what had happened. Had she broken things off? Or was she still in love with the loser?

The very thought of her being in love with someone else made him feel sick to his stomach. By all rights he should want Molly to be happy, yet somehow he only wanted her to be happy with him.

And Josh.

He donned his tux, which he'd had to dig out of the

back of his closet, eyeing himself critically in the mirror. He'd asked Gemma to stay overnight in order to watch Josh, something he hadn't needed her to do since he'd taken his leave of absence from the hospital. Normally, Gemma only stayed overnight on the weeknights and weekends he was on call.

Luckily, she hadn't said anything about the fact that he was spending the time going out rather than working.

"Don't go, Daddy," Josh whined. "Stay home with me."

He paused in the act of drawing on his jacket. This was the first time Josh had ever asked him to stay home. The first time his son had indicated he might prefer his father's company over that of his nanny.

"I love you, Josh," he said, coming over to crouch down next to Josh's wheelchair. "More than anything in the whole wide world."

"I love you, too, Daddy." Josh leaned against him, burying his face in his father's chest.

Dan kissed the top of his son's head, his heart swelling with emotion. He considered calling off his plans. It wasn't as if anyone would really miss him if he didn't show up.

"How about I stay here until it's time for you to go to sleep?" he said, trying to compromise. "We can read another book."

"Really?" Josh visibly brightened. "That would be awesome."

"Really." He followed as his son wheeled himself into his bedroom. He knew the party would start without him. And he'd only be a little late.

His son was far more important. Seeing the progress Josh was making helped ease his guilt for having been distracted the night of the crash. He was beginning to believe Josh really would walk again.

Now, for the first time in a long time, he had his priorities straight.

Molly paid the taxi fare and then walked into the Ritz Carlton Hotel. For several long moments she stood in the opulent lobby, gazing at the impressive high-domed ceilings and ornate white woodwork trimmed with gold as she waited for Kara to arrive. She smoothed a hand down her slinky green dress, and smiled as a couple walked by, wondering for the tenth time if the gown was too revealing. Not that it was extremely low cut or anything, but the way the fabric clung to every curve didn't leave much to the imagination.

She took a deep breath and let it out slowly, glancing down at her watch. It was barely eight o'clock, so it wasn't as if Kara was late. But she couldn't help feeling conspicuous, standing here alone.

A tall, handsome man with jet-black hair walked into the lobby, talking on his phone. "Hi, Callie, how is life in the great Down Under?"

Molly recognized him as Alex Rodriguez, one of the top neurosurgeons on staff at Angels. She turned away, trying not to eavesdrop on his conversation, although he wasn't exactly trying to be quiet. She noticed several other heads had turned in his direction, as well.

"I'm glad you're doing better, because I'm not," he said curtly. "Can you believe Layla Woods has been appointed as the new chief of Pediatrics? Seems no matter how hard I try to move on with my life, that woman keeps popping back into it."

Molly moved a few steps away, even though Dr. Rodriguez had certainly captured her attention. Apparently not everyone was thrilled to have a female in charge of the pediatric division. Was there some personal history between him and Layla? She didn't often pay attention to the hospital grapevine.

"Don't get involved?" Alex let out a harsh, humorless laugh. "Yeah, thanks for the warning, Callie. You and I are way too much alike, so I'll say the same right back at you."

There was another pause as he listened to something Callie said. "Thanks for the invite, but I'm not running away. Especially not from a woman."

Just as Alex Rodriguez finished his call, Kara walked in, looking very glamorous in a midnight-blue dress that displayed her slim figure to full advantage. Molly quickly crossed over to greet her. "Wow, Kara, you look amazing!"

Kara laughed and hugged her. "So do you, Molly."

"Maybe, but I think a certain doctor is going to be shocked when he catches a glimpse of you," she teased.

"From your lips to his ears," Kara said with a laugh. "And if he doesn't notice me, hopefully someone else will. So, are you ready to head up there?"

Molly took a deep breath and nodded, telling herself she needed to mirror Kara's attitude. "I'm ready if you are."

They took the grand curving staircase up to the main ballroom. A waiter greeted them at the doorway, holding a tray of drinks. Molly and Kara both helped themselves to glasses of sparkling champagne.

"This is the life," Kara murmured. "I see David is here, over by the bar."

"Maybe you should wander over?" she suggested.

"Maybe in a bit," Kara said. "This place is amazing, isn't it?"

"Absolutely." Sipping her champagne, Molly gazed out over the audience, quickly verifying that Dan wasn't among the mingling crowd. Not that she'd expected him to be here. She knew he was likely to be at home, spending time with Josh.

"I've heard Jack normally doesn't flaunt his wealth, but he and Nina are using this party as a way to collect donations for her pro bono clinic," Kara continued, filling her in on the latest gossip.

"I'd be happy to donate," Molly murmured. She'd gotten the emerald-green floor-length gown at a steeply reduced price, so she had a little extra money to spare.

"Let's go say hello to the guest of honor," Kara murmured, drawing Molly toward the large group gathered in the center of the ballroom. Kara was far more outgoing than she was, and she often wished she had the same confidence.

After signing the pledge card to donate funds for the clinic, she smiled and chatted with the other guests, feeling a little like a fraud. This wasn't the type of place she normally hung out at. No, she was far more at home eating pizza at places like Fun and Games.

She caught sight of a familiar dark-haired woman in the crowd and stopped dead in her tracks. Sally? Was that really her sister, Sally, standing there with her fiancé?

Before she could turn away, Sally glanced over and saw her. There was momentary confusion on her face before recognition dawned. Instantly, Sally took her fiancé's arm and dragged him over to where Molly was standing.

"Molly! What a surprise to see you here!" Her sister gave her a quick hug before turning toward her fiancé. "Mike, you remember my sister, Molly, don't you?"

"Of course. How are you, Molly?" Mike asked.

She forced a smile to her face, trying not to point out that the last time they'd talked had been three months ago, at Christmas. "I'm fine, doing great. Busy at work as usual."

"Yeah, Sally's been busy at work, too," Mike said. She wasn't surprised, as Sally worked on the orthopedic floor as a nurse. "Angel's is always hopping, that's for sure."

"Molly, guess what?" Sally gushed. "Mike and I are officially engaged!"

She didn't let on that she'd already seen the engagement notice in the paper. "Really? Oh, Sally, that's wonderful. I'm so happy for both of you."

"Thanks." Sally held out her hand, and Molly oohed and ahhed over the sparkling diamond.

"He totally surprised me, didn't you, Mike?" Sally said with a laugh. "Not that I'm complaining or anything."

"Aw, that's so sweet. Congratulations to both of you," Molly said, meaning every word. Even though they hadn't included her when they'd first gotten engaged, she was truly thrilled for them. Her sister deserved to be happy.

"Thanks, Molly. We had the best Valentine's Day ever, didn't we, darling?" Sally linked her arm with Mike's. "Oh, look, there's Aaron Carmichael. Come on, Mike, I'll introduce you. See you later, Molly," her sister tossed over her shoulder, before dragging her intended away.

For a long moment Molly couldn't move. Couldn't breathe. Valentine's Day? Sally and Mike had gotten engaged on Valentine's Day? Almost a month ago?

And no one had called her? Not even her parents?

Tears burned her eyes and she spun round and hurried out of the ballroom, intending to seek privacy in the ladies' room. But in her hurry to escape she plowed into a broad chest. "Excuse me," she murmured, trying to pull away.

But strong hands gripped her shoulders. "Molly? What is it? What's wrong?"

Belatedly, she recognized Dan's voice and his familiar musky scent. In some part of her mind she was surprised he was there, but at the same time she was too upset to wonder about that. And when he wrapped his arms around her, holding her close, she closed her eyes against the tears and rested her forehead against his chest.

"Shh, it's okay. Whatever happened, I'm sure it will be okay," he murmured.

She wished she believed him, but she knew firsthand there was no way to make someone love you. To care about you. She was so steeped in her misery she barely noticed when he led her away to a small private alcove out of range from prying eyes.

Dan had nearly swallowed his tongue when he'd entered the ballroom of the Ritz Carlton and seen Molly dressed in a figure-hugging emerald-green dress, revealing curves he'd only dreamed about.

But then he'd realized she was crying and he'd immediately scowled, searching for the person who'd upset her. He figured it was the guy who'd broken things off with her last year.

The jerk.

Although he was glad the jerk was a jerk because otherwise she wouldn't be available. Just then she'd barreled into his chest and he'd caught her close, more than willing to hold her in his arms.

Although he wished she was here for some other reason than the fact that she was struggling not to cry. After Suzy, he'd avoided women's tears like the plague. After all, his ex had turned them on and off at will, using them like a weapon.

But Molly's tears were different. For one thing, she was hiding them from him, as if she was embarrassed. And for another he could feel her body tense, deep breaths shuddering through her as she struggled to get herself back in control.

"I'm sorry I got your tux wet," she whispered, pulling away and sniffling loudly. She brushed her hand over his suit, as if to wipe away the evidence of her tears.

"I couldn't care less about the tux, Molly," he chided softly. He used his thumbs to wipe the dampness from her cheeks. "I hate seeing you so upset."

She tried to smile, although he didn't have the heart to tell her it was a pathetic attempt at best. She straightened and glanced around. "Where's the bathroom? I need to fix my face."

There was nothing wrong with her face that he could see. "Molly, you look beautiful, as always. But if you really need to go into the ladies' room, it's across the hallway."

"Thanks." This time her smile was genuine as she

touched his arm lightly. "I'll be back in a few minutes, okay?"

"I'm not going anywhere," he promised before she hurried away.

And he didn't move, not even an inch, until he saw her emerge from the bathroom a few minutes later. As before, she took his breath away, only now she was truly radiant as she smiled and nodded at a couple walking past.

His mouth went dry as she approached and he was glad to see that all evidence of her brief crying jag had vanished from her face. Except for the hint of sadness shadowing her eyes.

"I lost my glass of champagne," she announced. "How about we go in and find one of those cute waiters carrying trays filled with glasses?"

He chuckled and took her hand in his so they could stroll back into the ballroom side by side. "Far be it for me to stand in the way of you and a glass of champagne."

They found a waiter without too much trouble and Dan picked up two glasses, handing one to Molly. "Here you go. Did you come alone tonight?" He was proud of his casual tone.

Molly took a big gulp of champagne and shook her head. "No, I met up with my friend Kara Holmes. She's here, someplace."

He frowned, trying to place the name. "Does she work at Angel's, too?"

"Yes, she's a nurse in the neonatal unit. She's over by the bar, talking to one of the new doctors on staff." Molly took another sip of her champagne, catching his gaze over the rim of her glass. "Do you mind if I ask you a question?"

He raised his eyebrows. "Of course not."

"When you asked me if I had plans on Friday night..." She hesitated, then said, "Were you planning to come here all along?"

For some odd reason he wanted to grin. "Yes, I was planning to ask you to come with me tonight. And you shot me down before I even had a chance to ask." When her expression fell, he hastened to reassure her. "But none of that matters as we're both here now." He was glad, very glad he hadn't canceled out at the last minute.

"Yes, we are."

Molly drained her champagne and was looking around for another waiter, so he quickly reached for her hand. "Come on, let's dance."

The band was playing a slow number, and he was grateful for the excuse to pull Molly back into his arms. She was several inches shorter than he was, even with her heels, yet somehow she managed to fit into his arms perfectly.

"Wow, you're a great dancer," Molly murmured, tipping her head back to look up at him.

It took every ounce of willpower not to lower his mouth to kiss her. He tried to remind himself that she deserved someone better than him, someone who knew how to laugh and love, but logic flew out the window when she gazed up at him like that.

As if she cared not about his money but about him. As a person, not a meal ticket.

He cleared his throat and tugged her close. "You're a great dancer, too."

When the song ended, she moved away and he reluctantly followed her over to the side of the room.

"Molly!" A dark-haired woman came rushing over. "Introduce us to your…*friend*."

He sensed Molly stiffen beside him, but her smile didn't waver. "Oh, sure. Sally and Mike, this is Dan Morris, one of the cardiothoracic surgeons at Angel's. Dan, this is my sister, Sally Shriver, and her fiancé, Mike Drake."

He made sure that none of his surprise that this woman was Sally's sister showed on his face as he slid a casual arm around Molly's waist. "Pleased to meet you."

"Aren't you going to ask why we don't look anything like sisters?" Sally demanded with a slight slur to her voice. She staggered a bit and he sensed she'd already had several glasses of champagne.

"Hey, Sally, watch out there. Are you okay?" Mike stepped in to steady his fiancée. "Come on, honey, I think you need to eat something."

"Good idea," Dan murmured. "Molly, let's dance again before we eat, okay?"

She acted as if she hadn't heard him, and she didn't say anything when Mike eased Sally toward the buffet table set up along the far side of the wall. She stared after them for several long moments, before blurting out, "The Shrivers adopted me when I was four years old."

That explained the difference in their looks, but why did she seem so upset by that fact?

"Molly, look at me." He waited until she turned to face him. "I don't like the way your sister managed to upset you. Was she the reason you were crying earlier?"

When she nodded, he was glad to know she hadn't been pining over her last boyfriend.

"I didn't know you were adopted, but it's not the end of the world, is it? Do you think something like that matters to me? I don't understand why you look like you just lost your best friend. Do you think being adopted is something to be ashamed of?"

"No, I'm not ashamed," she said slowly, her gaze thoughtful. "But it just occurred to me that maybe Sally is."

"If so, that's her problem, not yours." Dan tried to keep the edge of anger out of his tone. "Besides, why would you listen to her when she's half-drunk?"

"You're right, she's not herself. Although I guess I always hoped we'd be close friends." Molly sighed and shook her head before she glanced up at him. "Never mind my sister. If you meant what you said a few minutes ago, I'd love to dance."

As if he needed to be asked twice. "My pleasure."

He escorted her onto the dance floor and pulled her into his arms. This time, instead of keeping a proper distance between them, she cuddled close, slipping her hand up and around his neck.

His pulse tripled as she pressed against him, her unique fragrance filling his head. For several long moments he could barely think, probably because all the blood in his body had headed south. But he wasn't dreaming. Molly was really here with him. Because she wanted to be. Not because she was drunk, as he was pretty sure she'd only had the one glass of champagne. After seeing her sister staggering after her fiancé toward the buffet, she seemed to have lost her taste for bubbly.

He smoothed his hand down her back, thinking he would be content to spend the rest of the night like this. Dancing with Molly.

Holding her.

Kissing her.

When she lifted up her head to look at him, he wondered if she had the ability to read his thoughts because she rose up on tiptoe and pressed her sweet mouth against his.

CHAPTER NINE

MOLLY'S BREATH HITCHED in her throat as Dan angled his head to deepen the kiss. The crowd on the dance floor faded from her consciousness, making her feel as if there were only the two of them in the room. Nobody and nothing else mattered.

Dizzy with desire she pressed herself closer against him, wishing she could run her fingers over his muscles. Not that he didn't look absolutely amazing in a tux, because he did. But she still longed to touch him.

Abruptly he let her go, lifting his head and taking gulps of air. She smiled and rested her cheek against his chest. It was nice to know she wasn't the only one aroused beyond what was decent.

One song ran into the next until she had no idea how long they'd spent dancing. Or swaying, as, honestly, their feet didn't move much.

"Molly," Dan murmured, drawing her gaze. "As much as I don't want to stop, you should probably know the band is taking a break."

She stopped, and blushed when she realized they were the only ones still on the dance floor. "Oh."

"Are you hungry?" he asked, drawing her over toward where the buffet was set up.

She was, but not for food. “Not really. But I should try to find Kara.” Guiltily, she remembered her friend.

“She’s over there, standing next to David Jacobson.” When she glanced over in the direction he indicated, she realized he was right. Kara caught her eye, raised her eyebrow and smiled, raising her champagne glass in a silent toast.

Molly knew the way she’d danced with Dan hadn’t gone unnoticed, and she wanted to grimace at the thought of how Angel’s grapevine would be rumbling with gossip by morning. But then again, she was single. And Dan was single. So what was the big deal?

“Do you want something else to drink?” he asked. She liked the way he kept an arm around her waist, leaning down to talk to her so that only she could hear him.

For the first time in too many months to count she felt beautiful. Special. Sexy. She glanced up at the most good-looking guy in the entire room. “Dan, would you mind taking me home?”

“Of course not,” he said, although she thought she saw a flash of disappointment in his eyes.

Obviously she hadn’t made her meaning clear. She wanted him to take her home, but she didn’t want him to leave.

She hoped he’d stay.

As they made their way toward the doorway, they were stopped along the way. “Dan, how are you?”

“Great, Marcus. Just great.”

“And who’s this pretty little thing?” Marcus asked, gazing at Molly with interest.

She couldn’t help smiling when Dan’s arm tightened around her waist. “This is Molly Shriver. Molly, Marcus is one of my colleagues.”

"Nice to meet you," she said, dutifully shaking his hand.

"Excuse us, Marcus, but we need to leave. I'll check in with you next week, okay?" Dan drew her away, but before they cleared the ballroom they were stopped again, this time by Alex Rodriguez.

"You're not leaving already, are you?" Alex demanded.

"Afraid so. Alex, this is Molly Shriver. Molly, Alex Rodriguez is Head of Neurosurgery at Angel's."

"I'm familiar with Dr. Rodriguez, he refers lots of patients to me." She held out her hand, hiding a smile as Alex stared at her, obviously trying to place her name.

"Of course!" he finally exclaimed. "Molly Shriver, the physical therapist. It's great to meet you. You have an outstanding reputation."

"Thank you," she murmured, embarrassed at how much he was gushing over her. It was great to know she had recognition, even though no one apparently knew what she looked like. She was starting to feel a bit like a ghost.

"Did you hear the news?" Alex said in a low voice. "Layla Woods has been named the new Chief of General Pediatrics."

"Yeah, I heard," Dan said with a wry nod. "I was a little surprised but, then again, she has a decent reputation."

"I'm still not over the shock," Alex muttered, tossing back the rest of his champagne as if it were straight whiskey.

"You'll be fine," Dan said, clapping Alex on the shoulder. "Excuse us, we're just leaving."

They finally made it out of the ballroom without

being stopped by any more of Dan's colleagues, and when they stepped outside, she shivered. "It's cold out here!"

Dan cuddled her close as he waited for his car to be brought out by the valet parking attendant. "Where's your coat, woman?" he asked, rubbing his hands up and down her arms in an effort to keep her warm.

"I wasn't going to buy a long coat for one evening," she said, half under her breath. Her waist-length jacket would have looked out of place with the emerald-green dress.

"Take mine," he said, shrugging out of his jacket and draping it around her shoulders.

Dan's sleek black BMW arrived less than five minutes later, and she slid into the passenger seat gratefully. Dan tipped the parking attendant and then climbed in beside her. He immediately cranked up the heat.

Now that they were alone in his car, nerves set in. What if he didn't want to come up to her apartment? What if he thought she lived in a dump? What if she'd misunderstood how he felt toward her? What if he wasn't as attracted to her as she was to him?

She'd initiated the kiss. Granted, he didn't pull away. In fact, he'd kissed her like he wasn't planning on stopping any time soon.

The memory was enough to make her heart race. She tried to take a deep breath to calm herself, but Dan must have noticed as he reached over to take her hand.

"Relax," he murmured. "Did I mention that Josh's nanny was spending the night at my place?"

For a moment she gaped at him. He tells her to relax and then he springs that on her? "She is, huh?"

"Yes, she is." A smile played around the corners of

his mouth and that hint of humor was enough to make her relax.

Because she hadn't imagined his response to their kiss. "Sounds like it's your lucky night," she teased.

He tightened his fingers around hers. "You have no idea," he said in a husky tone.

"Oh, I think I do."

Thankfully, the drive to her apartment didn't take long. Finding parking, though, was another thing altogether. She was appalled at the fee he was forced to pay but, short of taking his car back to his place and taking the subway back, they didn't have a choice.

She unlocked the door and led the way inside. They didn't get very far when Dan caught her hand and pulled her close.

"Kiss me," he murmured.

She was happy to oblige. This time she slipped her hands beneath the jacket of his tux, causing him to groan low in his throat.

"Molly," he said between kisses. "Which way is your bedroom?"

"This way," she said breathlessly. Tearing herself away from him wasn't easy. As soon as they crossed the threshold of her bedroom, while she was thanking her lucky stars that she'd had the foresight to make her bed and clean up, his cell phone rang.

Dan froze, and looked down at her. "I'm sorry, Molly, but I need to make sure it's not about Josh," he said as he reached into his pocket for the phone.

"I understand." She made sure her disappointment wasn't reflected in her expression.

He glanced at the screen, sighed and pushed the

button to answer the phone. "Gemma? Is everything all right?"

Molly could hear Gemma's reply. "Josh is having a nightmare. He keeps calling for you."

"I'll be home in fifteen minutes." Dan snapped his phone shut and let out a heavy sigh. "Molly, I'm sorry, but Josh is calling for me and I really need to be there for him. I know the timing is terrible but for once he's not calling out for his mother."

"Don't be sorry. I totally understand." And she did understand—if Josh had been her son she'd leave in a heartbeat. "I'm okay, really."

Dan muttered what sounded like a curse as he ran his hand over his close-cropped hair. "Will you let me make it up to you? Say, with dinner tomorrow night?"

"That's not necessary—" she started to say, but he stopped her with a kiss.

"Yes, it is necessary," he said in a low, strained voice. "Very necessary. Please?"

How could she say no? "All right, call me tomorrow."

"Count on it." He kissed her again, and then turned to leave. She followed him to the door, making sure she locked it after he left.

She leaned against the door, wondering if she'd truly lost her mind. She couldn't sleep with Dan. He was a big-shot open-heart surgeon at Angel's!

Not to mention the father of her patient. But that argument didn't hold much weight as she wouldn't be Josh's therapist forever.

Still, what did she have to offer someone like Dan? Nothing that he couldn't get with any other woman and, heaven knew, New York was full of single women, any of whom would be thrilled to be with someone like Dan.

She couldn't bear it if he abandoned her the same way James had.

If she was smart, she'd find an excuse to avoid seeing him again.

If she was smart, she'd stop the madness before she got hurt.

Dan was grateful Josh's nightmare had pretty much faded by the time he'd gotten home from Molly's, but he stayed up for a while longer, making sure his son was resting quietly before he crawled into his own bed.

Falling asleep wasn't easy, though, as he still ached for Molly. He almost considered heading back over there, but knew that wasn't fair. She'd be asleep by now, and even if she wasn't, Josh might wake up again. No, he couldn't take the risk. Besides, she'd already agreed to go to dinner with him on Saturday night. Tonight, as it was already past midnight.

He wasted a good hour staring up at his ceiling, thinking about where to take her. He wanted her to feel comfortable, yet he also wanted the evening to be special. He thought of the perfect place and finally fell asleep.

Thankfully, Gemma let him sleep in, taking care of Josh until he crawled out of bed. After he finished in the bathroom, Josh came to greet him. "Hi, Daddy."

"Hi, Josh." He was thrilled to realize his relationship with his son had gotten so much better and was deeply touched that Josh had called out for him in the night and not his mother. He swept the boy into his arms for a hug.

"Gemma's in the kitchen," Josh said importantly.

"Have you already eaten breakfast?" he asked.

Josh nodded. "Yep."

"I hope you left me some, 'cos I'm hungry," he confided, heading toward the kitchen. As he approached, he heard Gemma on the phone with her daughter. "Sure, honey, I'll be happy to babysit tonight."

No! Wait! He needed Gemma tonight! He rushed forward but too late. When she hung up the phone, he knew he was out of luck.

"Good morning, Dr. Morris. Now that you're up, I'm going to leave. I have a lot of things to do today."

It took everything he had to smile. "No problem. I take it you're babysitting tonight for your granddaughter?"

"Yes, I love spending time with Emily. My daughter and her husband want to go out for dinner," she admitted, sealing his fate.

Dammit, he wanted to go out for dinner, too!

"Well, have fun, then." He watched her leave and then scrubbed his hand over his bristly jaw. He didn't want to cancel his plans with Molly, but what choice did he have? Unless he could find another babysitter?

He didn't want to leave Josh with a stranger, so he went back to his list of former nannies and found the number for Betsy, the one Josh liked best.

Unfortunately, Betsy was busy. So he went down the list. After calling several former nannies without success, he was about to give up when Josh's tutor called to follow up on Josh's progress.

"Mitch, I know you're a tutor and not a babysitter, but would you be willing to stay here tonight with Josh?"

"I have a biochemistry exam on Monday, so my only plans were to study, so why not? I can always study after Josh falls asleep."

Dan closed his eyes and thanked his lucky stars that

Mitch had a biochem exam rather than a date that night. "Thanks, I'll pay you your tutoring fee for the entire night."

"Heck, Dr. Morris, that's not necessary. The standard babysitting fee is fine."

"I insist." Dan could barely contain his excitement. Not only was he going to see Molly again tonight but Josh would be in good hands with Mitch.

A win-win situation all the way around.

He ate a quick breakfast and then called to make reservations at Valencia's, a very small yet expensive restaurant that he'd stumbled upon by accident several years ago. Once he'd finalized his arrangements, he dialed Molly's number, feeling more nervous than he had in a long time. She didn't answer, so he left a message.

"Hi, Molly, I've made reservations tonight for eight o'clock. I'll pick you up at seven-thirty if that's okay. Please give me a call back to confirm."

Having finished up what he needed to do, he went over to help himself to more coffee. He glanced up as Josh rolled his wheelchair into the room.

"Can we play Molly's games, Daddy? Can we?"

He nodded, squelching a flash of guilt at knowing he'd leave Josh with Mitch tonight. So he decided to make sure Josh had a lot of fun today. "Sure thing. And afterward we can go to another movie if you'd like."

"Really?" Josh's face lit up like a neon sign. "Awesome."

He sipped his coffee and waited, figuring Josh was going to ask again about inviting Molly along, but when Josh didn't, he decided to count that as another win.

It was humbling to realize his son didn't mind spending time with him alone now.

And he vowed to make sure that even once he went back to work, he'd still set aside plenty of family time with Josh. Maybe he hadn't known much about love and family when he and Suzy had first got married, but he was determined to rectify that mistake.

Josh would always know what it was like to be loved. And wanted. Not like an inconvenience, the way his mother had treated him.

His own mother had blamed him for ruining her life after his father, an officer in the army, had died in Vietnam. Granted, his mother had gotten pregnant on purpose so that her officer would marry her, but being pregnant and widowed at the age of nineteen had been far more than she'd bargained for.

And throughout the years she'd made sure Dan had known that her misery was all his fault. Thankfully, he'd been able to lose himself in books and later in his studies, earning him the title of valedictorian of his high school graduating class.

He'd been lucky, he realized now, that he'd earned a full ride at New York's top university. He'd worked hard to get where he was today, but somehow, with all he'd accomplished, he still felt empty. As if there was something inside him that made him unlovable.

Sure, Josh loved him. But Suzy hadn't. And his mother certainly hadn't.

Playing with Josh eased his thoughts about his upbringing, and as they played Molly's kick-the-ball game, he was amazed that Josh was able to move his legs from side to side with far more strength than he had previously. For the first time in a long while he began to believe that Josh really might walk again.

His phone rang, and he jumped up off the floor,

nearly tripping over his own two feet in his haste to answer it. When he saw the caller was Molly, he ducked into the kitchen for some privacy.

"Hi, Molly, how are you?"

"I'm good, thanks. How's Josh?"

"He's fine. Slept well after his nightmare and seems to be back to normal today."

"That's good. I'm sure that it was hard on you not being there for him."

"Yes. But it was hard leaving you, too."

There was an awkward pause and his gut clenched with fear. Was she going to try and cancel on him?

When she didn't answer, he spoke in a rush. "Josh's tutor Mitch has agreed to stay here tonight, so I hope the dinner plans I made are okay with you."

"Oh, that's wonderful. I'm glad Josh will be spending time with Mitch. Dinner sounds good and I'll be ready by seven-thirty."

His shoulders sagged with relief. She hadn't cancelled their plans. "Great! I'm really looking forward to seeing you again."

"Me, too," she admitted in a voice so soft he had to strain to hear her. "I have to go, but I'll see you later, okay?"

"Sure thing." He hung up the phone, knowing there was a goofy smile plastered on his face but unable to find the energy to care.

He believed Molly cared about him, and not because he was a surgeon. Like him, she'd been hurt in the past, and he found he was desperate to see her again. To share a nice, romantic dinner together. Only this time, with a little luck, they wouldn't be interrupted by any sort of crisis.

He could hardly wait.

* * *

Molly had spent the morning lecturing herself on getting involved with Dan more than she already was, and had fully intended to back out of their tentative dinner plans. But once she had been on the phone with him, she hadn't been able to do it. For one thing, he'd already arranged for a babysitter, and she was glad that Josh would have fun with Mitch.

But the real reason she didn't back out was because once she heard his deep voice resonating in her ear she realized how much she wanted to see him again. She'd been thinking about Dan when she'd fallen asleep, and he'd been the first thing on her mind when she'd woken up.

Doomed, she thought with a wry shake of her head. She was doomed and too far gone to turn back now.

Sally had called to apologize for embarrassing her at the fund-raiser. Of course Molly accepted her apology and they'd ended the call on better terms. But deep down she knew she and Sally would never be as close as blood sisters.

Or even sisters of the heart.

Dan would say that was Sally's loss and she wanted to believe he was right. But she was the one who'd always wanted a family. Sally had no idea how lucky she was to have parents who doted on her and a fiancé who loved and adored her.

Enough with the pity party! She spent the rest of the morning cleaning her tiny apartment, which obviously didn't take long, and then took the subway to do some window shopping.

She couldn't really afford to buy another dress for her dinner tonight with Dan, but that didn't stop her from looking. She found lots of cute dresses, but in the end she decided to wear her old standby black skirt with a nice teal-colored sweater.

She was ready to leave well before seven, and tried to read, but ended up nervously pacing the tiny length of her apartment instead.

When her buzzer rang at exactly seven-thirty, she grabbed her coat and purse before crossing over to the intercom. "I'll be right down."

She took the elevator and caught her breath when she saw that Dan was dressed in a pair of charcoal-grey slacks and a black crew-neck sweater. Although she liked the way he filled out a tux, she was finding that she liked the way he looked no matter what he wore. "Hi," she greeted him shyly.

"Hi, Molly." He gave her a hug, surrounding her with his musky scent mingled with a hint of aftershave. "You look fantastic."

"Thank you." She didn't bother telling him how he'd now seen the full extent of her dressy wardrobe.

He opened the car door for her, and after sliding in she had to smile when she noticed that once again he'd cranked up the heat for her. Taking pity on him, she turned the knob down a few notches.

"I want you to know that Josh's leg muscles are getting stronger," he said, as he swung into the traffic. "We played kick the ball and he did amazingly well."

"That's great news," she said with a smile. "See, I told you the games were worth it," she teased.

"Yes, you did." She was surprised when Dan reached out to take her hand. "And you were right, I should have trusted in your judgment all along. I don't know how I'll ever be able to repay you."

"No payment necessary," she murmured. "There's nothing more rewarding than watching a patient's progress toward his or her goals. It's one of the reasons I love my job."

"And you're damn good at it, too," he said, still holding her hand.

She smiled. "I told you so," she teased as he put his hand back on the steering wheel. But she couldn't help feeling a twinge of regret at knowing that her time with Josh and Dan would eventually come to an end.

All too soon they wouldn't need her anymore.

"Hey, what's wrong?" he asked, as if sensing her disquiet.

"Nothing." She pushed the melancholy away. "In fact, my sister called me today and apologized for her behavior at the Ritz."

Dan's lips thinned. "She should apologize," he muttered ungraciously. "She had no right to hurt you like that."

She was touched by his concern on her behalf. "She doesn't mean to hurt me, it's really my problem. I've never felt as if I was part of the family."

He glanced at her. "I'm sure they adopted you for a reason, Molly."

"Yes, but shortly after they brought me home they found out they were pregnant with Sally, and from then on things changed." She lifted a shoulder in a careless shrug. "She became the center of their world, and I was more of an afterthought. Still, I know I should be grateful for what I have. I could have easily been sent from one foster home to another."

He was quiet for a long moment. "I'm sorry that you had that experience, Molly. But living with a blood relative, a mother who gave birth to you, doesn't automatically bring unconditional love," he said. "Unfortunately, some people just aren't capable of feeling that deeply about anyone else."

His words stopped her cold, and she had the distinct impression he was talking from personal experience. About his own mother? Or just his ex who had married him and given birth to Josh yet hadn't loved either one of them enough to stay?

"I feel sorry for those people, Dan. They'll never know what they've missed." She reached over and took his hand, vowing to prove to him that his ex had been stupid and wrong.

He and Josh were both special and very much deserved to be loved and cared for.

CHAPTER TEN

DAN WAS TOUCHED WHEN Molly reached for his hand, and he mentally cursed himself for allowing talk of their respective pasts to dampen the mood. He wanted tonight to be special. No sadness or regret allowed.

He gave her fingers a gentle squeeze. "Hey, will you please do me a favor?" She glanced at him in surprise, nodding automatically. "Smile, Molly. I want tonight to be about us, two people having a nice time together. I want you to have fun tonight."

She smiled and just like that the shadow that hovered over his soul was gone. "All right. So tell me, where is this place you're taking me?"

"Valencia's." He grinned. "It's one of the best-kept secrets. They have great seafood and they're located in the West Village."

"Sounds perfect."

"Have you ever eaten there before?" He didn't want to assume she hadn't. For all he knew, that guy she'd been seeing had taken her there. The thought made him scowl.

"No, although I've heard wonderful things about it."

Selfishly, he was glad she hadn't been there before. He parked his car at a very expensive structure and they walked the rest of the way.

"Oh, my gosh, this is a cobblestone street!" Molly said with a gasp of surprise.

"Yeah, this is a colonial building that was once used as a carriage house." He put his hand in the small of her back as she walked into the restaurant.

"Wow, fancy," she whispered, as they waited to be greeted by the maître d'.

"We have an eight-o'clock reservation," he said. "Dan Morris."

"Of course, Dr. Morris. Right this way, sir. You requested a table by the fireplace, correct?"

"Yes. Thank you." He smiled when Molly took the seat closest to the fire. "Would you like wine?" he asked. "Or maybe you'd prefer champagne?"

Molly blushed, or maybe it was the heat from the fire. "Wine would be great. I think I should stay away from champagne for a while."

"Do you have a wine preference?" he asked, studying the wine list.

"Anything you choose is fine with me."

He ordered a French red wine and watched Molly peruse the menu. Her eyes were as wide as saucers as she glanced over the options.

"The prices are outrageous," she whispered in horror.

"Molly, relax. Splurge a little." He hadn't brought her here to intimidate her—he wanted her to enjoy herself. "What would you have if money was no object?"

She worried her lower lip between her teeth, making him want to kiss her. "I have a secret love of lobster," she confessed. "And I also love a good steak."

"Then have both," he urged. "I promise you'll love it."

They placed their order and he noticed Molly relax

as she sipped her wine. "This is very nice, Dan. Thanks for bringing me."

"You're more than welcome. Besides, you deserve special treatment. Do you have any idea what a great reputation you have at Angel's?"

She arched a brow. "Do you have any idea what a great reputation *you* have at Angel's?" she countered. "Your patients love you."

"So do yours." He reached across to take her hand in his. "Your bright, sunny attitude is amazing. I don't think I've ever met anyone who enjoyed their work as much as you do."

She blushed and took a sip of her wine. "I'm sure you enjoy your work," she countered. "Saving small children's lives by doing open-heart surgery is far more important than what I do each day."

He cocked his head to the side, wishing he could find a way to convince her how special she was. "Your work is just as important. We both give hope to our small patients and their parents."

"Giving hope," she murmured with a smile. "I like that comparison, even if you're exaggerating my expertise."

"Molly, believe me when I say that no woman has ever talked to me the way you did after Josh's first therapy session," he said with a wry grin. "Your passion for your work is unsurpassed by anyone I've ever met."

"I let my temper get away from me," she admitted with a deep blush, making him want nothing more but to take her into his arms. But the waiter arrived with their first course and he had to settle for watching Molly enjoy her salad.

"What made you decide to become a pediatric heart surgeon?" she asked, when she'd finished.

Unwilling to ruin the mood, he gave her the light version. "I always wanted to be a doctor, and once I started my surgical residency I knew cardiothoracic surgery was my area of expertise. Yet once I finished my pediatric rotation I knew that working with kids was equally important. Luckily, I landed a job at Angel's that allows me to do the most with my little bit of talent."

"Little bit of talent?" she echoed dryly. "I say you're underestimating your ability."

"Giving kids the opportunity to have a normal life is important to me." He stared at his empty salad plate for a moment. "Yet I almost screwed up with Josh, big time."

"Josh loves you," she protested quickly.

He forced a smile. "Yeah, we're getting back on track. And I'm thrilled he's getting stronger every day. Today we went to another movie and for the first time in a long time he didn't ask for you to come with us." When he realized how that might have sounded, he tried to backpedal. "I mean, he loves having you around, but—"

She interrupted him with a laugh. "Don't worry, I understand. It's okay, he should want to spend time with you. You're his father."

As he gazed at Molly across the table, her red-and-gold hair glowing from the light of the fire, he realized that Molly would be an excellent mother. Far better than Suzy. Far better than his own.

And he was one lucky son of a gun to be here with her. Especially when she had no idea how unique and special she was.

He was sure his food tasted wonderful, but he didn't really pay much attention, having more fun watching Molly as she enjoyed every aspect of their meal.

He forced her to split the chocolate mousse for dessert and longed to lean forward to taste the chocolate from her lips instead of just from the spoon.

After they finished dinner, he followed her back outside to his car. "Thanks for the lovely dinner, Dan," she said as they approached his car.

He hoped, prayed the night wasn't over yet, but he didn't say anything as he closed her passenger door behind her and then walked around to slide into the driver's seat.

The ride back across town to her apartment didn't take long. When he was within a block or two of the parking garage he glanced over at her, feeling a little bit panicked at the thought of letting her go. "Molly, I don't want the evening to end."

She went still, before she glanced up at him. "Is that your way of asking if you can come up?"

His gut clenched. "Yes, Molly. I want to come up with you, spend the night making love with you. But only if that's what you want, too."

When she didn't answer right away, he figured he'd pushed too hard. But then she nodded. "I'd like that," she murmured in a low voice.

He let out his breath in a soundless sigh. Last night they'd been carried away by the slow dancing and champagne. Tonight it was a deliberate decision, on his part and on hers. One that he didn't want her to regret.

"I'm so glad," he said. "I was afraid you were going to make me beg."

"Never," she murmured with a laugh, and the last of his tension eased away.

He'd never looked forward to being with anyone the way he wanted to be with Molly.

Molly couldn't believe Dan had spoken so bluntly about how he wanted to spend the rest of their night. As they rode the elevator up to her apartment, she was tempted to pinch herself to make sure she wasn't dreaming. He'd been so wonderful, so attentive at dinner. For the first time in so long she felt beautiful, special.

And she wanted to hold on to that feeling for at least a little while longer.

She couldn't believe this was a mistake. Not when it felt so right. They were going to make love. She knew it. He knew it. For some reason, inviting him up last night had been easier but, oddly enough, she found tonight to be more romantic.

At least now she knew that he truly wanted her. Almost as much as she wanted him.

Still, she was nervous about taking this step, knowing that once they made love there was no going back. As they stepped into her apartment, she mentally kicked herself for not going out to buy some wine today, rather than window shopping.

"I only have soft drinks to offer you," she said apologetically, when he'd closed the apartment door. She turned to go into the minuscule kitchen to get something for them to drink out of the fridge.

"Molly..." The way he said her name made her heart melt, and when he stopped her and pulled her close she didn't resist. "I didn't come here for something to drink. I came here for you."

Before she could say anything more, he lowered his head and kissed her. Instantly, she forgot everything except how much she loved his mouth taking possession of hers.

Somehow he slid her coat off without her knowing, gathering her close as he deepened the kiss. She clung to his broad shoulders, enjoying the combination of sweetness and strength.

When he lifted his head and led her down the hall toward her bedroom, she gasped for breath and tried to gather her scattered thoughts.

"Are you sure Josh is all right?" she asked, when they entered her bedroom. Was she crazy to be here with him like this? "Maybe you should check on him."

Dan yanked her close and kissed her again. "Are you stalling?" he asked a minute or so later. "Nothing short of a tornado is going to stop me from making love to you tonight."

She laughed, but then her mouth went dry when he gently pulled her sweater up and over her head. In mere seconds he'd loosened the waistband of her skirt until the garment fell and pooled at her feet. Her bra and panties quickly followed.

For a moment she wanted to cover herself, but then his eyes darkened as he gazed at her. "You're so incredibly beautiful, Molly," he said in a voice husky with need.

She couldn't speak, but tugged at his clothes until he was as naked as she was. And then he kissed her, and kept kissing her, even as he picked her up and carried her over to the bed.

Warmth radiated from his skin and she trailed her hands up and over his biceps, enjoying the sensation of springy hair as she reached his chest, softening the strong muscles. She loved being able to touch him. All over.

Everywhere.

When she trailed her hands down to his magnificent butt, he growled low in his throat and left a trail of kisses as he made his way down to her breast.

She gasped and arched her back when he licked and suckled her nipple. Moving restlessly beneath him, she tried to pull him closer.

"Plenty of time," he murmured between kissing the tip of one breast and then the other. "I want to taste every inch."

Dear heaven, she wanted that, too.

"Molly." He lifted his head and stared at her. "You're sure about this, right? You haven't changed your mind?"

And just like that her nervousness faded away. She reached up to rest her palm against the side of his face, the same caress he'd given her after falling out of his wheelchair. "Yes, I'm sure. I haven't changed my mind."

"Thank God," he muttered, and lowered his head once again to her breast.

And then all ability to think vanished as he proceeded to make good on his promise to kiss her all over.

Molly closed her eyes and hugged Dan close as their ragged breathing gradually slowed. The intensity of his lovemaking was unlike anything she'd experienced in her entire life.

After a few minutes Dan groaned and rolled over onto his side, taking her with him, apparently unwilling to let her go. She tucked her head into the hollow of his shoulder, and inhaled deeply, filling her nose with his scent.

She must have dozed even though she hadn't intended to. But she woke up when she felt Dan ease away from her and roll off the bed.

"Where are you going?" she asked, before she could bite her tongue.

"I'm sorry, I didn't mean to wake you."

She clutched the sheet to her chest and squinted toward the blue illuminated numbers on her alarm clock. "It's barely five o'clock in the morning."

"I know, but I need to get home before Josh wakes up." He sounded apologetic but drew on his clothes. "I was trying to decide if I should wake you up or just let you sleep."

He'd obviously chosen the latter, although he couldn't know she was an extremely light sleeper. She tried not to feel bad that he was leaving. Logically, she knew he needed to get home to his son. For some foolish reason she'd envisioned them sharing a quiet breakfast together.

"Go back to sleep, Molly," he murmured, leaning over to kiss her. "I'll call you later on today, all right?"

"Sure." She forced herself to get up and grab her robe, so that she could lock the apartment door behind him. She clutched the lapel tight and tried to smile. "Good night, Dan."

"Good night, Molly." He kissed her again before he left. And she locked the door behind him and went back to bed.

But she didn't sleep. Being all alone in the aftermath of the intense pleasure they'd shared brought all her earlier doubts back. Had he been anxious to leave?

Had he planned all along to leave before she'd woken up? Was he regretting staying with her even as long as he had? Had he realized she was nothing more than a plain Jane with nothing special to offer?

Had she just made the biggest mistake of her life?

It was entirely possible, because right now she felt worse than the day James had told her that he loved someone else.

Molly got up and made herself a bowl of cereal and a pot of coffee. She read through the Sunday paper, determined to keep up with the news. After she'd completed a few loads of laundry, she decided to go over to see Dan and Josh. She didn't call ahead, simply deciding to take the subway.

She got off at the stop that was near Angel's and paused for a moment to gaze up at the impressive hospital overlooking Central Park. The history of the hospital's origin was humbling. Back in the dark days after the Depression, after his little boy had died of polio, Federico Mendez had established New York's first children's hospital, known for giving charity care to those children in need. In the years since then Angel's had become well known all across the country. Rich or poor, every child in New York was welcome to be cared for at Angel's. Even on Sunday it was busy, and she watched a medical helicopter land on the roof, no doubt bringing another small patient to Angel's house of hope.

She started walking toward Dan's condo, but stopped abruptly when she caught sight of two people in wheelchairs heading down the sidewalk on the other side of the street. She recognized Dan and Josh, arms pumping hard as they propelled their wheelchairs down toward the park.

She stepped back so they wouldn't see her, and watched as Josh laughed when he pulled ahead of his father. They were obviously enjoying some father-and-son time, which was good.

After watching Dan and Josh head into the park, she turned and retraced her steps to the subway. She shouldn't feel disappointed that they hadn't included her. Wasn't this what she'd wanted all along? For Josh and Dan to become close?

When she'd been with James, he'd always included her in all family outings. She could look back now and realize he'd used her more or less as a surrogate mother for his sons. They really hadn't had very much alone time as a couple. Which hadn't exactly helped their personal relationship. Was it any wonder they'd grown apart? Was it any wonder he'd fallen in love with someone else?

She should be glad that Dan wasn't doing the same thing. Obviously, he'd made love to her last night because he'd wanted to. He'd arranged for a babysitter so he could take her to a lovely dinner. So why did she still feel left out?

Determined to stop wallowing in self-pity, she headed over to see her parents. They always had a standing Sunday brunch invitation and today she'd surprise everyone by stopping by.

Twenty-five minutes later she arrived at her parents' place and wasn't entirely surprised to find Sally and Mike there, as well.

"Molly, it's so good to see you," her mother said, giving her a big hug. She clung to her mother for a long minute, before letting go to hug her father.

"It's good to see you, too," she said, hoping they didn't notice the dampness around her eyes. "Hi, Sally, Mike. How are your wedding plans coming along?"

"Wonderful!" Sally said, as they gathered in the kitchen. "We have our church and the hall picked out."

"Really? And when's the big day?" Molly helped herself to a glass of orange juice.

"August twenty-first. We were lucky that the hall had a cancelation."

"Wow, that's only a few months away," she murmured. Obviously the wedding plans had been going on for quite a while.

"Food's ready," her mother called.

Even though the conversation centered around Sally and Mike's upcoming wedding, Molly was glad to be here, surrounded by her family. For a brief time she didn't feel so much like an outsider.

Although she couldn't help thinking about Dan and Josh. Wondering how they were spending their day. Had they gone to another movie after their trip to the park? Or had they gone back to Fun and Games?

It was ridiculous to keep thinking about them when she'd see them both the following morning.

She stayed at her parents' house as long as she could, before heading back home.

There was no message from Dan waiting for her, and she wondered if he'd regretted spending the night with her.

Had he said those nice things to her at dinner just to get her into bed? Had she been hopelessly naive to believe him? Her stomach clenched as she couldn't help thinking the worst, especially as it was clear that he hadn't followed through with his promise to call.

It was her fault for getting emotionally involved with Dan in the first place. And it would be up to her to get over him, the same way she'd managed to get over James.

One painful day at a time.

CHAPTER ELEVEN

DAN CALLED MOLLY a half-dozen times, but when she didn't answer he hung up before her machine kicked in. He didn't want to leave a message. After the way he'd been forced to leave earlier that morning, she deserved better than to hear him say *"I'm thinking of you"* on a machine.

Leaving her warm bed had been one of the hardest things he'd ever done. If not for Josh being home with Mitch, he would have stayed longer. The rest of the weekend, if she'd have let him.

He ran his hands over his hair and told himself Molly wouldn't hold being a single father against him. After all, she loved kids. She understood that he'd needed to get home for Josh.

So why did he feel as if he'd let her down?

After he'd returned home, he'd caught another couple of hours of sleep before the rest of the household had gotten up. Once they'd eaten breakfast, Mitch had left to return home and he'd decided to celebrate the mild weather by taking Josh down to Central Park. They'd both used their wheelchairs, much to Josh's amusement.

As much as he tried to spend quality father-and-son time with Josh, he'd often become distracted by thoughts of Molly. He couldn't remember the last time a woman had dominated his thoughts.

Suzy didn't count as she'd once dominated his thoughts in a bad way. Molly's fresh laughter was the complete antithesis of Suzy's bitterness.

Yet he was forced to admit that maybe some of his ex's bitterness had been justified. He had worked a lot of hours. He could have spent more time with her. At the time he'd thought maybe he simply wasn't capable of love.

But being with Molly and Josh proved that theory to be false. He loved Josh. And he cared deeply for Molly. He knew she cared, at least a little, about him, too.

Maybe he wasn't so unlovable after all.

Once they'd returned home from Central Park, he spent some time working on Josh's surprise birthday party, and he called Molly again.

This time she answered. "Hello?"

"Finally we get to talk," he said. "I've been getting your machine most of the day."

"Really? Why didn't you leave a message?"

"Because I wanted to talk to you." And now that he was talking to her, his nerves settled down. He took the phone into the other room, out of Josh's hearing. "How are you? What have you been up to?"

"Had brunch with my parents, ran a few errands. The usual."

Was it his imagination or did she seem to be a tiny bit standoffish? Was she upset with him? "I wish I could have stayed with you this morning," he murmured. "I wish you were here right now."

There was a moment of silence before she spoke again. "I've been thinking of you, too."

The admission made him feel better. "I'd like to see you again. Soon."

"You and Josh are coming to therapy in the morning, aren't you?" she asked in a teasing tone.

"Yes. But what I meant is that I want to see you alone. Maybe we can do dinner one night this week?"

Another small silence and he wished she were here in front of him so he could read her facial expressions. He didn't like having to second-guess her thoughts. "I don't know if that will work. I generally try not to stay up too late on work nights."

Was she really worried about getting up for work in the morning? Or was she trying to put distance between them? "How about Friday night, then? Josh's party is on Saturday and it would be easier if you just stayed here overnight. You can sleep in the spare bedroom, if you're worried about Josh being here."

"Hmm, let me think about that," she said evasively. "Speaking of Josh's birthday, how is the party planning coming along?"

"Great." He injected enthusiasm into his voice when really just the thought of being in charge of all those kids was as daunting as hell. "Most of the kids in his class have responded that they're coming, which makes me feel better."

"Oh, Dan, that's great news." Molly's excitement was contagious. "Josh is going to have a wonderful time, you'll see."

"And he'll owe it all to you for coming up with the idea." He gripped the phone tighter and wished once again she was there with him. Especially when she laughed softly.

"No, you need to take the credit for having this party,

not me. After all, you're doing all the work." There was a brief silence, and then she added, "I have to get going. See you tomorrow, Dan."

"All right. See you tomorrow, Molly." He disconnected the call, wondering how he was going to manage to wait until Friday night to be alone with her again.

Molly did her best to keep things on a professional level when she saw Josh and Dan the following morning. She was already too close to falling for him, and didn't want to make the same mistakes she'd made in the past. But it wasn't easy when Dan stood close, his arm lightly brushing hers.

She eased away, concentrating on Josh. "Wow, you're doing very well, Josh. Look at how high you can kick your feet!"

Josh beamed. "We've been practicing, right, Dad?"

"Right," Dan agreed.

She was glad, very glad that the two of them were so comfortable around each other now. A far cry from their first day of therapy, that's for sure. She went through her list of warm-up games, and then decided it was time to move onto the next step.

"Okay, now we're going to try to stand again," she said, gesturing for Josh to follow her in his wheelchair over to the small platform nestled between parallel bars. "Are you ready, Freddie?"

Josh giggled, as she'd hoped he would. "I'm not Freddie," he said, as he set the brakes on his wheelchair.

"Are you sure? Because you look like a Freddie." She was proud at how bravely he faced the challenge of standing. His leg muscles were getting stronger, but they still had a way to go before he would be walking again.

Although there wasn't any doubt in her mind that he would accomplish that task.

"Wait for me," she said quickly, when Josh pushed up on the padded armrests of his wheelchair. His upper-arm strength had grown by leaps and bounds since Dan had agreed to let him use a wheelchair. "Steady now," she warned, as he stood up on his own two feet.

Josh didn't say anything, his face scrunched up with fierce concentration. She put her elbow under his armpit and took some of his weight.

"I can do it myself," he said testily.

"Okay." She eased back, allowing him to support his own weight but staying close by in case he lost his balance.

"Look, Dad," Josh said excitedly when he managed to grip the parallel bars and balance between them. "I can stand!"

"You sure can, Josh," Dan said in a husky voice. Molly didn't dare take her eyes off Josh to look over at him, but she knew he had to be thrilled with Josh's progress.

"How are your legs feeling?" she asked. His muscles were quivering beneath the strain, but he seemed determined to stay upright.

"Fine," he claimed, although the quivering got worse.

She waited a full minute before stepping forward. "Okay, Josh, let's have you sit back down, slow and easy."

He didn't argue this time, and soon he was seated once again in his wheelchair.

Dan came over and crouched beside Josh. "I'm so proud of you, Josh. Your hard work is really paying off.

The way your leg muscles are getting stronger is nothing short of amazing."

"Thanks, Dad," Josh said, throwing his arms around his father's neck and squeezing tightly.

Molly had to blink back tears, watching the way father and son clung to each other. And then Josh pulled back and glanced up at Molly. "Is it time for the massage yet?" he asked.

She had to laugh. "I suspect that's your favorite part of the day," she teased, as she headed over to the table set up near the ultrasound machine. "Either that or you just want to get through the rest of your therapy so that you can pick out a lollipop."

"I'm betting it's both," Dan said with a broad smile.

As she started her massage Dan's cell phone rang. He glanced at the screen, frowned and then glanced at her. "My colleague Marcus," he said, before he left the room to take the call.

She wondered why Marcus was calling. Did he have a question about patient care? Did they often talk about their respective patients?

Dan was still on the phone when she finished with Josh's massage and then moved on to the ultrasound treatments. She'd finished one leg and had started on the other when he finally returned, his expression grim.

"Problems?" she asked.

"Sort of. There's apparently a particularly challenging patient who needs surgery," he admitted.

She sensed he didn't want to talk in front of Josh, so she refrained from asking more as she finished up the ultrasound treatments. "All finished," she said cheerfully, as she put the machine away and began scraping the gel from Josh's legs. "Are you ready for a lollipop?"

Josh nodded and then contemplated the flavors left in the candy jar. “Grape,” he said, pulling out the last one. He wasted no time in tearing off the purple wrapper and popping the candy in his mouth.

“Molly, do you have a minute?” Dan asked in a low voice.

“Sure.” She turned to Josh. “I’ll be right back, okay?”

Josh nodded, sucking on his lollipop with such force that his cheeks were sunk in, making him look like a fish.

“What’s wrong?” she asked, the moment they were alone.

“I need to return to work,” Dan said. “I was planning to be off this week, but unfortunately this patient can’t wait.”

She hid her dismay, knowing better than to ask for specifics. “Who will bring Josh to therapy?”

“Gemma, his nanny, or maybe Mitch.” Dan blew out a breath and shook his head. “You need to understand that I wouldn’t make a decision like this lightly. This patient needs my expertise, or I wouldn’t cut my leave of absence short.”

Deep down, she wanted to ask why Marcus couldn’t do the surgery, but she managed to hold her tongue. After all, what Dan chose to do wasn’t really her business.

One night together didn’t mean much in the big scheme of things.

“Just make sure you keep spending time with Josh,” she said lightly. “Because he needs a father as much as your patients need a top-notch surgeon.”

“I know. Watching him stand was amazing. After the accident…” He paused then cleared his throat before continuing, "I don't know if I'd be able to forgive myself for that brief moment of inattentiveness just before the crash."

"Oh, Dan, it's not your fault," she soothed, trying to make him understand. "Your car was T-boned because the other driver ran a red light." She remembered reading about the crash in the newspaper. Scary stuff.

"Thanks for saying that," he murmured. He stared at her for a long moment, as if he wanted to say something more, but then turned away. She followed him back to where Josh was already waiting for them in his wheelchair.

"Goodbye, Josh, I'll see you tomorrow."

"Bye, Molly." Josh waved cheerfully, before following his father out of the door. She watched them leave, wondering what Josh's reaction would be once he discovered his father was planning to return to work.

Her heart ached for him. And for herself.

Because she couldn't help being afraid that once Dan was fully entrenched back in his old life, he'd revert back to his old ways. Being stern and serious, rather than taking the time to enjoy life. Yet he'd promised to maintain his relationship with his son, so she tried to take comfort in that thought.

Of course Josh would always come first. Which was the way it should be. And if he didn't have time for her, then obviously a relationship between them wasn't meant to be.

Dan went to the hospital early on Tuesday morning, and it seemed strange to walk through the lobby of Angel's after being gone for so long. His long white coat flapped against his thighs as he quickened his pace to reach the elevator.

He hurried up to the labor and delivery unit, where a pregnant woman was about to give birth to a baby with tetralogy of Fallot, a birth defect in which the infant's heart was essentially turned backward in its tiny chest. Normally this type of condition required surgery at some point during the baby's first year of life, but in this instance the unborn baby had been diagnosed with an additional complication, hydroplastic pulmonary arteries, which required bypass surgery to assist in oxygenating the infant's lungs. In years past these babies died, but now they could be operated on as soon as the infant was born and these children were now living well into their thirties and beyond.

The biggest catch was that the complex bypass procedure had to be started as soon as the baby was born or the child would die. And it was easily a ten- to twelve-hour procedure.

When he arrived in the labor and delivery suite, there was already a group of physicians and nurses filling the room. One of the nurses noticed him. "The cardiothoracic surgeon is here," she announced.

"Good. Nice to see you again, Dan. If everyone is ready, let's get this show on the road," Rebecca Kramer said briskly, pushing forward the gurney with the pregnant mother.

Rebecca Kramer was one of the neonatology experts on staff at Angel's and they'd worked together before, but there wasn't time for small talk as Dan could tell by the fetal monitor tracing that the baby was in trouble. They'd planned this C-section early, and it was obviously a good thing as it seemed the baby would have been born today, regardless. He made several phone calls of his own, making sure the O.R. right next to the one that Rebecca would use was equipped with what he'd need for long, grueling open-heart surgery.

"I want to see my baby," the pregnant woman sobbed, as they wheeled her into the O.R. suite. "I want to see her, to hold her in my arms before she has surgery."

Dan was used to this request, and had to steel his heart against her pleading gaze. He glanced at her name on her hospital bracelet. "I'm sorry, Mrs. Thompson, but your baby girl won't live if we wait," he said gently. "Have you chosen a name for her yet?"

"Erica," she said with a sob. "Erica Marie. After my husband, Eric. He's stationed in Iraq. Are you sure we can't wait for him? He's on his way home, he promised to be here soon."

"I'm sorry, but we can't wait. The minute Erica is born we're going to start surgery. The quicker we get started, the better her outcome will be. I've had a lot of success, so you and your husband just need to be patient, okay?"

She nodded, but tears continued to stream down her cheeks. "Okay."

He scrubbed while they prepped the pregnant mother's belly. Jennifer Thompson wanted to be awake during the C-section so the anesthesiologist topped up her epidural. There was a sense of urgency in both O.R. suites because there wasn't a moment to waste. Lives were on the line and as always the staff of Angel's took the care of their young patients very seriously.

He was gowned, gloved and masked when he heard the shout. "We have the baby out."

"We're ready," he called back. And seconds later

the neonatal team rushed in, with Rebecca holding the baby in her hands.

As they set the infant on the O.R. table, the anesthesiologist put a tiny breathing tube in place. As soon as the airway was secured, the circulating nurse quickly scrubbed the chest as Dan took the scalpel and cleared his mind, focusing entirely on baby Erica and the complicated heart surgery she needed in order to stay alive.

Ten and a half hours later he lifted his head and stretched his neck muscles with a heavy sigh. It was over and Erica had come through the entire ordeal like a trouper.

He stared at the cardiac monitor, watching her heart rhythm flash across the screen in a fast but relatively steady beat. Her blood pressure was adequate, too, and there wouldn't be a better time to transfer her upstairs. "Call the NNICU and let them know she's coming up."

"Will do," one of the circulating nurses said.

He broke scrub, knowing the anesthesiologist would take care of the transfer. Erica would need to remain on the ventilator, not to mention on several different medications, as they waited for her body to heal from surgery. It was late now, not likely that Rebecca would still be around. No doubt she had someone else covering the evening shift.

As much as he wanted to head home, he knew he couldn't leave until he was certain little Erica was stable. The first few hours were the most critical, and if she started bleeding, he'd have to take her back to surgery.

He changed his scrubs and then took a few minutes to call Josh, as it was just past dinnertime. "Hi, Gemma, is Josh there?"

"Sure. I'll get him."

He could hear her yelling for Josh and soon his son picked up the phone. "Daddy? Are you coming home now?"

He closed his eyes and wished more than anything that he could go home just for a few minutes to give Josh a hug. "Not yet. But if everything goes well, I'll be home before you go to bed."

"Promise?" Josh asked.

He hesitated, hating to promise anything he couldn't deliver. "Josh, I promise that I'll try very hard to get home before you go to bed. A lot depends on how well my patient is doing. Okay?"

"Okay." Josh sounded distant, and Dan wished more than anything he could have had this last week at home. But at the same time tetralogy of Fallot, complicated by hypoplastic pulmonary arteries, was his specialty. Erica had the best chance with him as her surgeon.

As always, the tug between doing what was best for his patients and what was best for his son was difficult to navigate. He didn't want to let either of them down.

But when he did, it was invariably his son who suffered the most.

"How was therapy today?" he asked in an effort to prolong the conversation.

"Good."

Another one-word answer. He strove for patience and tried again. "Let's see if I can guess what flavor lollipop you chose for today. Hmm," he murmured dragging out the suspense as he pretended to ponder. "Cherry? No, I bet it was root beer."

There was a gasp. "How did you know it was root beer?" Josh demanded with awe.

Dan grinned. “I have superhuman powers,” he teased. Glancing at his watch, he realized baby Erica was already up in the NICU by now. “Look, Josh, I have to go and check on my patient. I’ll try to be home in a couple of hours, okay?”

“Okay. Good night, Daddy.” At least this time he sounded as if he meant it.

“Good night, Josh.” After Josh hung up, he stared at his phone for a moment, before slipping it into his pocket and heading over to the elevator. He always hoped and prayed his patients did well after surgery, especially since they were so small and vulnerable.

But this time he hoped and prayed twice as hard because he didn’t want to disappoint his son.

He had been wrong about Rebecca, who was still there, and he found her studying Erica’s lab results intently. “Hi, Dan,” she said, somewhat distractedly.

“Rebecca. How’s she doing?”

“Good so far. Her hemoglobin is stable for the moment.”

“Glad to hear it.” If Erica’s hemoglobin stayed stable, he’d make it home in time to say good-night to Josh after all.

“I can watch her, if you want to head home,” Rebecca offered. “I have to be here, anyway.”

It was tempting, oh, so tempting to take her up on her offer but his rule was to wait for a least an hour. If patients were going to start bleeding it was generally within the first hour or two.

“I’ll wait.” He settled in a chair next to Erica’s isolette.

“Your choice.” She dropped next to him and they

spent the next hour monitoring Erica's vital signs and lab values.

"This baby girl is a true star," Rebecca said, pushing away from the isolette well over an hour later. "Go home, Dan. Your son needs you."

He didn't have to be told twice. Erica did indeed look like a star. Or at least she was stable. And he didn't live far from the hospital if something happened later.

He crossed the threshold of his home fifteen minutes later, giving him thirty minutes before Josh usually went to bed. "Josh? Gemma? I'm home."

"Gemma's not here, Daddy," Josh said, wheeling into the living room.

His jaw dropped and his heart squeezed in panic. "What do you mean, she's not here?" he said in alarm. "Are you telling me she actually left you here all alone?"

"No, she didn't leave him alone." A female voice from the doorway made him swing round in shocked surprise. Molly stood there, looking wonderful. And nervous. "I—um—agreed to come over as she had to leave. Something about her daughter needing to go to the hospital."

"You did?" He stared at her, tempted to rush over and haul her into his arms, to prove she was real. Because having Molly waiting for him was something he'd secretly coveted.

"Yes. I hope you don't mind."

God, no, of course he didn't mind. In fact, this just might be the best news of his entire day. He reverently hoped Erica would remain stable back at the hospital as he flashed a grateful smile and gently closed the door behind him. "I don't mind at all."

CHAPTER TWELVE

MOLLY TRIED TO HIDE HER uncertainty about agreeing to come over to pinch-hit for Josh's nanny. Deep down, she'd figured this was a bad idea, but she hadn't been able to refuse Gemma, as the nanny's daughter had been taken to the hospital with suspected appendicitis.

She sat on the corner of Josh's bed, listening as Dan read Josh a bedtime story. Dan was doing a pretty good job, changing his voice to match the characters.

After the story, Josh wanted to hug and kiss both of them good-night. Dan went first, and then she stepped forward. As she bent over, giving him a hug and a kiss, and receiving the same in return, she couldn't help remembering how she'd often done the same thing with James's boys. She tried to tell herself this was different, but at the moment she had an undeniable sense of déjà vu.

"Molly, I don't know how to thank you for coming over on the spur of the moment like this," Dan said huskily, after he'd closed the door for Josh's room and led the way into the living room. "I owe you, big-time."

She forced herself to relax and smile. "It's no problem. Gemma was so upset about her daughter needing emergency surgery, there was no way I could turn her down. Besides, you know I care about Josh."

"Something I'm very grateful for," he said humbly.

She was secretly relieved he didn't seem to think she was chasing after him, considering the night they'd spent together. It had been her biggest fear in agreeing to cover for Gemma. Fortunately, the moment Dan had realized she was there, he'd looked happy to see her.

Still, she couldn't help wondering why Dan had left her name and number to use in case of an emergency in the first place. She didn't want to think that he was taking advantage of her.

She smiled, determined to leave on a friendly note. "Well, now that you're here, I'll head home. Good night, Dan."

"No, wait." He stepped forward and took her arm. "I'm sorry, Molly, but I was planning on Gemma spending the night in the guest room, in case I'm called back to the hospital."

She tried to hide her dismay. Of course, Gemma hadn't mentioned that small detail. "Even after working all day, you're still on call?"

"I have to be available in case Erica needs to be taken back to surgery," he explained patiently. "She's still in a very critical condition, after being taken to surgery mere moments after she was born."

Her eyes widened in shock. "Really? I had no idea that was even possible."

"It's not something we have to do often, but her case was very complicated. Only a few pediatric cardiothoracic surgeons in the country do this particular procedure."

And Dan Morris was one of them, she thought with a tiny thrill of pride. But then reality sank in and she glanced around with a sigh. "I didn't pack an overnight bag."

"There's plenty of extra toiletries here." he said gently. Before she could respond, he surprised her by coming forward to pull her into his arms. "I've missed you, Molly," he murmured before taking possession of her mouth in a deep kiss.

Her ability to think was severely hampered by the way he kissed her so thoroughly. She soon became lost in his embrace. He'd actually started tugging her toward the bedroom and, heaven help her, she wasn't resisting when his phone rang.

"Dammit," he muttered, pulling away from her to fumble for his phone. "Yeah? Hi, Rebecca, what's going on?"

Molly took several deep breaths and smoothed her hair, trying to calm her erratic pulse, as she listened to the one-sided conversation. She'd managed to convince herself that a relationship between them was impossible, yet one kiss and she'd been ready to toss her fears and insecurities aside.

She must be going crazy. Granted, he'd called her on Sunday, but by the time they'd talked, she'd already convinced herself she must get over him.

Now she wasn't sure what to do.

"Okay, give her ten ccs of blood to run over an hour and I'll be there in ten—fifteen minutes tops."

She tried to hide her dismay. "Has the baby taken a turn for the worse?" she asked when he'd hung up.

"Not terrible, but she has been bleeding, so I really need to go in to see how she's doing." His dark brown eyes were full of regret. "I'm sorry, Molly."

"That's okay, I understand," she said lightly. And she truly did understand. Clearly a tiny life hung in the balance. She would do a lot for her patients, too.

He came over and gave her another hard kiss, before turning back toward the door. But then he paused and glanced over his shoulder at her. "I don't expect you to wait up for me, because I don't know when I'll be back." He hesitated, and then added, "Make yourself at home, either in my bed or in the guest room. Wherever you're most comfortable." He said the last few words in a rush, and then left without waiting for a response.

She stared at the door long after he'd gone. Did he really mean what she thought he'd meant? That if she wanted to pick up their relationship where they'd left off on the weekend, she could sleep in his bed? Or if she wanted privacy and or distance she could use the guest room?

And what about Josh? He was old enough that he probably wouldn't wake up in the middle of the night and his inability to walk meant he wouldn't wander into Dan's room. Still, Josh could get up early and use the wheelchair to come in. Or would Dan expect her to sneak out in the morning before Josh was up?

She collapsed on the sofa and stared at the ceiling, her thoughts in turmoil. What was the right answer? What should she do?

No matter how badly she wanted to, she couldn't come to terms with the idea of crawling into Dan's bed. Not while Josh was so close.

But she didn't go into the guest room, either, worried that she might send the wrong message. Instead, she took her book and settled in the corner of the sofa, using a quilt for warmth. Soon the book slipped from her grasp, falling to the floor with a soft thud as she drifted into sleep.

* * *

"Daddy, shouldn't we wake her up?" Josh asked in a loud whisper.

Molly shifted and let out a low moan at the shaft of pain that shot through her neck from sleeping at an awkward angle. She prised her eyes open and found Josh's face scant inches from hers.

"Good morning," she murmured as she tried to unwrap herself from the quilt cocoon. She lifted her gaze to Dan, who stared at her with an enigmatic expression that she couldn't interpret. "Hi. How's your patient?"

A smile curved his mouth, softening his expression. "She's a true champ. Thankfully, she stabilized enough that I didn't have to take her back to the O.R."

"I'm so glad," she said, truly happy that the tiny newborn was doing so well. "Um, what time is it?"

"Six forty-five. I wasn't sure how long to let you sleep, because I didn't know if you had an eight o'clock patient or not."

"Six forty-five?" She shot up to her feet, having momentarily forgotten that today was Wednesday, a work day. "I don't—you're my first appointment of the day, but I still have to get ready."

"I'll make breakfast while you shower," Dan offered. She belatedly noticed that he must have already done that as his short hair gleamed with dampness.

"Thanks." She didn't like the thought of putting her same clothes back on, but at least she had a spare set of scrubs at work for emergencies like when a patient threw up or bled all over the place. She would have to make do with what she had.

But as she washed her hair in the shower, she couldn't help wondering what time Dan had gotten home, and if he'd been disappointed when he'd noticed she hadn't chosen the option of sleeping in his bed.

And why she cared so much in wanting to know.

Dan suppressed a yawn as he drank more coffee, trying to compensate for fewer than three hours of sleep. He couldn't deny having been sorely disappointed to come home at two-thirty in the morning to find Molly asleep on the sofa. Fantasies of coming home to nuzzle her awake for some gentle lovemaking had instantly dissolved in a puff of smoke.

He'd stared at her for several seconds, tempted to lift her up and carry her to the guest bedroom, but then worried he'd only wake her up. So he'd left her alone, the way she'd apparently preferred, and gone to bed.

Where he'd wasted a precious thirty minutes he could have been sleeping, with tossing and turning and missing her.

Josh had woken him up at six, which was good because he hadn't been sure what time Molly needed to be at Angel's. And he'd taken time to do a quick check on Erica.

It wasn't until he'd started making breakfast that he'd realized that if Molly had slept with him, Josh would have come in to see them together. Not exactly something that would make him a candidate for father of the year.

The knot of tension between his shoulder blades eased, as he convinced himself that obviously that possibility had been what had caused Molly to avoid making herself comfortable in his room. Once again she'd proved she knew more than he did about kids, as he hadn't even considered that possibility until now.

And, worse, he suspected she might think less of him for even suggesting it.

For a moment he braced his hands on the counter and stretched the kinks from his neck. Being a single father in a relationship was much harder than he'd anticipated. Thankfully, Molly seemed to roll with the punches.

"I'll give you a back rub if you return the favor," she said from behind him. "My neck is killing me."

He swung round to face her. "I'll take you up on that offer any time," he said in a low voice. Just the thought of her hands on him made him tighten with need.

"What's for breakfast?" The way she shied away from the subject helped cool his desire.

"Just cereal today, hot or cold. Josh wants maple and brown sugar oatmeal."

"Sounds good to me. Make that a double."

"I'll make it a triple, since that's easiest all the way around. Just give me a few minutes to heat it up."

"I'll get the brown sugar, if you tell me where to find it," she offered.

"Third cupboard on your left." Within ten minutes they all sat down at the table and he was struck by the fact that even that first year, when Josh had just been a baby, he and Suzy had rarely shared breakfast.

Maybe an indication their marriage had been doomed from the start.

"If you want to drop me and Josh off at the physical therapy gym, we can start the session while you check on your patient," she offered.

"That would be great, thanks." As they finished their meal and then worked together to take care of the dishes, he wondered if this was how other families lived.

Or if this was just another of his fantasies that had no basis in reality?

* * *

Dan left Molly and Josh in the therapy gym and headed up to the NNICU to see Erica.

He found Erica's parents wrapped tightly in each other's arms, gazing at their tiny daughter in the isolette.

For a moment he had to look away. The love in their gazes was so intensely private, he felt like the worst kind of intruder. But he couldn't stand here forever, he had to check on their daughter's progress, so he cleared his throat and stepped forward.

"Dr. Morris," Jennifer greeted him tearfully, breaking away from her soldier husband. "Thank you for saving our daughter's life. This is my husband, Sergeant Eric Thompson."

Her husband was still wearing the fatigues he must have worn on the flight home. Dan stepped forward and offered his hand. "Pleased to meet you, Sergeant."

"I'm the lucky one," the young man said, shaking his hand. "I have you to thank for saving my family."

Uncomfortable with the praise, Dan brushed it aside. "Your daughter is a fighter. She's doing great. If she stays this good over the next twenty-four to forty-eight hours, we'll be able to get that breathing tube out."

"That would be wonderful," Jennifer said. "I want to hold her in my arms."

He understood. Obviously putting gloved hands through the windows of the isolette to touch their baby wasn't nearly as satisfying. "Soon," he promised. It was on the tip of his tongue to remind them that Erica would need more surgery down the road, but he decided there was plenty of time to broach that subject after they'd successfully gotten through this crisis.

According to the electronic medical record, Erica's

vital signs were stable. She hadn't lost any more blood and the rest of her labwork was good. He used his pediatric stethoscope and reached through the windows of the isolette to listen to Erica's heart and lungs.

Satisfied the baby girl was holding her own, he stepped away. "She's doing fine," he said to reassure her parents. "I'm going to order some weaning parameters later on this afternoon, to see if we can turn the ventilator down a few notches."

"Thank you," Eric murmured, hugging his wife close.

Dan wrote the orders, chatted with Rebecca's replacement and then looked for Erica's nurse. He scowled a bit when he didn't recognize her and glanced at the nametag she wore on her scrubs. "Scarlet?" he asked. "Are you new here?"

"Yes, I'm the new head nurse, but I'm taking care of patients today." She wore her chocolate-brown hair pulled back from her face, and jutted her chin stubbornly. "Why, do you have a problem with that?"

"Depends on how well you do your job," he said, refusing to back down. "Marcus is covering for me, but if Erica takes a turn for the worse, I want you to call me directly, okay?"

"No problem. And don't worry—I have a lot of experience with neonates. I promise Erica is in good hands."

He gave a terse nod and turned away because he believed her. And it was time to pick up Josh.

As he left he glanced back at the young couple at Erica's isolette, impressed once again at how they physically and emotionally supported each other through this difficult time.

Would they make it over the long haul? Or would the

endless toil and stress of life with a sick child eventually force them to part?

Cynically, he assumed the latter.

Then he stopped and turned back one more time to watch the young couple. Maybe, just maybe he needed to give them the benefit of the doubt. Just because he'd never experienced the type of love that lasted forever, it didn't mean that type of love didn't exist.

Molly was just finishing up with Josh's therapy when Dan arrived. She glanced up at him while she was running the ultrasound machine. "How's your patient?"

He was touched by her concern. Suzy had resented his pediatric patients, treating them like annoying inconveniences. "Much better. Should be able to start weaning her off the ventilator soon."

"That's wonderful. I'm sure her parents are relieved."

They were, so he nodded, but he didn't say anything more as he couldn't really talk about his patients much. All those privacy rules tended to get in the way. "How are you doing, Josh?" he asked, turning his attention to his son.

"We had fun. And I stood up again, right, Molly?"

"Yes, you did," she agreed with a soft smile. It struck him in that moment how much she'd bonded with his son. "Your muscles are getting stronger every day."

"I'm glad." He took a seat on a stool next to Josh. "I'm sorry I couldn't be here this morning, Josh."

"That's okay," Josh said pragmatically. "Molly told me there's a baby with a sick heart that you need to take care of. That's way more important."

His chest tightened and he slowly shook his head. "No, that's not true. I do have to take care of kids that have sick hearts, but they're not more important than you, Josh. You're the most important thing in my life. But sometimes I do have to take care of sick kids, like today. Especially because I knew that you'd be okay here with Molly for a little while. But I want you to know that I'll always love you best."

"All finished," she said, and then shut off the ultrasound machine. "I, um, have to check on something. Excuse me." She hurried out of the room, without even wiping the gooey gel off Josh's legs.

Dan took the towel and did the task himself. "You're not mad at me, are you, Josh?" he finally asked, breaking the silence.

"No. I think I understand."

He was tempted to spring the news about the surprise birthday party on Saturday, but forced himself to keep silent. The look on Josh's face would be well worth the wait.

"What flavor lollipop do you want today?" he asked, reaching for the candy jar.

For a moment Josh simply stared at the various flavors. Then he turned his head up to face him. "What's your favorite flavor, Daddy?"

He was touched that his son cared enough to ask. "Lime. The green ones are my favorite."

"Then I'm going to have a green one," Josh said, digging his little fist in the jar until he grabbed a lime sucker. He ripped off the wrapper and stuck the candy into his mouth.

Dan glanced toward the doorway and saw Molly hovering there. He realized she'd purposefully left them alone to give them time to talk.

"So I'll see you tomorrow, then," she said lightly, as Josh levered himself into his wheelchair.

"Don't forget about Friday night," Dan said, following her out into the hallway so Josh couldn't overhear.

She froze and then shook her head. "Look, Dan, I don't think Friday is a good idea," she said, avoiding his gaze.

He frowned and glanced back to make sure Josh was still preoccupied. "Why not?"

She took a deep breath. "I came over last night to help out because you and Josh needed me, but I don't want to be a convenient surrogate nanny. Been there, done that, don't want to do it again."

He was startled by her revelation. "I want to see you, alone, Molly. Certainly not as a surrogate nanny. And I had no idea Gemma was planning to call you."

"Yet she did, because you left my name and number to be used in case of an emergency."

He couldn't quite hide the flash of guilt, but he wanted to know more about this previous relationship of hers. "What do you mean, been there, done that?"

"The last guy I dated was also a single father, and he used me as a surrogate mother for his boys all the time. Yet when I thought he was going to propose, he told me he loved someone else. He never cared about me the way he should have."

That guy was just plain stupid, he thought, but managed to keep it to himself. "But I haven't been doing that with you, Molly. I do care about you. I want to take you to dinner so we can spend some time alone. I swear to you, making you a surrogate nanny was never my intention."

But she shook her head, not giving an inch. "Dan,

I'll help you with…Saturday's plans because I promised I would, but that's all. I have to go, my next patient is waiting."

And before he could protest or ask anything more, she turned and walked away.

CHAPTER THIRTEEN

MOLLY TRIED TO ERASE the stricken expression on Dan's face from her mind, but it stuck with her as she worked with her patients throughout the day.

Logically, she knew she'd made the right decision. Getting involved with Dan hadn't been very smart in the first place. She should have known better than to make the same mistakes she'd made with James.

Wasn't he already using her as a replacement nanny? Soon he'd leave her at home with Josh while he went out on dates. She had no doubt he'd find someone else to fall in love with, breaking her heart in the process. Just like James had done.

The organ in question ached in her chest as she rode the subway home. The newspaper she'd brought along to read didn't even come close to holding her attention.

Two more days of therapy and then Josh's birthday party on Saturday. After that, she probably wouldn't see Dan anymore. He'd go back to work full time, as Josh had gotten through the worst of his crisis. She'd continue to see Josh as a patient, but wouldn't see Dan. Wouldn't be forced to make small talk with him, as if she wasn't slowly bleeding to death inside.

She loved him.

The realization made her blink in surprise, although

now that she'd admitted it she was surprised she'd fooled herself for this long.

She loved him. She loved the way he'd turned his relationship with his son around. She loved the way he cared about his tiny patients. She loved the way she could make him smile and laugh.

And most of all she loved the way he centered his intenseness on her when they were alone, as if she was the only person on the planet who mattered.

But they hadn't been alone together much. The night of Jack's going-away party and the night he'd taken her to dinner. Two nights out of two weeks.

Ridiculous to think she could fall in love in such a short time. She cared about Dan, but love? How could that be?

She didn't know how it had happened, but it had. She loved him or she wouldn't be so upset about leaving him.

She got off the subway at her stop, holding the newspaper she hadn't read over her head when it started raining. She shivered and practically ran the rest of the way to her apartment.

Inside, she quickly changed out of her damp clothes into a pair of warm sweats. When her phone rang, she leaped to answer it, trying not to be too disappointed when she recognized the caller as her sister. "Hi, Sally, how are you?"

"Great, I'm great. Hey, listen, I know I should have asked you about this earlier, but will you be one of my bridesmaids at my wedding?"

Molly hesitated, wanting nothing more than to be included, but she knew her sister really would rather have one of her friends.

"I'm sorry I didn't ask you sooner," Sally said in a rush, filling the awkward silence. "And I don't blame you for being upset. I ran into your boyfriend in the cafeteria yesterday and he told me I should be ashamed at how I'm always taking you for granted. That I should be grateful for having a sister. And he's right. I am grateful, Molly. So will you please consider standing up with me at my wedding?"

Tears burned her eyelids as her heart swelled with joy. "Yes, Sally, of course I will. I'd love to be a bridesmaid at your wedding."

"Oh, I'm so glad, Molly. Thank you." She thought it must be her imagination because she thought she heard Sally sniffling on the other end of the line. "We're going shopping for dresses a week from Saturday. Do you want to come along? That is, if you don't have other plans."

"I'd love to come along, and of course I don't have other plans." She was still reeling from the knowledge that Dan had approached Sally at work, just to stick up for her. And she was glad they weren't shopping this weekend, as this Saturday was Josh's birthday. "Let me know what time and what store you're planning to meet at."

"I haven't figured that out yet," Sally admitted. "But I will soon. Thanks again, Molly. I love you."

Her heart almost folded in half at the second shocker of the day. "I love you, too," she managed to choke out.

"Bye, Molly." After her sister had hung up, she stared at the phone for several moments before she set it down, grinning like a fool. She'd mentally prepared herself to be left out of the wedding party, had even wondered if she'd make the invite list. But thanks to Dan, Sally had realized that being sisters was important.

Maybe their relationship wouldn't be completely fixed overnight, but this was a good start. A really, really good start.

Her smile faded. She wondered who in Dan's life had made him aware of how important he was? Certainly not his ex-wife. And he didn't have any brothers or sisters, because he'd mentioned being an only child.

The ache in her heart returned, and she wondered if she'd been too hasty in her refusal to see Dan again.

Molly looked for opportunities to have a personal conversation with Dan, but as the week went on she hardly saw him at all. According to Josh, his dad had been on call again, leaving Mitch to spend the night and subsequently accompany Josh to therapy.

She should have been glad to hear Dan hadn't used her as one of his nannies but instead she couldn't help feeling guilty at how she'd left things between them.

Telling herself that putting distance between them was for the better was one thing. But the lingering doubts wouldn't go away.

After rain during the week, the sun came out by Friday and according to the weather reports, temperatures were supposed to get up as high as sixty degrees by Saturday. Perfect weather for Josh's surprise birthday party and the wheelchair football game.

She'd been thrilled to see Dan on Friday afternoon, but he was all business as they stored the wheelchairs in the truck he'd rented.

"That's the last of them," he said, stepping down from the truck. "Thanks for your help, Molly."

She tried to smile, even though she missed the easy camaraderie that they'd once shared. "No problem. I'm going to head out to the park early to hide the prizes. What time are you going to have Josh there?"

"The party starts at one, so I thought we'd get there about one-fifteen." They'd already agreed that the other kids should all be there, holding a big birthday banner, before Josh arrived. "Unless you think we need to wait a little longer?" he asked uncertainly.

She pursed her lips, considering the timeframe. "No, I think one-fifteen should be fine. I suspect some of the kids will get there early, anyway."

Dan reached out to take her hand in his. "Molly, I've been thinking a lot about what you said earlier this week. If you don't want to help me with this party, I can handle it on my own," he said, his eyes dark and serious. "I don't want you to think I'm taking advantage of you."

"You're not taking advantage. I want to help. I want to be there for Josh." Seeing him now, after missing him for several days, she wondered if she'd been wrong to compare him to James. "Besides, I owe you for the way you stood up for me with my sister. She told me what you said to her in the cafeteria."

Dan scowled. "She needed to hear the truth. But that doesn't matter, because there isn't a score card, Molly. Friends help friends without expecting anything in return."

"I know." She kept the smile on her face, even though she feared her cheeks might crack from the pressure. Her instincts were screaming at her that she'd been wrong, but this wasn't the time or the place to discuss their personal issues.

He let out a heavy sigh. "I have to go, but I hope

maybe after Josh's party you and I can talk. There are… some things I'd like to share with you."

Now he'd intrigued her. "All right."

He flashed a lopsided grin and then nodded. "See you tomorrow, Molly."

"Until then, Dan." She couldn't understand the sudden sadness that nearly overwhelmed her when he walked away.

She had trouble falling asleep that night, thinking too much about Dan and Josh, and then overslept. When she realized it was almost ten in the morning, she shot out of bed like a rocket.

Thankfully, she'd already wrapped her present for Josh, hoping he'd like the Yankees sweatshirt she'd bought him, a miniature replica of his father's. She'd been tempted to get the full uniform, but since she knew he wouldn't be playing much this year, she'd chosen the sweatshirt instead.

But she still had dozens of gifts to hide near where they were going to play wheelchair football. She quickly showered and changed her clothes. Once she was ready, she tossed the items in a large reusable grocery bag and then headed down to the subway.

The ride to Central Park didn't take long, and she relaxed when she realized she had almost two full hours to get the gifts hidden and the banner ready. Hiding the gifts didn't take long, and she spent some of her extra time lining up the wheelchairs into two teams.

As she'd suspected, several kids came early. "Where's Josh and his dad?" the first mom asked, craning her neck as if to search him out.

"They're not here yet. He's bringing Josh at one-fifteen. The party is a surprise."

"Oh." Her face fell in disappointment.

Molly tried not to scowl at how the woman was clearly interested in Dan, considering she'd shown up at the birthday party dressed to kill in cream slacks and a red blouse that dipped low enough in the front to show off a fair amount of cleavage.

"I guess I can wait, then."

Molly's gaze narrowed but she simply shrugged. "Suit yourself."

"What did you say your name was again?" the woman asked as she turned to greet the next child.

"Molly Shriver." Maybe it was small of her, but she didn't label herself as Josh's physical therapist. She turned to the next new arrival. "Hi, welcome to Josh's surprise party. Thanks so much for coming."

By ten after one a large crowd of kids had gathered in the park in front of the wheelchairs. Molly took charge, unrolling the banner and getting all the kids together to hold it up for Josh.

When Dan and Josh arrived, Josh's eyes widened in shock as everyone yelled, "Surprise!"

"Happy birthday, Josh," Dan said, as he got Josh's wheelchair out of the trunk. "Guess what? We're going to play wheelchair football."

"We are?" Josh looked as if he was shell-shocked as the kids crowded around and wished him happy birthday before picking out their own wheelchairs.

"We are," Molly said, crossing over to give him a hug. "And you're going to have the advantage in this game," she whispered, giving him a secret wink. "You know how to use your wheelchair, they don't."

"Oh, yeah!" Josh's eyes glittered with excitement.

"Dan? Hi, Dan, remember me? Stephanie Albert?"

The woman in the cream-colored slacks that were distinctly out of place here at the park came rushing over.

"Oh, uh, yeah, sure," Dan said in a vague, distracted tone. "It was nice of you to bring your son to Josh's party."

"Well, of course I brought him. He's friends with Josh, isn't he?" The way Stephanie beamed up at Dan made Molly curl her hands into fists. Not that she had any right to be upset.

Or jealous.

"Hey, Molly, what do you think? Should we act as referees?" Dan asked, as the kids started piling into their wheelchairs.

She hid a grin as the nicely dressed woman wrinkled her nose in distaste. Clearly she wasn't offering to referee, the way she'd dressed. "Sounds good. We can each coach one of the teams, too."

"Excellent plan," Dan said, ignoring Stephanie as if she didn't exist. "I brought us whistles," he said, handing her one of the shiny metal whistles on a chain. "Let's go."

"I'll pick up Craig later," Stephanie called out, as if desperate for one last fragment of attention.

Dan lifted his hand, but didn't turn around so he didn't see the way Stephanie frowned and stomped away, like a spoiled little kid who hadn't gotten her way.

But Molly sensed that the woman had only retreated for the moment. It was clear she had every intention of trying to be the next Mrs. Doctor Dan Morris.

A plot that Dan seemed completely oblivious to. Which made her feel ridiculously happy as she hurried after Dan onto the football field.

* * *

Dan couldn't have asked for a better day for Josh's birthday party, and he had nearly as much fun as his son. The look of excitement in Josh's eyes was worth every minute of the seemingly endless preparations.

"Go, Josh, go!" he shouted, when his son went racing out toward the end zone for a pass.

"Get him!" Molly screamed to her team, but it was too late. Josh caught the ball and then rolled in for the winning touchdown.

"Way to go, Josh," Dan shouted again, all attempt at being impartial gone. "Way to go!"

Molly threw up her hands in disgust, but she didn't look too upset when she went over to give Josh a high five.

"This was too hard," Craig Albert said, letting go of his wheelchair wheels in a deep sulk. "We should have played regular football."

Dan had to bite his tongue to stop himself from pointing out it was Josh's party, and Josh couldn't play regular football. He did his best to ignore Craig's whining. "Good game, everybody, good game," he said, slapping his hands against each team member's in a high five.

"There are prizes hidden around the park," Molly said, when the kids had gathered in the center of the football field. "You might want to stay in your wheelchairs to find them and there's one for each of you, so once you find a prize, you need to come back here, okay?"

"Yay, prizes!" Craig rolled across the grass, but then was the first to abandon his wheelchair, so that he could look for the best hiding places.

"That kid grates on my nerves," Dan muttered to Molly, keeping his tone low so that the other kids couldn't hear him.

"Really? I thought you were friends with his mother?"

He stared at her in shock. "Are you crazy? That viper? Where do you think that poor kid gets his attitude from?"

She laughed and he basked in the musical sound for a moment.

"I've missed you, Molly," he said softly. "You have no idea how much."

Her laughter died away and she looked down as if she felt guilty. "I know, because I missed you, too."

Her words gave him a flash of hope. Maybe he hadn't totally ruined things between them after all? He tried to think of a way to help her understand. "Look, Molly, I know I'm not very good at being in a relationship, and I'm sure I've already made tons of mistakes, but I'd like you to give me another chance. I think, no, I'm sure I can do better."

She glanced up at him, surprise reflected on her features. "Dan, you haven't made any big mistakes, not really. It was my fault. I shouldn't have overreacted."

"You didn't overreact, you had every right to be upset." When she'd mentioned how the jerk who'd left her had two sons and had used her as a surrogate mother, he'd been extremely angry. And desperate to prove he wasn't doing the same thing. "I care about you, Molly. But I'm not sure how to show you. It's been a long time..." He stopped, unwilling to admit how ignorant he really was.

What did he know about love? He hadn't ever experienced it before. Not until Molly.

Stunned, he felt his heart squeeze in his chest. Was he really falling in love with Molly?

"Oh, Dan," she murmured, but then stopped whatever she'd been about to say when Josh came wheeling over.

"Daddy! Craig has two prizes and Amy is crying because she doesn't have one."

"Figures," he muttered. When the sound of Amy crying grew louder, he broke into a jog. "Don't leave yet, I'll be right back," he called over his shoulder, resenting Craig for being a brat and for interrupting his conversation with Molly.

A conversation he had every intention of finishing before he let her slip away.

Thankfully, he needn't have worried. Molly didn't leave. In fact, she stayed, helping him serve twenty kids pizza, punch, cake and ice cream.

When it came time for Josh to open his presents, Dan watched with pride as his son did so with glee, tearing into one package after another. And when Craig tried to grab the remote control to Josh's new truck, he swiftly intervened, snatching it away and handing it back to Josh. "I think the birthday boy should be the first one to try it, don't you?" he asked through gritted teeth.

Craig went back to sulking, but Dan didn't care. And when the parents of the kids started to arrive, he wanted to weep with relief. Even Stephanie Albert was a welcome sight if nothing more than to get Craig out of his hair.

"Did you have fun, sweetie-pie?" Stephanie asked, ruffling her son's hair.

"Our team didn't win and he wouldn't let me play with the remote-control car," Craig said, shooting Dan a dark look.

If the kid thought he was going to apologize, he was wrong. "Thanks for coming," he said cheerfully. "And don't forget your prize."

Craig snatched the mini pinball machine he'd won and stalked off, with his mother trailing behind.

"Good riddance," Molly muttered.

"You have that right," he said with heartfelt relief.

More parents streamed in and soon everyone was gone. As the wheelchairs had been picked up earlier, the cleanup job didn't take long.

Dan stared at the stack of presents Josh had accumulated. "I'm not sure we'll be able to fit all this in the trunk of my car, along with Josh's wheelchair," he muttered. But he'd rather cut off his arm than ask Molly for help, even though he wanted to finish their conversation more than he wanted to breathe.

"I'll help you. Between the two of us we'll get the car packed up, no problem," Molly said.

"Only if you're sure," he said, looking down into her bright green eyes. "There's no scorecard, Molly. If you want to go home, we'll handle it. You and I can always talk later."

Her tremulous smile tugged at his heart. "I know you can handle anything, but I'd like to help, if you'll have me."

Have her? Little did she know he wasn't about to let her go without a fight.

CHAPTER FOURTEEN

MOLLY WAS IN AWE OF HOW well Dan had handled the wheelchair football game, along with the subsequent meal for Josh's party, especially the not-so-nice kids like Craig Albert. Scary how much that kid was like his mother.

Just thinking of the way Dan had stared at her in horror when she'd mentioned Stephanie Albert made her feel warm and gooey inside. Clearly, he wasn't attracted to the woman, not even one little bit. And he wanted a second chance.

With her.

And, heaven help her, she wanted that, too.

She let out a little sigh of relief when Dan pulled into the parking garage beneath his fancy high-rise apartment building. "You don't have to carry those," he protested, when she gathered a bunch of Josh's presents into her arms. "I can make a few trips."

The way he was falling over himself trying not to take advantage of her made her smile. "Dan, it's fine. No scorecard, remember?" she chided lightly.

He grimaced and pulled Josh's wheelchair out, before loading up on gifts and leading the way to the elevator. Josh wheeled himself alongside, with his remote-controlled truck sitting on his lap, as if he wasn't about to be parted from the gift. She'd noticed that one was from Dan, and she silently approved of his choice. Perfect for now, with Josh being wheelchair bound, yet something he could still use once he was walking again.

Once inside Dan's home, they stacked the gifts in the corner of Josh's room.

"You realize you need to write thank-you notes for these," she said to Josh.

He wrinkled his nose, his face falling in dismay. "I do?"

"Yes. You do." She fought a grin as Dan sighed heavily at the news. "I'm sure your dad can get them to your teacher, who can hand them out to the kids at school."

"We'll work on them tomorrow, Josh," Dan assured him. "The sooner we get them done, the better."

"That's probably best." She glanced around, and noticed that Josh was bending over in his wheelchair, trying to massage his calf muscles. "What's wrong?"

"My legs are sore," Josh admitted.

"Really?" Dan scowled a bit and knelt beside his son's wheelchair to feel his legs. "That's strange because we didn't play the ball game very long this morning. I would think your arms would be sore after the game of wheelchair football, not your legs."

"Actually, using a wheelchair does exercise the core muscles along with the upper arms," she felt compelled to point out. "But even with that, it's possible Josh was unconsciously tightening his leg muscles while he played, especially when he was making those sharp turns on the field." She turned toward Josh. "You'd better let me massage them for you."

Dan looked relieved and nodded. "If you wouldn't mind, that would be great."

"Of course I don't mind." She helped Josh get settled on his bed while Dan brought in the bottle of lotion she'd used last time. "Do you have a heating pad?" she asked. "Heat helps to relax tense muscles, too."

"I'm not sure, I'll check."

As Dan went in search of the heating pad she instructed Josh to roll over on his stomach. She began to massage his lower legs, starting with the gastrocnemius and then moving onto the soleus, which was only slightly less tense.

"Feels good," Josh murmured groggily, as if he was half-asleep. She smiled, suspecting that the excitement of the day was catching up with him.

"I'm glad," she said, soothing the angry, tense muscles with her fingers. As before, his right leg was far worse than his left.

"I found it," Dan said in a low voice, bringing in the electric heating pad. He set it up while she finished the massage. She applied the heating pad to Josh's right leg and within moments the boy was out for the count, sound asleep.

She followed Dan from Josh's room, partially closing the door behind her. When they reached the living room, he surprised her by drawing her toward the sofa. "Please sit down for a moment."

She sat, knowing he meant to continue the conversation they'd started during Josh's party. She linked her fingers together to hide her nervousness.

He sat in the chair to her right so that he could face her. "Molly, there's so much I want to say to you, I don't even know where to start. First of all, thanks for everything you did today. Your idea for Josh's birthday party was brilliant. And I'll never forget the look on Josh's face when he saw all of you standing behind the banner, yelling, 'Surprise!'"

She couldn't help but smile. "The look on his face was priceless, wasn't it? And you did a lot of the work, too." She paused, and then added, "I'm so happy when I see how you and Josh are together now, compared to the day we first met. You've accomplished a minor miracle, Dan."

"You're the miracle, Molly," he said in a low, husky tone. "I owe everything to you."

"No, Dan, I'm sure you would have found your way back together again, even without my help." She lifted her gaze up to meet his. "You're a good father. You love Josh and I'm convinced your love can get you through anything."

"Molly." He reached over to rest the palm of his hand against her cheek. "You have to understand something. I don't really know much about love. My mother—well, let's just say I was a major inconvenience in her life. She never once let me forget how everything that was bad in our lives was my fault."

She felt herself pale, and brought up her hand to cover his. "That's terrible, Dan. How terrible of her to say those things to you!"

He rubbed his thumb across her cheek, but then pulled away, rising to his feet and turning his back as he began to pace. "Leaving home, going to college and then getting into medical school was the best thing I ever did. Everyone kept telling me what a great doctor I was, how much talent I had. I was at the top of my class, and then quickly rose to the top of my career. And when I met Suzy she claimed to adore me, so I married her."

He turned to face her, his gaze full of despair, and

her heart ached for him. "But she didn't love me, she only wanted my money. I basically went from one loveless existence to another. Until Josh was born."

"I know you loved your son the moment you saw him," she murmured.

"Yes, I did. I do. I've been wrestling with guilt over the accident that put Josh in the wheelchair, even though I know the other driver was primarily at fault. Still, I've been trying hard to move forward."

"Dan, surely you realize that the accident might have happened even if you hadn't been distracted. The guy ran a red light, right?"

"Yes, you're right. And I'm getting better there, but I'm afraid that without you I'll fall back into my old patterns."

"You won't, Dan. I believe in you. And to be honest, I feel like having me around will only get in the way." Saying the words, remembering how Josh and Dan had looked as they'd wheeled themselves down to Central Park that day, made her realize why she needed to leave.

Now. Before she lost any more of her heart.

"What are you saying?" he asked hoarsely.

She steeled her resolve. "I'm saying you need to take the time to concentrate on your relationship with your son." She ignored the cracks rippling through her heart, breaking it into zillions of pieces. "Without allowing anything else getting in the way."

"Is that really what you think?" he asked, his face pale.

She forced herself to nod. "Yes, that is exactly what I think." She rose to her feet and forced herself to take a step toward the door. "I care about you and Josh. And I only want you to be happy."

"Don't go," he said, and the tortured expression on his face nearly brought her to her knees.

"I have to." She lifted one shoulder in a helpless shrug. "I'm sorry, Dan, but I think you need to come to grips with your past and your present before you can even begin to contemplate a future."

He froze, as if pierced by her words. And in that moment she knew her gut instincts were right.

He wasn't ready for a true give-and-take relationship. Wasn't ready to be vulnerable enough to fall in love. For a moment her resolve wavered, because she could see just how clearly he needed someone to love him.

The way she loved him.

Yet didn't she deserve that same love in return? She'd given herself to James and his sons, and for what? No, she couldn't bear to have her heart broken again.

So she turned and left his apartment, intent on taking the subway home. And she wasn't sure which hurt more. Leaving him when she so badly wanted to stay or the grim knowledge that he hadn't tried to stop her.

The moment Molly left, Dan stared at the closed door, feeling more alone than ever before in his entire life. Worse than when Suzy had left him with their one-year-old son.

But the truth in her words resonated deep within him. Maybe she was right. Maybe he did need to resolve his past and his present relationship with Josh, before he could contemplate a future.

She'd told him he was a good father, but he wasn't sure if that was really true. His relationship with Josh had come a long way, and he wasn't about to lose the ground they'd gained, but instinctively he knew that having Molly around wouldn't distract him. He fought a rising sense of despair. He needed Molly to help show him the way.

He needed Molly to love him.

The way his mother and Suzy hadn't.

He'd grown beyond his mother's bitterness, had managed to come out with a great career in spite of her, but for some reason Suzy's betrayal seemed worse. Because he'd stupidly believed she'd loved him, even though she hadn't.

He still resented her. For leaving him. For the way she'd spent his money and then tossed him aside as if he wasn't good enough.

For distracting him the day of the crash. A crash that had almost killed Josh and had left him in a wheelchair.

He sank onto the edge of the sofa, cradling his head in his hands as bitter anger sloshed in his gut like bad whiskey. Maybe Molly was right. Maybe he needed to let go of his anger and resentment before he could move forward.

The image of baby Erica's parents holding each other, drawing strength from each other, as they'd sat next to the tiny isolette flashed into his mind. He remembered doubting the ability of their love to survive the stress of having a sick infant.

But maybe he had it backward. Maybe the reason his and Suzy's marriage had fallen apart after Josh's birth had been because they hadn't loved each other the way they should have in the first place.

Maybe true love held couples together during times of stress, rather than pulling them apart.

He'd known that things between him and Suzy hadn't been great even before Josh had been born. She'd made no secret of the fact that she'd hated everything about being pregnant. He'd hoped things would change once the baby was born, but instead they had gone from bad to worse.

He'd loved Josh the moment he'd first seen him, but he hadn't been an easy baby. Josh had suffered from colic and for those first few months he'd cried for hours on end.

Suzy hadn't been able to stand it, so he'd walked the floor with Josh, trying to soothe the colicky baby at night, while building his pediatric cardiothoracic practice during the day. He existed on little to no sleep, and it was by sheer luck he'd discovered that putting Josh in the baby swing and running the vacuum cleaner, of all things, had soothed his son more than anything else. Finally, they'd had at least a couple hours of peace and quiet.

Josh had grown out of his colicky phase by the time he was six months old, turning into a smiling, happy baby. But Suzy had still left just after Josh's first birthday. And he'd tried to manage on his own.

With his growing surgical practice he'd ended up spending less and less time at home, leaving Josh to the care of his nanny. Except for his days off, of course, when he'd had to haul Josh from one sporting event to another. Something he'd started to resent until that fateful crash, where he'd almost lost the one thing most precious to him.

Which brought him full circle, to the day he'd met Molly. The petite firecracker who'd dared to yell at him, had ordered him to get a wheelchair and who'd shown him the importance of having fun.

And what had she wanted in return? Nothing but for him to love his son.

No, wait. That wasn't exactly true. Over these past few weeks he'd learned a lot about Molly. He knew that deep down she wanted love and a family.

The knowledge hit him in the head like a brick. Of course Molly wanted love. She deserved love.

He was an idiot for not telling her how much he loved her!

He stood, and actually started for the door to follow Molly, before he remembered Josh was sleeping in his bed.

Spinning round, he went to find his phone. Okay, so he'd arrange for a babysitter. Josh might sleep the rest of the night anyway, and he wanted to talk to Molly. Now. Before it was too late.

Too late for what, he wasn't sure, but the sense of urgency wouldn't be denied.

He dialed Mitch's number, hoping and praying the college kid had another exam coming up. Or at the very least, wasn't already out partying on a Saturday night.

And if Mitch wasn't home, he'd call every babysitter he knew until he found someone who would come over. Because he desperately needed to see Molly again.

She deserved to know the truth.

He loved her!

Molly was reading in bed, finding it difficult to focus on the murder mystery while trying not to think about Dan. When her apartment buzzer sounded, she started badly. With a frown she pulled on her robe over her pajamas and went over to the intercom. "Who is it?"

"It's Dan—will you please let me come up?"

Dan? What on earth was he doing here? She glanced helplessly over her shoulder at her messy apartment, but pushed the intercom button again. "Uh, sure. Come on up." She pushed the middle button, which unlocked the door, and then ran her fingers through her tousled hair.

She probably looked awful in her ratty robe and no makeup, but there wasn't time to make herself look presentable. Besides, why should she care what she looked like? She'd spent the last two hours trying to forget about Dan and Josh, convinced she'd done the right thing by walking away. Giving them the time they needed. That they deserved.

So why was he here?

He rapped on her apartment door, startling her from her thoughts. Full of apprehension, she opened the door. "Hi, is Josh okay?"

"He was still sleeping when I left." Dan stepped inside, forcing her back a few steps, and then closed the door behind him. "Thanks for letting me come up. I really need to talk to you."

She glanced at him uncertainly. "Dan, I'm not sure there's anything more to say—" she began.

"I love you," he interrupted.

She blinked, opened her mouth and then closed it again. Was she dreaming? She must be because she couldn't believe what she was hearing. Somehow she managed to find her voice. "Excuse me?"

"I love you." He took a step toward her, and she instinctively took a step back. "I love you, Molly Shriver. I know you think I need to concentrate on my relationship with my son, and I will. But I don't want to lose you, either."

Her knees went weak and she tried to wrap her mind

around what he was saying. She desperately wanted to believe him, but what if she was wrong? "I don't understand."

"Then I can't be saying it right," he muttered, and before she realized what he was about to do he pulled her into his arms and slanted his mouth over hers in a hot, deep kiss.

She melted against him, wanting to be in his arms more than she wanted to breathe. When he lifted his head a few moments later, she swallowed a protest.

"I love you, Molly," he said again, for the fourth time. And, heaven help her, she was actually starting to believe him. No one, not even James, had ever looked so serious and sincere when saying those three little words. Dan's love beamed from his heart up to his eyes. "You've brought sunshine and joy back into my life. I know I don't deserve you, but I can't bear the thought of losing you."

The conviction in his voice and the expression of hope on his face shook her to the core. Here was this dear man who'd never had anyone love him offering his heart to her. She felt awed and humbled to be on the receiving end of such a gift. "Oh, Dan—you haven't lost me. I was only going to give you and Josh some time to be together, that's all." She realized that by walking out on him she'd done the same thing as his ex-wife. She couldn't prevent her eyes from filling with happy tears. "I love you, too, Dan. So much that it scares me."

"You do?" He looked almost afraid to believe her. "My career is time-consuming, but I want you to know that I plan to put my family first. You and Josh will always come first."

"I know your patients need you, Dan. Josh and I

will always support you, no matter what, because we love you."

"Molly..." His voice broke and he swept her into his arms again, burying his face in her hair. "I love you so much."

Before she could say anything more he picked her up, strode into her bedroom and kicked the door shut behind them.

The next week passed in a blur as the work that had stacked up while Dan had been away now teetered over him like a potential avalanche. He didn't get nearly enough time to sneak over to share lunch with Molly or to get home in time to share dinner with Josh.

Thankfully, he wasn't on call the following weekend and was determined to make up for lost time with Molly and Josh by inviting her over for dinner on Friday night.

He was grateful to Gemma, who'd made a beautiful pan of lasagna, which meant all he had to do was to toss a salad together and open a bottle of wine.

He was nervous because he'd purchased an engagement ring and was planning to ask Molly to marry him. Tonight. Which was probably rushing it.

He should wait. But he didn't want to. He wanted the whole world to know she belonged to him.

When the door buzzer went, his heart leaped into his throat. "I'll get it," Josh shouted, as he hurled his wheelchair toward the door.

"Hi, Josh. Hi, Dan," Molly said, as she stepped into the living room.

Conscious of Josh's keen gaze, Dan gave her a quick kiss, despite how badly he wanted to linger. "Hi, Molly."

"Something smells delicious." Her warm gaze, full

of love, settled his nerves. "What can I do to help?" she asked.

"Nothing. I have everything ready to go."

As they wandered into the kitchen, she asked his son about his day, listening intently as Josh described how he'd managed to pull a B on his latest math test. As Dan poured the wine and then started the salad, he found he enjoyed listening to them.

"Mitch helped me a lot," Josh said. "Some of the mistakes I made were stupid."

"Well, don't beat yourself up over them," she chided. "Just remember next time to go slowly and double-check your work."

As they sat down for dinner, Dan was struck by how much they already seemed like a family. His love for Molly overwhelmed him.

When they'd finished the meal, he took the dirty dishes into the kitchen, leaving Molly and Josh alone. When he returned a few minutes later he stopped in the doorway when he heard Molly talking to his son. "Josh, I have something very important to ask you."

"You do?" Josh's eyes widened, as if sensing the seriousness in her tone. Dan stood stock-still, just out of sight, wondering what she was about to say.

"Yes." Molly actually looked nervous as she took Josh's hand in hers. "Josh, I love you. And I love your dad. I want to ask you if you'll let me marry your dad and become your new mother."

"For real?" Josh whispered, his brown eyes growing even larger. "You're going to marry my dad and be my new mother?"

She nodded slowly. "If you'll let me."

"Yes! Of course we'll marry you!" Josh cried, and

he launched himself at Molly, who caught him in a huge hug.

Dan watched them, his heart swelling with love, respect and pride. He stepped forward, capturing her gaze with his. "I think I'm the one who's supposed to pop the question," he murmured with a smile. He pulled out the small velvet box holding the engagement ring, opened it and slid it over to her on the table. "I was hoping to ask you later tonight."

"Really?" she gasped, and her eyes welled up with tears. "I'm sorry."

"Don't be." He reached over to pull the two most important people in his life close to his chest. "Just say yes."

"Yes," she whispered, burrowing close. "A thousand times, yes."

He smiled with satisfaction as he held his future.

His family.

EPILOGUE

Six months later...

DAN STOOD AT THE ALTAR of the small church that Molly's parents still attended regularly, waiting patiently for his bride to appear. Molly had chosen to have a smaller service, after her sister Sally's more lavish affair.

And he was fine with that. Molly knew, just as he did, that the ceremony was only the beginning. He caught a glimpse of white and held his breath. When the music swelled and everyone in the church rose to their feet, he stepped forward eagerly.

The two attendants came first, and he recognized Molly's sister, Sally, and her best friend, Kara. But he didn't spare them more than a second glance as he waited for Josh.

When he saw his son, standing right in front of Molly, on his own two feet, no wheelchair in sight, his chest tightened with a mixture of love and fear. Maybe they'd rushed this? What if Josh's legs weren't strong enough to hold him? What if he tripped and fell when walking up the aisle with the braces on his legs?

As Josh stepped forward, though, he realized he needn't have worried, because his son was smiling widely as he made his way down the center of the aisle, his gait clumsy with the braces but each deliberate step like music to his ears just the same. When Josh reached the front, he came over to stand right next to his dad.

"Good job, son," Dan murmured, putting his arm around Josh's shoulders. "I love you."

"I love you, too, Dad." Josh flashed him a broad smile but then focused his attention on watching his soon-to-be new mother, Molly, as she walked down the aisle toward them.

"She's so beautiful," Josh whispered.

"Yes, she is." And all his, he thought humbly as he moved forward to take Molly's arm, so they could approach the altar together. With Molly at his side, he could face anything the universe had in store for them. This was the beginning of a new life together.

As husband and wife. As a family with Josh.

And he knew, deep down, that their love would only grow stronger with each passing day.

* * * * *

NYC ANGELS: THE WALLFLOWER'S SECRET

BY

SUSAN CARLISLE

This one is for you, Drew. I love you.

First published in Great Britain 2013
by Mills & Boon, an imprint of Harlequin (UK) Limited.
Harlequin (UK) Limited, Eton House, 18-24 Paradise Road,
Richmond, Surrey TW9 1SR

Special thanks and acknowledgement are given to Susan Carlisle
for her contribution to the *NYC Angels* series

ISBN: 978 0 263 89886 6

Harlequin (UK) policy is to use papers that are natural, renewable and recyclable products and made from wood grown in sustainable forests. The logging and manufacturing process conform to the legal environmental regulations of the country of origin.

Printed and bound in Spain
by Blackprint CPI, Barcelona

Dear Reader

I've spent many hours over numerous years in a children's hospital. What I've learned is that it takes very special people to work with sick kids. The doctors, nurses and support staff are true angels when it comes to the care of children and their families. Lives of the young are saved and enhanced by their dedication. Still, these professionals have issues and problems of their own. My characters Ryan and Lucy are no different.

Change is often hard. Most people fight it. Sometimes they discover later that they're grateful they were forced to make a change. It pushes them into finding a happiness they might have otherwise missed. Ryan and Lucy are two people who must change, but do so kicking and screaming. I encourage you to be open to change. You never know what's just around that next bend.

The evening bus tour to Brooklyn that I describe in the story is a real one. It is breathtaking.

I can't fail to mention how honoured I am to be included among the wonderful authors that are involved in the *NYC Angels* series. I'm in super-outstanding company.

I hope you enjoy Lucy and Ryan's story. I love to hear from my readers. You can contact me at www.SusanCarlisle.com

Susan

NYC Angels

Children's doctors who work hard and love even harder…
in the city that never sleeps!

Step into the world of NYC Angels and enjoy two new stories a month

Last month New York's most notoriously sinful bachelor Jack Carter found a woman he wanted to spend more than just one night with in:
NYC ANGELS: REDEEMING THE PLAYBOY
by Carol Marinelli

And reluctant socialite Eleanor Aston made the gossip headlines when the paparazzi discovered her baby bombshell:
NYC ANGELS: HEIRESS'S BABY SCANDAL
by Janice Lynn

This month cheery physiotherapist Molly Shriver melts the icy barricades around hotshot surgeon Dan Morris's damaged heart in:
NYC ANGELS: UNMASKING DR SERIOUS
by Laura Iding

And Lucy Edwards is finally tempted to let neurosurgeon Ryan O'Doherty in. But their fragile relationship will need to survive her most difficult revelation yet…
NYC ANGELS: THE WALLFLOWER'S SECRET
by Susan Carlisle

Then, in May, newly single (and strictly off-limits!) Chloe Jenkins makes it very difficult for drop-dead-gorgeous Brad Davis to resist temptation…!
NYC ANGELS: FLIRTING WITH DANGER
by Tina Beckett

And after meeting single dad Lewis Jackson, tough-cookie Head Nurse Scarlet Miller wonders if she's finally met her match…
NYC ANGELS: TEMPTING NURSE SCARLET
by Wendy S. Marcus

Finally join us in June, when bubbly new nurse Polly Seymour is the ray of sunshine brooding doc Johnny Griffin needs in:
NYC ANGELS: MAKING THE SURGEON SMILE
by Lynne Marshall

And Alex Rodriguez and Layla Woods come back into each other's orbit, trying to fool the buzzing hospital grapevine that the spark between them has died. But can they convince each other?
NYC ANGELS: AN EXPLOSIVE REUNION
by Alison Roberts

Be captivated by NYC Angels in this new eight-book continuity from Mills & Boon® Medical Romance™

These books are also available in eBook format from www.millsandboon.co.uk

CHAPTER ONE

PEDIATRIC NEUROSURGEON DR. Ryan O'Doherty's attention remained on the child lying in the ICU bed of Angel Mendez Children's Hospital in New York City as he spoke to the father. "I removed as much of the tumor as possible. I didn't get it all because I couldn't risk additional impairment."

This father wasn't the first person to hear those words and he wouldn't be the last. Ryan made a point not to gloss over the truth when speaking to parents. Despite the fact that Ryan knew he possessed more than competent skills, he'd done all he could for the child. He couldn't fix them all. Parents had to accept that.

"I understand. His mother and I will take him home and love him for as long as we can," the father said in a voice filled with tears.

The father had courage. He'd have to cling to it down the road.

The sharp, shrill sound of Ryan's phone filled the air. He tapped the screen, stopping the offending noise, and looked at the message. Human Resources. He'd forgotten all about being expected down there. What could possibly be so important in the paper-pusher department that he was needed so urgently?

He glanced at the father again. "The neurologist will

re-evaluate your son's case. I'll be here if needed," he said curtly. "Now, if you will excuse me..."

"Thanks for all you've done."

Ryan nodded. It was his job.

Ten minutes later, Ryan walked through the network of gray hallways on his way to the human resources department. Hospital leadership was notorious for putting HR departments in the basement of the oldest section of the hospital and in the furthest corner, if they could accomplish it. Angel's was no different. Ryan hadn't seen this particular region of the building since he'd become an official employee five years earlier.

He wasn't sure why he'd been summoned, but he'd received an email the day before, requesting his presence. When he'd called to say he was too busy to make the meeting, Matherson, the HR director, had stated it was mandatory that he attend. Ryan was sure the trip down would be a complete waste of his time. Whatever he was needed for, surely could be handled by email.

Despite technically being an employee, he still wasn't used to being called into someone's office. If there was something to be said he was typically the one doing the calling. Expected for a surgery consultation in just a few minutes, he needed to get this over with. He made the final turn in the hallway and pushed the faux woodgrain door open, entering the functional waiting area that would have been drab if not for the colorful framed pictures of children hanging on the wall.

Ryan headed straight to the middle-aged woman sitting behind the L-shaped reception desk. "Dr. O'Doherty here to see Mr. Matherson," he said with a smile he didn't feel. He'd learned long ago that it paid to mask your emotions.

"He's expecting you," the woman at the desk chirped, as if she'd said it hundreds of times.

Not bothering to sit, he stood over the receptionist as she picked up the phone and spoke into it, and looked around the room.

A young woman, maybe in her late twenties, sat facing the entrance in one of the three utilitarian chairs set against the office wall. She glanced up at him. Her large blue eyes reminded him of a summer afternoon, but held a sadness that contradicted their lovely color. With a single blink, the melancholy was replaced by an unwavering stare before she looked away.

"Dr. O'Doherty is here, Mr. Matherson." The receptionist listened a moment then glanced at the woman sitting in the chair.

Ryan followed the receptionist's look. The woman sat with her ankles crossed and her hands laced primly in her lap. There was little outstanding about her apart from those large eyes and a rope of hair that fell over her shoulder. She wore a business suit of light gray with a flimsy peach blouse beneath. A little too schoolmarmy for his tastes.

He could tell her clothes were of a fine quality. He snorted quietly. Must have been all those long-suffering shopping trips he'd made with his sisters that had given him that knowledge. He quirked a corner of his mouth. Should he be proud of that?

"Ms. Edwards, Mr. Matherson would like to see you and Dr. O'Doherty now."

Who was this Ms. Edwards and why would she have anything to do with him being here? Ryan's focus sharpened when she stood. The woman was tall, with a willowy frame that spoke of someone who took care of herself. Her gaze met his. The sadness he'd seen early in her eyes had been replaced by a resolute look. She held his gaze a moment before her attention turned to the HR man.

Mr. Matherson, a round bodied man with a balding head, had come round a corner. "Dr. O'Doherty and Ms. Edwards, please come back to my office."

Ryan stepped back and allowed her to go ahead of him. Her head reached his shoulder. Her wheat-colored hair was controlled by a braid. What was it called? He'd heard his sisters talk about them enough. Something foreign. A French braid, that was it. Even with the braid her hair went midway down her back. Did it touch her hips when free?

Ms. Edwards's eyes narrowed. Had she guessed his thoughts?

"Please come in and have a seat," Mr. Matherson instructed as he stepped around the desk facing the door and remained standing. Ms. Edwards took one of the burgundy vinyl chairs and Ryan sat in the other before Mr. Matherson settled in his seat.

"Dr. O'Doherty, this is Lucy Edwards, and she's just recently joined the Angel family."

Ryan offered his hand and a half-smile. "Ryan O'Doherty."

For a flicker of a second she hesitated before her small fingers slipped into his. Her grasp was firm, her hand soft and the touch brief. He liked the feel of her hand.

He gave Matherson an expectant look. They needed to get a move on with this meeting. His colleague was waiting on that consult. "So what brings us here?"

Matherson regarded Ryan as if he wasn't comfortable with others taking over his meetings. Clearing his throat, the HR man said, "Ms. Edwards is a family counselor. She comes with the highest credentials and praise from her last position. As I understand, she was the person the families regularly requested."

The woman beside him shifted uncomfortably. Pink touched her cheeks. She obviously didn't enjoy being the center of attention. That came as a surprise. In his experience, woman generally enjoyed being the main focus. What made this one different?

Matherson continued as if giving a great oratory to be remembered. "Angel's is setting up a new program called Coordinated Patient Care, where we're pairing a counselor with a doctor. Ms. Edwards is your partner. You'll be working with her on all your cases."

What was this? Another hospital bureaucratic feel-good project? Ryan leaned forward, piercing the rotund little man with a look. "Didn't we try something like this a couple of years ago and decide it didn't work?"

Matherson had the good grace to look contrite. "Similar, but this is a little different. You two are the beta test. If it works then we'll require other departments to follow suit."

"Is all this necessary? I'm sure Ms.…uh—"

"Edwards," the woman supplied.

He sensed more than saw her stiffen. "I'm sure Ms. Edwards and I could both use our time more wisely."

"Please don't speak for me." The woman who had been sitting stiffly beside him said, shifting direction. "Doctor, I can assure you that the closer the doctor-counselor relationship is, the better it is for the patient."

Her words were said in a soft Southern drawl laced with an edge of steel. So the woman had some backbone. Interesting.

He cocked a brow and smiled. "So-o-o." He dragged

out the word to match her drawl. "You believe that working closely with the doctor is important."

She rewarded him with a blush that added a brighter touch of pink to the ridge of her cheeks.

Matherson cleared his throat, but Ryan chose to ignore the man. He gifted her with a smile. The identical one he used when making an effort not to ruffle the nurses while at the same time trying to get his way.

"I didn't mean to imply that your job doesn't have merit, it's just that I don't think we need to personally discuss each patient. In fact, I don't discuss the same type of issues with my patients that you would be concerned with. You can make notes on their charts about any matters you think I should know about and I can read from there." Ryan stood. To his surprise, Ms. Edwards rose to face him.

"I can assure you, Doctor, our relationship will be strictly professional," she said through clenched teeth. She took a breath and continued, "Patients, as well as their families, need reassurance and comfort that you can't provide."

She couldn't have been more correct.

"That's my job and I do it well." She squared her shoulders, punctuating the statement.

"I'm sure that is true but I'm not going to waste my time in meetings when there is a perfectly good computer system we can use for correspondence. Now, if you'll both excuse me..."

"Dr. O'Doughty," Matherson said with a pointed look at Ryan, "I don't know if you fully understand what's being asked here. This is a trial program. The board's supporting it unanimously. Your *co-operation* would be noticed and to your advantage."

Ryan compressed his mouth. Matherson was making a veiled reference to the fact that he hadn't been offered the head of neurosurgery position and that his co-operation would look good on his CV. By rights the department head job should have been his. Instead, they'd hired Alex Rodriguez.

Drawing his lips into a thin line, Ryan looked directly at Matherson for a long moment. The hospital pencil-pusher did have the good grace to lower his eyes. If going along with this ridiculous time-consuming co-ordinated patient care idea would make him look good on paper to the powers that be, then he'd make some form of an effort. He'd at least give it lip service, but based on his experience it would be a waste of time. Shrugging a shoulder, he said, "Okay." He looked at Ms. Edwards. "I guess we're a team, then."

Ms. Edwards angled her head, mistrust written all over her face. Was she questioning his motives? Would she let him get away with doing as little as possible? Maybe there was more to this unassuming woman than he'd originally supposed. If nothing else, it would be a challenge to see if he could get her to smile. Find out if he could make that sadness in her eyes disappear.

"So it's settled." Matherson sounded far more cheerful than Ryan felt. "Then I'll let you two get started."

Lucy glanced at the self-absorbed doctor walking half a pace ahead of her up the hall. It had been hard enough to leave her entire life behind to start a new job in an unfamiliar city but being forced to work with a person who resented her being foisted on him made it almost impossible. Left no choice, she had to make this partnership work somehow.

Matherson, with the syrupy smile still on his face, had inquired if the good doctor was going back up to the neuro floor. When he said he was, Matherson had the nerve to ask him to show her the way. She'd been horribly embarrassed that Matherson had relegated this surgeon to a tour guide but didn't know a graceful way to say she'd find her own way.

As they left the HR department, Dr. O'Doherty held the door for her to go ahead of him. Someone had at least instilled manners in the self-absorbed man. She'd seen little else to impress her. That wasn't exactly true. She hadn't failed to notice his wide shoulders, piercing blue eyes and height. Even now his long legs were eating up the well-worn tile floor beneath them. Not often did she find a man that she couldn't meet almost eye to eye.

Gripping her purse, Lucy found herself tagging along behind him. With each step she became more irritated with his attitude. He walked as if he couldn't leave the HR or her quickly enough. Regardless, she appreciated him leading the way as they made one turn then another, past another bank of elevators. She had no idea where she was in the vast hospital.

That morning when she'd stood across the street in Central Park, facing the front entrance of Angel's, and had looked up, she hadn't begun to count the number of floors. The building spread across an entire block. To say she'd been intimidated would have been an understatement. Still, there had been something about the mixture of old and new architecture that had appealed to her. If nothing else, the bright yellow and red awning leading to the front door had made her think the place had warmth.

Being employed by a large hospital wasn't new to her. Most children's hospitals were attached to a larger teaching hospital that was affiliated with a big university. But compared to Angel's, those she'd worked in were dwarfs in size. She liked the nickname Angel's. Glancing at the man beside her, she decided he didn't act very angelic or hospitable.

Dr. O'Doherty finally stopped in front of a set of elevators and pushed the 'up' button.

Her job required her to read people. Dr. O'Doherty's rigid stance and unyielding demeanor said he wasn't pleased with having to answer to the HR department and now to her in a lesser way. She wasn't surprised. Typical surgeon. Highly typical neurosurgeon. Confident, in control and with minds closed to anyone's ideas but their own. Still, she had a job to do, and that meant co-operating with this guy. She had no choice but to make it work.

Clearing her throat, she said, "I understand this arrangement isn't really your idea of a good plan."

He moved to face her. "No, it isn't."

His displeasure didn't encourage her. If this was the way he acted over a simple request, she couldn't imagine his reaction to a serious issue. She was well acquainted with life-altering experiences. She wasn't going to waste her energy getting upset over anything as mundane as being partnered with the egotistical doctor.

"I'd like to make my end of it as painless as possible for both of us."

The elevator arrived, putting their conversation on hold. The doors opened and they stepped into an already crowded car. Dr. O'Doherty's solid frame brushed hers as they turned to face the front of the elevator. A prickle of awareness spread through her body.

On the ride upward, they stood close enough that the heat of his body warmed her down one side. It was the first time in months that the Arctic cold buried deep within her had melted even for a second. The numbness returned the moment the elevator doors opened and he moved away. She stepped out behind him, then paused.

He stopped and looked at her. "Something wrong?"

"No, I'm just always amazed at how completely different patients' areas are from the business parts of the hospital. These bright yellow walls are like coming into sunshine after being in gloom."

"I've never noticed."

She wasn't surprised.

"Can you get to your office from here?"

She glanced around, recognizing a framed picture of a child's artwork on the wall. "I know where I am now." He turned to leave and she asked, "So how're we going to handle this coordinated care plan, Dr. O'Doherty?"

Stopping, he turned back to her. "I'm going about it like I always have. Check the charts, Ms. Edwards."

"Mr. Matherson made it clear that wouldn't do. You might not like the idea but I expect you to do your part. Your patients are now mine also. I'm determined to give them the best care possible."

Dr. O'Doherty stepped a pace closer, leaned forward and pierced her with a penetrating blue stare. "And you don't think that's what I do?"

"I'm sure you're a more than capable surgeon, but there's always room for improvement where patient care outside the OR is concerned."

"Ms. Edwards, are you questioning my ability to be professional?"

She met his look squarely. "No, but I'll not let you dismiss me or my abilities either. I was approached by this hospital to do a job so someone must have thought I had something to offer the hospital and the neuro department in particular. I expect you to at least recognize that."

His attention remained on her long enough that her knees started to shake. Had she stepped over the line? With a huff, he said, "I do rounds at five. Promptly." With a curt turn he went down the hall as if he'd spent all the time he deemed necessary on her.

Lucy passed a number of patient rooms, rounded the large corner nurses' station and dodged a child in a wagon with a parent pulling it. Her heart tugged. Every small child she saw made her think of Emily. With relief, she finally reached the hall her office was on. Maybe going back to work in a children's hospital hadn't been one of her best ideas. But it had been the only job available when she'd needed to leave.

As bright, open and modern as the patients' floor was, in contrast her office was little more than a cubby hole. She shared the area with two other family counselors assigned to the neuro floor. Three desks were lined up side by side against a wall and if all three were working at the same time, they wouldn't be able to get to their desks without one of them stepping out into the hall. That didn't concern her. It was a fairly typical arrangement for support staff. She was happy to have her position and she'd work in whatever space provided.

Lucy checked her watch. There were a few hours before she had to meet Dr. O'Doherty for rounds. That gave her time to review his patient load and familiarize herself with each child's diagnosis. She'd make sure the doctor didn't have anything to complain about in regard to her work. It was her goal to make this partnership as stress-free as possible despite his opposition of the plan.

When she'd learned about this job she hadn't thought twice about taking it and had every intention of succeeding in it. She needed this position if she was going to survive and get her life back on track.

One of Lucy's officemates, a woman with pepper-colored hair and a generous smile, was coming in the door as Lucy was heading out. "Hey, how's it going?" Nancy asked.

"Fine."

"I heard you were teamed up with Dr. O'Doherty."

Lucy gave her a questioning look.

"Learned it from the hospital grapevine. Even from the basement news travels fast."

"I see." Lucy picked up her notepad.

"Ryan's such a cutie. We all love working with him. Kind of keeps to himself but he's a favorite among the nurses. More than one of them has a crush on him."

Lucy didn't know how to respond to that statement so she remained silent. She didn't see that ever becoming an issue for her.

"You know the kind of patients we see on this floor often break our hearts, but with Ryan around it sure makes it easier. That goes for the patients and us. He's a brilliant doctor. Not hard to look at either."

Lucy had to agree with the latter. Even so, he'd not made a great first impression as far as she was concerned. She had a new life to build and being a groupie of a doctor who already had a posse of female admirers didn't fall into her "need to do" list.

"Well, I'd better review some charts before rounds." Lucy gave her co-worker a wary smile and left the office.

She'd never been one for hospital gossip and actively stayed away from it when she could, but her officemate's chatter had caught her interest. The more she knew about Dr. O'Doherty the better off she'd be.

She slipped into a vacant chair behind the nurses' station desk. Facing the state-of-the-art computer screen, she typed in her password and queried Dr. O'Doherty's in-house patients. A list containing five names came up. One by one she reviewed the patients' charts and made notes. She'd just finished scanning the last chart when a deep-throated laugh followed by the high-pitched giggle of a child came from down the hall.

"Dr. O'Doherty is at it again," the nurse standing beside her said with a smile.

Seconds later, he slow-galloped into view with a young girl on his back. His white lab coat had been discarded. The light blue knit shirt he wore stretched tautly across his broad chest. The man either had good genes or he worked out regularly. The child had a happy smile on her face and her arms were wrapped tightly around his neck. Her head was bound in white gauze.

He stopped at the nurses' station where Lucy and the nurse stood watching. "Ms. Edwards, I'd like you to meet Princess Michelle."

The girl giggled.

"She buttoned her shirt all by herself today and got to make a wish." He glanced back at the girl. "Princess Michelle," he said.

The girl giggled again.

"Can you tell Ms. Edwards what your wish was?" Ryan asked.

"I want a horsy ride," the girl said with a shy grin.

"Well, that sounds like a fine wish." Lucy smiled up at the child. "So how far are you going on this ride? Over the mountain? Across the river?"

The girl snickered and pointed. "End of hall."

"I see."

"This horse can't go too far away from the barn." He winked at the young nurse and she blinked and grinned.

The sting of pain Lucy experienced when she'd not

been included in the flirtatious action surprised her. It was a visual reminder he didn't consider her part of his circle. She was once again an outsider.

An easy lilt in his Brooklyn accent became more prominent as he continued to speak. "I'd better finish this princess's ride and get her home. It's almost supper time." He turned his head toward the girl, "What do you say to get the horse to go?"

"Giddy up," Michelle said with another round of giggles and off they went.

A smile covered her lips.

"Why, Ms. Edwards, is that a smile I see?" Dr. O'Doherty asked with a brow raised. "I wondered if it was possible."

To her amazement, she was smiling. Something that had happened rarely in the last few months. How had that exasperating man managed to make her smile? Maybe there was more to him than she had originally given him credit for. His bedside manner might not extend to her but apparently he cared about his patients.

The horse and rider set off down the passage then returned, and she waved. Her chest constricted. It wouldn't be long until Emily would be the same age as Michelle. Sadly, Lucy would never hear the sounds of Emily's childhood delight.

Half an hour later, Lucy asked one of the nurses which end of the hall Dr. O'Doherty usually started his rounds on. The nurse pointed to the right and Lucy headed in that direction. A group of six led by Dr. O'Doherty exited a patient's room as she approached. The crowd circled around him. Lucy stopped just outside the ring.

He looked over the head of a female intern wearing

a lab coat, with her head elevated in a worshipful manner, to glower at Lucy. "Everyone, this is Ms. Edwards."

The assemblage turned to inspect her. She shifted uneasily under the scrutiny.

"She's our newest family counselor. Please introduce yourself later. We have patients to see." His mouth tightened briefly but his words didn't falter. "Please see that she stays in the loop on all cases." His intense blue gaze pinned her again. "I'll have to get you up to speed later on the patient you missed."

She looked away.

Dr. O'Doherty made a few more comments as they moved down the hallway to the next patient, then the next, stopping in front of another door. He paused. His attention focused on her again. "This is Brian Banasiak. I removed a blood clot three days ago. This is one case I believe that it might be beneficial to have you involved in."

Might? Lucy wasn't sure she needed his seal of approval but she didn't say so. Neither was she certain how she felt about the left-handed compliment. In her last position she'd been considered the "go to" person when a family was having a difficult time coping with their child's illness or injury. Her role was seen as important in overall patient care.

Apparently Dr. O'Doherty viewed her work as a sideline to his godly power. She'd do her job effectively then maybe she could change the narrow-minded man's opinion.

"I understand his head trauma occurred during an auto accident," she said quietly. "I'm going to discuss the benefits of therapy at home with the parents. Also assistance with home schooling. These parents have a long road ahead of them. The adjustment of having gone from a perfectly normal child to one who needs help eating and dressing will be difficult at best to accept."

Dr. O'Doherty's look of surprise along with similar ones from the others made her want to pump her fist in elation. She'd managed to wow the man. Why it should matter she didn't know, but it felt good.

He pursed his lips and nodded as if he might be impressed. "Thank you, Ms. Edwards. You've obviously done your homework."

"The family clearly cares about their child and I gather are willing to do what it takes for Brian to recover. I'll be speaking with them first thing in the morning to determine any additional needs."

Dr. O'Doherty gave her a quick nod and with a rap of his knuckles on the door entered the room. Along with the rest of their group, Lucy moved to stand next to the boy's bed.

The parents of the boy came to stand across the bed from the group. Dr. O'Doherty paid them no attention.

"Brian, how're you feeling today?" Dr. O'Doherty asked.

The eight-year-old boy offered a weak smile. His entire head was swathed in white gauze. His eyes had dark circles under them and there was puffiness about his face that lingered from having surgery.

"Okay, I guess," the boy said with little enthusiasm.

"Well, from all I hear from your nurse, you're my star patient," Dr. O'Doherty stated. "So give me a high five."

That managed to get a slight smile out of the boy. He raised his small hand and met the doctor's larger one with a smack.

Dr. O'Doherty pulled his hand back. "Ow! See, you're already getting stronger."

Brian's smile broadened.

The doctor did have a way with kids.

"I'm going to take a look at your head. Maybe we can give you a smaller bandage."

"It's itchy." The boy wrinkled his nose.

"Yes. That means you're getting better. I'll see if we can't help with that problem."

As he removed the gauze, Lucy watched the parents' faces to gage their reactions. Death wasn't the only time people experienced grief. A major life trauma could bring on the emotion. Lucy knew that all too well. She'd run to get away from hers.

"Will he be able to ride a bike?" the boy's mother asked. "Do we have to worry about him falling?"

Dr. O'Doherty didn't look at the mother as he said, "Ms. Walters, my clinical nurse, can answer those questions for you." He continued to unwrap the bandage.

The mother looked like she'd been struck. She stepped back from the bed.

He continued to examine the surgical site then spoke to the floor nurse standing next to him. "I believe we can place a four-by-four bandage over this." He looked at the boy. "You'll look less like a pirate but it won't be so itchy."

That statement brought a real smile to the boy's face.

"I'll see you tomorrow," Dr. O'Doherty said, before turning to leave. He shook the big toe of the boy's foot as he moved toward the door

The mother followed him out into the hall. "Dr. O'Doherty, we were wondering what to expect next," the mother said, tears filling her eyes.

"My nurse will answer all your questions."

Lucy compressed her lips. Where had all the charm that had oozed from him seconds before gone?

"Will he ever be like he was?" The mother's eyes pleaded to know.

"I don't make those kinds of promises," Dr. O'Doherty clipped.

The mother looked stricken again.

This man had a sterling bedside manner where his patients were concerned but he sure lacked finesse with the parents. Why was he suddenly so cold?

Lucy stepped forward, not looking at Dr. O'Doherty for permission. She placed an arm around the woman's shoulders. "Mrs. Banasiak, I'm Lucy Edwards, the family counselor. I think I can help answer some of your questions."

The mother sagged in relief. She shot a look at Dr. O'Doherty and then said to Lucy, "Thank you, so much."

Dr. O'Doherty progressed on down the hall with his group in tow without a backward glance. Lucy hung back to speak to the parents further. The watery eyes and fragile smile of the mother touched Lucy's heart. These were the type of people who needed her. It felt good to be using her skills again.

Ryan paused in front of the last patient-to-be-seen door. Turning, he waited for the group to join him. Ms. Edwards was missing. Should he really be surprised? He discussed the patient, while his frustration grew. She could speak to the parents on her own time.

"We're glad you could join us," he said when she finally walked up.

Her eyes didn't meet his. The woman didn't like having the spotlight on her. By the way she dressed and spoke so softly, he guessed she spent most of her time in the shadows. "I needed to reassure the parents," she said quietly.

Pushing the door of the patient room open, he stepped in. "Hi, Lauren," he said to the ten-year-old sitting up in bed, watching TV. "I believe you'll be ready to go home tomorrow. How does that sound?"

The grandmother, who was the girl's caretaker, stepped to the bed. "That's wonderful. What do we need to do about getting her back in school when the time comes?"

A soft but strong voice beside him said, "I'll help with that."

"This is Lucy Edwards," he said to the grandmother. "She's my family counselor."

The only indication that Ms. Edwards didn't appreciate the word "*my*" was the slight tightening around her lips. That had been entirely the wrong thing to say. He didn't know how to repair the faux pas gracefully in front of a patient's family so he continued speaking to the grandmother. He'd apologize to Ms. Edwards later.

This quiet, gentle-voiced woman wasn't *his* anything. She wasn't even his type. He was used to dating freer-spirited women, who thought less and laughed more. Those who were loud and boisterous and were not interested in emotional attachments. Ms. Edwards had already demonstrated she was the touchy-feely type.

He left the room while the grandmother rattled off a list of questions for Ms. Edwards.

After answering a page, he returned to the nurses' station in search of Ms. Edwards. Not seeing her, he was forced to ask where her office was located. He'd never paid much attention to the family counselors. He knew they had a job to do and as far as he was concerned they did it. Rarely did he interact with one outside other than when they asked him a question or left a note on a chart.

He knocked lightly on the nondescript door with a small plate that showed he was in the correct place. The door was opened by a woman he recognized. "Hi, Ryan. What's up?"

"Hello, Nancy. I was trying to find Ms. Edwards."

"Yes-s-s." The word being drawn out came from inside. He'd found the right place. Ms. Edwards put far too many syllables in a word. He glanced around the woman in front of him. Ms. Edwards looked at him with wide, questioning eyes.

"I'll get out of your way. It's time to head home anyway," the older woman said. "Nice to see you, Ryan."

"You too." He smiled as she left and stepped into the doorway, holding the door open. "Do you mind if I come in a minute?"

The new counselor looked unsure but nodded her agreement.

He'd received warmer welcomes but guessed he couldn't blame her, considering their less than congenial start. She sat at the desk furthest away from the door. Her eyes resembled those of a startled animal as he pushed the door closed behind him. The look eased when he sat down in the chair furthest from her. Was she afraid of him? He conjured up one of his friendliest smiles.

She gave him an inquiring look.

"I just wanted to say I'm sorry for the comment about you being my family counselor. I misworded the statement. It won't happen again."

Her bearing softened. "Dr. O'Doherty—"

"Please call me Ryan. I'm a pretty casual guy generally." She looked unsure about the idea. "May I call you Lucy?"

She nodded slowly. "Uh, Ryan, I know you're not a fan of this coordinated patient care arrangement but I'd really like us to work together with as little conflict as possible."

He liked the way his name sounded when she said it. Kind of easygoing and warm. "I'll do my part but there have to be some ground rules."

She pursed her lips and her delicately shaped brows drew closer together. "And those would be?"

"I expect the people that work for me to be punctual and to stay with me as I make rounds. I don't wait."

"Dr. O'Doherty, I don't work for you. I work for the hospital, and ultimately for the patients. If I understood Mr. Matherson correctly, we do coordinated patient care. Which means we work together."

"My OR schedule, which the hospital dictates, means I don't have time to stand around waiting for you."

"And my job, which the hospital and the human heart dictate, is to care for the patient and the family during a difficult time. My job is to help the whole family. We…" She waved a hand around, broadly including him. "This hospital should care for the whole person. That's my job and I would appreciate you letting me do it."

He flinched. "My job is to be a surgeon, I fix the problem. I don't need to hand-hold patients or their families to do my job well."

"No, you don't, but it would be nice if you would at least try to on some level."

His body stiffened and he gave her a questioning look. "The parents of my patients need to hear the truth."

"I don't disagree with that. I just question the delivery."

"I thought that was why you were here?"

"It is, but parents like Brian's like to hear reassurances from the doctor."

She met his direct gaze for the first time for longer than a second. He stood. "Point taken."

"What time's your first case in the morning?"

"Seven. Why?"

"I like to be here when the child leaves the parents to go into surgery. It's when they need the most support. Many want to talk. They're scared. I'll walk them down to the waiting room."

He'd never given any thought to how difficult it was for parents to watch their child go into surgery. Didn't want to think about it. He opened the door.

"It's hard to let go," she said with wistfulness in her voice.

Did she know that from personal experience? Her eyes glazed over. Where had her thoughts gone? Thankfully she recovered, the hopeless expression disappearing, to be replaced by that of a trained professional again. That he was more than capable of dealing with.

"I guess it is." He closed the door between them. What was the woman with the sad, serious eyes hiding?

CHAPTER TWO

THAT EVENING LUCY arrived home later than she'd planned. To be at the hospital early for four mornings out of the week meant she had to stay late in the evenings to prepare. On top of that there was the time she spent getting to and from work. Accustomed to the freedom of driving a car, she found using the subway system restricting and oftentimes frustrating. Never good at reading maps, she had a tendency to take the wrong train far too often. This was one aspect of living in a huge city that she'd not thought through.

Her heavy-set, dark-haired landlord, who was standing outside the building, called, "Hello," as she started climbing the stairs to her studio apartment.

"Hi, Mr. Volpentesta," she returned with more enthusiasm than she'd had in a long time.

He presented her with a big, white, toothy smile.

Lucy made her way up to the third floor above the Italian bistro. She didn't mind the climb. It was good exercise and she'd always enjoyed being fit. Staying in shape and eating right were important to her. She sucked in a tight breath. That had been one of the many reasons she'd had no trouble carrying Emily.

Emily. The hurt throbbed deep. She had to get beyond the pain somehow.

Unlocking the door, she pushed it open and stepped into the studio apartment. A nice window allowed light into the space. A bed faced it and there was a small sitting area. In one back corner was a kitchenette, functional but tiny, and in the other corner was the bathroom, which included a tiny closet.

She'd managed to make the place homely with the few things she'd brought with her. When she had time she'd give it the care it deserved. It wasn't much by most people's standards but she enjoyed the multicultural, tree-lined neighborhood. She'd been lucky to find a place within her budget.

Alexis, her sister, didn't understand Lucy's need to move so far away and Lucy had no intention of ever sharing the real reason she'd left. It was her deepest shame. It had almost killed her but she'd had to get away. It was better for everyone that she leave, despite how much she missed her sister, and Emily. She wanted Alexis and her family to be happy. For her to hang around, wishing she was a part of their close-knit group, hadn't been healthy for any of them.

Dropping her purse on the table, which had obviously been confiscated from the bistro, she put the kettle on to heat water to make tea. Sweet iced tea was her drink of choice. No matter where she lived she took that small pleasure with her. Even in the cold early spring weather she couldn't give up that small part of her growing-up years. It was one of the passions she and her sister shared. She wouldn't go there. Spending her evening crying wasn't part of her plan.

Taking a deep breath, she moved to her bed, pulled off her business suit and replaced it with sweatpants and sweatshirt, then she tugged on slouchy socks.

The streetlight below her windows flickered on, washing the room in a warm glow that only added to her loneliness. She clicked on a lamp on her way back to the stove and after pouring the hot water over the tea bags and sugar she reached for a can of soup from the open cabinet.

She'd gone from carrying a baby and living in her sister's home, where love abounded, to a shabby room in an enormous impersonal city. She sank into one of the two chairs she had and put her face in her hands.

Stop it. Get a hold of yourself. You can survive this. You have to make your own life.

The next afternoon, she entered Daniel Hancock's room to find Ryan leaning back in a chair as if he made social visits to the teenage boy's room regularly. Ryan had removed a tumor from the sixteen-year-old's brain stem the week before.

"Ah, Ms. Edwards, just the person we were looking for," Ryan said, as if he was genuinely glad to see her, which created suspicion in her mind.

He'd made it clear the day before that he wasn't interested in her being involved in his cases unless he thought she was needed. Now he acted as if they were old friends and he was planning to ask her a favor. She was unsure how to read his attitude change. Up until this moment she would have characterized their relationship as two dogs circling each other, trying to decide how not to get in each other's way.

She'd play along. Approaching the end of the bed, she smiled at Daniel. "What can I do for you two gentlemen?"

"I was just telling Daniel that he can't return to

school right away. That he'll need to be home-schooled for a while until his site heals. Can you help to arrange that?"

"I'll see about it right away."

"Did you know that Daniel's the star of his high-school baseball team?"

"I had heard that." In fact, his future had begun to disappear when he hadn't been able to control his hand movements. Now, because of Ryan's skill, Daniel had a chance at his dream again. She could forgive some of Ryan's brashness for that alone. He might lack empathy at times but he had major surgical skills.

Ryan stood and, grinning, said to Daniel, "I hope to see you playing for the Yankees one day soon. I'll leave orders for the teacher to be cute and like baseball—how does that sound?"

Daniel gave him a weak smile but seemed pleased.

Ryan offered his hand to the teen. Lucy appreciated the way Ryan showed his respect for the young man by treating him as an equal. It was a way of giving Daniel a sense of control in a place where he felt he had none. Why hadn't Ryan given the same consideration to the mother the evening before?

She followed Ryan out of the room. "You know, Lucy, having you readily available may be a good thing after all."

"It isn't my job to be at your beck and call."

"Maybe not, but so far it's working out well." He grinned and walked off.

And she'd thought moving to New York was going to make her life easier. How long was this coordinated patient care agreement supposed to last?

Hours later all she wanted to do was go home and fall asleep. Instead, she was hunting down Ryan for a signature on a couple of forms. She knew the vicinity of his office but she'd never been there. Punching the automatic door-opener on the wall, she waited then passed through a set of doors that led into a short hallway. Here she was no longer in the sunny land of the patients' hall. Instead, it turned into the practical world of business. She searched the uniformed name plates until she found Ryan's beside the second door on the right. It read: "Dr. Ryan O'Doherty, Associate of Neurosurgery".

She'd heard talk about Ryan not getting the department head job. Most of the nurses were surprised. They'd all thought he would be a shoo-in. Apparently popularity wasn't the deciding factor. If it had been and the staff had voted, it would have been unanimous. Even in the OR, where the pressure was greater and personalities sometimes clashed, the staff all seemed to appreciate Ryan's skill and winning ways. She just wished some of those winning ways would spill over when she had to deal with him.

His office door stood partially open. She knocked and waited. No answer. The forms had to be signed tonight or first thing in the morning. Maybe she should page him? No, she didn't want to do that. She'd just leave the forms on his desk and text him, asking him to sign them before he went into the OR. She rolled her eyes. She was sure he'd be *real* glad to hear from her.

Apprehensive about entering Ryan's private space without permission but thinking she had no choice, she stepped into his office. His ever-present lab coat lay across the back of his desk chair. He must have gone for the day if he didn't have it on. On the other hand, his office door was open.

She placed the papers on his desk and picked up a

pen lying there to write him a note. Maybe he would see them before she had a chance to text him.

Ryan stepped out of an adjacent doorway into the room.

She squealed, jumped. Her hand went over her heart before it settled with a thump. "Oh." Heaven help her, he wasn't wearing a shirt. She gulped. Coming into his office hadn't been a good idea.

Ryan's slacks hung low on his hips and his belt was undone. She couldn't take her eyes off his chest. An expanse of muscle covered in a light dusting of hair.

"What're you doing here?" he said brusquely. His tone stated clearly he wasn't pleased to see her. He stepped behind his desk and pulled out a drawer. Removing a shirt, he slipped it on and began to button it.

She followed his movements as he worked his way up the shirt. His long, tapered fingers moved swiftly. Ryan was a large man to be doing such delicate work as brain surgery. She'd heard he had a gentle touch with the scalpel.

What would it be like to be caressed by him? What kind of question was that? She shook her head. The last thing she needed to do was get moony-eyed over Ryan O'Doherty.

"Lucy, did you need something or did you just stop by to gape? Or maybe snoop?" His tone had turned teasing but still held an edge of distrust.

She straightened and moved away from the desk, trying to gather her poise as she went. "I do not snoop!"

His mouth quirked at one corner. "Then gape? Because you've yet to tell me why you're here."

"I need you to sign these forms so I can get Daniel's home schooling set up before he's discharged. These..." she pointed to the papers to prove she was telling the truth "...have to be in by tomorrow to make the deadline. That's if you still want him to have a cute teacher. They'll be all gone by tomorrow afternoon I was told," she said with the most insincere saccharine smile she could muster.

"Why, Ms. Edwards, you surprise me. I had no idea you had a sense of humor."

Ryan should've been livid at finding Lucy in his office without permission. This was his private domain and he wanted it to remain that way. The look of surprise on her face and the widening of her eyes when she'd seen his state of undress had defused his anger. She hadn't immediately turned away. Instead, her eyes had grown darker, her gaze fixed on his chest. It hadn't been one of her shy looks but one of bold appraisal. Pure male satisfaction had won out over his irritation. His ego officially skyrocketed.

She huffed, stepped over to the desk and picked up the papers. "If you would just sign these, I can get out of your way."

For some reason he was a little disappointed at the idea. This was the most entertaining time he'd spent with someone in a long time. Who would have thought he'd find the quiet, ordinary woman interesting? No, ordinary was the wrong word. There was nothing ordinary about Lucy.

Ryan picked up the forms and reviewed them. Setting them down again, he took the pen she'd dropped and signed a form. Out of the corner of his eye, he saw her looking around. He had learned quickly that she was observant, almost intuitive about people. What was she learning about him?

He glanced at her as he pulled the second form to

him. She studied his shelves filled with books intermingled with pictures and baseball memorabilia. Her gaze moved on to the opposite wall. There hung a framed picture of a Yankees baseball game in progress, which took up most of the space. Putting down the pen, he turned to sit on the edge of his desk. Lucy's consideration had traveled to the framed pictures on his desk.

Before he realized it, he'd said, "Those are my nieces and nephews." He pointed toward a picture with two dark-haired women in it. "My sisters." He rarely volunteered personal information to anyone. No wonder Lucy was so good at her job. Something about her made people want to tell her their secrets.

His gut clenched. He didn't want her to know his. "Is there anything else?" His words sounded more dismissive than he'd intended. He handed the forms to her.

All business again, she said, "I'll see that they are faxed before I go home."

He watched her leave his office. Why all of a sudden was he looking forward to coming to work the next day?

Ryan's running shoes made a rhythmic sound as he took the turn in the paved path on his way back to the hospital. He slowed when he saw Lucy sitting on a park bench. Her head was tipped back, her face held up to the sun. That golden rope of hair gleamed in the light. She'd removed her heavy cardigan and had her legs stretched out in front of her. He hadn't known her long but he suspected this was the most uninhibited she'd been in a long time.

She really was an attractive woman who seemed to want to blend in, go unnoticed. It hadn't worked where he was concerned. He'd noticed too much.

As he grew closer, he could see that her eyes were

closed. He wouldn't have disturbed her but just as he approached she shifted and sat up as if jolted awake.

"Hey," she said, drowsiness in her voice.

"Hey." He liked this off-guard Lucy. When she had her full faculties back in a second she'd close off fast. She acted as if she was wary of everyone and everything.

"Been running." She stated the obvious as he was standing there drenched in perspiration and wearing a sweatshirt and shorts.

"Yeah, one of the perks of working at Angel's is that the park is so close."

"I think so too. I already miss the lakes, forests and the spaciousness of the suburbs of Atlanta. Somehow knowing I can come to the park helps." She began to put on her sweater.

What had caused her to make such a drastic move? He couldn't ask that type of question if he wasn't prepared to share in return. "Have you had a chance to explore the park?"

She laughed. "It may not surprise you to hear that I'm afraid I might get lost. So I don't get out of sight of the hospital."

He smiled down at her. "Maybe I can give you a tour some time. We'll leave breadcrumbs if necessary."

"If I'm along, it'll be necessary."

"Well, I'll leave you to your sunning."

"I've got to go in too. I need to get some lunch before I meet you for clinic."

"I don't know if it's necessary for you to be at clinic today."

She stood and faced him with an unwavering look. "Why not? I thought we were past having this discussion."

He held up a hand. "It has nothing to do with me not

wanting you there. I'm only going to be seeing patients who were discharged before you arrived."

Her face relaxed. "I see. Just the same, I'd like to be there."

She started towards the hospital without a backward glance at him. He'd been dismissed, something he wasn't used to having happen from anyone other than his sisters.

Lucy entered the doctors' shared clinic building attached to the hospital. Ryan's day of the week to see patients was Wednesday. She looked around the waiting area of the clinic. It had large glass windows that provided a view of Central Park. Painted on the walls were murals with happy-faced animals. The orange furniture and light green carpet created a happy effect. Toy tables sat in an open space to the side. It was a place where children wouldn't be afraid to come.

She found Ryan waiting in the hall of the clinic. "I'm sorry, I'm late. No matter how much time I allow myself, I still eat it up having to backtrack everywhere I go." Lucy said as she caught her breath.

He smiled. "I'm starting to expect it."

"I'm getting better. I can get to work without getting off the subway and doubling back a station. I do get my exercise, though."

Ryan gave her body frank consideration. "I can see that you do."

Warmth washed over her. It felt wonderful to have a man look at her with interest. In the past few days they'd managed to develop a working relationship that was at least doable if not comfortable. On her part, she'd spent longer than normal getting to know Ryan's patients and their families. On his, he seemed to at least tolerate having her around.

"You know, I've been meaning to tell you that I like that Southern drawl."

The grin on his lips and the dimples it brought to his cheeks made him the sexiest man she'd ever seen.

"But you talk so slowly that I forget what you said at the beginning of the sentence by the time you get to the end of it."

She thrust her chin out and looked at him hard. "Are you making fun of me?"

The laugh lines around his eyes grew more prominent. "I would never do that."

Lucy couldn't help but return his teasing smile. Something she hadn't done in a long time. It felt good to have some humor in her life again.

A nurse came down the hall. "You first patient is in exam two, Dr. O'Doherty."

Ryan took the patient chart from the nurse and Lucy followed him. The man could turn on the charm when he chose. She'd have to watch out or he might use it against her.

Lucy joined him during each examination. All the patients were there for sixth-week post-op visits and would be released from Ryan's care after this clinical appointment. Neither he nor she would see them again unless the patients required additional surgery. Maybe that was why Ryan didn't invest more effort into getting to know the families. They weren't normally long-term patients for him.

"This is the last patient," Ryan told her as he pulled the chart out of the holder on the door. "Amanda Marcella. Three years old. "

He tapped lightly on the door then entered. Lucy

followed and he introduced her. "So, how's Amanda doing?" he asked the far-too-young mother.

"Okay, I guess."

Lucy cringed. If she had a child who was sick she wouldn't be treating the child's heath so nonchalantly.

The little girl had an external shunt located on the right side of her head. Ryan removed the bandages. He really had a tender way about him.

"This shunt isn't positioned correctly. The site needs to be checked and rebandaged. I'll show you how I want it done," he announced, engrossed in what he was doing.

"I don't like doing that sort of thing. My boyfriend has to do it," the mother said.

Ryan looked up. "This isn't something that you have a choice about. You have to take responsibility for your child."

He didn't wait for the mother to respond before he turned and left the room.

At the girl's stricken face, Lucy stepped toward her. "Do you have any one else who can help you?"

The girl shook her head slowly, her eyes filling with tears. "My parents kicked me out when I got pregnant with Amanda. I try to do what I can but I'm no good at being a nurse."

Ryan returned with a nurse in tow. She carried a disposable suture kit. "I'm going to put in a couple of stitches to secure the shunt. It'll still have to be bandaged and cleaned regularly." He looked at the mother to punctuate his point.

The mother's eyes grew larger and she screwed up her face with displeasure. Couldn't Ryan tell he was scaring the girl? If he did notice, why didn't he care?

"Why don't we wait outside while Dr. O'Doherty

is working?" Lucy suggested. The mother nodded and Lucy led her out into the hall.

"I know Dr. O'Doherty wants me to see about Amanda's head but I just can't. It makes me so sad to look at it."

Minutes later Ryan opened the door, letting them know that he was finished. Lucy and the mother returned to the room. Ryan looked at the mother and said, "The nurse will show you how to bandage the site. You'll need to bring Amanda back again next week. I'll expect to see that the wound has been cared for."

The girl mumbled, "Okay..." and took her whimpering child from the nurse.

Ryan left and Lucy gave the girl's shoulder a reassuring pat and joined him.

"I hate it when I perform surgery and the patient is improving but the parents won't take care of the child," Ryan said through clenched teeth, softly enough not to sound unprofessional. Lucy had no doubt that he wished he could say it loud enough that not only the mother could hear but everyone else as well.

"Can we go to an empty exam room and talk a sec?" Lucy asked.

He gave her a frustrated look but nodded his assent.

When they were in the room with the door closed behind them, she turned to him and said, "Ryan, you can't be so hard on that mother. She's little more than a child herself and terrified. She has no help at home and a sick child to care for."

"She has a duty to her child. She has to see that her child gets the care she needs."

"Her grief is so great she can't stand to look at her baby, it scares her," Lucy flung back. "Haven't you ever been in a spot where you thought you couldn't handle it?"

He went pale for a second but soon recovered. Still, she'd seen it. His reaction to the mother had been over the top—was his cool relationship with his patient's parents masking something more?

"What do you suggest?" he asked in a tight voice.

"I don't think forcing the girl to do the wound care is the answer. She needs help. Which I will see about getting her. Until then, if you would write an order for home health a couple of times a week, I think it would be best for her and the child."

She was shocked when a slight grin formed on his lips. "I'm starting to feel manipulated but I think you're right this time. I'll write the order." Taking the chart he held, he turned and left the room.

She'd eased one aspect of the girl's issues but she'd hit a nerve in Ryan's. Why?

The knock on her office door told her Ryan stood on the other side. Even the rap of his hand was distinctive. Her officemates had gone home long ago. She might have left sooner if she'd had more to go home to. Instead, she was busy trying to see what services were available to Amanda Marcella. Going to the door, she opened it.

"Hi, I was just wondering if you might have dinner with me tonight. Let me say thanks for helping out this afternoon and apologize for making you feel less than welcome on your first day." He grinned.

Ryan could slay dragons and carry off a princess' heart with that movement of his lips.

"Just doing my job. No thanks necessary. I appreciate the invitation but I think I'd better just go home." Why in the world wasn't she accepting an opportunity to go out with a good-looking, smart man? Because she could be one of those slayed by his grin. Because it couldn't go anywhere. But why did it have to?

"You don't think you can take a few minutes to keep a hard-working colleague company while he eats?" His grin widened.

She was starting to fall for his charm. "I guess I could for a few minutes. I am hungry. But do you mind if I pick the place?"

"Sure. Just so long as it's not a beans-and-sprouts place. I want meat and cheese and more meat."

Lucy smiled. Something she was doing more often when he was around. It felt good. "There's meat, along with great salads."

"Perfect. Let's go."

He stepped through the doorway and waited for her in the hall. For heaven's sake, what was she doing? She had no business going to dinner with Ryan O'Doherty. He was far too likeable. And he made her far too angry sometimes. She secured her scarf around her neck and pulled on her coat. Stepping into the hall, she pulled the door closed behind her and prepared to lock it.

Ryan was no longer there. It was late enough that most of the patients were in bed for the night. One lone mother spoke softly to her child and Lucy's heart constricted. She'd thought distance would ease her feelings about Emily but with each baby she saw there was a fresh stab of pain. Would it ever go away?

She looked around and found Ryan standing in front of the nurses' station, talking to one of the staff. The nurse was snickering. He looked in her direction and grinned.

His smile pushed the heartache away. She needed her mental faculties just to deal with him. The man had the ability to turn that charm on and off at will. All the nurses seemed to go calf-eyed whenever he walked down the hall. More than one had requested to care for his patients in order to have his attention for a few minutes.

That laughter and fun-loving attitude covered the seriousness of his job and the caring heart that she only glimpsed when he was dealing with the children. She'd seen him displeased and she was beginning to think few saw the emotional side of him. That he'd let it slip when she'd been around was something to ponder.

Ryan smiled and started toward her. The nurse saw Lucy and returned to her duties. When she reached Ryan he said, "I just got a page. I need to stop by the nursery for a few minutes to check on a child, if you don't mind."

No, she couldn't do that. It would kill her to see the babies. She would cry. "Um, why don't I just meet you in the lobby?"

"I would've thought you might want to meet the family, if they are there."

"I'll just wait and see if you are assigned the case."

He gave her a quizzical look. "Okay. I'll see you in the lobby as soon as I can."

Lucy breathed a sigh of relief as Ryan walked off. She just wasn't ready to face the nursery.

In the taxi, Ryan grinned when Lucy had to give the address of the restaurant for a second time. The cab driver didn't quite understand her sweet Southern drawl. He himself liked it, a lot. Her slower, softer accent was soothing. He especially liked it when she said his name.

Lucy had a way about her that relaxed him, and others as well. She wasn't authoritarian when she spoke but people listened to her. Plus her manner implied that everything would be all right given time. He'd seen it first hand when she talked to his patients' families. She'd given of herself. At one time, he'd done that more freely but now he had nothing left.

If he ever discovered he had something to give, he hoped someone like Lucy was around to share it with. But now wasn't the time. He'd never confided in anyone from work and he wouldn't be starting now, no matter how tempting it might be.

Lucy sat beside him in the back seat, staring out the window. He wasn't sure if she was avoiding looking at him or was just engrossed in the lights of the "city that never sleeps".

"Have you been to New York before?"

"Once, when I was a kid. With my parents. I don't remember much about it, though." The wistful tone in her voice made him think that it hadn't necessarily been a happy memory.

"I bet you never thought you'd be living here."

She glanced at him. "No, never," she said, before turning back to the window. "And with your accent, I'd guess you've never lived anywhere but here."

"Brooklyn boy, born and raised," he said proudly.

"So that's why you have the baseball picture in your office."

"Yeah. I'm a big Yankees fan. Do you keep up with baseball?"

"If you live in Atlanta you have to follow the Braves. My brother-in-law gets season tickets so I've gone to a few games."

"I have season tickets to the Yankees. Maybe you'd like to go to a game some time?" He shifted uncomfortably. What in the world was he doing, inviting her out to a game? That sounded too much like a date.

The taxi pulled up at the curb.

"Volpentesta's. That's some of the best pizza pie in the city. For someone who has been in the city no longer than you have, you sure know where to get a good meal."

Lucy smiled as she climbed out of the taxi. When she offered her share of the taxi fare he said, "It's on me. My idea for the pizza."

She didn't fight him, just waited on the brick sidewalk gone wavy with age. She tensed a second when he lightly touched the curve of her back but she eased just as quickly. As they came to the door of the restaurant, he reached around her to open it.

"Someone taught you good manners. That's the second time you've opened a door for me."

The dull pain that he carried in his chest sharpened for a second. "My father was very old school. He would say, 'Ryan, my boy, you treat a woman like you want your sisters to be treated. It's the O'Doherty way.'"

"Kind of got off track when you first met me, didn't you?"

"Hey, I showed you up to the floor."

"Yeah, but you would've liked to drop me down the elevator shaft."

"Was I that bad?"

She nodded.

"Then I'll try to make up for it over dinner, okay?"

She smiled. "I've really gotten over it, so don't let it worry you."

A man who was almost as round as he was tall approached them, his hands outstretched. He asked with a strong Italian accent, "Miss Lucy, how are you today?"

Her smiled reached her eyes. Ryan felt a hot stab of jealousy. What would it take to have her smile at him like that? He wasn't going to analyze that thought.

"Mr. Volpentesta, I'm doing fine. We would like a table."

"Anything for you, my dear."

Ryan gave her a quizzical look. The wait even on weeknights for a table at Volpentesta's was long and she'd just waltzed in without a reservation.

The restaurant was an authentic Italian bistro right down to the red checked cloths and the candle on the table. The room was dark enough to make for a pleasing ambiance but not so dim that he couldn't appreciate Lucy's incredibly expressive face.

She wore little make-up. On occasion he'd noticed that she'd applied a gloss to her lips that made them dewy looking. Her hair was always contained by a ribbon or clip or was braided. More than once he'd pictured what it might look like free. She was unique. He'd give her that.

It had been a long time since he'd found a woman so interesting. She reminded him of Irish coffee. Sweet, fresh cream on top with a stout bite beneath. What kind of magic was this woman conjuring over him?

"Come this way, my dear." Mr. Volpentesta led them to a table for two in a far corner of the room.

"How do you know him?" Ryan said close to her ear.

"I live upstairs." She turned and followed the man again.

"Good choice," he said, more to himself than her when they were given a cozy spot. What he'd had in mind had been more of a friendly meal than a lovers' evening. He looked around the room but not finding a better option he accepted his fate. He held her chair out and waited until Lucy was settled before he sat.

"Your father has left nothing out." She spread her napkin in her lap.

"He was a thorough man."

"Was?"

Left no choice, he said, "He died." He couldn't keep the heartache out of his voice.

At her stricken and pitying look, he wished he'd lied. She placed a hand on his forearm and gave him an earnest look. "I'm sorry."

Her touch and concern diminished his feeling of loss for a moment. For the first time he actually felt comforted by another human being. Why was it that this Southern belle touched more than just his arm? "I'm doing fine."

Mercifully, the waiter came to take their order and bought them a bottle of house wine. Ryan wasn't surprised when Lucy ordered a salad. When the waiter left he leaned forward and said, "Do you have any idea on how many levels of wrong it is to order a salad in a place like this?"

"I'm just not that hungry."

He gave her a speculative look. "If I were to guess, you haven't been eating like you should."

She shrugged and toyed with her silverware.

"Not going to comment on that one?"

"No," she said with less zeal than she had earlier, confirming he'd been correct.

He fished for something to keep the conversation going that wasn't too personal. He didn't think she'd answer more questions if they were. "So, did you grow up in Atlanta?" That wasn't as impersonal as he would've liked but he wanted to know more about her.

"Sort of, but mostly at a boarding school in northeast Georgia."

He cocked his head in question.

"My parents divorced. It was easier to send Alexis and me off than to take care of us."

His mother had died when he'd been young. Before his father had gotten too sick he'd been there to take care of Ryan and his sisters. They had never doubted that they were wanted and loved. "Alexis?"

"My twin sister."

"So you're a twin. Interesting. I bet you're close. My father said more than once that 'Family's everything. Without family you have nothing.'"

Clouds formed in her eyes. "I guess for some that's true," she said, sounding more resigned than wistful.

But not for her? "I shouldn't have said that." He took a swallow of his wine. The melancholy in her voice made him wish he'd not quoted his father.

"Alexis and I had each other. We were our own family..." She let the words trail off.

He had to find another subject. "You know, it turns out we're a better team than I anticipated."

"Even as slowly as I speak, I'm still worthwhile." She smirked.

Despite her making fun of him, he enjoyed her quick mind. "Truthfully, I like your accent. Makes me think of lazy, hot days and ice-cold drinks."

She blinked then her eyelids fluttered down. "Now you're embarrassing me." She looked at him. "You know something about me. How about telling me about you?"

"Brooklyn, and more Brooklyn. Med school NYU, intern Angel's, Angel's today."

"I see. The source of your clipped dialect, with a hint of Irish burr occasionally."

"Guilty. My father was second-generation Irish. My accent isn't anywhere near as strong as his was."

Was. He hated that word. Every time he said it, it just reaffirmed that his father was gone.

Their meals arrived. He inhaled the smell of the steaming pie. "This is going to taste wonderful." He glanced up as he bit into a slice of pizza. Lucy watched him. She looked down at her salad. "What?"

"Nothing."

"You were thinking something. Tell."

Her eyes slowly lifted. "I've never seen a man enjoy his food quite as much as you do."

He grinned around the warm pizza at his lips. "I told you I was hungry and this is darned good pizza. Thanks for bringing me here."

"You're welcome."

"You want to share?" He raised the slice in his hand. Somehow the word share took on an intimate connotation when it included her. "Come on, you should at least try your landlord's pie."

"I guess I could stand a bite."

He leaned over the table, holding the slice to her lips. She took a mouthful next to where he'd bitten. Somehow it made it far too familiar. As if their lips had touched. He was captivated by the change in her facial expression when it became one of ecstasy as she experienced the taste and texture of the morsel. His gaze remained glued to her lips when the tip of her tongue peeked out to caress the breadth of her full lips, seizing every particle of pleasure, leaving her pink mouth wet and glistening.

He shifted uncomfortably as his body reacted to the sight. Her utterly innocent look said she had no idea how incredibly erotic her actions were. Making her even more mesmerizing.

"Another?" He couldn't have stopped himself from

asking if he'd been offered a million dollars. He wanted her to repeat that sensual gesture. The downside was he wasn't sure he could leave the restaurant without embarrassing himself, or, worse, her.

"It was good, but, no, thanks."

Disappointed, he accepted her decision without pressing her to change her mind. With an effort he prevented his discomfort from showing. Based on her innocent appearance and just as enthralling was the fact she had no idea what she did to him.

He took another bite, hoping to clear his head, but it didn't help. She really was an enigma. In her slacks and sweater, she looked at if she had never experienced much of life, but he knew better.

They were finishing their meal over a discussion of the latest movies when Lucy's attention was drawn to something across the room. He turned to see what it was. A mother a few tables over was holding a baby of about six months old. What was it with her and babies? He still didn't understand her reaction to going to the nursery. He would've thought she'd have jumped at the chance to meet a new family.

"Something wrong?"

She looked at him with glassy eyes. "I was just missing my family."

He identified with missing loved ones. But those feelings could and should be managed. Dealing with a weepy woman was something he wasn't going to do. "I'm going to call it an evening. I've—we've, got an early morning. I'll walk you to your door."

"Go on. I'll be fine. I need to speak to Mr. Volpentesta anyway. I'll get the check."

"That won't happen. A gentleman pays the bill. It's the O'Doherty way."

* * *

Lucy climbed the stairs to her apartment. The place seemed less inviting after spending time with Ryan in the bustling restaurant. The solitude was stifling. She'd left everything that truly mattered in her life behind when she'd moved to New York. Maybe out of desperation she was hoping she and Ryan were becoming friends.

Their relationship had been rocky initially but they'd developed a mutual understanding in the last few days. He did what he needed to do and she tried not to get in his way. Up until today they'd shared nothing of their personal lives. Their work had forced them together but that hadn't made them friends. Maybe that was changing.

She unlocked and entered her apartment. Flipping on a lamp, she pulled the curtains closed, something she often forgot to do, not yet being used to living so close to others. She began to undress.

She'd enjoyed her meal with Ryan. It had been nice to eat with someone for a change. While living with Alexis and Sam, they'd eaten the evening meal together every night. It hadn't taken her long to miss that camaraderie, the feeling of being included.

Lucy had felt that same fellowship with Ryan tonight, but had he?

CHAPTER THREE

FRIDAY NIGHT, LUCY hadn't been home thirty minutes when her phone rang. The deep voice on the other end spoke so swiftly she didn't catch what he said. It sounded like Ryan but she wasn't sure.

"Ryan?"

"Yes. Lucy, we have a case coming in. You need to meet me in the emergency room."

"I'll be right there."

She dressed again quickly in jeans and a warm cream-colored pullover sweater. Wrapping a dark blue scarf around her neck and pulling on her coat, she headed out the door. After a subway ride and the usual couple of missed turns in the hospital, she found her way to the ER. At the nurses' desk, she asked what room Dr. O'Doherty was in.

"He's seeing a patient. Are you the parent?"

Lucy flinched. That question hit too close to home. That wasn't her job. "I'm the family counselor for Neurosurgery. Dr. O'Doherty is expecting me." She showed the clerk her badge.

"He's in exam room nineteen," the nurse said, indicating Lucy should go down the hall.

Lucy found the room and knocked on the door.

Pushing it open slightly, she stuck her head inside the dim room.

Ryan wore a heavy red sweater with a hint of a white T-shirt showing at the collar and dark jeans that fit his trim hips perfectly. His lab coat was nowhere in sight but, despite his dress, the air of authority around him said he belonged.

A young Hispanic boy of about six months lay on a pristine white sheet on top of a stretcher as if asleep. Lucy worked to make the golfball-size lump in her throat disappear. The boy was so close to Emily's age. This case was already hitting too close to home. The temptation to turn and run was great. The child's unnatural stillness indicated he'd been medicated. If anything like this happened to Emily…

Ryan lifted one of the boy's eyelids and directed a penlight into it. A couple stood nearby, the old man's arm circled the woman's shoulders, holding her close.

Taking a bracing lungful of air and letting it out slowly, Lucy slipped quietly into the room and stood nearby so not to interrupt Ryan's examination. She would get through this. See about the family then go home and regroup. That way she would have her emotions under control by morning.

An anxious-looking woman stood nearby, clutching a purse in a grip that could have strangled a living thing. Lucy's heart went out to her. Would she herself act the same way if it was Emily lying on the bed? She had to stop thinking in that context. This wasn't Emily and if it had been, she wasn't Lucy's to worry over.

In what must have been her nervousness, the woman broke into rapid Spanish. Ryan gave the mother a perplexed look. Apparently he had no idea what the woman was saying.

It was time for Lucy to brace herself and be the professional she was trained to be instead of the quivering mass of emotions she'd morphed into. She stepped closer, lightly touching the mother on the arm to draw her attention. In a low, even voice Lucy explained who she was in Spanish. The woman visibly relaxed as Lucy continued to speak. "I'm Lucy Edwards and I work with Dr. O'Doherty. Your boy's in good hands. What's your son's name?"

"Miguel."

"That's a nice name. Why don't you come over here and sit?" With a shaking hand Lucy directed her toward a metal straight-backed chair near the wall. The man followed them and stood close. She glanced to where Ryan's wide shoulders still leaned over the child. Taking a cleansing breath, she said, "As soon as Dr. O'Doherty is through examining Miguel, he'll be able to tell you more." The woman nodded, her eyes reflecting all the fear she was feeling. "What's your relationship to Miguel?"

"His mother. No, I'm really his aunt."

The words bit into Lucy and a swirl of agony formed in her stomach. Could things get any worse? Her hand came to rest over the spot. *She was Emily's aunt, not her mother.* Pressing her hand down, she hoped it would ease the building torment but knew it couldn't. Would she ever recover? Accept?

"His mother ran off and left him with me."

She'd run off and left Emily. But it had been different. Her sister was Emily's mother. Why wasn't there another chair for her to sit on? She had to grasp her emotions to hold them in check. She'd break down later and let the tears flow. Something she'd sworn never to do again. Lucy almost missed what the woman was saying as she reminded herself to breathe.

"Miguel's mother didn't understand his illness. It scared her. This…" the woman placed a hand on the forearm of the man standing beside her "…is my father. Miguel and I live with him."

With fortitude Lucy would never have thought she possessed, she managed to continue consoling the woman and her father. Maybe if she focused on their needs instead of her own, the anguish would diminish. She continued to tell herself that lie.

Having finished his examination, Ryan approached them. Lucy looked up to find his eyes on her. He nodded with what she read as his appreciation and respect but his brows crowded together seconds too long. Was the agony she felt written on her face? She tried to school her appearance not to show her feelings. The question in Ryan's eyes was replaced by a grave look.

"Ms. Edwards, may I speak with you a moment?"

She nodded then told the woman and her father she'd be right back. Ryan waited for her outside the door. When she stood close enough that he wouldn't be overheard by others in the ER, he said, "This child needs surgery."

"I understand."

"I won't lie. This will be a tough one."

"Then you need to explain it to them. Reassure them."

"I'm not going to do that." Ryan didn't think getting run over by a sixteen-wheeler truck could have knocked the wind out of him more completely. He couldn't and wouldn't provide the care Lucy was pushing him toward.

"They're scared. They need the reassurance that you can give them."

"Lucy, I do surgery. Not feelings. That's your department," he said, his voice rising. "You do your job."

She flinched but didn't move. "I am doing my job by seeing that you do yours. I'll translate. All you have to do is explain what's going to happen. Parents need to know their doctor cares."

He had cared. That was the problem. He knew the hurt it caused. He knew pain so great that if he let it out of the box it would groan, snarl and devour him.

"No. You handle it." He turned to walk away.

She grabbed his arm. "Look, someone has to tell this family something right away. I'm not the doctor. I don't have the medical knowledge. You're an excellent surgeon, just let them know that. Give them some hope. That's all you have to do." They stared at each other for a long moment before she said quietly, "I'd hate to tell Mr. Matherson that you refused to co-operate on the coordinated care project."

"The hell you will," he bellowed, and shook his arm out of her grasp.

Lucy's head jerked around toward the ER desk. His gaze followed. The staff behind the desk and in the hall had stopped in place to look at them with astonishment, curiosity and anticipation on their faces.

Great. If this got back to Matherson or, worse, Rodriguez...

He looked at Lucy. "Okay. But I do it my way," he growled.

Lucy nodded. At least she didn't smirk. If she had, he didn't know how he would've reacted. He'd talk to the parents but he'd leave feelings out of it. He'd survived his father's death and illness on his own and others could handle their problems. He offered his medical skills to his patients, performed surgery to the best of his ability but he couldn't get involved outside his work in the OR.

They re-entered the room.

The family remained seated and he stood over them as he spoke. Lucy translated. "As I understand it, Dr. Matthews, your son's neurologist, has explained that the child has experienced a *grand mal* seizure. The drugs that he has been taking are no longer working effectively. The seizures your son is having now will only get worse as time goes on. Your son—"

"Miguel," Lucy offered.

That was just like Lucy to make it personal. Something he didn't want. Ryan glared at her then turned back to the mother. "Miguel's going to need surgery to slow these down. At first Dr. Matthews thought the surgery might need to be done right away. I believe that Miguel needs to stay in the hospital and be monitored for a few days. But he will need surgery. Even after that the seizures will continue, but they shouldn't be as severe."

The mother was openly crying by the time he'd finished. All he wanted was to get out of there. Nothing he could say or do would make it better for them. He wasn't going to try. No matter how hard Lucy pushed.

He looked at her. "I need to make some arrangements and a couple of calls. I'll have to see about setting up a surgery time and date. Right now, I want him to remain sedated and rest. Dr. Matthews has already started the admission process."

"I'll see that they understand." She mouthed, "Thank you."

That wasn't going to smooth over how he felt about being forced to talk to the parents. His stomach was one big mess of knots. He left without a backward glance.

Thirty minutes later and still seething from the earlier ordeal, Ryan stalked to the family counselors' office. For a person who couldn't have told anyone where it was at the beginning of the week, he was actually visiting it for the third time. Lucy had made him go through the wringer and he intended to make it clear he would not allow it to happen again.

It was late enough that the floor was quiet and the lights had been turned down in the hallway. A light glowed beneath the office door. He rapped on the door with enough force that the nurse at the end of the hall looked up from where she was charting.

There was movement in the room and the door remained closed. Lucy must be in there. He'd raised his hand to knock again when the door opened.

"Yes?" She met his gaze. "Is something wrong?"

"As a matter of fact, there is. I will not be blackmailed."

Both their heads tuned toward the shushing sound coming from down the hall. The nurse had her finger held across her lips.

"Let's go into your office." He gave her a nudge. Her uncertain look brought his anger down a notch. He hadn't intended to scare her. "Please, Lucy."

She backed into the room but didn't meet his eyes. He entered and closed the door, and Lucy moved as far back in the room as the tiny space would allow. She didn't sit, so neither did he.

He shoved his hands into his pockets. "Just what was that all about down there in the ER? Why the big push to get me to be so concerned about the family's feelings? You went too far tonight, Lucy." He stepped a pace closer as he spoke.

She stood her ground. "Because the least they deserved was to have their doctor's, and especially their surgeon's, concern. They want to hear the good and the bad from *you*. They want to feel they can trust you with their loved one's life. To do that they have to know you. They have to have a relationship with you, even if it is only a surface one. They're putting the most precious thing in their lives into your hands and that takes real courage.

"Do you have any idea what it is like to hand your child over to someone? To trust them to give them the care and attention that you would?"

Her large, dramatic eyes glistened. Was she going to cry?

"Are you so insensitive that you can't have any compassion for the parents of your patients? It's a good thing you're not a thoracic surgeon because I don't think you'd even recognize a heart if you saw one."

Ryan recoiled as if he'd been slapped. He'd come here with the intention of getting an apology and instead he was getting a dressing down. Where was all this venom coming from?

She turned to her desk, putting her back to him. "I've had enough for today. I'm headed home. We can talk about this tomorrow."

"No, we can't." He used his OR hand-me-an-instrument voice. "We're going to talk about it now. I don't think that entire tirade was to do with me or what happened in the ER tonight."

She pulled out the desk drawer and brought out her purse. "Look, Ryan, I'm too tired to hash this out tonight. I'd just like to go home."

"We're not going anywhere until you explain to me—"

"You can't keep me here."

"I can." He moved so that he leaned against the door. "But I'd prefer not to." Her luminous eyes pleaded with him and his heart caught. The part he'd thought had died with his father. Lucy was pulling him, kicking and screaming, back to life.

"Something is wrong. Don't tell me you're just upset about the boy because I won't buy it. Even with your tender heart, you wouldn't be this upset."

"Not only a brain surgeon but a psychiatrist too. My, you must've been a genius in med school to be as young as you are and pull off two degrees."

"Not a genius but I do pride myself on being perceptive. Or at least I used to be." That had been until Alex Rodriguez had been brought in to take the department head position that Ryan had been so sure was his. "Anyway, we're not talking about me."

She pulled her coat and scarf off the back of her chair. "I'm sorry if I hurt your feelings but it needed to be said. Now, if you'll excuse me…?" She stepped toward him as if hoping to intimidate him into letting her pass.

He shook his head. "Not until you explain."

She dropped into a desk chair. He took the chair closest, propping his elbows on his knees and facing her.

"Sharing wasn't outlined in the co-ordinated patient care manual. Can't you just let it go?"

"You owe me an explanation for your attack." That at least got a contrite look from her. Was he losing his mind? He didn't confide in people and he didn't get involved in another person's personal life.

"You're going to make me say it?"

He nodded.

"Miguel's mother isn't really his mother."

"Miguel?" His brows dipped. He was completely lost.

"Your newest patient." Her voice had a tone of impatience and a touch of disappointment.

He was catching up. What did Miguel have to do with her problem? "Oh, yes, Miguel Rivera."

"His mother is really his aunt."

She wasn't usually this vague. His puzzled look must have indicated he had no idea of the significance of that statement.

"I carried a baby for my sister and her husband. I had in vitro fertilization," she said quietly.

Being a surrogate for her sister had been Lucy's ultimate pleasure. Handing over the baby she'd carried her greatest pain. In order to survive emotionally, she'd left. Emily was her sister's baby, not her own. No matter how much her heart screamed differently.

She stood and said in a flat voice, "Now can I go?"

Ryan's eyes widened. He blinked and shifted slightly, as if he was formulating his words carefully. "Of all the things I might have thought you'd say, that wasn't one of them."

To voice the words had been painful, but there was something freeing about having said them. She couldn't believe she'd told Ryan of all people. He'd more than once proved he couldn't connect on an emotional level. If she had been going to confess to someone, he wouldn't have been her choice. She'd only shared her pain because he'd caught her in a weak moment and he'd insisted.

Still, being new to town and working long hours, he was the closest person to a friend she had. He was the only soul other than Mr. Volpentesta that she saw regularly. That thought was so sad she didn't take time to analyze it for fear she would start crying. Here she was revealing her deepest pain to someone who hadn't wanted her even taking up his time just a few days earlier.

Ryan stood. "I've heard of women being surrogates, but I've never known anyone that has done it."

She'd obviously shocked him. For some reason she felt the need to make him understand. "My twin sister Alexis and her husband Sam tried to conceive for years. When Alexis asked me if I would carry their baby, I couldn't turn her down. Didn't want to..." The words trailed off. *If I'd known...*

His eyes widened as if he suddenly saw the picture clearly. "So when Miguel's mother said she was really his aunt, it hit too close to home?"

She nodded. "It almost killed me to give Emily up." She looked at her hands clasped around her purse.

"Emily?"

"My ba—uh...niece."

He placed a large hand on her shoulder. The heat from him seeped into her, easing some of the ache. As if he'd realized what he was doing, he let his hand fall away.

"That must have been hard."

Ryan sounded sincere but a little unsure. Her head spun. Was this the same doctor she'd had a heated confrontation with just an hour earlier about being compassionate? She'd never seen this side of him with the families. Maybe what happened tonight had knocked some of that crustiness off. She looked into his gorgeous blue eyes that compelled her to continue.

"My head said she didn't belong to me, but my heart said differently. I made the fatal mistake of starting to think of her as mine." She'd shared all she could. Her nerves were raw.

"You didn't want to give her up."

She couldn't have been more surprised. He understood. "That's why I took this job, to get away. Had to figure out how to get my life back. I'd like to go home now."

He opened the door. "Put on your coat. I'm going to see you home."

Ryan delayed until he was sure Lucy had made it safely inside her apartment. She'd insisted that he not walk up with her so instead he'd had the taxi wait until he saw her light come on.

He was on an emotional overload. If it had been a warmer day, he'd be sweating. He'd felt more and cared more than he'd wanted to in the last twelve hours. Taken a double shot. All of a sudden he'd been forced to support a family and had later become Lucy's confessor.

He'd been more in touch with others' emotions than he had been since his father's death. His father's debilitating disease had not only taken him but had slowly taken Ryan's soul as well. He couldn't let himself be pulled into that eddy again. He would be back to going round and round. If he didn't feel, didn't care, then it didn't hurt. Supporting someone emotionally was beyond his ability any more.

Today he'd stepped too close to the edge. At Lucy's pronouncement and the troubled look in her eyes, he'd almost gone over that edge. Only through fist-clenching control had he not taken Lucy in his arms.

They'd both stepped over the professional line today. After the emotional flood Lucy had experienced, would she be able to handle her job? She was supposed to be there to support and care for Miguel's family. Could she maintain that openness that made her so effective?

Lucy was worming her way into his life so effortlessly that she would begin to expect something he couldn't give to both her and his patients. She'd want everything and he had nothing. He had to step back a pace. Keep their relationship professional only. It was up to him to make it happen.

The problem came down to whether he had the strength to remain distant when he looked into those stunning jeweled blue eyes misted over with unhappiness.

Lucy hadn't heard from Ryan over the weekend. She'd not really expected to but she'd hoped he would at least call and check on her. It had felt good to share her burden with him. Just talking about Emily had made it easier. There had been a time she couldn't have uttered the words. Now at least she could think about Emily without crying. If Ryan hadn't insisted she talk, she might still be stymied by the pain. It wasn't gone but it had eased.

On Monday she didn't see Ryan until evening rounds and there was no opportunity to talk to him outside of giving reports on the patients.

They were just finishing up when Ryan announced to the group, "Miguel Rivera's surgery is scheduled for tomorrow first thing."

"I helped walk the mother through the insurance process and found them a place to stay while Miguel's in ICU," Lucy reported.

Ryan gave her a curt nod that held none of his usual humor. It was as if they were strangers again who knew nothing about each other and never intended to. He laughed and joked with the other staff members but hadn't even spoken to her directly. This was worse than his reaction to her on the day they'd met. She hadn't expected them to be best friends but she hadn't anticipated being thoroughly ignored either.

She didn't make it a habit of confiding in anyone other than her sister, and now that was gone she had no one. It disturbed her that the single time she'd stepped out beyond her safety zone she'd been treated like she didn't exist.

Maybe she should give him the benefit of the doubt. Was he worried about Miguel's surgery? Ryan had already proved that he was the kind of guy that compartmentalized. Still, she'd come to expect a certain attitude from him and she missed his easy grin.

Miguel's surgery was an all-day affair. Lucy came to the hospital early so that she'd be available if the family needed her. She had to work harder than usual to keep her emotions in check. Miguel reminded her so much of Emily that she had to call on her professional persona and do what she'd been trained to do. During the day, between seeing to her other cases, she checked in with the family. She happened to be sitting with them when Ryan came in after surgery to speak to the family.

The dark blue scrubs he wore brought out his vivid eyes. He hesitated a second when he saw her. He looked tired, the lines around his mouth a little more evident. After giving her a brief nod, he turned his focus on the mother and grandfather waiting anxiously to hear what he had to say.

"You will translate?" Ryan asked, again without looking at her.

"Yes."

Ryan didn't go down to the mother's eye level, but instead stood away from her. She looked up at him from where she sat. Disappointment filled Lucy. She'd hoped that what had happened the other night would make a difference in his rapport with families.

"Miguel's doing well. He came through surgery fine but it will not be an easy recovery. He'll be in ICU for a few days. If all goes well he'll go out to the children's ward after that. The first few days we have to be very careful."

"Thank you," the mother gushed, jumping up to wrap her arms around his waist.

Ryan looked shocked but patted the woman's shoulder. "You're welcome."

Lucy might have found it comical if it hadn't been for Ryan ignoring her.

He pushed away from the woman, shook the man's hand and left without a backward glance. Lucy understood this time wasn't about her but she still couldn't help the disappointment she felt that Ryan hadn't said something to her.

She'd planned to stay late in order to go into ICU with Miguel's family for the first time. The boy's nurse spoke enough Spanish to answer simple questions, allowing Lucy to leave without worrying about the family being on their own. She followed behind the Riveras as they left the unit. Ryan was sitting behind the unit desk. He looked up briefly and met her gaze before his eyes returned to what he was doing. A prickle along her spine said that he had watched her walk out the doors.

Where was the guy she'd thought might be a friend? She'd had enough of the cold-shoulder treatment. She was going to find out.

Ryan had just finished rounds for the evening. He'd done them later than usual. His clinical staff always knew that it would be a late night after he'd had a big surgery and made plans accordingly. Today was one of those days. He'd had his clinical nurse notify Lucy.

She was waiting along with everyone else in the hall, looking efficient and fresh despite the late hour. It had been a long day for her also. She'd been there every step of the way with the Rivera family. Ryan had been impressed with how well she seemed to be holding up under what had to be a difficult situation for her. To his discontent, he'd found himself worrying about her. Wondering how she was doing. That was a road he didn't want to travel.

When she'd visited ICU with the family he had been aware of every move she'd made. She'd looked tired, but every bit as committed to the family as he'd hoped she would be. A couple of times she'd looked in his direction with questioning eyes that had also held disappointment. It had been far more difficult not to engage with her than he'd anticipated. Still, he thought it was for the best.

He made every effort to make it through rounds as efficiently as possible. Lucy spoke to each of the families before she left the patient's room. The families had smiles on their faces when the door closed behind him and his group. She'd turned out to be a real asset. Without a word, she turned toward her office with determined steps.

Having finished on the floor, he headed to his office for a quick wash up before checking on Miguel. There would be no going home for him tonight.

There was a knock on his office door. A nurse coming to get him this late at night wouldn't be good news. "Come in," he called.

Lucy stalked forward, stopping in front of his desk.

“There’s a problem?” By the determined look on her face there must be. He had a nagging idea he knew exactly what was bothering her.

“Yes, I’d like to discuss something with you.”

Discuss? Lucy didn’t look like she was in a discussing mood. He’d never heard her sound so forceful, even more so than she’d been a few nights earlier. She’d shared her heartache with him the other night. That had scared him. He didn’t want to know anything else. “Lucy, it’s been a long day and I’m not really up for some major discussion if it’ll wait.”

“It won’t,” she snapped.

Apparently she was on a mission. “Then you can have a seat while I finish cleaning up.”

“‘I’ll stand.” She pulled her sweater tighter around her chest.

“As you wish.”

Her lips tightened. What would it be like to kiss those full lips into a smile of pleasure? Make her forget why she was here? Hadn’t he promised himself that he wouldn’t allow those thoughts? What he needed to do was find some nurse and take her out on a date. Have a good time.

He’d managed to keep Lucy at a distance for the last couple of days but he still couldn’t get the sad look she had when she’d told him about Emily out of his mind. He even remembered the child’s name. He was already far too involved.

After toweling off, he rubbed a hand over his more than five o’clock shadow and decided to shave. Stalling all he could in the hope that Lucy would leave. Five minutes later he stepped out into his office again.

Lucy still remained rooted in the same spot she’d been in when he’d left her. Her brows were drawn together and her mouth had eased but remained in a thin line. She pulled the ever-present cardigan tighter around her and crossed her arms. Her look said she might boil over at any minute.

"So what's the problem? I know this can't be about Miguel. He was doing fine when I called to check on him a few minutes ago."

"No, this is about us."

"I wasn't aware there was an 'us'."

Before that moment he couldn't have imagined her standing any straighter or looking more out of sorts, but he'd underestimated her. The blue in her eyes went diamond sharp. If she'd had the capability, he was sure she would've sliced him up into small pieces. He moved behind his desk and faced her.

"There isn't an *us*. Not the kind you're insinuating." Her southern drawl had lost its gentleness, taking on an edge that showed she had a strength she kept hidden. She took a deep breath that made him curl his fingers into fists to keep from touching her.

"What I'm trying to say is that I don't appreciate the cold-shoulder treatment that you've been giving me the last couple of days. I shared something incredibly personal. Painful. At your request. Then you start acting like you don't know me."

There was no volcano in any part of the world that could've looked more furious and spat more sparks than the woman standing in front of him. But he couldn't let that sway him. "So, because you told me your life story I'm supposed to be your best friend?"

Lucy jerked back as if she'd been physically slapped.

For the first time in her life she thought about striking another person in anger. She clenched her teeth.

Hitting him was the least of what she'd like to do. Run him over with a car, set him on fire, pull his fingernails out with pliers. *Ooh, the man!*

She was through being the peacemaker, the one who bent over to make everyone happy. "Look, you egotistical, arrogant man, I don't expect you to be my best friend but what I do expect is for you to be civil.

"The staff has noticed how you treat me. I've been asked what I did to make you mad. For some reason, not obvious to me, you're well liked. Your attitude towards me makes my job more difficult because the staff assumes I have done something wrong. I'm the new kid on the block so they'll side with you." She stopped long enough to take a breath.

When he opened his mouth to speak she held up a hand, stalling him. "What I want—no, demand—is that you show me the professional respect that I deserve. I will never make the mistake of believing that I'm anything other than a colleague you are forced to work with. Until we are told differently, I will do my job in the most professional manner possible and I expect the same from you."

He took a step toward her. "Are you finished?" he said between clenched teeth.

She hesitated. "No. Actually, I'm not." Her voice rose, which she almost never allowed to happen. "Fear not, I'll never confide anything of a personal nature again to you."

With that said, she turned and stalked out the door. Her hands shook and her knuckles had turned white where they were balled beside her. The clacking of her heels on the tile hallway matched the beat of her racing heart.

Boy, that had felt good. Liberating. She'd had no

idea how much pain and anguish she'd kept bottled up. Maybe Ryan didn't deserve the full blast of the emotions she'd kept in check over the last few months. Heck, yeah, he did. He'd been a real jerk. The release had been freeing. She'd been stupid to ever think they could be friends.

It had been empowering. To let go for once. To fight for herself.

She would've dealt with her feelings about him backing away from her in private, but when it came into the patient care area she'd had to draw a line. Then she'd had to say something. She smiled. She'd lectured, more like.

Heading for her office, she passed a nurse who said, "Hi, Lucy." She gave her a bright smile. The nurse gave her a funny look but returned Lucy's smile. She was relieved to find her office empty. She didn't want to discuss what had just happened with anyone while she was still feeling mad. If she did, the other person would be so surprised to know she had just told off the wonderful, charming, friend-to-all-the-nurses-and-patients Dr. Ryan O'Doherty. Haw!

That was, everyone but her.

Was she jealous because he didn't treat her the same? No, that couldn't be. Maybe it was. He had at least made it known that he appreciated her contributions in the last week. She had just read him wrongly. He didn't like her. She could deal with that. What really annoyed her was that she liked him.

The light on her computer blinked, indicating she had a message. Tapping a key with more force than necessary, her email inbox opened. She scanned it. The message was from Mr. Matherson in HR. He requested that she and Ryan attend Jack Carter's going-away party together as a sign that the co-ordinated patient care program was working.

"Great. Just great." She was starting to agree with Ryan's negative view of this program.

A new message came up. The address indicated it was from Ryan. She clicked. His terse message read: "*Assume you received same email. Will pick you up at seven.*"

CHAPTER FOUR

RYAN STEPPED ONTO the landing of the third floor above Volpentesta's Restaurant and studied the glossily painted doors. Lucy's response to his email had been "*Third floor, red door.*" That had been the sum total of their personal communication since she had stalked out of his office.

During rounds she'd made it a point not to stand near him. To make the Siberian, dead-of-winter, glacial temperature between them worse, she seemed even sunnier and happier to see the patients and the other staff members than usual. None of that sunshine fell on him.

If she'd had a question about a patient she'd turned to his clinical nurse for answers. Even when Miguel had had a high fever while still in ICU and Ryan had had a real concern that the boy might require another trip to surgery, it hadn't been him Lucy had turned to for information in order to reassure the parents.

He'd been concerned about her reaction to Miguel's downturn but he wouldn't let himself ask her about it. He wasn't going to that place he'd been during his father's illness. But, still, he cared.

Lucy couldn't have made it clearer that she had no use for him if she'd shouted it over the intercom. It had been the longest week of his life.

Wasn't that the way he'd wanted it? Yeah, but living in exile hadn't turned out to be as easy as he'd thought.

For heaven's sake, he did brain surgery for a living, on children no less, and the quiet, unassuming woman had rattled his world. He suspected this would be the least agreeable date he'd ever been on. With resigned steps he approached her door and paused for a second before knocking. He'd not been this nervous since he'd done his first solo surgery. This woman wouldn't intimidate him, he refused to allow it.

Taking a deep breath and letting it out slowly, he tapped on the door. It opened with a suddenness that startled him.

"I'm ready," Lucy said in a snippy voice.

Her anger hadn't cooled. Instead of making him mad, she'd managed to make him feel guilty. He didn't like that feeling at all.

Lucy stepped out into the landing and pulled the door closed behind her. Her coat was already on and buttoned. A scarf in shades of pink orbited her neck. There was a faint smell of wildflowers about her.

Recovering from the shock of her sudden appearance, he found his breath caught in a stranglehold with the realization that Lucy's hair was down. He'd never seen it anything less than under control. Tonight it hung in honey-gold ringlets around her face and down her back. Way down her back. He'd imagined, more than once, what the mass would look like set free but none of his ideas had come near the reality. Her hair was outstanding, glorious, mesmerizing. If he could only touch…

He lifted a hand. She jerked back as if burnt.

That hurt. Could the little boy caught with his hand in a cookie jar have felt any more humiliated? Disappointed? "After you," he mumbled as he moved back to let her precede him.

He watched in fascination as her wheat-colored mane bounced across her back as she went down the stairs. Her hair stood out in contrast against the chocolate color of her coat. He'd always thought of himself as a leg man but in this case that might not be accurate. What would it be like to have that curtain of gorgeous hair hanging above him while her eyes twinkled at him and her mouth lowered to his? He groaned low in his chest.

She glanced back at him. The unwelcoming look on her face said *Don't you dare* before it continued down. The woman couldn't possibly know his thoughts, could she?

He had to get control of his libido or the night would be even more difficult than he'd originally assumed. Lucy was already angry with him and lusting after her wouldn't make her happier. Grateful for the cold blast of wind that met him straight on when he stepped out of the building, he squared his shoulders. He could do this. If he had to, he'd walk outside when the need to touch her became too strong. Maybe they could get away with putting in an appearance then leaving.

Lucy turned and looked at him as if asking what came next.

"This way." He stepped toward the restaurant valet attendant, resisting the urge to cup her elbow. She walked beside him but not so close that they touched. He handed the parking slip to the attendant.

Her eyes went wide. "You're driving? I thought we'd take a taxi."

"Not tonight."

When the attendant pulled the low, two-seater sports car in front of them Ryan had the pleasure of watching as Lucy's mouth form an O. He grinned. She liked his car. Lucy allowed his touch as he helped her into the car. A ringlet of her heavenly hair curled along his arm. He took his chance and touched it briefly. *So soft.*

Closing her door, he walked around the vehicle, bracing himself to be confined in a small space with a woman snapping mad at him. Could her anger and his lust coexist without turning to fireworks before they made it to the Ritz?

Lucy looked away from the stop-and-go traffic as they worked their way up Fifth Avenue. She studied Ryan's profile by the glow of the city lights. The luminous yellows, greens, oranges and blues flashed across his straight nose and firm jaw. By anyone's definition Ryan was handsome. When he smiled, breathtakingly so. But being attractive was only surface deep. Where it really counted, he'd let her down. He'd pushed her away. She didn't like someone playing tug of war with her emotions.

Ryan glanced at her and she quickly looked away. "Everything okay?"

"You mean besides us being forced to attend this party together?"

"You do know it wasn't my idea." His words were as flat as a table.

She sighed. "I know." Silence filled the space between them as if they were strangers.

Minutes later Ryan said, "I had no idea you had so much hair. You always keep it up or in a braid."

"Too much. I grow it for Locks for Life."

"What's that?"

"I give my hair to make wigs for cancer patients."

Had he mumbled "What a shame"?

"Does your twin have the same kind of hair?"

"No. We're not identical."

"It's beautiful, you know."

Warmth that had nothing to do with the car heater blanketed her, but she wasn't going to be pulled in by him again. She no longer trusted him but she couldn't deny it felt good to receive a compliment from such a virile man. "Thank you, but you do know that you don't have to pay me compliments. I'm not your date who needs to be charmed. This is a business party."

"I'm sorry if giving you sincere praise and making conversation disturbs you."

"Let's just get through this evening with as little personal conversation as possible."

"I'm not promising that."

They had stopped at the next light before she spoke again. "I didn't think anyone who lived in the city drove."

"I don't drive often but I like to when I can. You know, this could almost be considered a personal topic." The smile in his voice shone through clearly.

Lucy huffed. The man was making fun of her. Typical male. Have it out and move on as if nothing had happened. That didn't work for her. She was still upset with him.

Getting through the party was going to be a challenge, with Ryan's charm swirling around and his talent for exasperating her. The evening could go one of two ways. She could blow up at him again or fall at his feet. The latter she couldn't let happen. Compounding the problem was that if she'd noticed how handsome he was on a daily basis it didn't come close to how fine he looked tonight.

His jet-black tux fit his shoulders to perfection. A tall

man, his formal dress had seemed to make him tower over her as he'd helped her into the car. The stark white of his shirt accented his dark skin. The entire package screamed man of power. His haircut didn't completely control the thickness of his locks. Was it soft or bristly to the touch? Those thoughts were better left in a drawer. She gulped and held her purse in a death grip as she resisted the urge to touch him.

She made a resolution. Her goal was threefold: get through the party; return home; and prepare herself to be professional again on Monday. The other day Ryan had made it clear he wasn't interested in discussing anything close to being deeply personal. She'd be glad to honor that.

There was no doubt in her mind that she wouldn't have been his date if it hadn't been necessary to keep in the good graces of the hospital. She just hated the tension that hung between them. It was a strain to always be on guard. At one time she'd thought they might be friends. Could have been if he'd not treated her as if she'd done something wrong by showing her feelings.

Ryan pulled the car skillfully to the curb in front of the brass doors of the Ritz. The attendant opened her door but Ryan was there to help her out. He offered his hand and she placed hers in it but let go as soon as she was on the sidewalk. She liked his touch too much. He opened the door of the hotel for her like the gentleman he'd been taught to be. The O'Doherty way didn't extend to friendship apparently.

Only by hanging onto her anger did she manage not to step closer to him and breathe in his scent. He smelled of tropical islands and salt breezes. It would've been heavenly to be escorted by such a dazzling man if he'd wanted to be with her. But he didn't.

She was relieved Ryan didn't offer his arm but instead followed a half a pace behind her as they entered the hotel. Close enough for her to feel protected by his large body but not overpowered. The zing she'd experienced when she'd touched his hand as he helped her out of the car still lingered. She could only imagine the extent of her reaction if she'd held his arm.

They walked across the marble-tiled hotel lobby towards the ornate circular staircase. She glanced back at Ryan. His attention was on Dr. Rodriguez, who was pacing nearby while talking on his phone.

When Ryan met her look his lips were tightly compressed. He cupped her elbow and they continued forward. "I'd like us to get through this evening as civilly as possible," he said as they climbed the stairs. His relaxed attitude had been replaced by one of a man on a mission. "This is important to my career and yours as well, I'd guess."

She looked at him. It hadn't been a good idea to look into his beautiful persuasive eyes. After swallowing hard, she said, "I don't see a problem. I'll play my part."

His brows took a downward turn as if he wasn't completely pleased with her response. "Then there shouldn't be an issue."

"Agreed."

As couples passed them on the stairs, Ryan moved closer to her to accommodate them. "Smile. You look like I'm escorting you to the guillotine." She gave him a wry smile.

"See, that isn't so hard." His breath whispered across her cheek.

A shiver shot through her. Being drawn in by his charisma wasn't part of the plan. She had a part to play that couldn't include falling for him.

Reaching the top of the stairs, they walked through the double doors into a room filled with people mingling. Attending this function with Ryan had not been her choice but she was still grateful to have him there. In a twisted bit of irony he was her anchor in a sea of unknown people. "I'd like to check my coat."

"Sure. While you're doing that I'll get us some champagne."

She didn't usually drink, or at least hadn't in a long time. While she'd been carrying Emily it had been off limits. At that time, everything in her life had revolved around the pregnancy. Now her life rotated around trying to get past it. Lucy handed her coat to the girl behind the counter and slipped the check ticket into her sequin-trimmed handbag. Fanning her scarf out, she adjusted it across her shoulders.

She'd had to shop on the fly after receiving the emails from Matherson, then Ryan. The second-hand consignment store a block away had saved the day. With pure relief, she'd found her dress. The instant she'd tried it on she'd known it was the one.

The salmon shade was the perfect color for her. It added life to her cheeks that hadn't been there for ages. The front dipped a little too low but it showed off her breasts to their best advantage. Two straps crisscrossed her back and the silky fabric fit snugly around the bodice and hips to drop into a cloud of folds. The dress bolstered her confidence, which she desperately needed tonight. She pushed her hair over one shoulder and licked her lips. Having done all she could to brace herself, she went in search of Ryan.

She spotted him leaning on an elbow at a high cocktail table. A champagne flute sat in front of him and the other he held by his fingertips. He was like James

Bond, dashing and just as dangerous. She'd have to remind herself constantly of how disenchanted she was with him or he'd sweep her off her feet before she knew what had happened.

Ryan watched a group of people standing across the room before his head turned and his focus rested on Lucy. He blinked then straightened to his full height. He stared. Lucy's heart fluttered. He took a long draw on the liquid from the glass he still held before he set the flute down. With long strides he came to meet her.

He stopped in front of her and leaned in intimately close. "You may get angry, and I know this will step over into the personal area, but, damn, you're beautiful."

Heat flooded her neck and face. Grateful for the low lighting, she smiled. "Thank you. I think I'll let you get away with it this time."

He laughed. The deep, rough sound flowed over her.

It was dangerous to be out with him. They'd been together less than an hour and she was already having difficulty keeping up her guard. To have someone tell her she was beautiful and look at her as if she belonged to him, as Ryan was doing now, was all she'd ever wanted. To belong. Be accepted. To have a little niche in the world that was hers alone. Like her sister had.

Ryan's pleasure remained on his face and her stomach did a loop the loop. That smile was for her.

"Come on, have some champagne. Then we'll make the rounds and do our duty." He led her back to the table where he'd stood and handed her a flute.

She glanced at the floor, forcing her emotions under control. How could he look at her like that while the words out of his mouth said he'd like to be as far from her as possible? She took the champagne. Maybe the liquid courage would help with the confusion she felt.

"Just try a sip or two. It'll help calm your nerves." Ryan raised his glass to his lips.

"How do you know my nerves need calming?"

"Your hands are trembling."

Great. After days of making her feel like a wall ornament he passed without notice, now he was paying attention to her. She did need to settle her nerves.

She sipped the gold liquid and enjoyed the bubbles playing a melody in her mouth before she replaced the flute on the table. Clasping her hands to appear calm, she said, "The email invitation implied that we should sign a pledge card to help raise money for the clinic in Harlem."

Ryan grinned. "Yeah. It didn't take Jack long to get on board, with Nina doing the convincing."

"I'd like to take care of that before I forget."

"Good idea. I think that's being done at a table over there." He pointed to the other side of the room.

"You lead," Ryan told her. Lucy turned and stared in the direction he'd suggested. Ryan placed a hand at her back and shock waves rippled through him. He'd touched bare skin. He jerked his hand away as if he'd been branded. One more surprise and he would be dragging her out of here to someplace private. She looked like sin and smelled like spring.

Lucy didn't slow down as she worked her way through and around the people standing in groups, talking. He drew in a breath and followed her. He'd have sworn he'd been sucker-punched when she'd walked towards him. The simply but functionally dressed family counselor had transformed into a sultry siren of sensuality. Nothing about her indicated she'd once carried a baby.

He didn't care if she thought it was being too personal to say she was beautiful. He couldn't help himself. He'd not been the only one staring at Lucy. And he didn't like it. Suddenly he wanted her all to himself. That wasn't a realistic wish.

Lucy and he had just broken out into an open area and were headed towards the pledge table when his name was called.

"Ryan O'Doherty. I had hoped to see you here."

He turned to find Alex Rodriguez standing behind him. "Alex," he said, more tartly that he should have.

Lucy waited patiently beside him. He guessed she wasn't missing a single nuance of his and Alex's interaction.

"We need to have a quick talk. Be in my office tomorrow morning before your first case." Alex's veiled dictate didn't go over Ryan's head.

The only answer he could give was, "Sure, I'll be there at six-thirty. I'd like to speak to you also."

They stared at each other like two alpha wolves deciding how they were going to share the same space. Ryan knew Alex had already won. He was the head of the neuro department now.

"Good," Alex said, and looked at Lucy.

"Have you met Ms. Edwards?" Ryan asked Alex.

"I have. Glad to have you working with us, Ms. Edwards."

"Thank you."

"Dr. Woods." Ryan waved at the blonde woman walking past.

She stopped. "Hello, Ryan." She smiled but when her gaze fell on Alex it dimmed.

Had Alex crossed swords with her also? "Layla," Ryan continued, "I'm sorry I wasn't here when the announcement was made that you're going to be the new pediatric head. Congratulations."

"Thanks, Ryan."

He looked at Lucy. "Have you met Lucy Edwards, the new neuro family counselor, and Dr. Alex Rodriguez, our new neuro head?"

"Hello, Lucy." Layla offered her hand to Lucy then turned to Alex, hesitating before she took the hand Alex extended. "Alex."

She gave his name a hard edge and their handshake was almost over before it had begun. Did they have some history? Interesting. Maybe Ryan wasn't the only one that Alex had rubbed up the wrong way.

"Hello, Layla," Alex said, his tone almost as cutting as hers.

"You two already met?" Ryan asked, looking from one to the other.

"Yes," Alex answered, but his attention remained on Layla. "How're you?

"Fine. And you?"

"Well."

If there was an iceberg between Lucy and himself, it was nothing compared to the frigid fog gusting off the two people in front of him.

"Is your husband here with you?" Alex asked, glancing around the room.

Even in the dim light Ryan could see Layla blanch. "No, we're divorced."

"I'm sorry to hear that," Alex said, but his response lacked a ring of sincerity. "If you'll excuse me, I see someone I need to speak to." He nodded curtly to the group and was gone.

"Lucy and I are on our way to sign pledge cards. Would you like to join us?" Ryan asked Layla.

"Thank you, but I've already stopped by. I need to speak to Jack a second so I'll see you around," Layla answered, not looking at him. Instead, her gaze rested on Alex's back as he moved across the room.

"Then we'll see you later." Ryan put his hand at Lucy's waist. A thrill went through him when she didn't move away.

"Nice to meet you, Dr. Woods." Lucy said. When Layla was out of earshot, Lucy whispered, "What was that all about?"

"I don't know but I'd say there's some history between them. And not the good kind."

"I'd say she isn't the only one that feels that way." She looked meaningfully at him. "I know you wanted the department head job."

"I did. Do." Once again she had him telling her things he should keep to himself.

"I would've thought you would've been the logical choice."

"Me too." He'd put in his time, paid his dues and had been confident he'd be the committee's pick.

"Do you have any idea why they didn't?"

"Yeah. Bad day for an interview."

She looked at him keenly. "How's that?"

"Who's getting personal now?"

She sneered at him. "This has to do with the hospital. It's not personal."

"Seems personal to me." He'd have to tell her or she wouldn't give up. "My father passed away the week before the interview. I left straight after the interview to attend his funeral. My mind hadn't been on impressing the committee."

His father's illness and death had not only destroyed Ryan emotionally but it had also damaged his career.

The timing of his bid for a leadership position couldn't have been scheduled on a worse date. He'd make sure when the next opportunity arose that he'd done everything he could to sway the decision in his direction. He was determined to make his father proud. That was why he'd agreed to be a part of the co-ordinated patient care program. Why he had brought the woman next to him to this party.

Lucy put her hand on his arm. "Ryan, I'm sorry. That seems so unfair." She looked at him with deep compassion.

Were her feelings always on display? "And that's life."

"That's a little more cynical sounding than I believe you are."

This conversation had already touched areas he wasn't interested in exploring. He gave her a twisted smile. "Come on, let's see about those cards and then get something to eat. Maybe have a dance," Ryan suggested.

Lucy wasn't too sure about the dance part. That would require Ryan to touch her and if he did so she was afraid she might make a fool of herself. "I'll go for the food. I'm not dancing with you. This is no date."

She glanced at him. Had Ryan said, "You want to bet?"

Minutes later they were making their way towards the hors d'oeuvres tables despite being stopped a number of times by greetings from people Ryan knew. He was flawless in his manners and introduced her every time. The charming O'Doherty way.

Ryan seemed to be popular with women and men alike. He was always ready with a witty remark and a quick smile. Why couldn't she and Ryan have that kind of relationship? Oh, no. She was letting him do it to her again. He'd made it perfectly clear how he felt and she'd do well to remember that.

"Why don't we sit down for a while and enjoy this without juggling the plates?" Ryan suggested, heading toward an empty table.

They lapsed into silence as they ate. Lucy's animosity had dwindled but she still wasn't at ease with him, afraid she'd share too much or, worse, sound needy. Her heart went out to him about his father. He'd obviously cared intensely for the man. And to have lost the department head job must've hit Ryan hard as well. For as little as she had shared with him on a personal level tonight, she'd managed to learn a great deal about Ryan.

While taking small bites, she looked around the room at the upper-level staff of a world-renowned children's hospital. In spite of dealing with life and death on a daily basis, they were still humans with problems of their own. She glanced at Ryan. He too had issues, even though he worked to hide them behind that facade of humor and charm. She couldn't point a finger. She also hid her pain.

Her gaze settled on a group that included Dr. Woods. She kept glancing toward the entrance, where Dr. Rodriguez had his arm around a pretty woman's waist and was leading her out the door. Dr. Woods shrugged a shoulder and turned to speak to the man beside her. Something about the way she'd been watching Dr. Rodriguez intently was in direct contrast to the nonchalant way she was acting. Lucy's belief was that Dr. Woods' look implied she wasn't pleased to see Dr. Rodriguez leave with a woman.

Their issues weren't Lucy's concern. She had enough

of her own, starting with the man sitting beside her. "How much longer do you think we need to stay?" she asked.

"Why?" Ryan popped another canapé into his mouth. "You in a hurry to get away from me?"

"I thought it was the other way around."

"Why would you think that?" His face took on a perplexed look. "I thought we were having a pretty good time."

"Well, you made it more than clear that you weren't interested in spending any more personal time with me than necessary." She nudged her half-empty plate to the center of the table and stood. "If you're not ready to go, I don't mind taking a taxi."

He stood. "We can go. We've done our duty. I'd just hoped to get one dance with you."

"This isn't a date. It's work," she said over her shoulder as she made her way to the coat-check counter. "Dancing comes under the heading of personal."

She claimed her coat. Ryan took it from her and held it while she slipped it on. He stood so close that his body warmed her back. She stepped forward on the pretense of putting her scarf on in order just to catch her breath.

As Ryan and Lucy descended the stairs she said, "By the way, I understand about the department job but that doesn't explain way you don't like Dr. Rodriguez. There's something more going on there."

"More?" He did not want to talk about this.

"Yeah. I thought you were supposed to be Mr. Happy-Go-Lucky and you were…what would be the word?…strident, harsh, displeased…" She stopped on the step and looked up at him as if trying to pull the right expression out of the air. "You don't care for the man. Why?"

"It's personal."

"Right. You're going to play that card."

"Why not? You've been throwing the word around all night."

They'd reached the bottom of the stairs when Lucy said, "Closing off when you might have to share more than a joke. Typical."

"Look, I'm sorry if you think I have no concern for your vulnerabilities, but I've done nothing wrong. I'm not your confessor. You spilled, I listened, and now we move on." He couldn't let her know that he admired what she'd done. If he did, she might use him as her confessor again. He desired her supple body and itched to caress her hair, but he wanted nothing to do with being involved in her life.

If Lucy could have produced steam, he didn't doubt it would be coming out of her ears right now. "Of all the contemptuous, uncaring things you could have said. You're nothing like people think you are."

"How many of us really are?"

"That's a pretty pessimistic way to look at life.'

They continued across the lobby. "It might be, but you can't deny that it's the truth. We all hide things from others." He should know. Most of his life he guarded closely.

"Yes, we do."

"But for some reason you think I should tell all. Is that little family counselor who wants to make it all better working after hours tonight?" Goading her was starting to be fun. At least, if she was mad at him he'd be less temped to explore his fascination with her. She was so beautiful with her hair cascading around her shoulders. Her eyes glittering with anger only heightened that beauty.

"Oh, you…you… You've managed to make it personal!"

That did it. He'd heard that word one too many times. As they passed a small alcove he took her waist and pulled her in. "I'm going to show you *personal*."

Combing his fingers into her hair, he brought his mouth down to hers. It wasn't a gentle kiss. He wanted to consume her. Wanted to get her out of his system, out of his life. The world slowed to nothing but Lucy and the moment. He'd not felt so free in a long time.

She jerked away and he immediately regretted the loss of her lips. He wanted more. The evening had certainly turned out far more positively than he'd anticipated.

Lucy's eyes were wide as she gazed at him blankly. She blinked and in that second she found reality again. With a quick look around, she checked to see if anyone had seen them. Relief flooded her features when no one was visible.

Her eyes flashed at him as she hissed, "You had no business doing that!"

"It wasn't business, it was personal."

She clenched her mouth shout, glared at him before she swung around and stalked away.

He caught up with her before she made it out of the main entrance. "The valet service is out the other door."

"I'm getting a taxi."

His fingers circled her arm. She stopped and looked pointedly at his hand. He released her. "Come on, Lucy. I apologize. It won't happen again. I brought you and I'm going to see you home."

* * *

Lucy said nothing as they rode back to her apartment. He glanced at her while they stopped in traffic. There was a pensive look on her face and her fingers touched her bottom lip. He grinned. So she wasn't as unaffected by his kiss as she acted.

Good, then maybe he'd get to kiss her again. One taste hadn't been enough.

When he entered her street she said, "Just pull up in front of the restaurant. It's not necessary to park. I can get in on my own." She raised a hand. "I know that goes against your raisin' but I've had enough tonight."

He hadn't had enough and he didn't think she had either but he wouldn't argue the point. Stopping by the curb in front of her apartment, he let Lucy out as she'd requested. "See you tomorrow, Lucy."

"Tomorrow," she said, as if she was parroting him instead of really thinking about what she was saying. She bit her lower lip.

His male ego took flight. Yes, there would be more kisses.

CHAPTER FIVE

LUCY STARED OFF into what little space there was in her office.

Ryan had kissed her. Had kissed her good. He'd kissed her like no one else ever had. Her lips tingled from the memory. She stuck the tip of her tongue out and licked the center of her bottom lip. Could she still taste him? With an effort she stopped herself from moaning.

"Lucy, you okay?"

"What?" She looked around.

"I've called your name twice. Something bothering you?" Nancy asked.

"Oh, no, I'm fine. Just thinking."

"How's it going with Ryan?"

Lucy's heart revved up. Her body temperature rose. Beyond a shadow of a doubt her face had gone beet red. "We're fine."

Nancy looked at her longer than Lucy found comfortable. "You aren't falling for the silver-tongued devil, are you?"

"No. We're just co-workers." Lucy tried to sound as convincing as possible, tried to convince herself that his kiss had meant nothing.

"I see," Nancy said, but disbelief ricocheted around

the room. She smiled knowingly at Lucy before she picked up papers off her desk. "Hey, it's Saturday night. Why don't you come to O'Malley's Pub for a drink before you head home? Everyone will be there. I'll introduce you around. Should have done it already."

Lucy wavered only a second between going home to spend the evening alone or getting to know other staff members better. "I think I'd like that. Thanks."

"Great. What time is Ryan usually through with rounds?"

"Today it should be about six."

"Perfect. I'll meet you here."

"I'll be ready." Maybe going out with a group and having some fun would get her mind off Ryan O'Doherty. Still she couldn't help but have a fluttery feeling in her middle at the thought of seeing him again.

"So, Alex, what can I help you with?" Ryan asked as he took a seat in one of the two chairs in front of Alex Rodriguez's desk.

"Ryan, I thought I should speak to you privately about a couple of matters that came up during the patients' review meeting yesterday," Alex said, leaning back in his chair.

Ryan looked at him expectantly.

"I heard that you and Ms. Edwards had a public shouting match in the ER the other evening." Alex's voice made it clear he wasn't pleased.

Ryan had let Lucy push him too far. His emotions had gotten away from him. Something he rarely, if ever, allowed to happen. Now he was being criticized because of it.

"Things like that reflect poorly on my department and you professionally," Alex finished with a note of reprimand. In a very unsubtle way Alex was making it clear he wouldn't tolerate it happening again.

"Ms. Edwards and I did have a heated discussion about a patient. We've worked out our differences."

"Good. That's what I wanted to hear. Do I need to speak with Ms. Edwards?"

Ryan shifted in his chair. He couldn't have Lucy telling Alex what they'd been arguing about. "That won't be necessary."

Alex nodded. "Now for the other issue. I understand that the Rivera kid's progress hasn't gone as expected."

The hair on the back of Ryan's neck stood at attention as he shifted into fighting mode. What was this guy getting at? With his background he didn't have any room to talk. Or accuse.

"*Miguel*—" Ryan stressed the boy's name "—is doing quite well now. He did have a setback in ICU but he didn't require additional surgery. His recovery has been slower than I originally estimated but he's coming along fine nonetheless. Why? Is there a problem?"

"All I'm doing is asking the question that was put to me. I'm not accusing you of anything. In order to have a solid, top-notch neuro department, I need to know what's going on. It's my job to protect my staff but also make modifications when necessary in patient care."

Ryan wasn't sure how he was supposed to respond to those statements. He glared at Alex. He didn't appreciate the implication that he couldn't manage the case or manage his job in general. He needed to get a handle on his ire if he didn't want to create a problem. Like it or not, Alex was his superior. Antagonizing him wouldn't be to his own advantage. "What exactly are you insinuating?"

"I'm not insinuating anything. I'm just voicing a concern."

"Just for the record, you should know that I've done my homework. I know about you and your malpractice case."

Alex leaned forward. The only visible sign that Ryan had hit a sore spot was the tic in Alex's jaw.

Ryan received a small amount of perverse pleasure from the other man's reaction. "I haven't shared this information with anyone else. I'll admit that I wanted your job but not if I had to act underhandedly to get it. I wanted it based on my merit and skill. The committee voted for you. You're a talented doctor and no matter how much I'd like to have your position; I can't fault your skills as a surgeon."

"I appreciate that," Alex said. "Thank you for clearing the air. It'll be my job to see that you are left alone to care for your patients. You can count on me standing behind you. If there's a problem regarding administration then we'll discuss it behind closed doors." Alex stood and offered his hand.

"Agreed." Ryan shook the other man's hand. He was pleased with the tentative plan he and Alex had established to stay out of each other's way based on mutual respect. Ryan still wanted the position of head of Neuro and one day he would have it.

Long hours later he found Lucy sitting in the surgery waiting room with the family of his most recent surgery patient. He'd stopped being surprised at the consideration she gave to parents.

Lucy looked up at him from under half-lowered eyelids as he finished speaking to the family. She really was a lovely woman. Her hair was pulled back, making him wish he could take it down and feel its silkiness one more time.

That evening, she showed up for rounds, adding information as necessary. He was hyper-conscious of every move she made. She held a clipboard against her chest like a breastplate, as if preparing to go to war for her patients. The free tentacle of hair she pushed at impatiently when she spoke intrigued him. Her lips captivated him the most. The urge to create an excuse to see her in his office was so tempting. Only because he respected her enough not to make her feel cheap or self-conscious had he not let his baser instincts run wild.

The woman had gotten to him. First it had been her gentle ways, then her strong backbone as she'd told him off, then her sexy looks and tasty lips last night.

"I think Miguel might be well enough to go home early next week. Ms. Edwards, will everything be in place on your end for that to happen?" he asked. Did the others notice her cute, shy ways? What was he going to be doing next, spouting poetry? He had the hots for the leggy family counselor and if he wasn't careful it was going to show.

"I have everything lined up. All it needs is your signature on the orders."

"Good. I'll take care of that. I understand there was some concern that the family might have difficulty getting him back here for the post-surgery check-ups."

"There's a group called Care Ride that helps patients with transportation to and from appointments. They either send a car or see that the family has a subway pass for X number of times. I've already signed up Miguel's family and they have been approved."

"Excellent." Ryan smiled at her. "Then I think we'll

send the young man home the better for his visit to Angel's."

The group standing around him chuckled and he winked at her.

Lucy's heart leaped and did a somersault. He'd included her. A warm feeling washed over her. She was starting to belong somewhere, even if it was just at her job. She was a part of Ryan's team.

Twenty minutes later, with purse in hand, she was on her way to meet Nancy in the lobby. Her co-worker needed to deliver some paperwork to a different department so they had decided to meet downstairs. Lucy circled by the nurses' station on her way out. Ryan sat behind the desk.

He rolled the chair back when he saw her and smiled. "Hi."

She tingled all over at the sight of him. It happened so often around Ryan she'd begun to think of it as her body's normal reaction. She'd given up fighting it and settled for not letting it be on display.

"It's more like bye. See you next week." She kept walking.

He stood and met her at the end of the long nurses' desk. "Hey." He scanned the area as if looking to see if anyone was paying attention to them. His blue gaze met hers. "How about we have some Volpentesta's pizza together tonight?"

She wasn't sure she could handle being alone with him again after last night. He was well aware of her loneliness and vulnerabilities. Would he take advantage of that? Could she trust him? She certainly couldn't rely on herself to stop him if he kissed her. Wanting to belong so badly, would she recognize it if Ryan didn't feel the same? Could she survive if he treated her like he had before? She was a basket of nerves.

With a sense of relief she said, “I’ve got plans.”

His look of surprise, then disappointment, made her heart flip. Ryan didn’t get turned down.

“I want someone to be interested in eating with me for me, not for the pizza my landlord makes.”

“That has nothing to do with it. I… I—”

“I’m kidding Ryan. You’re not the only one who can make a joke.”

He looked around again before his gaze came back to bore into hers. This time the crystal blue held a sauna-warm intensity. “I thought I proved last night that I like you. You taste better than any pizza I’ve ever had.” His voice had softened.

Heat filled her and she looked away.

“What’re you doing tonight?”

“Hey, Lucy, I thought you were going to meet me in the lobby?” Nancy said as she approached them.

“I was on my way. Sorry you had to come back up.”

Nancy looked from her to Ryan and grinned. “Ryan, we’re on our way to O’Malley’s for a drink. Want to join us?”

Only with supreme self-control did Lucy suppress a groan. No way would she ever relax with Ryan in the group. It was all she could do not to act like she had a schoolgirl crush around him as it was. She certainly didn’t want anyone else to notice. Nancy was already too suspicious for Lucy’s liking.

“Sure. I’ve got a couple of other things to see about here. I’ll meet you there.” Ryan grinned at Lucy.

“Great. We’ll save you a seat,” Nancy said.

O’Malley’s Pub was loud and busy when Nancy and Lucy arrived. Lucy was grateful for all the noise because it made it more difficult for Nancy to quiz her about Ryan. The questions had been free flowing since she and Nancy had left the hospital and during the short walk to the bar.

Nancy waved at a group in the corner. Lucy followed her as she weaved her way through the mass of people to the table. They settled in and Nancy introduced her to everyone. Some of them Lucy recognized, but others were completely new to her.

"We need to save a seat for Ryan," Nancy announced.

Those that heard Nancy turned to look at her in surprise. "Dr. O'Doherty? He never comes out with us. What gives?"

As popular as Ryan was with the staff, Lucy was surprised he'd not spent more time socializing with them. As she thought about the man, in he walked. Had she been watching for him? Even across the crowded room he'd managed to zero in on her. He smiled and headed her way.

Ryan had changed from his ever-present scrubs into worn jeans and a light blue sweater. The collar of his button-up shirt showed above the neckline. As he approached, women turned to watch him. Her insides trembled.

"Room for another?" he asked, standing between her and Nancy.

"Sure." Nancy scooted over and Lucy did also. Ryan squeezed between them on the wooden bench. The tight space meant Ryan's firm body was sandwiched against hers from hip to thigh. His heat branded her along the length of her leg. She squirmed, trying to put as much room between them as possible.

He looked at her, which brought his face much too close for her comfort, and whispered, "If you continue to wiggle like that, I might think you're issuing an invitation."

She sucked in a breath and jerked her head around to look at him.

He grinned.

The waitress circled by them and took their order.

"I'll get this round," Ryan said, smiling at Nancy then her, "just for asking me along." His look said he knew Lucy would have never invited him.

The conversation flowed around the table. She mostly listened. Ryan told a story and everyone laughed. He really was fun. Despite all his story-telling and jokes, he rarely shared anything personal about himself. What little she'd learned he'd been forced to tell her in order not to appear rude. Even his story tonight was about someone else.

Was he hiding something or was he just so closed off he couldn't share?

At one point, he leaned forward to hear what someone was saying farther down the table and Lucy had a wonderful view of his broad shoulders and back. The muscles across his back rippled beneath his sweater as he reached for a basket of peanuts. His hair brushed against the top of his collar and there was a line around the back of his head where his surgical cap had been tied. It looked like he'd tried to get rid of 'cap hair' by running his fingers through it, leaving it with a mussed look that had a boyish appeal.

Lucy folded her hands tightly in her lap, stopping if not completely relieving the desire to touch those irresistible locks.

He leaned back and looked at her. "Is something wrong?"

People were always asking her that when she thought

about him. She was going to have to work on not showing her emotions so much. In answer to his question, yeah, she was beginning to feel too much. She didn't trust herself. Didn't trust him.

"I'm fine. Just tired, I guess."

"We've both had a long day. Come on, I'll see you home."

"That's not necessary. I've learned to manage on my own. I wasn't late but once this week."

He leaned closer. "My, that is an improvement. Still, I'd like to see you get home safely."

She wouldn't have thought it possible but Ryan moved further into her personal space. Somehow it seemed safer to take her chances on her own.

Glancing away from his compelling look, she found the others at the table watching them. Did they think he was going to kiss her, like she was afraid he would? "Uh, sure."

He stood, stepping over the heavy bench, and waited for her to do the same.

"I'm going to see Lucy home. She isn't feeling well."

There were mummers of concern around the table. Lucy smiled at them weakly.

She couldn't refute Ryan's statement because it would make her look silly. Waving a hand, she murmured, "Goodnight."

The table quickly returned to their discussions. Ryan led the way, taking her hand. He used his big physique as a wedge through the crowd of people and pulled her along behind him. They picked their coats off a peg by the door and put them on. Soon they were out on the sidewalk, standing in the cool, windy night air. Ryan let go of her hand and she felt the loss immediately. She hefted her purse strap over her shoulder then stuffed her hands into her pockets in an effort to contain the warmth he'd left behind.

Lucy faced him. "You know that they all think something is going on between us."

"Isn't there?" He cocked his head to the side and gave her a slight grin.

"Not that I know of." She started down the sidewalk. He fell in beside her. "A week ago you treated me like I had the plague. You weren't even speaking to me. Why would I think anything has changed?"

"Maybe because I kissed you and you kissed me back."

"You think just one kiss is going to make a difference?"

He stopped and she did too. "I'm shocked that the tender-hearted, make-everyone-feel-better woman is really a skeptic at heart."

"You can't turn a cute phrase every time you don't like the subject matter."

He grinned. "I'm pretty sure I can."

"I wished I could stay mad…" she muttered.

"I heard that."

They fell into silence by mutual agreement as they walked. All the lights in Manhattan had been switched on. Lucy missed being able to see the stars in the sky but there was also something intriguing about living in a techno show. "I'm always amazed at all the lights and sounds here," she breathed.

"Yeah, it's pretty fascinating. And noisy. You should see the lights from my place. I think you'd be impressed."

"You sure that isn't some come-on line, like 'Would you like to see my etchings?'"

His deep-throated laugh made her think of hot fudge

over a brownie. Sinfully wonderful. He really had a magnificent, heartfelt laugh. She needed more laughter in her life. Ryan being the source both flabbergasted and unnerved her.

"Well, it could be but actually it's the truth."

They walked slowly down the street, occasionally dodging people. "So is that how the great Dr. O'Doherty lures women into his wolf's lair, by saying come look at my view?"

"I don't invite just anyone to my home." His voice had turned serious.

"Really? Why?"

"Because I like my privacy."

When the wind picked up and a light drizzle began to fall he said, "I'll get us a cab."

"No, I can get home from here. I'll take the subway."

"Okay."

"Okay?"

"Yeah, okay. I'll ride with you."

Lucy didn't try to argue. She'd figured out it wasn't worth the trouble. They found the subway entrance and used their passes to go through the turnstile. The station was crowded with the evening after-work foot traffic. As they waited, they were pushed closer and closer together.

Was everyone and everything conspiring to keep her shoved against Ryan? No matter where they went it seemed like his body was in contact with hers. She loved the warmth and security he provided but it was hard on her already edgy nerves. Maybe she should've agreed to the taxi. At least it would have allowed a foot of space between them.

When the train came, Ryan pulled her back against

him, wrapped an arm around her waist and held her close as the car unloaded.

"Let's go." He nudged her forward as the last person stepped off the train. He moved her in and down the car to stand next to a pole. All the seats were taken. "You're going to have to learn to be aggressive if you ride at this time of day," he whispered next to her ear.

He made the words sound far more suggestive than they should have been. They had her thinking of firelight, him, the floor. She shook her head. That was no place for her mind to wander. She searched for a handhold on the bar to steady herself for when the train launched out of the station. None were available.

"Brace yourself against me," Ryan said from behind her.

"I'll manage."

"Yes, and fall. Maybe hurt yourself or someone else." He widened his stance and again wrapped his solid arm around her. "Remember I offered a taxi."

"I think you're just using this crowd as an excuse."

"Excuse for what? To hold you? Come to think of it, it *is* working to my favor."

"Ryan, don't tease me. I don't need this."

She tried to pull away but he tightened his embrace fractionally before the beep sounded to notify everyone that the doors were closing.

"I'm not teasing. Give me a chance to make it up to you."

She sure wanted to. Would he treat her just the same again? This time she was afraid she'd have more invested. It could hurt worse.

They rode in the same intimately close position until they reached her stop. Since when had a ride on a dirty, hot, packed subway car become sexually exciting? Even with a crowd of people around them her world had narrowed down to just Ryan and the effect he had on her body.

"Isn't this your stop?" His breath brushed her ear.

"Uh?"

"You get off next."

"Oh, yeah."

"Where has your mind been?" His chuckle was low and suggestive.

Darn the man. He knew exactly what he was doing to her. The cold damp of the outside was a blast to her hyper-sensitive system. A welcome relief from the heat. It woke her from the blissful Ryan-filled trance and jerked her back to reality. She stepped away from him, putting as much distance between them as she could. Her body had reached overload and she needed to regain her perspective. He didn't leave her side or touch her as they walked the block to her apartment. She stopped at the foot of the stairs and faced him.

"Thanks for seeing me home, even if it wasn't necessary."

"My pleasure. I enjoyed it." He had a wicked look in his eye.

"I'll see you next week."

"You're not going to invite me up?"

"No."

"That hurts."

"I don't know what's going on here. What I do know is that you're playing at something. After tonight at the bar, all the tongues will wag about us. I need as little emotional upheaval in my life as possible. I have no interest in becoming part of the O'Doherty harem."

"The woman speaks her mind. For starters, I don't have a harem. Nice idea, but I work too many hours to keep a group of women happy. Second, you've been doing too much thinking. Why don't we just try being friends again? I don't have to take calls tomorrow so how about I show you around New York? Is there any place that you've never been but would like to go?"

"I thought we were friends—"

He put up his hands as if to warn her off. "Okay, I'll say it. I'm sorry. I messed up. Tomorrow will be no strings attached. No expectations, just two people enjoying a day off. How about that?"

She took so long to answer that his uncertainty that she would say yes started to show.

"Okay, then I'd like to see the Statue of Liberty." When she'd visited New York as a child her parents had been planning to take her and Alexis out to see it, but instead they'd gotten into a huge fight and that part of the trip had been forgotten. It would be nice to see the statue and share it with someone instead of going by herself.

"Perfect. I love the old girl. How about we sleep in and I pick you up around eleven?" He made it sound like he was issuing an order in ICU. As if Lucy would dare defy one of his directives. "Wear your fun clothes and something warm. It's cold on the ferry over to the island this time of year. See you tomorrow." He turned and raised a hand for the taxi that was passing by.

Had she just been sucked into the vortex that was Ryan O'Doherty?

Ryan couldn't remember looking forward to a day off more. At least, not since the time his father had surprised him with tickets to a Yankees game when he'd been a kid. It had been more than he could do to concentrate on his schoolwork that week, with thoughts of going to the big game. Thankfully he didn't have a week to contemplate spending the day with Lucy.

He'd asked her to his house. He took his solitude seriously and didn't share outside his family. He dated—after all he was a red-blooded man and had needs. He'd had his share of women but had never let them get too close. For some reason, Lucy had slipped under that barrier. He wanted her to see his place, wanted to share his home, his special view with her.

Most of his days off he spent with his sisters and their kids. In fact, they'd been shocked then pleased when he had told them he was taking Lucy out to the statue. There were far more questions than he was willing to answer about Lucy but they accepted for the time being what few he gave. He knew they weren't done. They worried about him and he didn't like that.

Ryan knocked on Lucy's apartment door right at eleven. There was a scuffle of movement before she opened the door. "I'm not quite ready. I'll only be a minute."

"Mind if I come in?" he asked.

Lucy paused longer than he would've liked to give her answer.

"I guess." She opened the door wider and he followed her into the small but neat apartment. The first thing that struck him was the lack of personal items. Even as a bachelor he had family pictures around his home. It was very telling. There was nothing there to indicate she had any family that she cared about, and he knew differently.

She wore jeans that fit her slim figure perfectly, not leaving a single curve untouched. Lean and fit, she looked lovely. He wished the bulky cream-colored sweater didn't hide her luscious breasts. He had told her to dress warmly so he only had himself to blame. She'd pulled her hair up and through the back of a baseball hat and braided it. She looked like a woman-child instead of the competent, mature woman he knew her to be.

After slipping her arms in to a pea jacket and looping a bright pink scarf around her neck that hung below the hem of the coat, she said, "I'm ready."

"Great. I think we've got a perfect day to visit. The sun's shining and the wind isn't up too high. We need to hustle to make the ferry. I managed to get us tickets on the one o'clock. We were lucky. They take reservations and there were only two left. Otherwise we might have had a long wait."

At Battery Park, Ryan paid the cab driver and grabbed Lucy's hand. "We better run for it." He loped so she could keep up with his longer stride. As they raced across the park to where the ferry was docked, he glanced back to check on Lucy. Her bright smile and rosy face made him grin like a foolish kid. She looked happy.

"I've not run like that in a long time," Lucy said, panting as they stood in line to go through security.

"Neither have I. It felt good."

Lucy looked up at him. "It did, didn't it?"

He wrapped his arm around her shoulders and gave her a quick hug. "We'll run back after we see Liberty if you like."

She grinned. "I think I'd be just as happy with a walk."

He laughed.

They made it past security and Ryan fished their tickets out of his pocket as the powerful engines of the ferry started to boil.

"Where did you get those? Do you have an 'in' with the port authorities?"

He waved the papers in his hand. "The internet is a wonderful thing."

They walked aboard and found a spot on top. Out in the open they could get a three-hundred-and-sixty-degree view of the city, the bay and New Jersey.

"It's amazing," Lucy said as she stood beside him and looked towards the statue.

"I love this city."

"You've never wanted to live anywhere else?" She looked at him as if his next words would be committed to memory.

"No. How about you? Anyplace special you'd like to live?'

"Not really. Other than my sister's I've not had a place to call home in a long time."

Her words drifted away on the wind as they crossed the harbor. He might have had it rough with his mother dying so young but his dad had always made sure that Ryan had a home. Just as he'd made sure his sisters had known they had one when his father had gotten sick. He didn't know what he would do without his family…

Lucy shuddered. He wrapped his arm around her waist and pulled her close. She didn't resist but relaxed against him. Ryan liked the feel of her next to him. "Having fun yet?" he asked as they closed in on Liberty Island.

"Yes. More than I thought I would."

He studied her a moment. "What exactly does that mean? You didn't think it would be fun to spend the day with me?"

"I wasn't sure."

"You could damage a man's ego."

"I think you have enough of one that it can take a hit."

He squeezed her tighter in retaliation. When she giggled he let her go. "Did you really think you wouldn't have a good time with me?"

"I'm not going to get the cold shoulder again after we share something personal, am I?"

"Funny, very funny. Coming from a woman I couldn't get a smile out of a week ago."

The ferry docked and they followed the other passengers down the gangplank. They spent the next two hours exploring the grounds of the statue and listening to a park ranger tell the history of the lady.

"Can we climb to the top?" Lucy asked.

"They're doing repairs. I'm sorry, it's closed. We'll come back when it opens."

"Oh, I had hoped to look out of her."

She had the sweetest pout on her face. He leaned down and gave her a quick kiss, unable to resist her pucker.

Lucy put her hand to her lips. "Why did you do that?"

"Because you look so sad."

"Oh."

He looked up at the top of the statue. If he didn't focus on something else he was afraid he'd kiss her again. She looked so adorable in her confusion. "My father brought my sisters and me here when we were kids. It was an experience to remember. Every year my father let us take turns picking some place in the city that we would like to go. This was mine. I wasn't nearly as happy with one of my sister's picks."

"What was that?"

"She wanted to go to the Met."

Lucy's laughter made him feel good deep down inside. "You don't like art?"

"I do. But as a twelve-year-old it was a punishment."

She giggled some more.

"Dad's rule was that we were to go as a family. I went but I wasn't happy about it."

"Those memories must be fun to share now." Her voice had taken on a melancholy sound.

He took her hand and gave it a gentle squeeze. "The holidays are something when we all get together. Loud and lots of fun." He stopped abruptly. His father wouldn't be here this year. That's the first time he'd allowed a thought like that to enter his mind.

This time Lucy returned his comfort. "You'll miss him."

She'd known without asking what was bothering him. He recognized her counseling voice and found it comforting. "I will." This was supposed to be a fun day for them both, and he wasn't going to let sad memories overshadow the day. "Hey, you interested in seeing Ellis Island?"

"Sure. If we have time."

"Then come on. I'll show you the name of the first O'Doherty to come to America. We can look and see if any of your family members came through too."

Lucy wasn't as confident that they would find any of her family noted as being on Ellis Island as Ryan was. Edwards was such a common name that if they did, there would be hundreds or thousands. It didn't matter. She was having such a good time that she'd go along with any idea he had.

Ryan's view of family was so different from hers. Her family life was so fractured that she could hardly remember the last time they'd all been in the same room. Could they do that now and be civil? No one had tried to get them together in a long time. Maybe it was time someone did. Yeah, right, she couldn't even face her sister.

She and Ryan stood atop the ferry taking them from Liberty Island over to Ellis Island. No other tourist braved the chilly air. The wind was cold but Ryan wrapped his arm around her shoulder and she burrowed into his warmth. He gave her a history lesson on the two islands and the museum over the roar of the engines. After he finished one story, she looked up at him and said, "You're a great tour guide but…"

Ryan raised a brow as if she'd dared to question his skills.

"Sometimes you talk so fast I only understand the first and last words." She grinned at him.

"Let me see if this is slow enough for you." His lips brushed hers, teased and tasted.

She was falling for the guy. Falling hard.

Was it that he'd offered her the first real happiness she'd had in months or was she just so desperate to be noticed for who she was that she'd fall for anybody who gave her attention? She'd always been the youngest, had stood in Alexis's shadow as the quieter one, had been the baby carrier, and now she wanted to be the one who stood out.

Ryan made her feel special. She was going to go with that feeling, revel in it, experience it, grasp it and hold it tight for as long as she could.

CHAPTER SIX

LUCY HELD RYAN's hand as they exited the boat and entered the Ellis Island National Monument. The warehouse-type building had housed immigrants who had funneled through on their way to gaining freedom and new citizenship. Still hand in hand, Ryan showed her around the different levels, wandering past black and white pictures of people who had stayed on the island.

She probably should have removed her hand but didn't want to. His friendly but secure clasp gave her a feeling of belonging. What would it mean to truly belong to Ryan O'Doherty?

"I often wonder what it must have been like to leave everything you know and love behind and pick up and move somewhere else," Ryan commented as they looked at a picture of a man holding a child in his arms. "I don't know if I could do that."

Hadn't she done that very same thing? Just not on as grand a scale as leaving the country where she had been born. In many ways, she was no different. She was struggling to find her place in the world.

"They had to work to rebuild their lives."

She was doing that also. The job was there but she floundered with the other aspects. Today had been the first day that she'd felt like her old self in a long time. She liked it.

"Let's go have a look at that book." Ryan directed her toward the center of the large building. He stopped before a glass case. Inside lay an old register with names written in faded ink.

"Come on." He grabbed her hand and gently pulled her towards a computer screen on a wall nearby. He sounded as excited as a kid wanting to show off a toy. "All you do is type your last name in and see what comes up."

"You do yours first." She didn't know much about her family tree. That hadn't been a priority when her parents had been together. Certainly hadn't been mentioned after their divorce. Even her grandparents had deserted her.

"All right." Ryan tapped the keys.

A list came up on the screen of all the O'Dohertys who had passed through Ellis Island.

"See, this is my grandfather." Ryan pointed with his index finger. "He was just a baby then. These are his siblings. All nine of them." He ran his fingertip down the list of names. "I can't imagine having nine children," he said in wonder.

"That does seem excessive." Her heart caught. She'd given birth to a child.

"A couple sounds like plenty to me," he said offhandedly.

Pain filled her. She'd already had a baby. "That sounds about right," she said dryly.

"I'm sorry. I shouldn't have said that."

She shrugged. "It's okay. I have to learn to live with it. Move on. It's a fact and I can't change it."

He gave her a quick hug. "I think you're doing a great job." He kissed the top of her head and let her go.

She appreciated his show of support. If she wasn't careful she could get too used to it. "Tell me about this grandfather or great-grandfather who picked up and moved his whole family."

"Well, he was pretty much like everybody else who came through here. He was Irish and wanted a better life. Settled in Brooklyn, worked hard but had little other than family. And family is everything."

"And your dad and mom?"

He looked away as if he wouldn't answer then he turned back to her. "Mom was the local girl who married the big Irish policeman who came into the café where she worked. Mother used to say she fell in love with his Irish brogue and the rest of him just came with it."

"So that's where you get the hint of an inflection intermingled with your Brooklyn clip."

He chuckled. "That's a nice way of putting it. Mostly the Brooklyn has taken over but every once in a while the Irish really shows through."

"How old were you when your mother died?"

"Thirteen."

She didn't miss the hitch of pain in the word. "Your sisters?"

"My sisters were a number of years younger. Dad became both parents."

"That must have been tough, on all of you."

"It was, but I think it was toughest on Dad. He'd lost the love of his life. He wasn't only the breadwinner but he had to be the stable factor in our lives when his was crumbling."

"Crumbling?"

He hesitated as if he didn't want to say more. "He got sick. He developed motor neuron disease."

"You had said he'd died but not that he'd died so slowly. That must have been horrible for him. You and your sisters." She grasped one of his biceps and squeezed, hoping to relay her sympathy.

As if he'd gone off into the past, he continued, "I saw him struggle to keep his job for as long as he could. Then be forced to give up one more thing he loved."

He needed to talk. She knew not only from her experience as a counselor but because she'd been in the same place when her parents had divorced and again when she'd left Alexis and Emily. Ryan and she had both known loss.

"I had to watch this rock of a man slowly die. He had to be put into a nursing home. I thought it might kill him to go but I was the one it almost killed. I hated it that he needed to be there."

Ryan was pouring out his pain like water that had been dammed and needed a place to go. How long had he been keeping all this pain to himself? No wonder he'd isolated himself from the families of his patients. She felt troubled. She'd pushed him to be more open.

"You carried the responsibility, didn't you? For everything. Him, your sisters. For holding things together."

He looked at her as if amazed. As if for the first time he recognized that someone understood.

"Yeah. I visited him as often as I could. Took care of my sisters."

Ryan's reaction to what she'd told him about Emily suddenly made sense. He'd supported others' emotions for so long that he didn't want to carry hers. She hadn't once heard anyone at the hospital talk about his father having just died. She bet he'd never let on to anyone what he was going through. He'd just shared a part of himself that few saw. She was honored to be one of those people.

"You're a good man, Ryan O'Doherty." She would have hugged him but she didn't think he would appreciate that much pity. He was also a proud man.

"Are you through?" a man with a wife and couple of kids standing nearby asked.

"Yes," Ryan said, stepping away from the computer.

He took her hand again and she gave his a squeeze. She didn't want him to close himself off like he'd done before.

As they walked toward the entrance, Ryan said, "We didn't look up your family name." He turned as if to go back.

She tugged on his hand. "We'll do it next time." Would there be a next time? It would be nice if there was. She was enjoying her day with Ryan.

They boarded the ferry that would take them back to Manhattan and found a spot inside, out of the late afternoon wind.

"Are you hungry?"

Lucy found to her surprise she was, in more ways than one. "I'm getting that way."

"If we have another hot chocolate, will that hold you over for an hour or so?"

"I think I can survive that long."

"Do you like Chinese?"

"I do."

"Then Chinese it is." He pulled out his phone and made a call before he left to order their hot drinks.

They said little as they sipped their hot chocolate. Lucy was surprised how quickly she'd become comfortable in Ryan's presence. They had bonded in a way she'd never expected they would or could. After their first meeting she would have said it was impossible for them to find common ground.

"Look here," Ryan said.

"What's wrong?"

He leaned over and kissed her, his tongue lightly brushing her upper lip. It was quick and warm and, oh, so short.

When he pulled away she said, "Why did you do that? You could have told me and I would have used a napkin."

His blue eyes danced with mischief. "If I'd done that I wouldn't have gotten that last extra sweet taste of chocolate."

"No, I guess you wouldn't have."

She was having fun. She looked into the eyes of the big, sensitive, caring and highly intelligent man beside her with the devilish sense of humor and knew she'd lost her ability to be rational about him. She had real feelings for the guy. It was an intoxicating while at the same time disturbing reality. Would there be more heartache in her future?

Ryan licked his lips as if getting every last drop of chocolate from them and grinned at her. "You have any more to share?"

"I do not." She looked so indignant that he laughed. She grinned at him.

He couldn't believe that he'd told Lucy so much about his father. He'd never confided to anyone outside his family and for the most part he'd not even done that. His father had been an intensely proud man and Ryan had been gifted with that same propensity, good or bad. It was an issue of pride for Ryan that he could handle his own problems. He'd never shared his innermost feelings with anyone before but Lucy made him feel secure enough to do so.

Why had he? He should feel naked and vulnerable now that she knew so much about him. Instead, relief had washed over him at being able to tell someone about the burden of loss and pain he carried. He found it rather liberating.

"Hey, I've been meaning to ask you where you learned to speak Spanish so well. I don't think of Georgia as the go-to place."

"I learned it from my father's Mexican housekeeper at his home in LA. Alexis and I spent a lot of time with her. I just picked it up."

He pulled her to him and smiled down at her. "And it came in handy a few times."

"Just a few?" She smiled shyly back at him.

He wanted to kiss her, not a quick peck or a teasing brush but a real kiss right there in front of everybody. He brought her against him. His lips met her soft warm ones that tasted faintly of chocolate.

She grabbed his coat and pulled, going up on her toes. Her acceptance fed his desire. He requested admission with the end of his tongue, and she granted it. Entering, he found a heated cavern of pleasure. This was a kiss.

"Hey, buddy. Get a room," someone called.

Lucy jerked away, but she still had handfuls of his coat. Her eyes were large and awestruck, her lips cherry red from his kiss.

"Was that a friendly kiss?"

He laughed. "The friendliest. Come on…" He took her hand.

"Where are we going?"

"My place."

"I'm going to see those lights?"

"Yes."

"Ryan, I don't think—"

"I said fun and no pressure, remember? I keep my word."

"That would be the O'Doherty way."

"Yes, it would."

Lucy was still reeling from Ryan's kiss as she followed him out of the subway into the early evening air.

They had shared a real kiss. The kiss of a man who wanted a woman. Was she stepping into water over her head? If she was, would she sink so far under Ryan's spell that she'd never come up?

They were in an area of small privately owned stores. People milled on the sidewalks in front of the stores. She'd never been to Brooklyn but she'd not expected to find the small-community feel within a large metropolis. Ryan's stride changed, became more leisurely, as if he'd returned home.

"I live about a half a mile from here. Would you like to walk or should I call for a taxi?"

"Walking would be nice. I'd like to see where you grew up."

As they strolled hand in hand Ryan spoke to a shop owner, introduced her to a former high school teacher and her husband. Others waved or called out to him. It was a community proud of their home-grown boy done well.

"You love living here, don't you?"

"What's not to love? And I've known nothing else."

"Never thought of moving on up? The super-neurosurgeon who outgrew his roots?"

"No, here suits me just fine."

And it did. What was it like to be that secure in those around you that you knew you belonged?

They walked down a small hill that had a line of new-looking condos that had not been constructed to look so modern that they didn't blend with the rest of the buildings along the waterfront. At the one closest to the East River, Ryan stopped in front of a door stained a dark color. He fished in his pocket and pulled out keys.

"You live here?" Lucy made no effort to hide her amazement. "What a beautiful spot." Across the East River was Lower Manhattan with all its enormous buildings, including those around Wall Street.

"Come on in," Ryan said as he opened the door. "Our Chinese should be here soon. We'll eat out on the deck."

He led her straight through the living room, stopping long enough to flip on a light in the kitchen before they went out a glass door to a deck. It ran the length of the condo out the back and had a privacy fence separating him from his neighbor. There was a small table with two chairs and an oversized and wide lounge that faced the city.

"I think we timed it just right for dinner and a show."

She put her hands on her hips and gave him a skeptical look. "So you're sticking with that story?"

"I am."

"We eat and then the light show begins."

The doorbell buzzed. "That will be our supper."

While Ryan was gone, Lucy looked across the river, watching the shadows begin to fall across the buildings and the orange of the western sky become the backdrop. Ryan had a lovely place to live.

He returned with two paper bags filled with wonderful-smelling food. "I thought we'd have a picnic. Eat out of the boxes. Share." Going back inside, he brought out two glasses and a bottle of wine. With minimal effort he opened the bottle and poured them both drinks. He then pulled boxes and other items out of the sacks and placed them on the table. "Have a seat."

She pulled out a chair and sat. "Is there a fork?"

"Fork! There are no forks with Chinese food." He grinned at her as he picked up chopsticks covered in paper and handed them to her with a flair of a magician. "Have any experience?"

"A little."

"I'll help you." He opened a box of rice, pushed it toward her and opened another for himself. A larger container with chicken and broccoli he placed between them. He stripped the paper off the chopsticks and manipulated them like a pro between his lean fingers. She shouldn't have been surprised. The dexterity he used to do delicate brain surgery would lend itself to using chopsticks to eat.

She followed suit with the chopsticks but her ability was much more hit and miss than his. Ryan laughed when she must have looked like a snapping turtle going after a morsel before it fell back into the box.

"You're going to starve at that rate and I'm going to look like a poor host. Let me help." He scooted closer and offered her a bite on the end of his chopsticks.

She continued to make efforts of her own while he filled in between them. Over one offering she looked up and found him looking at her intently. It was heady to be the center of his attention. One who loved those he cared about so totally. She could be overwhelmed by his magnetism with little effort on his part.

Ryan looked away, breaking the moment, and dropped his chopsticks into an empty container. He stood and put out his hand. "Come on, we're going to miss the show."

She put her palm against his and stood. He led her to the lounger. Letting go of her hand, he settled into the chair and stretched out his long legs. "Join me." He patted the space next to him.

The lounge should have been large enough for two but with Ryan's size it seemed far too small. "There's not enough room for both of us. I'll just pull a chair over here."

"I'll make room." He scooted over as if he planned to give her plenty of room. "The show's much better from here."

She sat alongside him. They touched from shoulder to foot. She pulled her coat closer around her. He picked up a blanket from beside the chair and spread it over their legs. "Lift your head." She did so and he slid an arm behind her neck, resting his hand on her shoulder. He tucked her closer. "Relax."

"I am relaxed."

"No, you're not. You're as tight as a guitar string."

She shifted and found a more comfortable position.

"You know, if you keep that up this may not remain just a light show between friends."

She stiffened. What had she been thinking to agree to this?

Ryan chuckled. "I'm kidding. I'm not going to do anything that you don't want me to."

Hadn't he kept his word so far? The problem was, she wanted him to do plenty. Settling next to him and clasping her hands in her lap, she looked at the horizon. The lights of the city began to flicker on. "Oh, this is amazing. I just saw the lights on the top of the Chrysler Building come on."

"It's beautiful." He fingered the tail of her braid, which was lying against her arm.

"Thanks for sharing this with me. It's everything you said it was."

"You're welcome."

They continued to watch until the kaleidoscope of colors from the buildings reflected off the water. Could anything be more wonderful than being in Ryan's arms and watching the sun set to a beautiful light show?

"Wow, this view is something. You must be in demand as a date for this alone."

"So you think my sex appeal is location-related?" He spoke so close to her ear that his warm breath brushed her skin.

She kept her focus on the lights of the city. "I think you're fishing for a compliment."

"Maybe. I thought I told you that I don't bring people home."

"By people, do you mean women?"

"Yes. Women. You're the only woman who has ever shared my view."

She sat up and twisted around so she could look down at him. "Why?"

His fingers played with the end of her braid, which now fell over one breast. His look met hers. "Because," he said, his voice low, "you're the only one I've ever wanted to share it with." Wrapping a hand around the mass of hair, he tugged gently, bringing her down to him. His hand cupped her head as he guided her mouth to his. His breath brushed her lips. "I'm going to kiss you. It won't be a friendly kiss. If you don't want this, you need to tell me to stop now."

"The O'Doherty way? A gentleman always." Her lips touched his.

He pulled her head closer, slanting his mouth and taking the kiss deeper. His tongue found the seam of her lips and demanded entrance. When she didn't immediately open he pulled back and placed small searching kisses along her bottom lip. He shifted her until she lay along him. Her body followed the contours of his.

Did heaven feel like this?

When the bill of her cap hit him in the forehead she reached up and pulled it off.

He ran his hand down her braid. "I love your hair. You have no idea how many times I've wanted to touch it."

She reached to remove the band. What little light there was spilled out from the kitchen.

"No, don't. I want to be the one who sets it free." His voice had gone low and gruff, creating tingles inside her.

Gently he removed the band from the end. He drew a finger between the sections of the braid, slowly releasing them as if he were opening a present he'd been eager to see for weeks. His sure, precise movements told of his skill as a surgeon. What she did to her hair every day he turned into a sensual experience.

"I know of no one who has hair as beautiful as yours." He fanned his fingers out and ran them over her head, finishing the job. The waves fell about her shoulders and flowed around them. Filling his hands, Ryan watched in fascination as it spilled between his fingers. He brought a long lock to his cheek, sliding it across his skin.

His mouth returned to hers and this time when he asked, she opened. His tongue entered, savored, sipped and swirled, while his hands burrowed into her hair to hold her head.

She squirmed.

"Easy, honey. We have all night if you wish." His tone was low and soothing but the tension in his body and the ridge below her hip said he was just as aroused as she was.

Her hands traveled up his chest and wrapped around his neck. Her mouth came down to his, then tugged on his bottom lip before she pressed her mouth firmly against his, letting him know just how much she desired him.

His hands spread her hair out along her back and moved to her waist. He ran a hand under her coat and lightly grazed the inch of bare skin separating her shirt from her pants.

She shivered.

He released her mouth and kissed his way across her cheek to nuzzle behind her ear. His hands glided over the hyper-sensitive skin of her back.

She moaned.

"You like that, do you?" He nuzzled her again while his hands pushed her shirt upwards. He released her bra, his fingertips grazing the under-curve of her breast.

She flinched at the shock of sensation that rocketed through her. His fingertips were prickling heat and softest torture as they trailed over her skin.

"Lift up, honey."

"We can't do this here?"

"Why not?" He hushed her opposition by bringing his mouth to hers and giving her another mind-altering kiss. "Are you cold?"

If he continued to kiss her like that, she'd do anything he wanted. She arched her back, allowing him to push her coat away. The movement brought her center into intimate contact with his rigid manhood.

Ryan O'Doherty wanted her. *Her.*

"Put your hands on my shoulders."

She did so and he stripped her shirt and bra away. Before she could lower her arms his mouth found a nipple. His lips dropped away with infinite slowness. His actions and the cold air touching her sensitive tip caused her to shudder.

His low chuckle was one of pure male satisfaction.

She hadn't recovered from the honeyed moment before Ryan showed the same mind-blowing attention to the other breast. His hands skimmed her waist then flowed leisurely upwards until his hands cupped both breasts. He lifted, and weighed them.

They'd changed while she'd carried Emily. Would he mind?

"Perfection," he murmured, before he kissed the tip of each one again.

Not recovered from his devotion, she sucked in a swift breath when his hands skimmed downwards and dipped below the waist of her jeans while he left kisses across her breasts. She whimpered.

"More?"

"Mmm." She sounded entirely too sensual even to her own ears. Ryan was making her feel more than she'd ever felt before and he'd done little more than kiss her.

She brought her hands down to his chest. He shifted so they lay facing each other and continued to fondle her breasts as if he found them extremely fascinating. She was grateful he couldn't see them well. They weren't as firm or high as they had been before Emily.

Her hand slid down to the edge of his sweater to play with the hem.

"You can touch me," Ryan said before he nipped at her earlobe. "In fact, I wish you would," he said as he found her mouth again.

She accepted his invitation and slid her hands under his pullover. It was warm there but his T-shirt still created a barrier. Touching skin was her goal.

Ryan must have heard her groan of frustration because he let go of her and pulled his jacket off and then his sweater. Jerked his shirt from his waistband. "I might lose my mind before you get up the nerve."

"I don't want to do anything wrong."

He leaned back so that he could look at her face. "This isn't your first time, is it?"

"No, but it's been a long time. I wasn't the girl with the most boyfriends."

A soft smile of satisfaction came to his lips. "I'm surprised there weren't hundreds." She gave him her best "I don't believe that" look, which he answered with another kiss.

"Honey, the only thing you can do wrong is not do." His lips went to her collarbone and moved lower.

She ran her hand under his shirt and upwards until he was forced to remove it too. "That's better," she said as she wrapped her arms around his neck and pulled him to her. "Cold?"

"No. How about you?"

"Mmm. No."

Ryan went willingly towards her. The touch of her breasts against his bare chest almost ended any further foreplay. Her hair dropped around them like a silk curtain.

He had to have her. Soon.

Her hands fluttered over his skin, creating tiny points

of pleasure as they went, but he wanted more. That shyness that he'd seen earlier had returned. It intrigued him that someone so sure of herself in some areas was so completely insecure in others. Cupping Lucy's bottom, he brought her snugly against his manhood, letting her know clearly what she was doing to him.

Lucy flexed in answer, making his heartbeat rise, his blood pound in his head. Her lips found his chest as if she'd discovered the perfect playground. Her cheek rested just far enough above his torso for her to rub against his chest hair. Her warm breath blew gently against his skin, driving his desire higher. The fascination and pleasure she found in him was like balm to his damaged heart.

Ryan stroked along the waistband of her jeans. Each time he dipped beneath he was rewarded with a hitch in her breathing. He brushed her hair away from her face so that he could watch as she explored him. When he went to unfasten her jeans she grabbed his wrist.

"What's wrong, honey? All I want to do is touch you."

"I've…uh…had a baby. Things have been…stretched, moved around."

He kissed her, showing her just how sexy he found her. "I'd be surprised if they hadn't been." He kissed her again. "Come on. I think it's time we go in."

At her stricken look, he grinned. "I said nothing about being done. We're just going to try a little experiment."

"I don't think I'm ready for that."

"I'm positive you are." He climbed out of the chair and stood. Grateful for the cool air circling him, he ached for want of her.

She reached for her shirt and he snatched it way.

"You're not going to need that. Wrap up in the blanket. I'll get our clothes."

Taking her hand, he opened the deck door, led her through and kicked it closed behind them. He had no intention of letting her go. With that rabbit-in-the-headlights look in her eyes, he was afraid she might run. He kept her hand firmly in his as they climbed the metal stairs with the cable-wire handrails to his bedroom.

CHAPTER SEVEN

LUCY'S BREATH CAUGHT. Ryan's bedroom had a large picture window that shared the same view as the deck. His bed faced the scene. He turned on a small lamp sitting atop a dresser. It gave off just enough light to see well but not so bright as to be harsh.

Ryan led her to the bed. He let go of her hand and rested his hands on each of her shoulders. He gently pushed down until she sat on the edge. He backed away, just out of touching distance. Despite still being wrapped in the blanket, she felt more undressed than he was. She wanted him close, close enough that she could run her fingers over his muscled chest before she lost her nerve. Lifting a hand, she reached out. Capturing it, he gently squeezed her fingers and backed up a pace. He grinned. "I've created a monster."

"Ryan—" She started to stand.

"Just listen a minute."

She sank to the edge of the bed.

"In this room there will be no barriers. Be it clothes, emotions or thoughts. We can do and say anything without it leaving these walls."

"O'Doherty law," she murmured.

"Yes."

The more he spoke the less she could control her

hands. They shook. She clutched the blanket, hoping he wouldn't see.

Ryan removed his socks and shoes, dropping them on the floor. His hands went to his jeans, flipping the button from the hole. She couldn't look away, her concentration on the movement of his fingers. The only sound in the room was their breathing.

He pushed his pants down to the floor and stepped out of them. The evidence of his desire tented his boxers as he stood in front of her. The heat between her legs, banked when they'd come in the house, flowed again. This time it grew stronger. Ryan looked like a god standing before a display of multicolored lights. She was speechless.

"You're scaring me, Lucy. But I love it."

She blinked. "There's that ego."

"Yeah, and the way you're looking at me only makes it and other parts grow."

Unable to help herself, she stared at his manhood, which stood tall and proud between them. She promptly blushed when her gaze met his pleased one.

Completely confident, he came toward her. Why shouldn't he be? She drew in a shallow breath. He was stunning. The total cliché Irish package—dark skin, expansive shoulders, thick hair and a grin to die for. The mind-boggling thing was that he was hers for the taking.

He stood so close, all bare and beautiful. She didn't know where to look, finally focusing on a spot on the wall. He reached out a hand. She placed hers in his.

He tugged her to him, giving her a kiss that started a fire in her. "Now you go stand where I did."

"What?" Her heart fluttered in her chest. She drew the blanket tighter.

"You heard me. It's your turn. I'm going to watch."

She shook her head. "I can't."

"I think you can. I went first so it's only fair that you go."

She dragged the blanket with her and turned to find him sitting on the bed where she had been.

"Let it go."

She shook her head. "I've never stripped before."

"Look at me, Lucy." His words were said so softly yet with such force that he left her no doubt he'd accept nothing less than her compliance. Her gaze found his.

"I want to make love to you. All of you. Your mind, body and soul. I want a strong, self-assured woman in my bed and I know you are that woman. Let the blanket go."

She fought a war in her mind. Part of her wanted to let the blanket fall but the insecure side screamed not to. Ryan's expression never wavered. He believed in her. Did she believe in herself?

Taking a deep breath as if preparing to jump off a cliff into water, she let go. Unable to stop herself, her arms covered her breasts.

"Put your arms down. I want to admire you."

Her confidence level wrenched upwards. Ryan wanted to admire, not just see.

"You are a goddess. Your hair is gorgeous. The way it falls over your breasts and flirts with your waist. I want to feel it all around me. Caress all the places it touches."

She bit her bottom lip.

"Now your socks and shoes."

Lucy bent to do his bidding. Her breasts hung before her and she knew without looking that his focus centered on them. In a fit of courage she pulled her hair away so that he had a clear view.

When her gaze met his again, his held a pained look. His eyes were hooded and his lips tight, as if he was working to restrain himself. Still she hesitated at the snap of her jeans. What if he didn't like what he saw?

"Lucy."

He wasn't asking, he was demanding that she meet him halfway. She flipped the button and unzipped her jeans. With a shimmy, they fell to the floor. Ryan's look flicked downwards but quickly returned to hold hers. She stepped out of her pants and stood before him in her pink panties.

"All or nothing, Lucy, your choice. This can start here or you can run and hide."

The last words made her loop her thumbs in her panties and shove them down.

She didn't miss his gasp in the silent room.

"Perfect. Completely perfect in every way. Come here."

She gradually moved toward him. His eyes held her mesmerized. He hadn't touched her but his gaze spoke of admiration, desire as it stroked each part of her body.

Ryan widened his legs and she walked between them until her knees touched the bed. He placed his hands on her waist. They trembled slightly. That encouraged her. It was empowering to know she affected this strong, highly intelligent man so.

He pressed his lips to her belly.

A quiver ran though her.

"You're a beautiful woman. Every silky inch of you." His lips slipped upward in a caress that made her skin tingle. "All glorious woman," he murmured against her ribs before his mouth moved down the curve of her hip. "Perfection."

He liked what he saw.

Lucy's hand cupped the back of his head and held it there. For the first time in a long time she felt like a complete woman, whole again. This man before her had just given her a precious gift.

Ryan leaned back on the bed and pulled her on top of him. "I want you, Lucy. Now. I don't think I can wait any longer." His lips found hers and his kiss was hot and demanding.

She shifted, settling more intimately against his hard body, and deepened the kiss in answer.

Minutes later he rolled, taking her with him so that she was beneath him. "Let go a sec." She did. He stood, found his pants and pulled a packet from a pocket.

"You were so sure of me you had a condom in your pocket?"

"Just a man with a dream."

Ryan lifted her against him. Carrying her to the top of the bed, he sat her down and pulled the covers back then eased her under the sheets. He came down beside her and she watched as he sheathed himself.

"We'll go slower next time, I promise. But right now I've got to have you."

He entered her. When she tensed he stopped and eased away but returned and went deeper with each movement. Lucy spiraled higher, higher until there was nothing but bliss.

Ryan was but one thrust behind.

Could she be in love? Yes, she already was.

Lucy woke to the sun shining and sounds of a steady heartbeat beneath her ear as her cheek rested on Ryan's chest. He lay on his back, one hand thrown across the huge bed and the other curling over her bare hip beneath the sheet. She wadded a corner of the material in her hand and pulled it up to cover her breasts.

He'd proved more than once during the night that he didn't find her post-baby body less than fascinating. In fact, he'd taken time to express with words as well as actions that he appreciated her body and found her desirable. No dip or crevice had been overlooked. He'd spent an inordinate amount of time along the insides of her thighs. She warmed deep within from the memory.

From where her head rested in the arch of his shoulder, she watched as she skimmed her palm over the soft mat of hair covering the center of his chest, seeing the individual strands dance. Lifting her hand a fraction of an inch higher, she let her hand just tickle the ends of each curly hair. She found all of him irresistible. Too much so.

Was this the beginning of something truly wonderful or was she headed for heartache all over again? She wanted what Alexis had but could she trust herself enough to know if this was real? Could her heart stand devastation again?

She sighed heavily.

"Hey, what was that for? You could make a guy feel insecure, sounding like that."

She placed her lips on his chest and turned to look up at him. "First thing in the morning and you're already fishing for a compliment."

"I don't have to fish. I know how good I am by the way you put all those extra syllables in my name as you climax."

She buried her face in his shoulder. A smile of pure satisfaction crossed her lips. The man knew how to make her feel wanted and special. She stroked his hair.

"And I found out when that Irish in your speech makes an appearance."

"Great." He kissed the top of her head. "I have a 'tell'?"

"Oh, I could tell all right." She giggled as her hand traveled lower.

"Lucy." That soft Irish burr became stronger, circling her name like a caress. "You want to hear more?"

"I think I just might."

A long satisfying hour later, Ryan asked, "Is there anything special you'd like to do today? I have to check in at the hospital but I'm all yours after that."

"I don't know…"

"How about I make breakfast then take you to the St. Regis Hotel for afternoon tea."

"You like tea? I think of you more of a baseball and hotdog guy."

"I am, but the season hasn't started yet. I've heard my sister talking about going to tea and how much she enjoyed it. I just thought you might like it as well."

"So you like froufrou? Amazing."

"Froufrou?" He curled up his nose.

"You know—tea, violin music, garden parties."

"Hell, no!"

She laughed at the appalled look on his face.

"Really, tea at the St. Regis sounds wonderful. I'd just like to be dressed appropriately. So while you're at the hospital I'll go home and change."

"Sounds good."

Ryan dropped Lucy off at her place and went to the hospital to check on his patients. He stopped in his office long enough to make reservations at the St. Regis Hotel. He already missed Lucy and it had only been a few hours since he'd seen her. She had an effect on him like no other woman had ever had. Snatching his sports jacket off the coat rack in his office, he went out the door with a smile on his face. A decision about where their affair might go didn't have to be made today. They'd just enjoy being together and see where that led.

He climbed the steps to Lucy's apartment two at a time, unable to wait to kiss her again. He'd made fun of his brothers-in-law and rolled his eyes when they'd acted like this about his sisters. He hoped they never found out that he was walking around with a syrupy smile on his face. If they did, he'd pay for all the times he'd laughed at them.

At his knock on Lucy's door, someone opened it. *Was he at the correct door?*

He'd expected a simple but elegantly dressed woman whose hair was in place and a shy smile of greeting. Maybe a slight blush from heated memories of their night together. Instead, the woman in front of him had hair that stood out in wild disarray around her face and shoulders as if she been tugging on it then running her fingers through it. Her mouth was pinched in a hard line and her eyes were red-rimmed. She wore baggy sweats and an old hoodie.

What had happened to the happy, smiling Lucy he'd left a few hours ago? She'd even volunteered a good-bye kiss without him asking. A delicious kiss at that.

"Lucy, honey, what's happened?"

"They're here in town!"

"Who?" Aliens, terrorists, the IRS? From the look of alarm in her eyes, he could only think the worst.

"Alexis, Sam and Emily."

He cocked his head to the side. "Alexis. Your sister?"

He made no effort to keep the astonishment out of his voice. Was that what this was all about?

She nodded.

"That's great. I'd love to meet them."

"It isn't great," she all but shouted before she turned to pace the room. Grasping her hair, she pulled it back and let it go to fall in wild array around her face again. The woman who kept tight control over her hair and didn't raise her voice had made an abrupt change.

He stepped into the apartment and shut the door behind him. As she came by him the second time, he caught her hand and pulled her into a hug. She stood inflexible in his arms for a moment before she wrapped her arms around his waist. He held her. It wasn't until her shoulders shook and spots on his chest felt damp through his shirt that he realized she was crying. "Honey, you're not making sense. You're going to have to tell me what's going on if you expect me to help."

"I don't expect you to help."

That hurt on a level he didn't want to explore. At a loss how to respond, he said, "I'd like to." To his surprise, he meant it. He placed his hands on her shoulders and pushed her away until he could see her face. She wore the classical look of panic. Taking her hand, he led her to the bed.

"Let's sit down and you tell me what has you in such a state."

She dropped to her bed. He took a spot beside her, close enough to touch her but not so close it was difficult to read her facial expressions.

"Look, Ryan, I don't want to go into it. I'm sorry about not going to tea, but I'd just like to be left alone."

"I'm not leaving you like this."

She made a movement to get up, but he grabbed her hand and held her in place. "Talk to me, Lucy."

It took so long for her to answer he was afraid she might not.

"Alexis wants to see me."

"Of course she wants to see you, you're her sister."

She buried her face in her hands. "I'll just have to tell her I'm too busy at work to meet them. I've only been here a few weeks and I can't get away." She spoke as if he wasn't there any longer.

"What? Why? I would think you'd be glad to see her. Especially Emily."

She flinched at the baby's name.

"I know it'll be hard but you don't want to live with regret in your life. If you really think about it, you want to." He stood and looked down at the top of her head. "Of course you're going to see her. They're your family. They came all this way."

Lucy jumped up and went to stand at the window. "If I see Alexis, she'll know."

"Know what? I realize you had a hard time giving up Emily but this has to go beyond that. You're an intelligent woman. You knew all along that was the plan."

She twisted away from the view of the top of a tree outside to look at him. Her face was contorted with pain. "You don't get it," she spat. "It's not just about Emily. It's about me." She poked at her chest a couple of times. "How I feel. About how I shouldn't feel."

He stepped toward her into her personal space in an effort to intimidate her into expressing her true feelings. If she got mad enough, maybe the truth would come out. "Then tell me how you feel."

She looked down at the floor. "I'm jealous of what she has. Her happiness. Her perfect little family. There's no place for me. I'm miserable when I'm around them. In the way. And worse than that, I hate myself for feeling that way." She spat out the words. "The best thing for them and me is to stay away from each other."

Ryan jerked back, his heart constricting. She couldn't mean that. Family was everything. No matter how hard you had to work at it, you stayed together, cared for each other, did what had to be done. "Lucy, you don't mean that. I took care of my sisters, my father as he slowly died, and I would do it all over again if I had to. That's what a family does."

Her head jerked up. She leaned towards him and looked him in the eye. "I'm not you."

"You're more like me than you think," he said quietly. Had he misread her? His family was the center of his life. How could he be interested in someone who didn't understand the value of family? He took a deep breath, getting control of his own emotions.

"Lucy," he said in a quiet, soothing voice, hoping his even tone would make her speak and think more rationally. "You cared enough to carry a baby for her. You put your life on hold, took a risk to your body. Those are not signs of someone who doesn't care. She's your twin. That bond will always be there. Even if you want to hide from her."

As if a bubble had been popped she deflated before his eyes. All the fight fizzled out of her. He enveloped her in a hug. She hung on as if he were her lifeline.

"Honey, you need to see your sister. Work through these feelings."

Her fingers dug in, then relaxed on his back. He could feel her struggle within herself.

"Go with me," Lucy said against his chest.

He'd never planned to become her emotional support but having her in his arms made him want to be there for her. He'd been the emotional rock for his family through the last ten years while his father had been dying. He'd had enough.

That had been until Lucy had come into his life, demanding he care again. To his astonishment, he wanted to be that rock of support for Lucy. He didn't know how she'd done it but there it was. He wanted her to be happy. She needed to see her sister if she was ever to let go and find contentment.

"I don't know. I think you need to see her alone. Work though this without me getting in the way."

"But if you came with me as moral support?"

He looked into her pale face and pleading eyes. "Your family doesn't even know me, honey. Under these circumstances, I don't think that would be the best time to meet."

"But you said you wanted to meet my sister."

That had been before he'd realized the emotional strain Lucy was under. He was just coming to grips with his feelings for her. He wasn't ready to make the commitment of meeting her family.

She gave him a pointed look as if this was going to be the make-or-break moment in their relationship. If he became her emotional support this time, would she expect him to always be there for her? Could he do that?

"I understand." She stepped back. Smoothing her hair and squaring her shoulders, she looked at him with her large eyes peppered with bone-deep pain.

Guilt washed over him. "Okay." Even to his own ears he didn't sound enthusiastic.

Relief filled Lucy. Having Ryan with her when she faced Alexis would help strengthen her. The shame formed a lump in her stomach, making her want to double over in pain. Admitting to Ryan her feelings about Emily had been difficult enough, but to have to confess her pathetic feelings of jealousy had been far worse.

How could she explain to Alexis she was envious of her? Her own sister? That it hurt to be around her and her family. She wanted to be a part of that unit but she wasn't. That she had seen her sister's resentment. If you really loved someone, you shouldn't be jealous of them. You should want the best for them. Be happy for them, but…

Lucy wrapped her arms around Ryan's neck and hugged him. "Thank you. I really appreciate it." This was one thing she didn't want to do alone.

He gave her a quick kiss. "You're welcome, honey." He sounded sincere but there was still an unsure look in his eyes. "So when do we see them?"

"They're staying in an apartment near Times Square. Sam's company keeps it for employee travel. Alexis wanted to come here but I told her it was too small and they didn't need to be hauling Emily up three flights. They want me to come to dinner this evening."

"Okay. You call and let your sister know that you're coming and make sure it's all right for me to come along."

"I'm really sorry I've dumped my personal problems on you."

"Stop saying you're sorry. We'll get through this."

A stricken look crossed his face for a second but soon changed to a gentle smile. He'd said *we*. Was she asking too much of him? Was this too personal, too involved for him?

Ryan held her hand while she spoke to her sister. Afterwards, his hands went to her shoulders. He turned her round and nudged her towards the bathroom. "Now go and get yourself together."

Ryan's deep voice speaking to a person at the St. Regis was the last thing she heard before stepping under the shower. Through still unsure how she'd handle seeing Emily or Alexis again, she felt reassured that Ryan would be there with her. Twenty minutes later she came out of the bathroom dressed in a robe with her wet hair twisted in a towel on top of her head.

Ryan sat on her small sofa, making it look very inadequate for his large size. One ankle was propped on the other knee. He'd removed his jacket, leaving it hung over the top of a chair at the table. Amazingly, he seemed right at home in the small apartment.

He had the phone to his ear. From the questions he was asking, he was speaking to someone at the hospital. His dedication to his job was one of the many facets of his personality she admired. Caring for his patients was his top priority. That compassion extended to her.

Looking up, he gave her a smile of encouragement. She made an effort to return it but she didn't think she pulled it off when his brows dipped in concern. The self-conscious feeling when he watched her intensified while she gathered her underwear. She wasn't used to that kind of scrutiny from anybody, particularly from a devastatingly sexy man.

She stepped into her tiny closet and pushed clothes around on the rack, unable to make up her mind about what to wear. A long arm reached past her. She squeaked.

Ryan pulled a hanger supporting an aqua-colored sweater dress off the pole. "I like you in this one." He hung it on the hook on the closet door. "You wore it the third day you came to work."

"You noticed?" She'd had no idea he'd observed her that closely.

"Yeah, I noticed a lot of things about you." Ryan reached an arm around her waist and pulled her back to his front. His fingers splayed over her robe to cover her stomach.

She rested against him, enjoying the warmth and strength of him that seeped through her. He kissed her neck. She shivered.

He moved upwards and found that spot behind her ear. The one he'd discovered the night before. He kissed it. "You're so tense. Honey, you've got to ease up on yourself or you're going to make yourself sick. I know just what to do to relieve that stress." The hand on her stomach pressed her back against him even more, leaving her in no doubt what he meant. He continued to nibble at her ear.

Her head fell against his shoulder. He slipped a hand beneath her robe and cupped a breast. She panted softly as his fingers teased, working their magic. His hand slid downwards as he pushed the robe open, leaving a trail of heat along her skin. Pulling at the belt of her robe, he gained access to her bare body. His hand inched further down. His index finger flirted with her opening then retreated. She moaned. Warm heat pooled in her.

"Lucy?"

"Mmm?"

He whispered against her ear. "What do you want?"

"More." She felt his smile against her skin.

His finger slipped in to find her core. She went up on tiptoe and leaned back against him.

"How do you feel?"

"Good."

"How good?" His finger moved again.

"Oh, so good."

Ryan watched as Lucy nibbled at her bottom lip. Her unease had increased as they'd waited for the elevator that would take them up to Alexis's floor. Letting go of his hand, she pushed at her hair. It wasn't necessary because she'd swirled and curled it, pulling the mass into a messy knot at the back of her neck. "How're you feeling?" he asked.

"I was better earlier."

She still sounded more stressed than he would have liked. She was going to scare her sister if she didn't lighten up some.

"Do we need to find a closet?" he asked.

He laughed at her stricken look. "We can't have sex every time I'm upset."

"I don't know. I'm available."

She gave a real smile for the first time since he'd left her at her apartment that morning. "Thanks for the offer. I'll keep that in mind."

He'd watched the movement of her lips and had immediately wanted to find somewhere private. Getting enough of her was becoming a problem.

As they rode up in the elevator, her frantic look became more pronounced. She fumbled with her purse, dropping it. Picking it up, Ryan handed it back to her. "Honey, take a deep breath."

She did so.

Where had the woman gone who had marched into his office and told him off in no uncertain terms?

"Now, give me your hand." He held out his hand palm up and gave her his most reassuring grin.

The door of the elevator slid open and they stepped

into the hall. Lucy's grip tightened as they neared the door of her sister's apartment, as if she was drawing strength from him. Standing in front of the door, she tried to pull her hand from his. She was going to run.

He brought her close, kissing her until she melted against him. "You can do this." He gave her another quick peck.

She nodded and squared her shoulders. Ryan knocked on the door.

CHAPTER EIGHT

LUCY WAS STILL under Ryan's spell until the door opened and Alexis rushed out, wrapping Lucy in a bear hug.

"Oh, Lucy, it's so good to see you. I've missed you." Alexis sounded as if she was choked up with happiness.

Shame washed over Lucy as she stiffened in her twin's embrace. Afraid Alexis would pick up on the slightest vibe, she returned the hug. She didn't want her sister to know, wouldn't let her know. She couldn't hurt her sister.

Alexis released her and looked at Ryan.

Lucy gathered her thoughts enough to say, "Alexis, this is Ryan O'Doherty. A…uh…friend of mine."

Ryan smiled his killer smile. "Hi, Alexis. It's nice to meet you. I knew you weren't identical twins but I still see the family resemblance in the eyes." The O'Doherty charm was flowing.

Alexis grinned.

Lucy appreciated him picking up the introduction. It gave her time to gather herself.

"Y'all come in." Alexis turned and opened the door wider.

Ryan's large warm hand rested on Lucy's back, a reassuring reminder that he was there for her. He had her back figuratively and literally.

"Your sister has a nice drawl but it isn't as sweet as yours," he whispered into her ear before closing the door behind them. As they entered the living area, a smiling Sam was carrying little Emily to meet them. Lucy froze. Ryan almost stumbled into her. Gracefully, he recovered and stood beside her. His hand brushed up then down her back, letting her know that he was aware of her response.

"Lucy, we're so glad to see you. We thought if you were too busy to come see us we'd just come see you."

"Hi, uh…Sam." She faltered with his name, her attention so completely focused on Emily.

"I'm Ryan O'Doherty."

She barely registered Ryan speaking. The two men shook hands.

Only because she'd lost the warmth of Ryan's hand did her gaze break away from the baby. She had grown so much and become more beautiful since she'd seen her.

Sam pulled her into a one-armed hug and she returned it quickly. She never wanted to see that unsure look on Alexis's face again.

Alexis's attention turned to Ryan. "So, are you the doctor who keeps Lucy so busy that she doesn't have time to call us?" She moved to stand beside Sam.

Ryan glanced at Lucy and winked. "We've been busy." His look suggested something different than hospital business.

Lucy couldn't help but give him a small smile. His wink always made her feel as if she belonged. He was trying so hard to ease her out of her worries but the intense jealousy stuck like chewed gum. Her attention turned back to the little cherub in Sam's arms. She itched to reach for Emily and pull her close to inhale her baby fresh smell. But she couldn't. It would be too hard to let her go. She stepped away to put some space between her and the child.

"This is Emily," Sam proudly said to Ryan. "Our baby girl."

For the first time the deep searing pain she normally felt when Sam made that statement wasn't as strong. Thankfully the ache was easing. Becoming what it should be. Although everything in her still begged to reach out and take Emily, but she dared not do it.

"Come on in and have a seat." Alexis directed them to the living area. Two sofas faced each other with a low table between them. "Let me take your coats. We thought we'd just have dinner catered in. It would be so much easier than going out with Emily. That way we can really talk." She placed the coats over a chair near the door.

"That sounds nice." Lucy forced out the polite comment as she took a seat on the sofa.

How had she let her feelings get so out of control that she had to make an effort to have a conversation with her sister? She didn't like it but didn't know what to do about it. It was as if she and Alexis were old friends trying to find common ground again.

They'd been everything to each other before Emily had come along. Alexis marrying Sam had changed things between them but that had been nothing compared to how they'd been after Emily had arrived. They'd once shared everything but now Lucy hid a crippling ugly secret.

Ryan sat beside her, not too close but near enough that his leg lightly touched her knee. The small contact fortified her.

"Before I settle down for a talk, I need to get Emily a bottle. Hope you like Italian, Ryan. It's Lucy's favorite."

"I shouldn't be surprised. She lives above an Italian restaurant."

Alexis looked at Lucy. "Really? I didn't know that."

"Yeah, I haven't had a chance to tell you," Lucy said.

"Well, you'll have to tell me all about it over dinner. It should be here soon," Alexis said, before going into the other room.

The doorbell rang. "That'll be our food," Sam said. "Hey, Lucy, would you hold Emily while I get that?" He handed the child to her without waiting for a reply.

Could she touch Emily and not break down? She cradled the soft, cuddly baby to her chest with trembling arms.

Sam left them.

She nuzzled Emily's neck, pulling her close.

"She's a cutie," Ryan said. "You're an exceptional person Lucy Edwards."

Her heart lightened. He thought she was special. She hadn't realized how much she'd needed to hear that. Ryan being the one who believed she was incredible made it twice as nice.

Ryan offered his finger to Emily and she clutched it with a chubby hand.

Lucy glanced at Ryan. He watched her intently with a mixture of concern and amazement on his handsome face. Was he judging her reactions?

"How're you doing?" he asked quietly.

"I'm making it." She turned to Emily so that she could see the child's face. Alexis's features were showcased there, not her own. Something shifted inside her, allowing her heart to let go. She no longer felt like a spurned mother but an aunt. Still, her envy for what

Alexis had still festered. She wanted her own child, a husband, family. To belong. To never be pushed out again.

"I'm proud of you." Ryan gave her a quick kiss on the temple.

Alexis returned. "I see that Emily's enjoying getting to know her auntie again. Hasn't she grown?"

She gave them all a bright smile and took Emily from Lucy, who let the baby go with less reluctance than she'd expected. Mercifully, Alexis was so caught up in Emily that she didn't notice how uncomfortable Lucy was. At least she'd been able to cover it well. Without Ryan's reassuring presence, she would have broken down and spilled her horrible secret.

"She *has* grown. Is she a good baby?" Lucy managed to ask, clasping her hands together.

"The best." Alexis sat, adjusted Emily and put a bottle in her mouth.

When Ryan's large hand covered hers, Lucy held on tight.

Ryan was impressed with how well Lucy was handling what he'd come to realize was an extremely difficult situation for her. She was making all the right noises and had even held Emily without breaking into pieces. He was proud of her. She was trying, but the strain showed in the tension around her lips and her rigid posture.

He'd been emotionally empty after his father had died and had kept it together only because his sisters had needed him. He never thought he'd willingly be anyone's emotional crutch again. Then along had come Lucy with her big blue eyes and quiet ways, and here he was doing everything in his power to support her, encourage her.

She could've done it without him. He'd seen her

spunk and determination when she'd told him off. It had made him feel like he was important to her when she'd asked him to come along here. She believed she needed him.

Sam brought the food to the table and came back to join them.

"Here. You finish with Emily," Alexis said, offering the baby to her husband, "and I'll take care of the food. Lucy, come help me and we can talk."

Lucy hesitated a second before she scooted away from Ryan to go to the dining table.

Lucy had given the impression she was shy when they'd met but in reality she had a backbone as sturdy as the Brooklyn Bridge and the sweetest way of showing a man that he mattered. She didn't give half. She gave all.

He glanced away from where Sam was settling in a chair with his daughter to the women moving around the table. As always his attention rested on the gutsy blonde woman. Lucy would be a fierce warrior and protector of anyone she loved. That's why she cared so deeply for Alexis and for Emily. It was who she was. She expected to receive the same in return. Would accept nothing less. Could he give it? He had no choice but to try, unable to imagine her not being in his life.

"Lucy's a special person," Sam said.

Ryan looked at him. Was that a warning? "Yes, she is. Very special." He glanced in Lucy's direction a number of times to check on her. The tension in her face had eased. He was sure that having something to focus her mind on helped.

Alexis obviously doted on Lucy. They shared some facial features but that was where the resemblance ended. Where Lucy was tall and unassuming, Alexis was petit and feisty. He liked Alexis but Lucy's gentle, easy way suited him much better. Even Sam had shown his affection for Lucy in his hug when they had arrived and his smiles in her direction. She had a family who obviously cared for her so why did she feel like she was on the outside?

"Okay, guys, food's on the table," called Alexis.

They gathered around the small table. He let his leg touch Lucy's. Just a reminder that he believed in her.

She gave him a weak smile.

Alexis spent most of the meal tending to Emily, who sat in a seat on the floor beside her mother. Sam watched the mother and child with a look of adoration on his face. Ryan now understood why Lucy felt like an outsider. Alexis and Sam probably had no idea of how they shut others out. Lucy would never tell them. She watched them also as if she couldn't pull her eyes away.

"Lucy, how do you like that great big old hospital you are working in now?" Sam asked.

"It's fine."

"She stays lost half the time," Ryan remarked smiling at her. "I've threatened to send a search party out for her a number of times."

Lucy grinned but it didn't reach her eyes.

"Sam, you interested in baseball?" Ryan asked, trying to steer the discussion away from her. Her face showed obvious relief when the conversation turned into a heated discussion about who would win the baseball pennant that fall.

During a lull, Ryan looked at Lucy. Her attention was on her plate as she pushed her food around. She had eaten little.

Alexis must have noticed also because she asked, "Lucy, are you feeling okay?"

"Oh, yeah. I'm fine." Lucy sounded artificially bright.

Just then Emily demanded Alexis's attention and she let the subject drop.

Sam, watching his wife and child, said, "Lucy, thank you so much for giving us this."

If Ryan hadn't been so in tune with Lucy he might have missed her barely perceptible flinch. That was the last thing she needed to hear. Emily was a gift she'd given her sister out of love and the Lucy he knew didn't want them to feel indebted. Being reminded of what she'd done made her feel uncomfortable. He found her hand under the table and gave it a reassuring squeeze. She gripped it back as if it were a lifeline.

"This little one has fallen asleep. It's time for bed," Alexis said. "Lucy, would you like to help me?"

"Sure," Lucy said, with little eagerness. Before she left the table she looked at him. He smiled encouragingly.

Ryan liked Alexis and Sam but couldn't they see how hard this was on Lucy? If Alexis wasn't so caught up in being a new mother she would notice Lucy was less than excited about being here. Lucy put on the same determined face he'd seen her wear when she was fighting for a patient as she followed Alexis and a drowsy Emily into another room.

He'd never been prouder of anyone. She was fighting an emotional battle like a champion. Heaven help him. He'd fallen in love.

It was a wonderful, scary and totally bewildering feeling. Yet somehow so right.

Lucy stood motionless in the doorway of the bedroom. Alexis would be destroyed if she ever found out her twin wanted to run.

Why couldn't she handle this better? Her job was to

help people through tough situations and she couldn't even be rational about her own problems. Known for her calming and forthright encouragement with patients' families, she was completely irrational where her own issues were concerned. She was such a fraud.

"Would you mind taking her dress off while I get her nightclothes together?" Alexis asked over her shoulder as she laid Emily in a crib. "I had no idea it took so much stuff to travel with someone so small."

Lucy took a breath. Just knowing Ryan was close had gotten her this far. She stepped to the bed and began to undress Emily. The sleepy-eyed baby looked up at her with complete trust. Unable to stop herself, Lucy leaned down and gave Emily a kiss on her forehead.

She wanted what Alexis had. Not this child, but her own. A family.

Alexis's bright sunny world was in complete contrast to the dark, lonely one Lucy lived in. Jealousy was a nasty emotion and Lucy wanted it to go away.

"I hate to wake a sleeping baby to change her clothes but I wanted her to look cute when you got here." Alexis came up beside Lucy, who gave the job of dressing Emily over to her.

Minutes later, as Alexis finished tucking Emily into her crib, Sam entered and came to stand beside the crib. Lucy stepped back, giving him room. He kissed Emily then, putting an arm around Alexis's shoulders, he kissed her temple. Together they looked down at their sleeping child. It was a poignant family moment.

A moment that Lucy wasn't a part of. She and Alexis had only had each other for so long, and now Alexis had her own family. Lucy had been pushed out.

Panic, fiery and foul, bubbled in her. Disgust rose in her throat. She had to get out of here. If she didn't she might burst. *I can't let her know.* It might cut that thin thread of a relationship she still had with her sister.

With blurry eyes, she rushed out of the room. Ryan met her, his forehead wrinkled, and his look penetrated her. Why couldn't she hide anything from him? "We have to go," she said tightly, reaching for her coat. "I have to go."

"You can't just leave," he whispered. "It'll hurt your sister's feelings." He took hold of her shoulders, stopping her frantic movements.

"If I stay I'll hurt her more," she responded in quiet desperation.

Alexis and Sam joined them.

Lucy kept her back to them as she gathered her and Ryan's coat from the chair. "We have to go. Ryan's been paged. He has a patient he needs to check on."

"Can't you stay, Lucy?" Alexis said. The disappointment in her voice grabbed at Lucy's heart.

"I have to go with him. We're part of a special program. We have to see all the patients at the same time. Co-ordinated patient care." She needed to slow down. Her words were running together.

"Surely you don't have to make every visit," Alexis insisted. "We haven't really gotten to talk. I wanted us to have a real visit."

"This is a patient in the ER." Lucy slid her arm inside the sleeve of her coat as Ryan held it. She glanced at Alexis and came undone. The disappointment in her sister's eyes made her heart clench. She was hurting Alexis, and she couldn't stop herself. Her feelings were a huge monster rising up to consume her.

"Oh, well, I guess I understand." Alexis didn't sound as if she did. "We'll see you tomorrow, won't we?"

Ryan shrugged into his jacket and joined Lucy at

the door. She looked at him and the worry in his eyes said he was only going along with her lies in order not to upset her sister further. The thin line of his lips said clearly he wasn't pleased.

As Lucy opened the door she said, "I'll have to see how it goes at work. I'll give you a call." She reached out and managed to give Alexis as brief and soothing a hug as she could manage.

Ryan waited until they were out of the apartment and in the dim light of the street before he asked, "Lucy, what happened?"

"I just couldn't stay there any longer."

She started down the street at a quick pace. Even with his long strides he had to work to keep up with her. "Come on, Lucy. Talk to me. I thought you were doing great."

Releasing a huff of indignation loud enough to draw the attention of others passing by, she said, "No, I wasn't. That…" she waved a hand in the direction they'd come from "…was my sister. She defended me. Took care of me. Supported and encouraged me all our lives. And me, I can't even be happy for her." The last few words came out almost as a sob.

Ryan grabbed her arm, stopping her in the middle of the sidewalk. "Lucy, listen."

She jerked her arm away and continued walking. "I don't want to talk about it any more."

He followed a few steps behind her, letting her work off her anger and frustration. When she'd cooled down he'd hail them a cab. Three blocks later she paused at the cross streets. She looked up at the buildings as if searching for a landmark, then at the street signs, before her head went down and her shoulders slumped. She had no idea which direction to turn. His heart broke for her. She was lost, both emotionally and physically.

The innate need to protect and support this proud woman who gave to and cared for others so wholeheartedly welled up in him. She'd given her sister the supreme gift of a child but couldn't see that because of the all-consuming dislike she felt for herself for desiring the same things out of life. Being around her had forced him to open up emotionally again. In that way, she'd even given him a gift.

He needed her. He didn't know how it had happened but it had.

Catching up to her, he pulled her securely against him and wrapped his arms around her. She didn't struggle. He held her a minute then raised a hand to get the attention of a passing cab driver. She said nothing as they waited for the yellow car to pull to the curb. "Come on, honey. It's time to go home."

Lucy used a determined voice to correct Ryan when he gave his address to the cab driver. "No, I want to go home." She told the driver her street. He looked at Ryan for confirmation. Ryan nodded.

She allowed him to hold her close, appreciating his strength. How could he possibly stand to be around someone who resented her own sister's happiness? She didn't like herself and she couldn't comprehend how he could either. Ryan was far too fine a man to have anything to do with a person who didn't have the capacity to love unconditionally.

The drive to her apartment was too short because she didn't want to lose the feel of being in Ryan's arms but too long because all she wanted to do was crawl into bed, curl up in a ball and pretend she didn't exist. As the driver pulled onto her street she said, "Ryan, keep the cab. I'll be fine going up myself."

"I'm coming with you." The tic in his jaw and the tone of his voice said he wouldn't be dismissed that easily.

Their feet made clomping noises as they climbed the worn wooden stairs to her floor. Ryan's hand rested at the slope of her back. She was exhausted in mind, body and particularly spirit. When she was unsuccessful at putting her key into the door lock the second time, Ryan took it from her and opened the door. He followed her in and closed the door behind him.

She went to her bed and sank down on it. He came toward her and she looked up. Why didn't he go home? "I'd like to be alone."

"Lucy…" He sounded so unsure. "Don't push me away. I want to help. But I don't know how."

"You did what you could by being there with me tonight. There's nothing more you can do."

"But you've got to work this through. Go back and talk to your sister. If not now, call her in the morning."

"I can't."

Ryan paced to the window and back. "No, that's not true. It's that you won't." He sounded disgusted.

She jumped up, faced him. "How can you say that? I did what you wanted. I went to see Alexis. Did you see what happened? I couldn't handle it."

Ryan's look didn't waver as he leaned toward her. "No, I didn't see that. What I saw was you trying despite your fear. You made the effort. You care about your sister. Emily. Even Sam. Everyone. And they care about you. You may not see it but I do. In fact, you wouldn't be this upset if you didn't care."

"I can't tell her how I feel. She wouldn't understand.

How can I explain what I don't understand?" She buried her face in her hands. "I'm just too ashamed."

He let out an exasperated breath. "Doing brain surgery is easier than getting through to you."

She glared at him. "You making a joke isn't going to make this one go away, Ryan. You can't make this all better for me. I've decided to stay out of my sister's life. It's for the best."

"This isn't the real you. Where's that woman who told me off and made it clear I wasn't her date at a party? The one so intriguing to me that I couldn't stay away from her? The one who made me want to get involved no matter how hard I tried not to? The one willing to fight for her patients?"

She sat on the edge of the bed again and looked up at him. "I don't know. Maybe she never really existed. I'm such a phony anyway. I tell families all the time what they need to do or how to act, and I can't even get my own life straight. I'm a mess.

"Ryan, you're a good guy. You cared for your father, your sisters and now I come along and you're stepping in to support me. I can't do that to you. I think I just need time alone to figure out my life. I don't want to ruin yours."

Ryan stepped back as if she had slapped him, hard. "Lucy, you're wrong. Way wrong. I swore never to carry the emotional needs of others ever again after my father died. I promised myself I'd never completely open up to my patients or anyone else again and then you came along. I want to be here for you. You're making a choice to be miserable. Your sister loves you. I care for you, and you won't accept either."

She raised her chin "You think Alexis is going to love me after I tell her how I feel?"

"I do. She showed how much she cares just by coming all this way to see you. I saw it when her eyes lit up when she opened the door. She's concerned for how you are doing. That's a plus in your life. Don't throw it away. Sometimes we just have to do some hard things because we love someone. Some really difficult things. Talk to her. Work through this."

"That's right, Mr. Bottle-Up-All-Your-Feelings wants me to bare my soul to my sister and hurt her more."

Ryan stalked toward her stepping into her personal space. "What do you want me to bare? That my father was the strongest man I've ever known and that I watched him slowly disappear? That I sat by his bed every minute I wasn't at school or working? That I saw fear in his eyes that I knew had to match mine? That I became responsible for my sisters during the worst time in our lives? Is that what you want me to share? Is that enough sharing for you? Enough to let you know I care deeply? That I do care about you?"

"Ryan, I just can't do this now. I don't know what to think."

Shaking his head, he looked at her. "You're a bright, sensitive, caring person, Lucy. Don't push Alexis away. And don't push me away."

"My sister was the one steady thing in my life. How can I feel this way towards her?"

Ryan sat on the bed beside her and put an arm around her shoulders. "I want to be the constant person in your life now. I know this isn't the perfect time, heck, it's probably the worst time in the history of mankind to tell you I love you. But there it is. I do. I'm here for you."

Her heart raced. She stared at him in disbelief. How could he? She was a mess. She didn't even love herself right now. "Please don't." She moved away from him and knew she'd regret it for the rest of her life but she had to.

He took her hand. "I understand you better than you think. I know how tough caring can be. What it's like to wish the person you love more than anyone else in the world would die quickly for their sake while at the same time wanting to hang onto them for as long as you can. I know what it is like to wish for something you can't have. Lucy, I'm offering you something you can have."

"No, Ryan, I can't let you love me."

He let go of her hand and stared down at her as if defeated. His beautiful blue eyes held shadows that she'd put there. "You don't get a choice in that," he said slowly.

She crossed her arms over her chest. "You don't get it. I don't know how to love. To really love. I've failed my sister. I'm failing you now. How can you love this messed-up, screwed-up me?" He just looked at her with a mixture of astonishment and sadness in his eyes. She studied his face, wanting with all her heart to give him what he asked for. But she couldn't.

He leaned over and kissed her cheek. "Goodbye, Lucy."

His kisses the night before had been all fire and passion, but the simple caress of his lips on her cheek held a devastating finality that filled her with a grief bone deep.

Apart from when Ryan had followed his father's casket down the aisle of the church, walking down the stairs and away from Lucy was the longest journey of Ryan's existence. For once in his life he'd opened his heart to someone and she'd shoved it back at him.

Lucy wasn't who he'd thought she was. He wanted the woman who'd shown such spunk when he'd made her mad. The one who'd had the fortitude to carry a child for her sister, the strength to move away from everything she knew to one of the largest cities in the world and to share her pain with him. Why couldn't he make her see that she had what it took to talk to her sister?

He pushed the door to his condo open. Dumping his wallet and keys on the bar in the kitchen, he climbed the stairs to his room. He stopped in the doorway and looked at the bed.

That morning Lucy had insisted, "We can't leave it undone. I make my bed every morning."

"And I have a housekeeper who comes in twice a week."

When she started shaking out the sheet, he'd taken the other side to help.

As he'd tucked a corner she'd said, "Hey, you can't just wad that up and put it under there." She circled the bed, reaching down to pull the material out.

"Don't tell me how I'm supposed to make a bed," he'd said, sounding as indignant as possible before he'd grabbed her and rolled her onto the bed. She'd giggled. He'd shared her mirth. He hadn't laughed so freely since before his father had become sick. Had almost forgotten how good it felt to be alive. Happily alive.

He'd kissed her and that was all it had taken. They'd not taken time to remove their clothes and she hadn't seemed to mind. In fact, his desperate need for her had seemed to fuel her own. She'd crawled on top and had taken over their lovemaking.

That's what it had been. Him loving her. He'd not recognized it then but it was clear now. So much so that it hurt to look at the bed, to remember. His body ached from the mere thought of her.

Walking to the dark brown chair that faced the window, he plopped down, put his legs across the matching footstool and crossed his ankles. The lights of the city had lost some of their luster. Scooting his butt forward, he braced his head against the back of the chair and closed his eyes. He wouldn't be sleeping in his bed tonight.

Lucy curled under her sheets still fully clothed and pulled her legs to her chest, becoming a ball. She buried her head in a pillow and let the tears flow. It had been horrible when she'd left Alexis and Emily behind and moved to New York. But nothing compared to giving up Ryan.

She'd hurt him. He'd said he loved her and she'd thrown it back in his face. She was unworthy of his love. She missed Ryan's arms being around her, his strong, calming presence. It had taken him no time to become embedded in her life.

She'd slept next to Ryan for only one night but she already missed his warm body pressed against hers. What did he see in her? She was a mess. Here she was supposed to be helping others and she couldn't even handle her own life.

How had her world spun so out of control? How could she ever face him at work again? Maybe she should speak to Mr. Matherson and see if she could be reassigned to another neurosurgeon. No, she couldn't do that. It might damage Ryan's career if she did. She couldn't hurt him like that. She'd just have to endure and be the professional she was known to be. But could she stand the pain of seeing him daily?

CHAPTER NINE

"THE PATIENT'S DOING as expected," Ryan informed the assembly around him in the hallway of the neurosurgery floor midmorning. The group didn't include Lucy. She'd excused herself as soon as they had come out of the patient's room. He had to make an effort not to watch her walk away. They'd not spoken since he'd left her apartment three days earlier.

It was up to Lucy to make the first move. She was the one who'd pushed him away. She'd never said she loved him. Despite being distraught about her issues with her sister, she'd sounded very clear-headed where he was concerned. Learning to live with her decision was going to be difficult. Even harder was accepting it. Compounding the issue was having to continue to work together.

She'd taken care of her responsibilities, making meticulous notes on patient charts. His clinical nurse questioned him a couple of times about an issue that Lucy had noted but which she hadn't directly spoken to him about. In fact, she refused to look at him. She was living by the letter of the law regarding their co-operative patient care but there was no spirit of partnership in her actions any more.

He grieved for her. Only by sheer iron will did he

not go in search of her or ask about her. She'd made her feelings clear. How could they have been so in sync and now have an ocean-wide chasm between them? He missed the peaceful, quiet way she'd had about her. How she'd made his hectic, often stressful life easier just by being near.

Helping her was impossible. She had to work out her issues on her own. He'd offered her love and his support and she'd pushed them away. He was paying dearly for it.

The worst was the physical ache. His body craved her, making his nights almost longer than his sanity could tolerate.

Having a few minutes before starting his weekly paperwork, he headed across the street and into Central Park. He needed to get out, away. Clear his head. As large as the hospital was, it still closed in on him, knowing that Lucy was so near but still so untouchable.

He strolled around a bend on the paved walkway and there sat his nemesis and love of his heart. She looked out over the lake, her face held up to the sun and her lunch spread out on the bench beside her. His body went on full alert. Every fiber of his being wanted to reach out and snatch her to him. Thankfully, his pride held him in check.

Her eyes opened, widened. Had she heard him or just sensed someone was near? She looked as if she was debating whether or not to ignore him. She squared her shoulders and looked directly at him.

"Hello, Ryan," she said. The sounds of the city were hushed by the foliage of the trees and bushes. The few voices he could make out were in the distance. It would have been a perfect opportunity to take her in his arms for a kiss. But if he did that he would want more. A little of Lucy would never be enough. He wanted it all and he wanted her to want it all too.

A thin smile came to his lips. She was tough. He'd give her that. Far tougher than he was. But, then, she didn't care about him as he cared for her. She had never once said she loved him. Forcing a foot forward, he came to stand in front of her. "Lucy." His traitorous body hummed, being near her. She'd crushed his heart and still he wanted her so desperately it was almost a living thing, crawling to be released. "Could I speak to you a minute?"

"I thought we'd said all that needed to be said." Her flinch gave him a second of satisfaction before it turned to guilt. It shouldn't be this way between them. "I'm sorry. That was uncalled for."

Lucy looked around as if checking to see if anyone was paying attention to them. Apparently finding they weren't, she said, "I understand. I've hurt you, and for that I'm sorry."

The North Pole would become a heated swimming pool before he let her know how badly she'd hurt him. "It didn't work out. We're both adults. We know the score."

She blinked then looked away.

He'd sounded harsh, he knew. But he couldn't continue to do his job, live his life if he didn't start getting a handle on his emotions where she was concerned. The first step was making clear to her that he was moving on.

"Ryan, about Miguel Rivera. His mother called. She's upset because she's having difficulty getting Miguel into a program designed for children with epilepsy this summer. It's too expensive for her to pay for and she wanted to know if you would consider recommending he attend. She believes he would qualify for a scholarship on your recommendation."

"Have you checked this camp out?"

"I have. I think it would be very beneficial for Miguel."

Ryan shouldn't have bothered to ask the question. Lucy was thorough, if nothing else. She looked at him, really looked at him, for the first time in days. Those beseeching eyes would have him doing anything. How he still wanted her! "Then I trust your judgment. See that the paperwork gets to my desk. If they don't get the scholarship, let me know. I'll pay for him to attend."

She sucked in a breath.

"Don't act so surprised. You're not the only one who can be philanthropic. Put the paperwork on my desk, and I'll sign it this afternoon."

"Thank you, Ryan."

"Is that all?"

"I'd really like to say one more thing."

Ryan shifted his weight from one foot to the other, waiting. Something about the hesitant way she said the words made him think he wasn't going to like what came next.

"I'm only saying this because I care about you."

His mouth quirked and took on a dubious line. Lucy had the good grace to look contrite.

"I'd like you to think about why you have such a difficult time talking to families—"

"I'm not going to discuss—"

"Ryan, you need to hear me out. You've retreated behind the pain and sorrow of your father's illness and death for so long that you can't bring yourself to be near anyone else in the same pain. You'd be a better doctor, even a happier person, if you would try, just try to see that and be a little more open with your patients' families."

He glared down at her. She'd thrown what they'd had together away and now she wanted to give him personal advice?

Before she could say more or he could respond, a nurse from the floor approached them. "Hi," she said with a smile.

As she passed Ryan asked, "Are you headed back in?"

"Yes," the nurse said, surprise in her tone.

"Mind if I walk with you?"

She gave him a brilliant smile. "Sure."

"Enjoy your lunch, Lucy." He turned and fell into step with the pretty nurse, whose eager, encouraging eyes made him wish that he could see that same look coming from Lucy.

Lucy had cried so much in the last few days that she didn't think she could ever cry again. She was wrong. As she watched Ryan walk away and heard the cute nurse's laugh, she was afraid another sobbing session was coming on. She wadded up her meal and shoved it into her sack.

Her days and nights had started to run together. She hadn't really slept since the night she had lain curled in Ryan's arms. Going through the motions was the only way she could describe her efforts at work. She'd managed to do what needed to be done for her patients but little else.

Most of her energy had gone into making sure her and Ryan's paths didn't cross. Working in such a large hospital had helped. It hadn't worked today, though. She'd been completely surprised to see him in the park.

Also the fact that Ryan spent so much time in the OR had helped.

She wasn't proud of the fact she'd checked the schedule each morning and planned her visits to the patients' rooms when she knew there was the least chance of running into him. Even though she made every effort not to see him, her body turned against her whenever she did. Heat rose in her every time she saw him.

Her life had gone from barely tolerable when she'd left Alexis's home to impossible. The only shining moments had been those spent with Ryan. Now even those were gone. Knowing she'd made the right choice didn't make it any easier to live without him. Seeing him daily at the hospital was a constant painful reminder of how much she cared.

She didn't have to look at him to know when his gaze was on her. She felt it. Hot, heavy and beckoning. When she glanced at him he made sure to be looking elsewhere. His sunny, ready smile had become almost non-existent. The nurses were making comments about how much he'd changed, speculating on the cause.

He wasn't happy and neither was she, but she didn't know how to change it. Even if she wanted to, would Ryan forgive her for all the things she'd said to him? Based on the ease with which he'd left her to walk with the nurse, she'd say she'd lost her chance.

Her efforts to dodge Ryan were working better than those she used to keep Alexis at bay. Where Ryan was silently accepting, Alexis was overt and demanding. There were twice-daily calls asking when they might get together. Lucy had ignored the first day's worth. The second day she'd actually spoken to Alexis but only long enough to say she was too busy to meet her.

She had to get control of her life. Did she want to

continually live like this? She'd shocked herself when she'd stood up to Ryan. Even more so when she'd undressed in front of him and all of Lower Manhattan. She should be able to talk to her sister. Ryan was lost to her but maybe her sister wasn't. She had to try. Nothing could be worse than what she had now.

She called Alexis as soon as she was out of bed the next morning.

"Alexis, can we get together tomorrow? I'm taking the afternoon off."

"That sounds wonderful. We're leaving the day after tomorrow and I've hardly seen you. I'll meet you at the hospital if you want."

Lucy couldn't risk her sister running into Ryan. "I'll come to your place. Take you out for lunch."

"I'm looking forward to it. I've missed you, Luce."

"Me, too," Lucy whispered, after Alexis had hung up.

Lucy pushed away the strands of her hair that had escaped from the tight bun she'd worn the last few days. Just thinking about how much Ryan loved her hair made her feel self-conscious. Having it down reminded her of how he'd played with it as she'd explored his body. If she kept tight control of her hair, maybe she could govern her memories as well. She shuddered. Those moments were events she shouldn't dwell on.

She raised her hand in the air to hail a cab. It surprised her how acclimatized to living in New York City she'd become in just a few weeks. Where she'd been intimidated by the large bustling city when she'd first arrived, now she could throw up an arm and hail a cab with ease.

Even the subway system was starting to feel familiar

to her and her on-time rate was improving because she wasn't lost all the time. She was starting to think of the city as home. Where she'd been a meek and mild person unsure of what to do and where to go, she'd become much more confident. That was empowering.

How often had she told her patient families that when they got out on the other side of the tough times they would find a bright spot? It was no different for her. She had lived her life not in the shadow of Alexis but with her leading the way all the time. Now she was her own person, having to fight her own battles. She was a stronger person for making the move to New York.

She could face Alexis. Would tell her the truth. With new resolve Lucy stepped out of the taxi and entered Alexis's building, making her way up to the correct floor. Could things between them be worse than they already had been? She loved Alexis and Alexis loved her. They would get through this. Wasn't it the same with Ryan? She wasn't so sure. Could she forgive him if he'd treated her as badly as she'd treated him?

She rapped her knuckles firmly against Alexis's door. Squaring her shoulders and lifting her chin to cover the jitters that felt like a flock of birds taking off in her belly, Lucy waited.

Too soon for her nerves the door opened and Alexis stood there. The warm smile of welcome Lucy had received days earlier had disappeared. Alexis pierced her with a look.

"Come in and tell me what's going on."

Lucy should have known she couldn't hide from her sister long. Nothing got by her. She knew Lucy too well.

Alexis closed the door behind Lucy, reminding her of bars closing on a jail cell. She wouldn't be released until Alexis got want she wanted. That suited Lucy just fine. She was ready to bare her heart. Would do what it took to get back what she'd lost.

Alexis headed toward a sofa, leaving Lucy to follow. "Emily's napping and Sam's at the office at a meeting. We have time to talk. Really talk," Alexis said, sitting on the sofa.

Lucy had always received a hug from Alexis when they hadn't seen each other in a while. It was telling that she hadn't offered one this time. Lucy would have to call on her new-found determination to get through this. She followed Alexis to the living room, taking the sofa opposite hers.

"What happened to you the other night? I know what you told me but I also know you well enough to know when you're lying. Something's going on and I want to know what it is."

Alexis had never been one to dance around what she wanted to know. Lucy had to tell the truth. Alexis deserved to hear the whole dreadful story.

She focused on the tip of her black dress boot, unable to make eye contact with Alexis. "I had to leave Atlanta."

"Had to leave? Why?" Patience was never Alexis's strong suit. Lucy had always been the one to wait and listen.

"Because I was too close to Emily. It was too hard. I thought you were starting to resent me."

Alexis's mouth fell open as she leaned forward. "I don't understand."

She didn't imagine that Alexis did. Alexis's thoughts had never wavered away from the fact she was going to have a baby to think about how it was affecting her sister. Lucy looked at Alexis, seeing her in a different light for the first time ever. Lucy had always revered Alexis, thinking she could do no wrong.

Now she recognized that Alexis had been so focused on her own needs that she'd had no idea of what Lucy had been going through. Lucy didn't love Alexis any less, she just recognized that Alexis's concern had more to do with her having a family than with Lucy's welfare. It was not a criticism. It was a reminder that Lucy had to build a life of her own. Move on.

"Alexis, we talked of Emily being yours. You made all the doctor's appointments. I knew in my head that she belonged to you and Sam, but as she grew and my body changed, it became harder to think of myself as just an incubator. As hard as I tried not to, I felt the baby belonging to me more and more."

Alexis's sharp intake of breath made Lucy flinch but she had to go on.

"Do you remember that day you came home and Sam had his hand on my belly? He was feeling her kick for the first time. I saw the look on your face. You resented me. I knew then I was going to have to do something drastic after the baby was born. I started applying for jobs then. My post partum emotions didn't help. You and Sam and Emily became this tight little unit that didn't include me."

"Luce, we didn't—"

Lucy held up a hand. "Let me finish or I might not be able to. I know my feelings were irrational. But I couldn't make them go way. The problem was I was jealous. Jealous of you with Emily. Jealous of you having Sam. Jealous that I had no family of my own."

"You had us. I'm your family."

Lucy looked away. "No, my own husband, child. The jealousy was eating me up inside. I had to get away.

When the job offer up here came I snatched it. My excuse was that I was feeling too attached to Emily when it was really that I was jealous of what you had. The longer I stayed at your house the more those awful feelings grew. I was disgusted with myself.

"I'm jealous of your happiness! You found it and I haven't. You and I were a team. It had always been us against the world. Then Sam came along. You still included me, things weren't that different, but Emily changed everything. You had your little family and I had nothing."

She looked up to find tears rolling down Alexis's face. They matched the ones on her own cheeks.

"I'm so ashamed, Alexis. If you love someone you should want them to have all the happiness in the world, not be jealous of them. I had no intention of seeing you the other day. Only because Ryan agreed to come with me did I show up. I just couldn't face you." She caught Alexis's gaze and said with all the sincerity she could muster, "I'm so sorry. For it all. Please forgive me. I love you, Emily and Sam."

Alexis's stricken look tore at Lucy's heart. Her sister was just as hurt as Lucy had feared she would be. Seconds later, Alexis popped up and came around the coffee table that stood between them. She sat next to Lucy and pulled her into a tight hug. "Aw, honey, I wish you'd said something. Sam and I love you. We want you to be happy too, not for us to be happy at your expense."

It felt good to have Alexis's understanding, concern and touch. "I don't want you to feel guilty. I've carried enough of that for both of us. Please forgive me." Lucy gave her a pleading look.

Alexis let go of Lucy enough that they could look at each other. "There's nothing to forgive. I had no idea what a toll carrying Emily was having on you. Sam and I had no idea. You gave us no hint. You should've said something."

"I couldn't. As jealous as I was, I still couldn't ruin your happiness."

Alexis took both of Lucy's hands in hers and looked at her with gloomy eyes. "Luce, I'm so sorry. We should've been more sensitive to your feelings."

"I don't want you or Sam to feel bad. As hard as coming here the other night was for me, it also made me face my fears and feelings. I'm stronger for it. I'm moving on, learning to cope, and I don't want anything to ever stand between us again."

Alexis wrapped Lucy in another hug, which she accepted and returned with every fiber of her being. She hung on until she and Alexis had moved from crying to laughing. With that came a sense of wellbeing that hadn't been there in the last few months, except for those precious moments in Ryan's arms.

"Enough of the crying. I'm going to call Sam and see when he'll be home. He can watch Emily while you and I go out and have a good old-fashioned girls' evening out," Alexis declared, in that childhood one-twin-is-more-dominant-than-the-other voice.

"I'd really like that," Lucy said, not hiding the emotion that crept into her voice. "I've missed you."

Alexis gave her a hug. "And I you. Do you know of any good places to do some shopping in this big city?"

"I think Macy's would cover everything we might need and more."

"Then Macy's it is."

A cry from the adjoining room announced that Emily was awake.

"Do you mind if I get her?" Lucy asked.

"I would love for you to."

Lucy reached into the crib and brought the warm child to her chest. Emily gave a whimper and quieted. Lucy inhaled the sweet smell of her. "Hi, sweetheart. It's your Aunt Lucy."

Hours later, with shopping bags in her hand and a smile on her face, Lucy asked, "Would you like to see where I live? It isn't much."

"I'd love to," Alexis responded, with more eagerness than the tiny apartment warranted.

"Come on, I'll show you how a real New Yorker travels." Lucy headed down the steps into the subway station. Half an hour later she and Alexis were strolling along the narrow, bumpy sidewalk of her tree-lined street.

"What a nice area to live in. If I had to live in a city this large, I'd like to live somewhere like this. It feels like a real neighborhood," Alexis commented.

"It is, but it doesn't have the view of the city that Ryan has from Brooklyn." He'd been on Lucy's mind all day, especially after she'd begun to adjust to being a doting aunt and loyal sister. She missed him with all her heart. If they couldn't return to what they'd had, she wanted them to at least be friends. No, that wasn't true. They couldn't go back to being friends. She wanted Ryan to be more than that. There had to be some way to make up for what she'd said to him.

"And you know about his view how?" Alexis put a suggestive tone in her voice. "I've been wanting to ask but was afraid to because of all the other emotions we've been drowning in today. But you opened the gate so I'm asking. What's going on with you two?"

Lucy touched Alexis's arm. "You can ask me anything. I'll never again close you out. Ever."

"I love you, Lucy."

"And I love you. Here's my apartment."

A short time later Lucy and Alexis were sitting at the table, having glasses of iced tea, when Alexis asked, "Now, tell me about Ryan. How do you know about his view exactly?" Her look was pointed enough to make Lucy squirm and blush simultaneously.

"I've seen it."

"You have? I knew there was something going on between you two." Alexis's seemed pleased with herself. She waited as if she expected Lucy to say more.

Under her watchful eyes, Lucy played with the moisture on the side of her glass.

"You really care about him, don't you?"

"Yeah. Too much. And I messed up big time."

"What happened?" Alexis put her glass down and leaned toward Lucy.

"Oh, Alexis, he told me he loved me."

Alexis squealed. "That's wonderful."

"I said he couldn't. I pushed him away."

Alexis's eyes widen in disbelief. "Why did you do that?"

"He told me right after we left your place. I was already upset. I didn't think he could or should love anyone who was jealous of her own sister."

Alexis huffed and reached across the table, taking one of Lucy's hands in her own. "Isn't that just like a man? To pick the worst possible moment, when we're not thinking straight, to say something like I love you for the first time."

"I've hurt him so badly. He won't have anything to do with me now."

"Honey, all you have to do is tell him that you love him too."

"What if he's changed his mind?"

Alexis snorted. "He'd be crazy if he did."

"We barely speak."

"I don't think you're giving him or yourself enough credit. He doesn't strike me as a man who gives up on someone he loves."

Could she convince Ryan of her love? "I don't know…"

"Lucy, you've changed. You're more self-sufficient. More confident. Almost outspoken. You do it the same way you came to talk to me. Make Ryan listen. If he doesn't, it's his loss."

Lucy's greatest fear was that it would be her loss too.

Ryan clicked a computer key, making the screen go black. Matherson's email requested that he and Lucy meet with him to discuss the co-ordinated patient care project. He and Lucy hadn't had a real conversation other than that short one in the park in over a week. She'd not even shown up for evening rounds the day before. He hadn't wanted to wonder where she was or, worse, worry about her. He'd done both.

She'd started to treat New York more like home but she could still easily get lost. As tender-hearted as she was, she could even be guided wrongly by someone in the subway. He loved her and was intensely concerned. Nothing between them had diminished since the night she'd pushed him out of her life. The separation made his ache for her bottomless. He wanted her not to matter but regardless of what he did he couldn't get her out of his mind and heart.

He hated to admit to the mountain-sized relief he'd

felt when she'd slipped into the clinic examination room that afternoon during Miguel Rivera's post-surgery check-up. Doing a double-take, he'd looked at her again. She'd cut her hair. It was loose and flowing, touching the top of her shoulders. His heart had skipped. She'd looked gorgeous. As much as he loved her hair, this version was every bit as breathtaking as the other.

Lucy had replaced her rather drab clothes with a straight skirt, a blouse of light blue and a multicolored sweater that showed off her breasts to their best advantage. Was she trying to kill him? He was confused. What was happening here?

Miguel's mother's face lit up when she saw Lucy. After she'd spoken to the mother, she looked at him and gave him a shy smile.

She kept the sucker punches coming. She hadn't met his look straight on in days, much less smiled at him. He didn't know what had happened to make her change her reaction to him but he wouldn't complain. Still, he couldn't let her super-sexy smile fool him into believing that she wanted anything more than a stable working relationship. He wouldn't let her stomp on his heart again. Heck, she was still stomping on it. His sense of self-preservation refused to let her know what she was doing to him.

What she'd said to him in the park about him letting his father's illness control his life had made him mad. He'd stewed over it. Where did she get off, telling him something like that? When his temper had cooled he'd realized that she might be right.

Ryan cleared his throat and said flatly, "Will you translate?"

Her smile faded. "Yes." Her professional armor slid into place.

He smiled at the mother. "Please tell her that Miguel's doing well. And that she's been doing a fine job in caring for the wound."

He waited while Lucy relayed his remark.

Miguel's mother smiled at Ryan. *"Gracias."*

It did feel good to have a parent look at him with something more than disappointment. With his examination completed he said, "Please bring Miguel in to see me again in six weeks. I hope you are taking care of yourself also." Lucy repeated his request in Spanish with a slight smile on her face. While she was doing so, he picked up Miguel. "He's a handsome boy." Ryan smiled at the mother again.

The mother said something to Lucy and giggled, before taking Miguel and heading towards the door. Lucy responded with a grin. He raised his chin in question.

"She said you're handsome also. I agreed," she said, so softly he wasn't sure he'd heard it.

"You got Matherson's email?"

Her smile slipped. "I did."

"I'll see you there, then."

"Sure." She looked at him as if she wanted to say more. When she didn't, he left. If he stayed any longer he was afraid he might do something he'd regret. Like take her in his arms and beg her to reconsider. Tell her he'd do anything to work things out between them.

CHAPTER TEN

LUCY CONTINUED DOWN the corridor, paying special attention to the signs directing her to the HR department. The enormous hospital still intimidated her when she got off her beaten path. She'd not returned to the HR department since the day she and Ryan had met. She didn't remember much about how she'd gotten there and certainly recalled little from Ryan's guided trip other than his displeasure.

She'd checked her emails in the hope he'd offer to walk down with her, but after their few terse words during Miguel's clinic visit she'd not been surprised when there had been none. She'd hurt him so deeply that his gentleman's manners were slipping where she was concerned.

He remained polite, which was the O'Doherty way, but there was a ten-foot-high, eight-foot-thick wall around him with no door for her to beat on. He still charmed the nurses and the children but there was a look in his eyes that she couldn't quite put a name to, or didn't want to. She'd give anything to see him grin at her.

With relief and only one double back, she pushed the HR door open to find Ryan already there. He reclined in a chair, his white lab coat unbuttoned. His tie looked as if he'd tugged on it in irritation and his hair was in disarray. He glanced at the clock on the wall. She smiled to herself. He knew she had a hard time finding her way around the hospital. It served him right to have to wait since he'd not offered to walk down with her.

He looked tired. There had been a number of new cases in the last few days but his weariness seemed to come from deeper inside. His eyes lacked that twinkle she'd grown accustomed to and loved. Had she been the cause of that luster disappearing? If she'd thought he would allow it, she would have taken him in her arms.

Was he sleeping as poorly as she was? Even though she and Alexis had cleared the air, her life still had a gaping hole. What she missed sat in front of her, but he might as well be a hundred miles away. Ryan had never looked less approachable.

Ryan glanced at her and she gave him a hesitant smile. He didn't return it. Would he ever forgive her?

She glanced to where the receptionist should be sitting and saw no one then looked at Ryan. "Where's the receptionist? Does Matherson know you're here?"

"No one was around when I got here. I knew you would probably be late so I was waiting before I looked for Matherson."

He stood. His somewhat unruly locks looked even more so, as if he'd been running his hands through it regularly. She wished she could. The thought did her no good. Only made her want what she couldn't have.

Ryan straightened his lab coat then stepped toward her. Her breath caught. Was he going to touch her? Instead, he stepped past her. Sorrow filled her.

"Come on, let's get this over with," Ryan grumbled. "I still have work to do and it's been a long week."

He didn't look at her after that statement. Had what

had happened between them affected his week? They had started down the short hall in the direction of Matherson's office when he stepped out of it.

"Good. Here you are," he said, all smiles. "Sorry you had to wait. My receptionist left early."

The man sounded far too cheerful for her liking. By the curl to Ryan's lip, he wasn't too impressed either. Maybe Matherson wouldn't drag this meeting out. As soon as she got this over with she was going home to a hot bath. She glanced at Ryan. Maybe a good cleansing cry as well.

"Come in. Have a seat," Matherson said as he took his chair behind the desk that was too large for the room.

Ryan stood to the side, letting her enter the office ahead of him. It was the closest they had been in days. As she passed, she caught a hint of the scent that was Ryan's alone. With great effort she managed not to step closer to him, though her body vibrated with the need to.

She was relieved when she sat as her knees had begun to wobble. Ryan waited until she settled into her chair before he took his. The chairs were situated so close that when he placed his arm on the rest, it came within an inch of hers. She moved her arm and clasped her hands in her lap, fearing the powerful urge she had to touch him.

"So," Matherson began, leaning back in his chair, "how's the co-operative patient care working out between you two?" He ended the question with a sappy smile.

Ryan shifted slightly in his chair at Matherson's use of the words "you two".

"Fine," she and Ryan said at the same time, not looking at each other.

"That's all you have to report?" Matherson looked back and forth between them, his brow contracting "Could you be more specific, Dr. O'Doherty?"

"I think it has gone pretty much as I expected. I thought little of the idea to begin with and still do. The only difference between how I handled patient care before and what I do now is that I have to call Ms. Edwards before I meet the patient. Which does take time."

She glanced at Ryan then scooted forward in her chair, gaining Matherson's attention. "He had to wait a couple of times for me. I'm new to the hospital and had to learn my way around. The same for the city. I don't believe that lessens my effectiveness."

"So you believe the project has merit?" Matherson asked.

"I do." She glanced at Ryan again and found him looking straight ahead. "I assisted in the patient's and the family's emotional needs. Something that surgeons often don't address. I thought from the total patient care aspect it has value," Lucy volunteered. "I was involved early on in easing family into the reality they were facing."

Ryan snorted. His manners had disappeared. She and Matherson looked at him. "Yes, but I'm not sure that the hand-holding is necessary when the patient is in the ER."

She swung to face Ryan. One of her knees bumping his hard thigh sent a shock wave through her before she pulled it away. "Really, Dr. O'Doherty? You seemed to appreciate my hand-holding just fine when you needed a translator." She couldn't keep the edge out of her voice.

Ryan didn't look at her but at Matherson. "I concede that. Ms. Edwards was of value then."

Ooh, the man! Lucy waited until Ryan and Matherson were both looking at her. Through clenched teeth she said, "Are you implying that what I do isn't as important as being the all-powerful, all-knowing surgeon?"

"What I'm saying is that we don't have to be joined at the hip," he said through a taut jaw.

She flinched at his choice of words. Was he baiting her? Reminding herself to remain professional, she responded, "You're right." She turned to Matherson. "We shouldn't have been required to attend Jack Carter's party together."

"So that didn't go well?" Matherson sat forward as if he was enjoying their exchange.

"There are parts that are better left not discussed," she murmured.

Someone called from the outer office. "Anyone here?"

"If you will excuse me a minute, I'll be right back." Matherson said, coming around the desk and heading out the door.

"So, do you have something particular in mind?" Ryan leaned toward her.

Two could play this game. "Yes, as a matter of fact I do."

"Then why not just say it? I'm sure Mr. Matherson would be interested. You've had no trouble speaking your mind before."

He was right. Since she'd moved to New York, no, met him, she'd taken to speaking up for herself. But this wasn't the time. The discussion was too personal.

Too heart-wrenching. "Ryan, please don't do this here," she whispered.

"Why not? I admit I kissed you. And what's more, you liked it."

"Please, Matherson can hear you," she whispered in desperation.

"You don't think I show my feelings enough," he said, standing and pulling her up out of the chair. "How about this for showing some emotion?"

His mouth came down on hers hard and heavy as if he wanted to brand her and consume her at the same time. Nothing in her life had felt more wonderful. She curved a hand around his neck, savoring the moment she'd thought never to have again. With a soft moan of bliss she leaned in and soaked in the feel of him. Her world turned, funneled into a tornado and Ryan was the eye. Nothing mattered but the feel of his lips on hers.

The loud clearing of a throat from the doorway broke them apart. Matherson stood there, a look of shock on his face.

Blood rushed up her neck. The stricken and surprised look on Matherson's face had to match hers. She glanced at Ryan. He was grinning like he'd just made the winning home run in the bottom of the ninth at a Yankees game.

What had just happened? She'd been kissing the surgeon she'd been assigned to work with in front of the head of the HR department! It hadn't been just any kiss. It had been an open-mouthed, moaning kiss. Could she feel more mortified? She'd learned to stand up for herself in the last few weeks but Ryan's—and admittedly her own—kiss had been far out of her comfort zone when done in front of an audience.

She couldn't meet Matherson's gaze, and she sure

wasn't going to look at Ryan. Appalled at their actions, she still wanted to step back into Ryan's arms and have his generous lips find hers again. She desired more than a kiss. Her body shook with the need to draw him to her. "I have to go."

Her knee hit the chair leg in her fervor to leave the room. Not sure how she did it, she made her way out of the office and the department. Wishing for her old sensible shoes back, she walked as fast as her new heels would allow. At the first bank of elevators she pushed the button for the eighth floor. Getting in the first door that opened, she rode up. Not until they opened again did she realize it was the eighth floor of a different wing of the hospital.

She wanted to stomp on the floor and scream *Ryan, Ryan, Ryan*. Instead, she took her frustration out on the down call button and punched it with the end of her finger. Why had he done it? Why had he kissed her in front of Matherson? She'd never been more embarrassed in her life. Did he mean anything by it other than to kiss her into submission? Regardless, it had been heaven to have his mouth on hers again.

Ryan lounged against the wall outside Lucy's office door. He crossed his hands over his chest and prepared to wait. This time he didn't mind doing so. The taste of Lucy lingered on his lips. She'd returned his kiss. Held nothing back, even in front of Matherson. Maybe there was hope after all.

When she turned the corner of the hall a few minutes later, he suppressed a smile. The Lucy that had stood up to him was back. He'd seen some evidence of it in Matherson's office but by the look on her face now, he knew he was in for it. The best part was that he was looking forward to the fight and hopefully the making up. The last week had been one of pure misery.

As she stalked toward him he said, "You got lost again."

He smiled when she mumbled, "Darned elevators." She stopped beside him and shoved her key in the door. "I don't need you making fun of me. You've hardly spoken to me in a week." She turned to face him. "Then you pulled that stunt in front of Matherson."

Lucy flung her hair back as she turned to fiddle with the key. "How could you?"

Her wildflower scent touched his nostrils. He wanted to bury his nose in that warm, silky spot on her neck that he knew so well and inhale all of her. Pushing down a groan, he leaned towards her. "If you don't talk sweeter to me, I just might do it again right here."

She jerked her head up to look down the hall toward the nurses' station. "Don't," she muttered.

"Why, Lucy? Because you're afraid you might like it? I thought you were the one who believes in sharing feelings."

She pushed the office door open and entered. He followed, not giving her a chance to close the door on him.

"You might not lose your job, but I could."

"No, you won't. I told Matherson I'd be glad to continue working with you. That I thought he made a much better matchmaker than HR director."

"You said that?" she squeaked.

He shut the office door behind him. For once he appreciated an automatic lock. "Okay, maybe I left that last part off."

She turned to face him, hands on her hips. "If we continue to work together you can't kiss me every time I voice my opinion."

"Yes, I can." He grinned, stepping a pace closer, grateful the office was small.

"Huh?"

"I think you love me."

She blinked. Then a smile formed on her lips. "Pretty sure of yourself, aren't you, Dr. O'Doherty?"

He moved closer until her breasts touched his chest. "Kiss me again, Lucy."

She placed her hands on his shoulders and looked into his dark blue eyes as she touched her lips to his. Heaven. He opened for her and she slipped her tongue in to meet his. He greeted and encouraged it. Her hands moved to wrap around his neck as he became master of the kiss, drawing her to him and heating her so that she melted against him.

Divine minutes later he pulled away and looked into her face as he combed his fingers through her hair. "You cut it." He groaned with disappointment.

"It was time and I needed to make a statement I'd changed."

His other hand went to her waist. "You did that with your wardrobe alone."

"You noticed? The way you've been giving me the cold shoulder, I thought you might not have."

He trailed his fingers over her hip. "Oh, I noticed and so did the male interns. I might have spoken a little harshly to one after I caught him watching you walk away."

"So, I'm not the only one who has jealousy issues." She cupped his face. "I'm sorry I hurt you. I just couldn't get things straight in my head. I was so eaten up with envy and confused about my life that I couldn't think straight."

"Have you got it figured out?"

"You were right." Her hands ran over his shoulders to stop at his biceps as she looked into his eyes. "Alexis had no idea. She and I had a long talk. I discovered I've being using her as a security blanket all my life. I needed to find my own identity."

"Do you still want what Alexis has?"

"No."

His heart fell, taking his hope with it. She didn't want a family any more. Which meant that even if she loved him, which she hadn't said she did, it would never work between them. He wanted children. He wasn't staying around to have his heart trampled twice.

He took a step back and let his hands fall to his sides. "I understand. I just came by to apologize for embarrassing you. I won't let it happen again."

"Ryan." She caught his hand as he turned. "I don't think you do understand."

He looked at their hands then up at her face.

"I don't want what Alexis has. I want more. A husband of my own and lots and lots of children."

His heart fluttered and started to live again. "And who do you plan to have father these children?" he asked, moving close again.

"I was hoping you might consider the job," she said with a flicker of shy lashes that he found alluring. "I love you, Ryan O'Doherty. With all my heart. Do you maybe still care for me?"

He swept her up into his arms again, holding her as tight as he dared. Joy surged through him. She wrapped her arms around his neck, holding him just as tightly.

"I love you," she said over and over.

He moved so that he could see her face. It was killing him to have to ask but he had to know. "You're sure that you're not just replacing Alexis with me?"

She cupped his cheek again. "I'm not. For the first time in my life I'm an individual. I could survive on my own. But I don't want to. I want you."

Ryan hugged her close. Minutes went by before he let her slide down him. His lips hovered close to hers. "I love you, too. Never stopped and never will."

Long, wonderful, contented and soul-filling hours later, Ryan rolled over in his bed to look at Lucy naked beside him. She'd come a long way, not once trying to conceal herself or prevent him from looking until he'd had his fill. Not even an argument when he'd wanted to make love to her with the lights on.

Unable to resist, he dipped down to kiss her rosy lips before he asked, "When do you think Alexis and Sam will visit again?"

Her brow wrinkled in confusion. "I don't know. Why?"

Leaning over her, he kissed away the crease. "I thought we might invite them to a wedding if they could come back soon."

"And if they can't come back soon?" She trailed fingers over his chest.

"Then they may miss it," he growled as her fingers traveled lower.

Her gaze left her fingers to come up and meet his. "Are you asking me to marry you?"

He grinned. "Lucy Edwards, I promise to give you that family you dream of. You'll always be a part of me, never alone again. You are my life. I love you. Will you marry me?"

Those blue eyes she loved expressed that love so clearly. She wrapped her arms around Ryan's neck and pulled him closer. Precious minutes later her lips released his. "Oh, yes, I'll marry you. Whenever you say."

She put her head down on his chest and listened to the steady beat of his heart. The one that held her in it. "I've been thinking."

"I'm not sure I like that idea.'

Lucy gave him a nip with her teeth. "Not funny." She rose so that she could see his eyes. "I was just thinking about how much I admire how close you and your family are. And how far apart mine has been for so long. I'd like to invite my parents to the wedding. It's time someone reached out and tried to build some kind of connection. Maybe a wedding is a good place to begin."

He covered her body with his and his mouth rumbled against hers. "I think that's a great idea. Now, how about we practice that having a family of our own idea?"

"You have to ask?" She gave him a quick kiss. "You make me happy, Ryan. Something I've not been in a long time."

"I aim to please."

"The O'Doherty way," she whispered, as his mouth took hers in a kiss warm with promises of tomorrows to come.

* * * * *

Welcome to the world of the NYC Angels

Doctors, romance, passion, drama—
in the city that never sleeps!

Redeeming The Playboy
by Carol Marinelli
Heiress's Baby Scandal
by Janice Lynn
On sale 1st March

Unmasking Dr. Serious
by Laura Iding
The Wallflower's Secret
by Susan Carlisle
On sale 5th April

Flirting with Danger
by Tina Beckett
Tempting Nurse Scarlet
by Wendy S. Marcus
On sale 3rd May

Making the Surgeon Smile
by Lynne Marshall
An Explosive Reunion
by Alison Roberts
On sale 7th June

Collect all four books in this brand-new Medical 2-in-1 continuity

Find out more at **www.millsandboon.co.uk/medical**

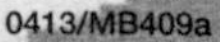

Join the NYC Angels online community...

Get all the gossip straight from the hospital on our NYC Angels Facebook app…

- Read exclusive bonus material from each story
- Enter our NYC Angels competition
- Introduce yourself to our Medical authors

You can find the app at our Facebook page

Facebook.com/romancehq

(Once on Facebook, simply click on the NYC Angels logo to visit the app!)

0413/MB409b